SECRETS OF OLD GIANTS

Kelly Virens

Port Fireflirt
Bindery

To those who know there is magic out there on those trails and in the trees.

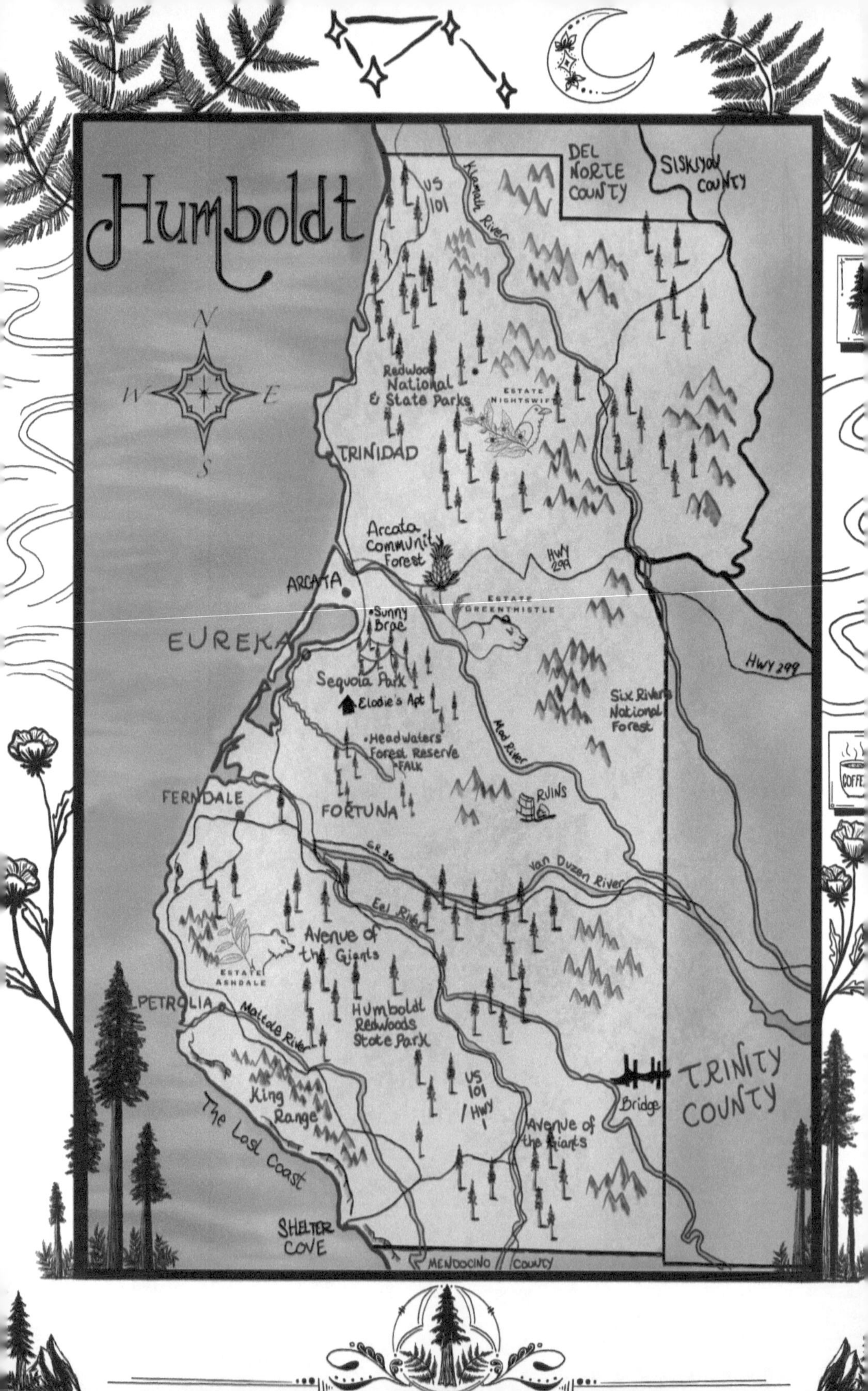

Humboldt
N W E S
US 101
Klamath River
DEL NORTE COUNTY
SISKIYOU COUNTY
Redwood National & State Parks
ESTATE NIGHTSWIFT
TRINIDAD
Arcata Community Forest
HWY 299
ARCATA
ESTATE GREENTHISTLE
Sunny Brae
EUREKA
HWY 299
Sequoia Park
Elodie's Apt
Six Rivers National Forest
Mad River
Headwaters Forest Reserve
FALK
RUINS
FERNDALE
FORTUNA
CR 36
Van Duzen River
Eel River
Avenue of the Giants
Estate Ashdale
PETROLIA
Mattole River
Humboldt Redwoods State Park
King Range
US 101 / HWY
Bridge
TRINITY COUNTY
Avenue of the Giants
The Lost Coast
SHELTER COVE
MENDOCINO COUNTY
COFFEE

Out in the forest, a mountain lion ran to a small clearing deep in the redwoods. A light and silent tread of paws springing back off the earth. Ferns brushed along its fur as it approached the clearing to meet a brown bear. The bear's amber eyes, with hints of gold, met the emerald green ones of the mountain lion. They both glanced up to see a raven swoop down and land beside them, doing a few little hops and tucking its wings. It cawed and tilted its head, sky blue eyes gazing between the two larger animals.

"Just an earthquake?" the bear asked the two animals through the mind link they shared.

"Yep, a big one. My sister will have her hands full with PR for Eureka. See anything funny up above, Cyrus?" the mountain lion asked, sitting back on its haunches.

"Nope. The forest is fine, the Old Giants are fine. Autumn might have a quiet day after all, depending on what happened in Arcata and Eureka," Cyrus said, adjusting his wings and glancing at the bear. "No damage to the south, Quinn?"

"Some spooked animals scurrying away from the remains of Falk. Another building collapsed from the sounds of it. I was near Avenue of the Giants so I passed it on my way into Ashdale's land, but didn't stop to inspect it."

The mountain lion let out a groan, then pushed a gust through its nose. "I will let my dad know the Falk project has yet another setback."

"Ahh, come on, Trevin. You know it's a lost cause. How is your dad sure that there is a tome there?" Quinn asked.

"I don't even know, but since I work for State Parks and Bureau of Land Management, it's my task." Trevin shrugged.

"I gotta say I'm glad it's Greenthistle's task and not Nightswift's. Can't imagine my dad would want to deal with that," Cyrus laughed out loud, his beak clicking.

"No mortals were around Falk, right? I wouldn't put it past some of them to try that hike at this hour," Trevin scoffed. "Wandering in the dark. I don't know why they do this," Trevin said, shaking his head as a certain scent came to mind. A scent of ocean breeze and lavender. He had caught it a few times when he had been out on the trails at night. Likely from a mortal, out too far and too late for it to still be safe. The scent stuck with him though, teasing his senses. He'd usually let out a groan or even a chuff toward the mortal back toward the safety of light. "Silly mortals, they are so fragile," he said.

"Nah. I didn't smell or hear any. A good bit camping along Avenue, though. Probably pissed themselves," the bear laughed. "Speaking of mortals, Cora's Halloween party, Saturday?" Quinn asked.

"Not for me. I have plans already. Ones that don't involve watching silly mortals dress up as fairies and ladybugs," Cyrus laughed.

"Trev? Cedar is going, Autumn too. It could be a whole Greenthistle family affair. You guys could all go dressed as cats?" Quinn laughed. "Maybe you can flirt with someone, get cozy with one or three."

Trevin shook his head. "Shut up. Seriously? That's the only reason you want to go is to eye the mortals? Are you going for a guy or a girl this time?"

"Depends what strikes my fancy. Why not see what strikes your fancy? Cora's Halloween party is always fun."

"I will go. But I'm not getting cozy with anyone. I don't need mortals fawning over me. It's pointless anyway."

"You could get cozy with your own kind, ya know? Fae? You don't even eye them much," Cyrus said with a grin.

Trevin shook his head. "Both are liars and manipulative. Mortals can lie to your face, and fae just care about our titles, heirs to the estates, one day hoping to be an estate lady or lord," Trevin said, rolling his eyes.

"Come on Trev, are you planning to be single forever? You can't. You gotta carry on the Greenthistle line at some point."

"I got an eternity to do that, besides Autumn and Cedar can carry it on just fine."

"Firstborn are always heirs, though. We all have younger siblings, but it's us that get to take the title of estate lord one day," Quinn said. "Besides, we are immortal as if any of them will be around when we do become estate lords. Let 'em fawn over you, they already do."

"One day, not today, not this year or decade or century," Trevin said. "I'm heading home to tell my dad we didn't find anything."

Quinn and Cyrus shook their heads and laughed.

"You need to glamour your eyes, Trev. Someone's going to notice this enormous mountain lion running around Humboldt with vivid green eyes," Cyrus pointed out.

"Yea, then you are going to get a mortal to fawn over a mountain lion," Quinn agreed with a laugh.

"Cedar's are green too, and Autumn's are blue. It's fine."

"Not like yours, though. They dull theirs to an olive or a gray at least."

"It's fine. Mortals shouldn't be close enough to see my eyes anyway. If they are, they're too scared to recall my eye color. I always forget that my eye color stays the same. Anyway, catch ya guys later." Trevin nodded, then took off into the forest.

Cyrus and Quinn gave each other a nod as one took flight north and the other ran south.

Chapter 1

When the ignition was off, she felt her ears, ensuring her costume was still on correctly. A smirk escaped her when she glanced in the visor mirror. A few nerves fluttered about since she hadn't been to one of Cora's parties before. Confidence hadn't really been her strong suit but she knew this was part of settling into her new life in Humboldt County, California. Two and half months in, and so far it was everything she had wanted and needed right now. A new beginning in a place she almost felt homesick for, despite having only visited a handful of times. The night was clear and the air was crisp. The fall season was certainly here in the home of the redwoods, a place she hoped to call home. Sounds of music and conversation grew louder as she walked in the door. Some people gave a nod in greeting, which she returned with a smile as she made her way to the drink table.

"Hey, Elodie. Glad you are here, girl." Cora walked up to her and set down some more red cups. Elodie eyed the bright fluorescent colors and Cora's crimped hair.

"Eighties, nice. I like it," Elodie said with a laugh.

"I had a few things I could piece together. You know where stuff is, make yourself comfortable."

"Will do. I'm glad nothing broke in the café with that earthquake. Everything in the house, okay?"

"Yes! Not a thing broken in either place. Such a relief. Hey, I got some pastries in the oven I gotta go check on. Don't be shy, everyone is really nice here," she said, running off as Elodie nodded. With a drink in hand, Elodie wandered through the house, taking in everyone's costumes. She noted all the usual ones but also some unique ones too.

As she made her way to the living room, she locked eyes with a stranger from across the room. His head tilted ever so slightly and she took in his green eyes. They were striking—he was striking. Her cheeks heated for a moment and then she attempted a small smile. He did not return it, instead turned his attention to the girl talking beside him. She observed the girl now, noting her costume was similar to her own, but she didn't have the fake ears. Maybe at some point she would introduce herself to them.

Elodie glanced at him again, watching his eyes roll in disdain. He shook his head as though he knew she was in awe of him. His expression said he didn't want to be here tonight. She took in his ornate, well fitted clothes—they looked tailored to fit him. He wore black pants and dark brown leather high top boots, with an intricately embroidered green vest over a black long sleeve shirt with two forest green buckles as accents on the upper left arm. A thistle plant stood out on the upper chest pocket. Elodie saw a satin, dark green cuff on his upper right arm with a rune embroidered in black. She recognized the rune meant strength. Her eyes widened as she took him in.

That entire outfit must've cost a fortune, it looks really well made and fits him amazingly, she thought to herself. *That is walking around Humboldt. Oh wow.* She took a slightly deeper inhale and exhaled.

"Hey, you're here!" someone said behind her.

"Charles, hi!" Elodie said, eyeing the pirate costume up and down, grateful for the distraction. "I guess I should say Captain Charles?" They both laughed.

Elodie had met him the very week she moved here and next to Cora he was the second friend she had made.

As they talked, her phone buzzed. Dread pooled in her gut at the name. She only checked it to see if it was her dad, but when she saw that it wasn't, she stepped into the bathroom and took several deep breaths.

"You do not need to explain anything to Ricky. You moved far away from him," she repeated to herself as though it was a mantra.

Shoving her phone back in her hip pouch, she walked out of the bathroom. She looked at the girl now chatting with Charles and noted his love-struck expression. Elodie smiled at them. The girl seemed to have so much charisma and a brightness to her.

Suddenly, oakmoss and amber permeated her nose. It was an intoxicating scent. With a deep inhale to savor the smell, she found herself walking towards the fireplace until she was standing awkwardly close to the attractive stranger.

Her body tensed as their eyes met once again. His stunning green eyes met hers with a razor sharp focus, as though she were being eyed by a mountain lion on a trail. She forced herself to blink.

"You are an odd one." His voice was smooth and coy.

She took a deep inhale and narrowed her eyes. That response rubbed her the wrong way. "I'm not the one staring as though you've never seen a high fae before." Sarcasm lined her voice yet her cheeks heated. Elodie wasn't sure why she had said that.

When he laughed she noticed it didn't match his coy tone. It sounded friendly.

Elodie started to smile, then her body went rigid as he gently cupped her chin. Her eyes shot wide and his head tilted. His gaze was far more intense than a mountain lion on prey. It was the gaze of someone analyzing a puzzle and searching for a solution.

Elodie could hardly process what she was feeling. A range of fear, caution, curiosity, attraction, and humiliation that she was getting lost in this creep's gaze all crashed into her. As if sensing she was about to cry out for help, he spoke, making her body freeze.

"Perhaps, dearly enchanted, I am staring because I'm seeing such a beautiful high fae." That smooth voice again. Her eyes fixed on his lips, now smiling like someone who had sampled a fine wine. His finger traced her jeweled wire ear cuff along the curve of her ear and up to the point. "Pretty little fae princess, with your pointed ears and shimmer on your cheeks. I do wonder how those glossy lips would feel against my skin."

Her eyelids went heavy, as though some magic trap had ensnared her. She reminded herself this was no fairy tale, this was weird. A chill scrunched up her neck and shoulders for a mere moment, then her survival instinct took over. Panic set in and she pushed him away with a hand on his chest with more force than she realized, than he had expected her to use. Yet they never broke eye contact. She watched him cover up his shock.

"You thought about it. I could see it in you. Kissing down my neck," he said, bringing his hand to his neck and biting his lower lip.

"Gross," Elodie snapped and stormed off. She heard him laugh.

Trevin laughed as he watched her walk towards the kitchen. "Suppose that was out of line," he said to himself.

That was the first time he had ever done anything like that to a stranger, to anyone really, mortal and fae alike. It gave him a rush. He recalled the conversation with Quinn and his sister as they watched her talk to the mortal male named Charles. Autumn had been worried the girl liked him and wasted no time walking up to him as soon Charles was alone.

Quinn had been quick to point out the stunned look of attraction the girl had given Trevin. He knew it too, but he was not here to hook up with anyone though. He certainly did not want to lead the girl on and figured that interaction would scare her off.

A smile formed as he smirked to himself at the absurdity of it. The jealousy he had felt when he noticed Quinn eye her. That too was something he had not expected to encounter. Of course his friend would call him out on it. They could read each other so well having grown up together.

The girl's energy and the scent confirmed it had been her on the trails late at night. Something bad was likely to happen to her. Of course she wouldn't listen if he told her that, mortals thought they knew so much about everything. He knew these forests though, far better than any mortal did. These redwoods and ferns were in his bloodline, he was fae after all.

Letting out a sigh he went off to find his younger brother.

"See anybody worthwhile, Trev?" Cedar asked, standing next to Quinn.

"Nah. No one worth my time," Trevin said.

"No one seems to be worth your time, here or there," Cedar responded.

Trevin knew here meant the mortal realm they were currently in and there meant their home on the other side of the boundary, the fae realm.

"Anyone catch your eye, Caleb?" Trevin gave his brother a light shove, remembering to use his pseudo name they used in the mortal world. Trevin never faltered and made a mistake with this; they never revealed their names to anyone. Nor did they enter the mortal realm without a glamour on to hide their pointed ears, vivid eyes and face markings. As far as the mortals knew they were all just mortal humans too.

Cedar laughed. "Haven't decided yet."

"Should we go then?" Quinn asked, glancing off toward the crowd. "This party is getting boring if there's no one to chase and flirt with."

"Shame really. Not even a kiss tonight," Trevin said as he thought about her, and her glossy lips. That had always been his weakness.

"Come on, you haven't actually had anyone's company in years," Cedar said.

"What's the point?"

"Trev, we are not looking for our vowed here. We are just here to have our fun. It's a release," Quinn laughed.

"Yeah, besides, it's not that they are not interested. Look around. It's not normal. How are you still sane? When was your last time, five years ago?" His brother followed up

"I don't need to do that stuff to stay sane."

"We are not leaving until we all get at least a kiss. I mean, Autumn seems to be the first one of the night," Cedar said.

They watched Autumn give her best starry-eyed gaze to the mortal male dressed as a pirate. Charles had a goatee and loose hair down to his chin.

Trevin drew the conclusion he almost certainly lived in an adventure van, or wanted to, but drove an Outback and went to Cal Poly Humboldt. Autumn loved this type. He rolled his eyes. While he was protective of his younger sister, he knew Autumn wasn't in any real danger. She was quick with her words and slyer than any in their circle of friends. He didn't think this guy had any inkling of who or what he was flirting with.

Charles had his hand on the small of Autumn's back as his other hand brushed back a lock of Autumn's chestnut hair. Her eyes, a sky blue-gray, gazed into his, completely enamored. She took after their mom a lot with her sky blue eyes. Cedar and Trevin had gotten the green of their dad's eyes. Pair that with his chestnut hair and tan skin, and Trevin knew he had his pick of any girl here, and probably most any mortal male here too.

He glanced around the room, listening to Cedar talk.

"No really, we all have to get a kiss and since we can't lie—not even to each other—we will know we did."

"By the time we all get a kiss, Anna will have left that one passed out in his van," Trevin groaned. Quinn and Cedar laughed in amusement.

"Only because you will hold us up, numb nuts. Go on, find a cute little thing to kiss," Cedar said before walking off.

Trevin sighed. "This is stupid. I'm not going to party with you guys again."

Quinn laughed. "Yet you always do, though. What else are you going to do, sulk around Greenthistle Estate?" he said, walking away.

Now annoyed, Trevin headed to refill his drink. When her scent grew stronger, his ears heard the conversation on the other side of the wall.

Chapter 2

"Elodie, meet Justine! She just moved back from the East Coast," Cora beamed. Elodie was grateful to be back in Cora's company.

"Hey! Nice to meet you, Elodie. How's Humboldt been so far? What brought you up here?"

"Hi! It's been good. I teach third grade. It's my first year with this school district," Elodie said jovially. "How about you? What do you do?"

"Oh, my brother, his wife, and kids live here. I work for a marketing firm and telework, so I usually move around a lot. Figured it would be nice to be closer to my nieces and nephews. They are starting high school. Fun times." They all laughed. "Where are you from?" Justine asked.

"I grew up in Marin, went to school in SoCal, and lived abroad for a few years. Came back, worked in the city, then back in Marin and—" She paused with a slight sigh recalling the phone call. "I moved up here about two months ago."

"Hope you are enjoying it. I hope Humboldt treats you well," Justine said.

"I love this area so much. My parents and I used to come up here and camp when I was little. It always felt as though I set a piece of my soul down somewhere up here and was a distracted little kid who left it behind. I guess it was time I got it back." Elodie always felt self-conscious talking about that. She hadn't told anyone about that feeling she had felt most of her life.

"Aww, that's wonderful. I missed it too when I was in New York. Cities are fun but, I guess you can't take the trees outta the girl," Justine said with a smile.

Elodie took an inhale, then spoke, "Random question, but everyone here is nice right? Anyone I should avoid?" Nerves hung in her voice.

Cora looked at her with concern.

"No creepers should be in my house. I take note of who is at these parties," Cora said. "Generally though, people try to look out for each other up here."

"Oh, okay," Elodie responded with a nervous laugh.

"Did anyone here make you uneasy?" Cora asked. Elodie paused and her eyes flashed down. "Oh, come on, Elodie. You really should let me know. I don't want anyone like that in my house! Speak up."

"It's nothing," Elodie said, feeling her cheeks heat. The awkwardness of the entire encounter made her recoil.

"Out with it. Who made you uncomfortable?" Cora insisted.

"I was in New York long enough. I will fight them," Justine said with a hint of a laugh.

Elodie laughed nervously again. "I don't know. It was a weird encounter. This guy had tan skin, dark brown hair, around six feet. His eyes though, were striking, like emeralds, as though he came out of the redwoods and ferns themselves. He was breathtaking." An inflection of a smile was apparent in her voice for anyone listening then nervously she said what had happened. "But I'm over the fuckboy phase and I get the feeling he knows that's what he is."

"That description sounds like Trev. Trevor Greenthistle. He is really nice, I've never heard of him acting so forward with someone. He's at the café a fair amount. His family is super rich and his dad holds a county seat. Three families have a lot of pull in what happens here. They live in these big estates out in the forests, Greenthistle, Nightswift, and Ashdale. I'm not sure I even know how to find them. Trev is cool though. His brother, Caleb, and sister Anna are here. Anna is super nice. He's friends with Q too, whose dad works up with Trev's at city hall. Caleb and Q are big flirts," Cora teased, smirking at Justine.

"What? I can't help it, Q is hot. We hooked up a few times before I moved." Justine smiled.

"My parties are safe. Don't worry I will make sure of it."

"Thanks. Glad I went to the café. I never noticed Trev before though."

"He's usually there during the day—I assume when you are teaching. Why do you ask?"

"No reason. I don't need a stalker. I just moved here, new place jitters and all."

"Trev isn't a stalker. Don't worry. He is attractive, but I've not seen him pursue anyone in a while. He hardly flirts with people. I will talk to him," Cora assured Elodie.

"Good to know," Elodie responded.

"Let's go sit near the pool?" Justine asked. Elodie was grateful for the topic change and followed the two outside.

"What are your favorite hiking trails here? I've done a few," Elodie asked.

Making mental notes of trail names and things to see nearby, she relaxed once again. The three shared hiking stories.

Then her phone vibrated again in her bag and her stomach filled with dread. This time it was a phone call. *Why do I let him stress me out?* she asked herself. *As if he would drive five hours. He couldn't be bothered to drive twenty minutes sometimes.*

With a deep inhale and determined to end this, she would tell him off tonight. She had moved away for a refresh, after all. The night had proven she was no longer in familiar territory, despite the redwoods calling out for her.

"Hold on. I just need to take care of some asshole," Elodie sighed and got up. Cora and Justine watched, concerned.

"I told you we were done, Ricky." Elodie's voice was hushed, trying not to draw attention to herself.

"Come on, babe. You seriously moved apartments?"

"Yea, I did. Three months ago." Affirmation rang in her voice.

"Just come over. What'd you do, go back to the city? East Bay? As if anything there is worthwhile," Ricky said.

Elodie narrowed her eyes at the video call. "I'm not in the city. Please stop calling me. We are done and have been for at least five months, probably longer with your escapes." Anger and spite laced her tone. "We are done. We are over. Leave me alone."

Elodie noticed the oakmoss and amber scent. Then she realized why in her peripheral vision.

"Yea, then why can I still call you? You haven't blocked my number. Come on, Elodie, I miss you. I miss what we had. Let me make it up to you," Ricky cooed confidently.

She watched Trev spin around and lock eyes with her. His jaw dropped. Some reckless urge came over her, paired with annoyance that he had followed her and heard this conversation. Her mind ran a mile a minute, weighing her options if he would help her out or be a complete prick. The night was unfamiliar territory, after all.

"Because I'm about to block it. I moved on. I found someone better," Elodie said, walking up to Trev. "Sorry to keep you waiting, Trev." Her eyes locked with his, never off her predator or her prey at this rate.

He looked at her, still stunned for a moment before that sly, clever gaze slid over him as if he had never once doubted himself.

"El, I wondered where you went," Trev's smooth voice purred.

Being this close to him again nearly took her breath away. Her eyebrows raised realizing he had been listening to her long before this phone call.

"El? He calls you El? Who is this asshole? In three months? Elodie!" Ricky snapped out.

Trevor held her gaze, still searching for whatever he hoped to find. For a split-second, Elodie wondered if he saw some strand tethering her to the redwoods. To these Old Giants that grew wild in his home.

"This asshole knows when he has a good thing right in front of him," Trevor said, cupping her chin just as gently as before, then kissing her.

When their lips met, Elodie felt her eyes go heavy, and something deep inside her pulsed. She felt the ferns and the redwoods embrace her, felt the mist and soil cradle her. That thing calling her to the forests. *Safe, comfortable, home.* The words seemed to echo through her.

Trev held that kiss as if he too savored this moment.

The moment was ripped away for them both by Ricky. "You just left your dad behind? Ran away from everything? Just to whore around?"

Elodie flinched as though a nerve had been ripped out.

Trevor grabbed her phone and glared at Ricky.

"Do not speak to her like that ever again! Listen to her. She's moved on." The tone Trevor took was as low and serious. He ended the call before Ricky could respond and watched her holding his smirk.

"He sounds like an asshole," Trevor said, handing her phone back.

Elodie was frozen, but felt her eyes water. Once again, they had not broken eye contact.

"What is going on?" someone asked in a hushed tone. It forced her to break his stare and glance just past him where people were watching.

"She's upset," she heard Cora say.

Her eyes cut down for a split-second. She took the risk, and it had attracted so much attention. Not once did she consider or expect he would *actually* kiss her, though. That feeling though when they kissed. *What was that?* She didn't know what to say or do.

"El, are you okay?" he asked, slowly reaching for her hand and placing her phone in her palm, his fingers gently cupping hers to grip it. "I'm sorry, if that kiss was too much, I hope he got the message. I assure you I am no fuckboy," he said with a confident laugh.

Elodie realized he had heard that too. Shock crossed her face as her eyes met his again, and her cheeks heated with embarrassment. She glanced at his lips briefly, then at her phone in her hand as he let go.

Elodie cursed herself for creating this awkward moment. Quickly, she wiped her eyes. "I'm fine! I hate him. He's an asshole, I'm sorry!" She fumbled over her words. Then she realized she didn't feel any fear being near him and didn't sense any anger from him about the situation.

He smirked. "Nothing to apologize for. Are you going to be okay? I'm sure Cora and Justine are wondering what happened." A sly little grin graced his lips.

She glanced back and met the concerned expression of Cora and Justine. She noticed a few other people still watching them and got uneasy.

"You're okay. It was a pleasure meeting such an interesting little mink," he said, his tone curious before walking back toward the house.

Elodie saw a guy taller than Trev pat him on the back with a loud laugh. "Nice, bruh, nice!"

She stood there still dumbfounded.

"Elodie, are you okay?" Cora asked. She turned to her friend and nodded.

"I'm fine. I don't know why I did that. I just wanted Ricky to leave me alone."

"That entire encounter was weird," Cora said. "I've never known Trev to act like that. It was protective? Possessive?"

"Was that guy that followed him inside his brother? Caleb, right?" Elodie asked.

"Yeah. Seems they all were busy tonight," Justine said, rolling her eyes.

"Elodie, I don't know what in his right mind possessed him to do that. I swear all three of them are really nice. They may flirt, but they never pressure," Cora said. "I will tell him to knock it off and leave you alone."

"I left a pretty toxic relationship back in Marin. I mean obviously if he's calling three months later thinking I just moved to East Bay." She laughed at the absurdity. "I saw him standing there and don't know why I said I moved on, with Trev," she said, putting her hand to her face. "I swear I'm not this impulsive or reckless. I don't do these things. I didn't even do it in my twenties."

"Your ex clearly wasn't getting the hint, and Trev seemed more than willing to help. I mean, he's hot. Go you. Trust me, they are not bad guys. Certainly not Trev." Justine laughed.

Elodie blushed but nodded, mortified by what she had done, what *he* had done.

Cora laughed and shook her head. "Come on, let's go inside."

Chapter 3

Trevin, Cedar, and Quinn sat around the fireplace in the Greenthistle Estate, finishing the night with wine. Trevin thought about Elodie. He had thought about her on the way home, too. Running through the events of the night as fast as his paws carried him through ferns and redwoods. Her outfit flashed in his mind first. The worn brown boots, teal leggings, and a black corset over a white flowy long sleeve button-up shirt. Not a real corset with an elastic string in the back. The light reflected off the fake diamonds and green rhinestones on the diadem she wore. *At least her ear cuffs looked well made—probably by someone with skills to properly wrap wire and stone. She had put some effort into that cute little fae getup,* he thought.

Trevin recalled his eyes traveling back over her, noticing the flowy shirt acting as a very short dress. *She does have nice curves though, if that shirt-dress was a tad shorter...*

Some sort of essence or power was in her, but it was blurred. There was an odd familiarity to it and yet it was foreign to him. He had to focus on her eyes to see past all her emotions to get to it. *Why did I grab her chin like that?* he still wondered. The sensation he felt around her confused him, and yet he wanted more.

He hadn't intended on eavesdropping, but the conversation in the kitchen grabbed his attention. His fae hearing let him hear far more than mortals could. Learning about her and the smile that graced his lips as he silently pronounced each syllable of her name. *Eh-lo-dee.* Then how his gut twisted when she called him a fuckboy.

From her conversation near the pool about hiking and camping, Trevin knew she had stamina. When his eyes fixed on her, the thought of kissing her neck up to her ear sent a spark through him. Then the realization of her rounded mortal ears halted that spark. Her conversation with Ricky made him seethe.

Trevin thought of their kiss. He had not wanted to play Cedar's game, but he seized the moment anyway. That kiss was far greater than a spark in him, it ignited something in him he had never experienced before. This was something he could not put into words, but he knew in his core he wanted. A desire to be better—to become what he knew he was destined for, but had never felt he was suited for. He wanted to follow it and wanted her to follow him down that path.

It did worry him—in fact, it outright scared him too. How badly he wanted it. That was his signal to run, not to embrace it, but force himself to rationalize.

All the thoughts rushing through his head, as plentiful as the ferns he ran through day after day. Only now these ferns felt different. There was a distinct presence in the air. This mortal girl was here in Humboldt. Elodie, with that tantalizing scent that did such odd things to him. He had to figure out what she was.

The grandiose French doors of the estate opening snapped him out of his daze. Quinn gave him a smug smile.

"How was your boys' evening?" Autumn asked, giggly. The three knew she had found some dark corner with a certain pirate.

"Good, and how was yours, Anna? Did he have an adventure van?" Cedar asked, saying her mortal name with a smug tone.

"Charles? He does, but he also has an apartment near the park," she said, "It's lovely. Just didn't want to impose too much. Next time I might stay the night." Autumn winked. Trevin rolled his eyes.

"Second date. Nice. How long do you think this one will stay?" Quinn asked.

"Oh, he's got like a year tops here. He's a music teacher, he's lived all over. Even Hawaii," she said dreamily.

"Aww, that's cute sharing all the stories. Did you tell him all about the Old Giants?" Cedar crooned.

"We talked about hiking trails and stuff," she laughed. "Anyone else get lucky? I saw Justine was back, Quinn," she said in a teasing manner.

"I saw. How could I miss her?" Quinn rolled his eyes.

"You'll be back with her within two weeks, tops," Cedar teased.

Quinn sighed, then noticed Trevin shaking his head with a laugh. "Whatever, but can we talk about the little scene Trevin caused? With the new mortal girl in town."

"Yes! Dang, talk about a scene. Of course, the girl dressed as a fairy with the ears and diadem!" Cedar laughed loudly.

"What happened? I didn't see it. The one talking to Charles? You hooked up with her?" Autumn asked, eyeing her older brother with brimming curiosity.

"Nothing happened. I didn't hook up with her," Trevin groaned, then took a drink of his wine.

"Yeah, okay. She walked out on the patio with Cora and Justine and caught my eye, but Trev here walked out and stared daggers into me. Clearly he had her locked in his sight," Cedar went on, retelling the scene and laughing. "You should have seen it. She just stood there frozen."

"The guy on the phone was garbage, the way he spoke to her. If she lives here in Humboldt, she's one of ours. We look out for our own."

"Oh, his kiss turned some heads, the way he cupped her chin and kissed her for some time. Then he made sure she was okay, and she just stood there, speechless. that Master Greenthistle kissed her," Quinn laughed.

"Shut up! Cedar made the dumb game and as if I'd be able to just leave without getting shit the entire rest of time if I didn't kiss some random girl," he scoffed, finishing his glass in a large swallow.

"She didn't look like a random girl. The way you glared when I eyed her seemed a *whole* lot like pissing on your territory," his brother retorted.

"You are horrible individuals. I hope you know that. Elodie is new. She doesn't need to have a bunch of dogs eye her like a piece of meat," Trevin said.

"You got her name?" Autumn asked, surprised.

Trevin sighed.

"Just leave the girl alone. She's got enough going on in her head. She doesn't need the estate kids messing with her."

"Okay, Trevy. Sure thing," Quinn said with a laugh. "I'm going to head home. Fun night for all it seems," he said, standing up.

"Later," Cedar said. Trevin nodded and went up to his room.

Elodie went home two hours later. A breeze picked up as soon as she got out of her car, sending a chill through her. She gazed up at the sky and the tree line as she stood at the base of the stairs.

Elodie. Elodie.

A voice called for her. She often heard it when she walked in this forest. Whenever she slid her hand along a fern, feeling the water on the leaves, a current pulsed inside of her. A voice that could have been in her head, or it could have been a whisper. Elodie never could tell, but she could not ignore it. She did not want to ignore it. She had told no one about it, nor would she, lest they deem her crazy.

It was becoming a more common occurrence. As though the Old Giants themselves were actually calling to her, beckoning her.

She felt compelled to walk the trail nearby. She had walked miles on it, even after sundown, but never this late. Another chill passed through her, and she hurried up to her door.

Once in the bathroom, she looked at herself in the mirror, then at the wire-framed wraps on her ears. She took the braids out and fluffed the waviness of her hair. The shimmer on her cheeks was still bright, and then she thought about Trev. Trevor.

A beautiful high fae princess. A good thing right in front of him. You are an odd one.

She snapped a selfie of herself with her hair down. "I'm too old for this. I'm too old for fairy tales." She laughed softly, and finished getting ready for bed.

CHAPTER 4

O n Thursday, Elodie went to Cora's café in the evening to draw. She'd go out for a short walk later. Friday lessons were always easy. She always asked her students to share one good thing that happened to them during the week to end on a good note. Of course, she had to share one too. She would say she went to a Halloween party and leave it at that.

That Halloween party. She laughed at the thought. How awkward she was. How awkward that night was. The things she said and had revealed, had done. This was not her usual self. She could not recall a moment in her life when this was her usual. The redwoods flashed in her head.

"Hey, how's the week going?" Cora asked.

Elodie blinked realizing she was at the counter and distracted. The distraction thing was not new. She had often daydreamed all her life. "It's going well. Thursday means the weekend is soon."

"Yeah, I'm looking forward to the bonfire. Dress warm," Cora said with a smile.

"Camping will be fun."

"You have a tent, yes? You could shack up with Charles. Though, from the sounds of it, he may have gotten lucky last Saturday night, with a Greenthistle too," Cora laughed. Elodie shook her head with a hint of a smile.

"I have a tent. I'll put my gear in the car after work tomorrow," Elodie said and placed her order. Once seated, she took her sketchbook out along with a pen and started to draw ferns. When she drew she often focused though, it was usually when she was not busying herself did her mind daydream. She read books just fine, was very invested in her lessons and work.

When her order came she thanked Cora and sat back in her seat. Her eyes roved the café and locked on one person in particular.

A few tables down and across from her was Trev. His head was down as he focused on some papers with a sly little grin.

She quickly cut her eyes down. *I hope he doesn't talk to me. It's a coincidence, nothing more.* Elodie pleaded in her mind. While she had thought about him, she didn't know what to even say should she actually run into him. She would really rather stay off his radar given what his dad did, given what his family name meant. Then she cringed remembering how much he had overheard that night.

She remembered the comment about not being a fuckboy and was mortified all over again. He called her El. No one called her that since her mom—she never let anyone else call her that. With a frown, she eyed the fern she had just drawn. *Maybe it's time to let someone else call me that, even if he's odd too.* The few times her mind had wandered to him were when she would see a fern pop against the dark soil. She frowned and propped her chin on her palm, elbow on the table. She mindlessly doodled and wrote the words 'one good thing' on the page in curly letters.

Trevin watched her. He went to the café to watch after all. It was a good time to change up his routine, to see what the evening crowd did, what she did. This was his third night in a row here this week. He watched her shift through every emotion, noting them all, while trying to figure out what she was. Trevin thought about Ricky. *The bastard,* he thought.

Whatever thought she had just come to her mind seemed to be one of defeat. How he wished he could read minds. She sighed, and he fixed his eyes on his notebook.

"Hey Elodie, how's the week going?" he heard a male say. Trevin glanced over before listening closely as Charles and Elodie talked. Trevin hadn't gotten an invite for camping, he hadn't really cared, as he couldn't go anyway. They had a big job to do on Saturday night. He did glance over when Charles mentioned he'd bring his adventure van with the bed in it. He watched her face.

"No, I'm okay. I've done Lost Coast and camped on the Sonoma Coast in December, plus all the Desolation Wilderness camping in the Eastern Sierra. I'm not going to get too cold. Besides, aren't you talking to someone—Anna, right?" she asked.

"Yeah, I mean, you can sleep in it. I will be in my tent too. It's open to anyone who gets too cold." He laughed. "Anna is out of my league, but she is amazing. You and her would get along great, I think," Charles said.

Trevin smiled, thinking of his sister and Elodie being friends. Not that he knew much about Elodie, other than she liked to wander out on trails alone, and she was pretty brave. Observant and loyal, too. The embodiment of the three estates, a perfect Humboldt resident, he hoped.

"You met her at Cora's party last weekend?" Elodie asked.

"Yeah, we really hit it off. She kinda just came up to me and started talking, though I did steal a glance at Anna before I saw you. Did you meet anyone of interest?"

Trevin wanted to glance up, but he kept his eyes down.

"Me?" She paused then laughed. "I met Justine."

"Yeah, I met her too. She seems cool. From here to New York—I couldn't imagine being in such a dense city again."

"There and now back again? The Old Giants are hard to leave, impossible to forget. I felt as though they were calling to me even when I lived on the other side of the ocean and was wandering old temples. The Old Giants are magical," she said with a laugh. "I sound like a crazy person, large old trees talking to me across the ocean. I swear I haven't done any drugs since undergrad."

Trevin couldn't help but glance over, puzzled.

"I wouldn't judge if you still did them. Though you've got a magic to you I think belongs here with those Old Giants," Charles said. Cora walked up and handed Charles his order and smiled at them. She glanced at Elodie's sketch book.

"What? How have I never seen your sketches? I've seen you with your sketchbook, but probably was too busy to notice. Want to do the menu when we update it? That fern is amazing and with the shimmer, like emeralds." She smirked at Elodie, who blushed and glanced at Trevin. He maintained that smug expression as he pretended to read.

"Yeah, the menu would be fun. It's been a while since I've done chalk stuff. I need practice, but there is no pavement at my place."

"Do it at Sequoia Community Park. Families love that stuff. I live across from there," Charles said.

"Oh, I live not too far from there. In Cutten."

"Nice. Well, I gotta run. Music lesson soon," he said, grabbing his bag.

"See ya later," Cora said. Elodie smiled and lifted her cup.

She drew ferns and added an emerald effect with a green pen. Like my eyes? The thought made Trevin eager, and he didn't understand why. *Why is she so interesting to me?* He heard a rustling of a bag and watched her close her sketchbook. He frowned as she put stuff in her bag and got up to bus her plate.

"Later, Cora. I'm going to squeeze in a short hike tonight."

"You and your night hikes. Be careful. Catch ya tomorrow."

"I will. See ya," Elodie said.

Trevin flipped the page over and fixed his eyes on the words as Elodie walked closer.

Elodie kept her head down, hurrying to the door. As she opened it, she glanced back, locking eyes with him for a moment before heading outside. He waited all of one minute before he grabbed his notebook and got up to set his cup on the cart.

"Trev," Cora said as though he were going to be scolded.

"What?" he scoffed.

"Care to tell me why you did that at my party? Why have you been here every night? Waiting for her?"

"Okay, first of all, I have training and office stuff during the day now. It's a whole different vibe at night, and you're here more in the evenings now. Besides, I don't want to miss any party invites or bonfire camping trips in Trinidad," he said in a sly tone.

"It's a smaller group thing and after how you acted at the party, I don't want her to be uncomfortable. I will invite you to the next one. Seriously, it's like five of us. You know the campground rules, you work for State Parks."

"I'm not upset that I wasn't invited. I have work stuff this weekend anyway."

"Okay, then tell me why you kissed her? What the hell happened?"

"I overheard the conversation with her ex, and it was obvious it stressed her out. Besides, Caleb made some stupid bet. We couldn't leave till we kissed someone, and I did. You know how the guys are," he said. No lies, all truth. He had a cocky grin plastered on his face.

"So, you used her? And now you realize you might like her?" Cora sighed in disappointment. "Trevor."

"No way. You and Anna are the same. I wanted to apologize, and I was going to, but she left," he said. Cora's disappointment was still apparent.

"Trevor, if you do like her, just talk to her. You saw how Charles acted with her."

"He doesn't like her, though. He likes Anna."

"What I mean is, you can start by being friends with her instead of watching her like a weirdo. You better not just be trying to get her in bed. You acted differently with her."

"She needed a hand. I mean, technically, she pursued me during that phone call. And come on, I'm not Russ," Trevin said with a smirk.

Cora sighed. "Just don't toy with her, don't make me hate you, okay? She's really sweet, and you don't need to be like Russ."

"Keep an eye on her this weekend. She hikes at night? Alone?" he asked, trying to play as though he didn't know that already.

"I don't know why she does. I mean, it'd be one thing if she was with someone or a group. National and State Parks arrange night hikes all the time, but alone? If she's too close to town someone dangerous could be out there and if she's too far out, a wild animal could get her. Honestly, she doesn't strike me as foolish—reckless, maybe?"

Trevin didn't want to think about finding her injured in the forest. It gave him a chill. "She's overly curious. That's all. Keep an eye out for her."

"Try being her friend. Keep an eye out for her too," Cora said, walking off. Trevin shook his head and left.

Heading to the park, Trevin assumed Elodie was likely on one of the trails. There were many people in the park at this hour, lots of older people, families, and friendly dogs. She would be safe here. Once down a road, he checked his surroundings before he changed into a mountain lion. Then, he took off toward the trail that would take him to the fae world. The scent of a nearby mountain lion halted him.

Way too close to town. He thought to himself and rolled his eyes. One of his biggest tasks was keeping the mountain lions away from mortals. Since mountain lions were Greenthistle's feral, it was their responsibility. One thing he was jealous of Cyrus for. Nightswift had it easy with ravens, though they caused some accidents.

Ocean breeze and lavender slipped into Trevin's nose, then a surge of energy followed. She knew she was being pursued. He chirped.

Leave her be, he said in his chirps. *Leave.* One quick chirp. The animal paused, then pursued again. He knew it was an animal and not another fae. There was a wild instinct in this one, no words. Other fae knew they would feel the estate's wrath if they hurt a mortal. The surge in her pulsed stronger.

Trevin repeated himself. *Leave her, leave this area. Never hurt humans. Never ever her. Listen to her, feel her,* Trevin said.

The mountain lion stopped and turned to Trevin. He was staring directly into its eyes. That energy passed over him and the mountain lion, confusing them both.

Never her. Watch out for her, that power. A few more chirps. He could hear Elodie's breathing now. The mountain lion left running the opposite way into the forest. Trevin sighed with relief and walked toward her, letting himself make noise.

Elodie kept walking as Trevin watched. The energy in her bubble and boil and the trees seemed to brighten, shifting ever so slightly toward her. A purr slipped out and she froze. He was hidden enough that she couldn't see him.

Elodie took a deep inhale and then walked again, turning left.

Slowly, Trevin followed at a distance and then watched her walk down a street with lights on it. When she was on the property, he changed back into fae, not bothering to glamour himself as he pulled his hood up. With slow, quiet steps, he saw her go upstairs and inside quickly then heard the locks click. He noticed a car near the stairs. A few national park stickers decorated the edge of the window and a Thule Box sat on top.

He stood there for a while, wondering what might have happened had the mountain lion moved faster. A sigh of relief escaped him.

"Do I need to keep an eye on you, El?" He groaned at the thought. Having to watch over a curious mortal just to figure out what was inside of her. What was coursing through her blood? He walked back to the trail, changed, and ran home.

Chapter 5

As Elodie got ready for work Friday morning, she thought about the previous night. When she was breathing hard and failing to keep quiet. She couldn't see the mountain lion, but knew it was near. With a mile between her and her front door, she knew there was no way she could outrun it. A gasp escaped her when chirps flitted through the air and she knew there were two. She grabbed a stick knowing she would have to make herself look bigger

Elodie. Elodie.

Those voices had whispered again. Her eyes slowly roved toward the nearest tree, a redwood with ferns surrounding it. As a warm breeze graced her, the ferns reached for her.

You are safe, you are watched over, you are home. Home.

More chirps, quicker this time. Almost a cat meow. A whimper slipped out of her and she forced herself to walk. With a shaky breath she kept her steps quick and hurried to her front door. Once she got inside she sat on her couch and wiped her eyes. Confusion cascaded over her.

Sometimes she would hear those voices. Part of her couldn't help but wonder if coming here was a mistake. She feared she was going insane, that pull, the longing to be here, she liked it here. Yet this draw to the forest was dangerous. She also recalled how she looked at her phone and tears formed. She couldn't help but wonder if Ricky's words held true. That she did run away. Her eyes looked at his number.

Knows a good thing right in front of him. Trev's words had played for her and she set the phone down. It was not the time for regrets or mistakes.

Elodie faced the window, her eyes fixing on those trees with the early morning fog. She didn't want to leave this place—she had always missed it. Trees couldn't make her crazy, they couldn't accelerate crazy either. Cora had told her to be careful, and she wasn't.

Home. Safe.

"Is this really home, not Marin? With Cora, Justine, Charles, Trev?" she asked herself, then laughed. "Not Trev." Shaking her head, she grabbed her keys.

The day flew by, the kids were happy, and she felt better. She felt as though everything would be okay. After work, she ran home, grabbed her gear, then headed over to Cora's house. Charles was there with his van.

"I must say, I am impressed with your setup," Charles said, looking at the sleeper set up in the back of Elodie's car.

"It's been around. Furthest was Sedona. Handles like a champ," she laughed.

Then they caravanned up to Trinidad and set up overlooking the beach. They ate and talked while Cora browsed through Elodie's sketchbook. Charles had lived in Chicago, then headed down to Memphis before making his way to Humboldt.

He spoke of Anna and how nice she was and how he hadn't met anyone quite like her before. "She reminds me of a forest sprite or something. She's so cute and passionate too, if you catch my drift," he said with a dopey smile. Elodie laughed, thinking of how sly and smooth Trev was.

"You remember me telling you she's Trev's younger sister, right?" Cora said, glancing at Elodie.

"It completely slipped my mind. That was such a wild night. Then suddenly he was at the café. He is so weird." Elodie shook her head.

"I think he might be interested, Elodie," Cora said. Justine and Charles listened with curiosity.

"No, I don't think so. He just likes to toy, and honestly, he saw an opportunity to play a cool guy and puff his chest out. I was glad he was there for that call with Ricky." She sighed. The previous night came back to her. She had almost called Ricky after the mountain lion encounter, yet Trev's words pulled her back from that. "Ricky is deplorable. He and I dated for about two years and he got into drugs. We were off and on for two more years—he cheated a lot and I never had the proof, so I stayed like an idiot. Then I walked in on him with some other girl and just turned around and left. Things worked out really quickly, and I moved up here shortly after. Only a few friends and my dad knew. I had wanted a fresh start, and that was the final push. I was burned out down there. I love it up here, but I don't know. I wonder if maybe I'm just running away from things when they get hard. Teaching makes it easy. Everywhere needs teachers," she said.

"It always feels like running from one place to the next, but it's not. A whole world of experiences are out there that can never be repeated. The trick is knowing that you've embraced the hell out of a place. Ready for the next unforgettable experience. Beautiful places, amazing people, good food and all," Charles said. Justine smiled and nodded.

"There's no rush. You'd at least stay through the school year, right?"

"Of course. It's a new set of challenges. It's fun up here and the kids are always excited with art and nature. I can't leave mid-school year without burning a bridge anyway."

"Good. You've become one of my good friends. I do hope you stay, but if you go, then keep in touch please."

"I mean, I don't think I'd leave the coast. I honestly don't want to leave the trees here. Trev, he doesn't have time for some awestruck city girl with some tree hugging tendencies. A politician's son, I would never." She laughed and shook her head.

"Oh please. His dad works in Humboldt. We are known as a bunch of tree huggers to the city folk," Cora said and they laughed. "Plus, he is acting differently. I'm pretty sure he likes you, and if I didn't know better, I'd think you might be keen on him."

Elodie shook her head with a grin, and they continued to talk about their lives. Charles gushed about Anna more and Justine listened while texting someone.

As they got ready for bed, Cora walked over to Elodie. "After you left the café yesterday, Trev asked me to keep an eye on you for night hikes. It's pretty safe here, save for falling off a cliff, but he was pretty alarmed that you hike alone at night. So, I guess what I'm asking is don't go on a night hike?" she said with a sweet smile. Elodie laughed.

"I won't. The waves are nice and calming. The most I might do is sit here and watch the water break under the stars. I promise."

"Well, don't freeze to death either. Honestly, Elodie, it will be a relief when the wonder of this place starts to fade," Cora laughed. Elodie did too and then glanced at the tree line. The trees on the coast were different. They were not redwoods but still recognizable to the North Coast. The Old Giants were near. She knew this because she could feel them.

She crawled into her tent and got cozy in the sleeping bag. She felt calm, she felt at home. And as Elodie drifted off to sleep, she recalled his words. *It's been a pleasure, little mink.*

"What's that even mean?" she asked with a small laugh to herself. She didn't care anymore. She could deal with coy smiles from a politician's son. Elodie would be more careful, and she would find what had been calling to her here. She wasn't going crazy. It was her embracing Humboldt to the fullest.

It was a good thing the crashing waves of the mighty Pacific carried Elodie into a deep, safe slumber. For the forests would not remain quiet anymore. The stars and the earth knew this, the redwoods and the ferns knew this, and soon the high estates would know it too.

Chapter 6

Cyrus flew overhead, aware of the bear and the mountain lion on the ground under him. They were deep into the Six Rivers National Forest. Their fathers, the estate lords, were out too, closer to the territory line of Humboldt and Trinity. Rumors were a mountain lion had gotten rabies and had gotten too close to towns. Since it was within Humboldt's territory, it was their responsibility to handle it before it ran into Trinity. Their lords and heirs stood ready in case it crossed the county line.

"Damn bro, you chased one off the girl's tail?" Quinn asked. He was a mass of muscle in bear form, and a mass of muscle in his fae and mortal form, too. He had pinned Trevin many times in sparring drills.

"Yea, I mean come on. It was way too close to the neighborhood," Trevin said.

"What were you doing there, anyway?" Cyrus asked. "Trying to get laid finally?"

"Shut up. She's new and she goes hiking at night alone, absolutely foolish," he scoffed.

"Silly mortals and their adrenaline rushes. So, you're on babysitting duty for this one?" Cyrus laughed, letting out a caw. "Seriously, just scare her one night and be done with it. Let her see you feral—growl, hiss at her and charge her, then run off. Convince her to stop being dumb," Cyrus said overhead. "Greenthistle doesn't need a manhunt for a mountain lion."

Trevin groaned. "I don't want to scare her."

"He's trying to get laid, remember? He's just going to stalk her in hopes he will," Quinn said, and Trevin knew by his tone he was smiling.

"He's got better odds of her packing up and moving on at that rate." Cyrus let out another caw, laughing in his head. "Do you want us to scare her so you can play the hero?"

"No! Just shut up. Let's focus on this mountain lion," Trevin growled.

He could smell it and knew it was near. He chirped, calling out the signal for his dad to tell everyone to be ready. He could sense only its rage; it just had the instinct to kill. He chirped this to his dad, too. His dad chirped back in confirmation.

Cyrus cawed out that he saw it running toward the territory line only two hundred feet in front of them. "It's just up ahead. Foaming at the mouth too. But this doesn't look like rabies, it feels darker, evil, old."

"Yeah, I feel it too," Quinn said.

"It's not the same mountain lion from last night," Trevin said. He chirped more frantically and his dad chirped back. They continued to close the distance.

Suddenly the mountain lion spun around charged Trevin, knocking the wind out of him.

"Trev!" Quinn called out. He barreled into the mountain lion, knocking him down. With an arched back, it growled at Quinn who pulled from the strength of any nearby bears. One of Ashdale's gifts as a high estate.

"Fuck," Trevin said, rolling over. He jumped back up and stood in front of Quinn, chirping at the mountain lion.

"Calm down, what happened?" he asked in his headspace, gazing into the enraged eyes. Pure malice bore into him. No response from the mountain lion's mind, a blank. Trevin didn't understand. Every animal had thoughts. This one was silent, though.

Cyrus landed on a low-hanging branch and its eyes shifted to Cyrus.

"Be careful. Cyrus. Stay up higher," Quinn said.

"Don't let him bite any of you, just hold it here. Our dads are on their way," Cyrus cawed out.

Trevin shivered and thought how lucky he had been last night that this was not the one stalking Elodie. How lucky she was to be safe on the beach, hopefully sleeping cozy and warm. The growl snapped him out of his thoughts. *Fuck, why does she cloud my head like this?*

The mountain lion lunged at Trevin, who pushed back. The two mountain lions fought with ferocity. Quinn grabbed the enraged animal by the scruff and slammed it into the ground. It charged and knocked Quinn back into a tree with alarming strength. It stunned Quinn. *No. it's not possible...* he gasped out. Cyrus was knocked off balance and threw his wings out.

In a heartbeat, the mountain lion pushed up on Quinn, digging claws into his chest and sunk its teeth into the raven's body. Quinn and Trevin gasped. Trevin lunged and ripped the mountain lion off by the scruff. Cyrus fell gasping as Quinn called for him.

"Cyrus! Hold on, hold on!" Quinn screamed.

Cyrus cawed violently as his blood oozed.

Trevin was still fighting while trying to see what happened to his friend. The mountain lion pinned him, still enraged, but less so. He could sense its wild instinct now—something had blocked it before. *Evil. Evil,* it growled. Trevin didn't understand why he couldn't see it before. This was just adrenaline from being attacked now. There had been a wall blocking the mountain lion's head space before.

Claws slashed across Trevin's face and he cried out. He fought back despite his face stinging with the cool sensation of air hitting open flesh and warm blood oozing. With a sudden blur, the mountain lion died—a loud roar, a yelp of pain and then silence save for the raven's pleading caws.

"No! Please! No," Cyrus screamed with garbled breaths. Trevin jumped up unsteadily. His dad changed and placed a hand on his son's back and winced at his son's wounds.

"Don't change. Deep breaths," he said, trying to remain calm but clearly shaken. Trevin was still in a daze as he watched his dad walk over to Cyrus.

"Please don't! No! No!" Cyrus screamed. Trevin watched the raven thrash and breathe hard, the rasp of breath escaping from his body. Quinn heaved, still in bear form. Their dads were all back in fae form. As the rasping breaths slowed and the screams quieted, Trevin's eyes shifted to the trees. They were still. Not bright, no ferns swaying in a warm breeze toward an odd little mink with a strange energy. Her name flowed through his mind. *Elodie.*

"It's okay. You are going to pull through this. Relax," his dad said, kneeling over the raven.

"No! Please, please!" Cyrus cried out, then Trevin watched the raven go limp, wings falling. Lord Greenthistle, being the oldest high estate lord, had the ability to sedate and heal.

Trevin's eyes shifted to the lifeless mountain lion, and frowned. It always hurts when one of their own dies. He glanced at the forest; it was so still. As though nothing dare stir tonight.

"Trevin," his dad said. "Come."

Trevin looked at Cyrus, the raven now cradled in Lord Nightswift's arms, lifeless and still. He glanced at Quinn, who finally was back on four paws. His cuts were deep and as Trevin finally realized, his face stung and blood dripped. He felt a pain in his throat and he wouldn't dare look at anyone other than Cyrus now. He felt like a coward. His gift was to pull emotions off those who needed it, but he was far too scared to do that for any of them. He was scared that if he locked eyes with any of them, he would impulsively pull their grief onto him. This was horrible.

"Is he going to be okay?" Trevin asked. He hadn't moved.

"Come," His dad repeated, stress heavy. Trevin wept. His tears stung him. Then he heard the others walk. Quinn changed back with a groan.

"Are you okay?" Lord Ashdale asked his son.

"The cuts are deep, but I can heal them. It happened too fast. It charged Trev, and I told Cyrus to fly higher. It had so much strength." Quinn groaned in pain.

"We were not prepared for this. We wanted you three to handle this task, it looked like rabies. We should have been the ones on the chase. Not you boys," Lord Ashdale said.

Lord Nightswift held his eldest, appearing utterly distraught at Cyrus's limp body. Trevin couldn't tell if the shine on the feathers was blood or the moonlight. He wasn't sure he wanted to change, for Trevin knew it would sting far worse.

"Trevin," his dad repeated in a sterner tone.

Trevin followed, his mind racing, as he followed his dad, letting muscle memory guide him home. He thought of Elodie and how the trees seemed brighter in her presence. He thought of the sheer rage and malice in that mountain lion's eyes over him. Cyrus's cry of pain, his thrashing and pleading after. Then he realized he was home.

"Trevin!" Autumn cried out. Still in his mountain lion form, he saw her hands come to her mouth and noticed Cedar's worry. Trevin was still too stunned to respond. "What happened to him, Dad? Is he going to be okay?" Autumn pleaded. Trevin noticed the blood drip from under him. The sting of the cuts started, driving Trevin crazy.

His dad changed from mountain lion to fae. "Silence. Trevin, in the study, now." His tone was low and serious. Trevin didn't know what was happening. Worry cascaded over him. Slow steps led him into the study and his dad closed the doors, then locked them. Trevin swallowed hard and sat back on his haunches. His dad turned and walked up to him.

Lord Greenthistle gazed at the mountain lion, which was his heir, his firstborn son. He saw the gashes across his muzzle, his split open lip. It had missed his eyes, one small grace in a sea of strife of tonight. He dropped to his knees, hugging Trevin tightly and cried into Trevin's chest. Trevin remained still, not sure what was happening. His dad had always been the strong, silent type and had only seen him cry once when his mom had passed. Lord Greenthistle always showed pride in his kids. He fell in love with Autumn the second she was born, daddy's little girl. Cedar always pushed harder and in turn maybe that was what made him stronger than Trevin. Yet when it came to Trevin, his dad truly beamed with pride. Trevin never had to be asked. He always stepped up, worked hard. His dad told him repeatedly how great he would be as an estate lord one day. When he didn't do well, his dad would express his disappointment in him and tell him to stop questioning why he was firstborn. He was firstborn because he would be great. His mom had always told him he would make Greenthistle better than his dad had made it, and do the bloodline proud. His dad never once had a doubt in him.

"I'm sorry. None of this should have happened. Cyrus shouldn't be in his condition. Quinn shouldn't have been touched, you shouldn't be injured. That was something far darker, old, evil, and I put you on death's watch," he cried. "I could have lost you, son. I'm sorry," he said, still hugging Trevin.

"I'm here, Dad," Trevin said, not sure what else to say.

His dad flinched, then gripped him tighter. "You were all hurt on account of me. I suggested you three work together to chase and use your strengths, and you all did. You did exactly what you all needed too. Yet you all paid a price for my miscalculation. Cyrus most of all."

"Is he going to be okay? He's going to make it? I've never heard him in that much pain," Trevin said, fighting the whimper back. "He sounded terrified."

"I put him in a deep sleep and healed what I could. His body will mend the rest. I can only fully heal fae, mortals, and mountain lions, since I have all three forms. I can't know for certain what it would do to Nightswift or Ashdale. I could severely mess them up in feral form."

"You don't know what that evil was?"

"I've never seen it before. I shouldn't have killed the mountain lion. I should have sedated it. Lord Ashdale ripped it off you but seeing your face and seeing what it did to Cyrus, knowing that could have been you. I snapped. I couldn't control myself and I killed it. I couldn't lose you—I couldn't carry your body back here for your siblings to see," his dad said, still gripping Trevin's fur.

"Please don't blame yourself for this attack. I wasn't thinking clearly. I was distracted, trying to figure things out. I should have focused more," Trevin said with remorse. *Stupid mortals.*

"And I ask you to not blame yourself for Cyrus or Quinn's injuries. I don't think any of us could have predicted this. You fought hard, you made me proud, you all made your estates proud," his dad said.

Trevin told his dad about what had happened with the encounter. Lord Greenthistle finally pulled back and nodded. His face strained at the gashes and busted lip.

"Deep breaths, son," Lord Greenthistle said, as he placed his palms on either side of the mountain lion's head. His index fingers and thumbs wrapped around his ears, fingers braced firmly on the back of Trevin's skull. Trevin took a deep breath and his eyelids went heavy. The sting of his face faded for a moment, then his dad's magic faltered. Trevin snapped back too, his face still sore. Shock washed over him and he watched his dad drop his head, sitting back on his knees and ankles as he wiped his eye. "I'm sorry. I don't have enough. This was taxing on me. I'm sorry, son, the wounds on you and Cyrus are not normal. They were deeper."

"Dad, it's okay. I'm still here. I can heal the rest on my own," Trevin said.

His dad flinched again and let out a defeated sigh. He finally lifted his head to see his son's face, still a mountain lion. The wounds were less severe.

Trevin swallowed and changed. He gritted his teeth at the sting and his dad sighed.

"Go get some rest, please. I will send food up with a medic to clean what I can't heal."

Trevin nodded, leaving his dad still slumped on his knees. Trevin could see his despair, could see how broken he was. He went to pull the emotions, but stopped suddenly when his dad spoke.

"Don't you dare pull this off me, Trevin. This is not your burden to bear." His tone was stern and serious. Trevin sniffed and nodded, then left the room. He pulled the door shut, knowing he could at least spare Autumn and Cedar from seeing their dad like this. He wasn't sure he wanted to see his dad that broken again. Once outside, he turned to Autumn and Cedar, who jumped at the sound of the door.

"What happened?" Cedar asked.

Trevin turned to face them finally, and they gasped.

"I will tell you later. I'm too exhausted right now. Dad is too. We are okay. We are home," he said. They both nodded. "Autumn? Have you heard from Charles or Cora?"

Autumn watched him, worried.

"He's fine, they are fine, I just want to know they are fine," Trevin said, assuring not only his siblings but himself too. Cedar and Autumn gave him a questioning expression.

"He texted saying they were going to sleep a few hours ago. They had a good night. No one asked to use his van," she said with a pause. "Do you want me to go check on them? I can, it's not that far," she offered.

"No. I don't. I want you both to stay here inside. Dad does too," Trevin said with a sigh. He then turned and started upstairs to his room, overhearing their conversation as he walked.

"I don't like any of this," Cedar said. "Why wouldn't Dad have just finished healing him?"

"I don't know, and why would he ask about Charles and Cora?" Autumn asked. "Something bad happened."

"I guess check in with your guy tomorrow and then let Trevin know when he gets up."

By Sunday, Cyrus was awake and able to walk around. He hadn't taken flight yet but was eager too.

"Just relax, you don't want to push it," Trevin said. His face is still tender. His lip was swollen, and the wound scabbed over.

"I see you couldn't get your face healed," Cyrus scoffed. He gave Trevin a sly little grin. Trevin looked at him with some surprise.

"I see you still got your spunk. Glad to see you recovered," Quinn said, hoping Cyrus was joking.

"And here you are, the biggest of the three of us, as though you weren't even touched," Cyrus snapped back.

"Like I said, none of us were prepared for that. I *did* try to fight it. Trevin did too. Those gashes on my chest are still there," Quinn said, slightly perturbed.

Just then, Cyrus flinched and grabbed his chest. Worry crept over his face as he met his friends' concerned expressions.

"Sorry, still healing and all. I'm glad neither of you took that much impact. I know you both fought. I wanted to. I tried, I am trying," he said, laying back with an exhausted sigh and a chill.

"Are you okay?" Trevin asked, watching him. He was confused by the sudden mood swing in Cyrus.

"Yea, I'm just exhausted. Like I said, it hurt. I wouldn't wish this on my worst enemy. Thanks for checking up on me. I will hopefully see you at drills tomorrow," he said. Trevin and Quinn's expressions grew concerned.

"Seriously, don't push it. We will check in with you tomorrow. Take it easy, okay?" Quinn said. Cyrus nodded and reached for his phone as a way of dismissing them.

Trevin felt something in the pit of his stomach. He stood up, as did Quinn, and they headed to the door.

"Cyrus, are you really okay? You look better but, I want to make sure," Trevin asked. Cyrus glanced at him with a mask of confidence.

"I'm fine. Just tired," he said. "Going to take more than a pathetic mountain lion to take me down." He smirked. Trevin nodded with unease and followed Quinn out of the door.

They headed downstairs and saw Lord Nightswift in the foyer with a small smile.

"Thank you boys for visiting. It will be a slow recovery for him. I think he needs you two a lot," Lord Nightswift said.

Trevin noticed Delia and Poppy—Cyrus's younger sisters—sitting on the couch, Poppy wiped her eyes. She was the youngest of all the estate children at only nine years but already acutely aware of her world. He assumed she was just as upset as he had been with what had happened to Cyrus. He hoped Delia didn't blame Greenthistle for this. She had little interest in the roles expected of high estate life. Though he could understand if she loathed him specifically. If anything happened to Cyrus, the succession of the estate would fall on her, and she was not prepared for that. It would also knock Nightswift out of second below Ashdale. Lady Nightswift walked over and sat by Poppy. She glanced at them and offered a small smile.

"He only woke up this morning, and he's exhausted. Night terrors were his only movement since Lord Greenthistle sedated him. I never want to see any of you kids experience that."

"I will let my dad know," Trevin said. Lord Nightswift nodded and watched Trevin and Quinn leave.

CHAPTER 7

The following Tuesday, Elodie walked into the café and saw Trev sitting there at a table. He was reading something intently with his sly little grin. She stared at him with narrowed eyes. He still had a number on his table, meaning he had gotten here recently. As soon as she looked ahead, she caught him glancing up in her peripheral vision.

Elodie walked up to the counter and met a big grin on Cora's face

"Silly games you two are playing."

"That is not what's happening." Elodie rolled her eyes.

Cora laughed and rang the order up.

"Oops, I put your order under number 14, but I don't have number 14, silly me. I think it's still out at a table," Cora smiled widely and glanced passed her to the side Trevin was sitting on.

"Cora," Elodie whined. "No."

"Here's your receipt. Should be out in ten." She smiled.

"Are you two plotting something?"

"Not at all. We are all friends here, right?" She laughed and turned her attention to the person behind Elodie in line. Elodie scowled and let out a sigh before walking to Trev's table. The one next to him was open, so she sat down next to him on the bench. From her peripheral vision she noticed him glance at her, a shocked expression on his face.

A small shake of her head and a smirk before she spoke. "Cora slipped up and put my order on yours," she said, and Trevin glanced over at Cora and sighed.

"Great," he said.

Elodie turned to meet his eyes with a glare and then gasped at the sight of his wounds. "Are you okay?" she asked.

He frowned and lowered his eyes. "Yes," he said shortly.

"What happ—I'm sorry. I shouldn't ask." Elodie cut her eyes down. "I hope it was nothing serious," she said, taking out her sketchbook and pen pouch. It was black with a crescent moon and a luna moth on it.

He casually tucked his papers under his notebook and she glanced over, but kept her eyes down. She saw something about the town of Falk.

✦✦✦

"It." he paused, remembering the mountain lion, how still the forest was, how quiet it was, and how alive the Old Giants were when Elodie was near. He sighed. "It was a thing." He damned himself for not being more prepared for this question. Someone was sure to ask about his face.

She fixed narrowed eyes on him again, but he focused his attention on his tablet.

"At least it appears to be on the mend?" she asked, trying to offer sympathy. He gave her a genuine smile, and she smiled back.

"At least there is that," he said with a frown. He thought about Cyrus and Quinn. He didn't understand what was in the mountain lion to block out his ability to communicate with it. Was he losing his edge? Was he the best for the Greenthistle line? He sighed again, forgetting for a moment who was sitting next to him. He went to rub his eyes and hit one of the tender spots on his face. He flinched and gasped in pain.

Elodie glanced at him with concern. She reached her hand out for a split-second and her eyes darted over his face as if assessing it, but then she dropped her hand.

Trevin watched her confused for a second, then looked back down at his tablet and they remained silent.

She stared at her sketchbook. When she sighed, he snapped back to the moment and saw her staring at it, but made no attempt to open it.

"I'm sure Cora told you I didn't do any solo night hikes this weekend. Obviously, I didn't get swept away by a sea siren or kraken," she said as if those were the obvious dangers wandering around here at night.

He looked at her again and felt that energy in her—something calm, quiet, and soothing. One that beckoned him, lured him, teased and tantalized his fae senses. He smirked slightly.

"I forgot to ask her about that. Gotta watch out for the sea sirens and the kraken. Though I feel as though you might be well versed in handling them for some reason."

"I've read a fantasy book or twenty," she answered.

Oh, that explains it. Are you looking for something? he wondered. "Suppose that's a good place to start," he said with a small laugh. They were interrupted when Cora brought their order at the same time.

"Here you both go. Silly me putting the same number in." She smirked. "You okay, Trev?" she asked.

"Yea. I'm okay," he said, glancing down.

"You're still beautiful. Don't worry about that." She smiled and glanced at Elodie, before walking back to the counter.

He shook his head. "But am I still breathtaking? That is the real question," he said, confident and smoothly.

Elodie rolled her eyes and shook her head. "You eavesdropped on that entire conversation, didn't you?" she asked.

"I might have heard some of it."

"That's weird," she said bluntly. The energy in her shifted.

"It was a pleasure to meet you that evening, Lady Elodie of Marin," he said with a grin. Her cheeks and ears heated.

"Don't please. You are no five hundred-year-old fae prince. Which I certainly don't need, by the way." He chuckled and she sighed. "I'm no princess or nineteen-year-old skilled renegade, either. I'm not looking for a prince or a knight in shining armor. Or anything," she continued, "You and your pet names too. What does little mink even mean?"

Are you really not looking for anything? Why would it matter if she is or isn't? He was grateful he was good at keeping his masks up. She'd think she was sitting next to a madman.

"You are curious. You watch a lot too. I see it in your eyes, which I find rather lovely, by the way. I think you are searching for something, though. And I don't mean a five hundred-year-old fae prince, but something you think is in the forest, in the trees and the ferns. The Little Mink can be brave too, but trust me when I say sea sirens and krakens are not the danger in the forests," he said confidently and smugly.

She sighed again and cut her eyes down.

Good, be scared, he thought to himself.

"I know," she said, "I will heed your advice, Prince Greenthistle." She added sarcasm to the last part. He laughed briefly before wincing at the pain from his wounds.

"Good, because those five hundred-year-old fae princes are probably all too busy saving the nineteen-year-old renegades, if they exist." Trevin laughed. He knew there were no princes in California when it came to fae, and there were few five hundred-year-old estate lords. The state wasn't even two hundred years old, but there were some areas with old estate families, before they called themselves estates. Far older than five hundred years.

She sighed and shook her head.

Trevin smirked at how easy it was to tell the truth most of the time. Mortals were always quick to shut out the magic world. Occasionally, a few would have a tiny bit of fae blood from many generations ago, giving them sharper senses. Any half human-half fae were kept on his side of the fae boundary. Only fae approved by the high estates could pass between the boundary for work. The three high estate families were required to integrate with mortals.

Trevin turned back to his papers and tablet when Elodie began to eat and sip on her drink. He glanced over when she opened to a random page in her sketchbook—a pirate ship and a lighthouse. He was impressed and curious about the drawing. He took a sip of his drink—a cold brew with cream. When he glanced over again, he couldn't help but smile slightly at the little mink she had drawn. She had started drawing a small teal and yellow flower crown on it, too. He felt such delight and again he asked himself why. He wanted to commit it to memory. She didn't even take a break, just moved and started sketching something else. As he watched her draw, he couldn't make himself look away, fascinated by how easily she was able to draw what was in her head.

Trevin finally snapped out of it when he heard a chair scratch against the floor. He turned back to his papers and unlocked the tablet screen, and focused on what he was doing. When she finally set her pencil down a little while later, he glanced over and his jaw fell agape. She had drawn a mountain lion sitting in a sphinx pose in front of a redwood on some rocks. His eyes moved to her, then back down to his papers. He couldn't concentrate on reading about the history of the town of Falk while sitting next to her. He heard Cora's footsteps approach and looked up.

"Since you two are getting along, I was thinking of another bonfire, local though, just for the night, no camping. Just over near Samoa. Trev, pass it on to your people, yeah?" she asked.

He nodded. "Will do."

Elodie gave Cora a nod.

"Tell them they better behave, too." Cora eyed Trevin. He smirked.

"Don't we always?" he said in the most charming voice he could muster. Cora laughed.

"Most of the time."

"I always do." His response was pompous.

"Sure ya do," she said, walking back to the counter.

The door opened and Trevin glanced over. His brother Cedar walked in with a smug grin on his face, dressed in black cargo pants, a sweatshirt, and his aviator sunglasses on his head.

"Trev," Cedar said in a sly tone. "I'm not interrupting your date, am I?" he crooned.

"It's not a date, Caleb. We are at separate tables. Elodie, meet Caleb, Caleb, Elodie. My younger brother. He works at the police academy and serves with Humboldt's finest."

"It's nice to meet you, Mr.—" she trailed off and Trevin realized she wasn't sure how to address them.

"Caleb is perfectly fine. Shall I call you Elodie or something else?" he asked with his most dashing smile leaning forward.

Trevin eyed him. Flirting with mortals was not out of character for Cedar, but he did not want him flirting with Elodie.

"Elodie is fine," she said in a small voice. Trevin placed his hand on her arm lightly. She looked at him, unsure.

"Don't let Caleb intimidate you. He's a shameless flirt," he said with a smile.

"You seem to be doing well yourself, Trev," Cedar followed up without dropping his grin.

Trevin felt the energy in her shift.

"There is no need for a pissing contest. I'm not interested in being eyed like a piece of fresh meat. I'm not even that fresh, it's been over three months since I moved here."

Trevin watched her, unsure what to do, and removed his hand before glaring at Caleb when he let out a sly little laugh.

"Nice, she's got some spark in her. I like that," Cedar said.

"Okay, that's enough," Trevin responded.

Cedar locked eyes with Trevin, holding his grin. "That little game we played at the party turned out to be quite the match for one of us at least, no?"

"Caleb!" Trevin hissed.

"What game?" She stared at Trevin.

"Just a little game we play where we see who can get a kiss first. I won, but he was a very close second." Cedar still had his smug tone.

"Caleb, what the hell?" he said, glaring at him. Cedar smiled back with mocking concern on his face. Elodie hastily put her belongings away. "El, I don't like to play those games. He does, but I don't," he said.

"But you did, figures as much, little fuckboys need their fun too," she spat out.

How Trevin had grown to despise that term as of late. He watched her stand, angered, and hated that he couldn't lie, because he couldn't make himself deny it. It was not the only reason for the kiss, but it was part of it.

"Thanks though. Guess I made that extra easy for you, didn't I?" she said, glaring at Trevin.

"No. El, wait I—" Trevin said, reaching out for her. He froze. Seeing a few other patrons watch, they shook their heads in disapproval. His heart was pounding, he realized.

"Don't call me El," she hissed and walked out the door.

"Honestly, those estate boys think they can do whatever they want. Poor girl seems nice," an older woman said in a hushed tone.

Cedar smirked again.

"I did you a favor. Now you can stop being weird and get back to your job."

"You don't need to paint me as something I'm not, though. I'm not a fuckboy. I'm not you or Russ."

"Come on, let's go. We got work to do," Cedar said.

Trevin glanced at Cora with dismay. She glanced back at him and shook her head in disappointment.

Chapter 8

E lodie got to her car and tossed her backpack on the passenger seat as she jumped in. She gazed up at the tree line.

Elodie.

They seemed to call out to her.

She sighed. "I'm not supposed to go out and wander the trails. Cora doesn't like it; Trev doesn't think it's safe. The mountain lion," she pleaded with herself. She drove north toward Arcata to the community forest at the edge of a neighborhood. It was dusk when she parked and a sigh of defeat escaped her.

"I should have known better. He thinks I'm stupid. Caleb thinks I'm stupid. I'm just a stupid game to them." She put her car in park and grabbed her phone, and reread the text message Ricky had sent earlier today.

Whatever that asshole has, you know isn't worth it. Just come over. Let's at least talk. Please. I'm sorry. You mean a lot to me.

She sighed. She deleted the entire message and his number.

"I don't need either of you pricks."

She scoffed then got out of the car and began walking on the trail. After walking on the gravel path for a little while, the trail turned to dirt and narrowed.

Elodie. El

The voices called to her again.

She took an inhale and walked deeper noticing the presence of the Old Giants. Her fingers brushed along the redwood trunks and the ferns. Moisture collected on her hand then silently dropped off.

"Maybe if you were a five hundred-year-old fae, I'd believe you. Fae can't lie. Maybe that is what I'm searching for?" she said to herself and laughed. "Not you, Trevor. Don't flatter yourself."

She kept walking deeper and deeper, and darker and darker it became.

Elodie. You are home. You are watched over.
He will watch over you.
Do not push this away. Awaken and you'll see.

Krakens and sea sirens are not the dangerous things in the forest. His words trailed through her head. She frowned, seeing the last of the light fading. Instead of turning back towards her car, something pulled her to go further—something beckoning her deeper and deeper into the forest. She set a timer on her phone for fifteen minutes and noticed she had no signal. Letting her fingers skim the ferns, Trevor's face flashed in her mind.

El.

The voice swirled through her, causing her to freeze. The timer went off, startling her. She still wanted to go further, but it was dark.

She sat down on a rock and listened, observing what she could hear. A raven called out.

You sought enough tonight. You are home.

The voices said and her eyes got heavy. The raven cawed, and she heard the flap of its wings.

She saw Trevin glancing at her sketchbook. He had smiled at the mink drawing. Then he was stunned as his eyes traveled to the redwoods and mountain lion sketch she had done. She then saw Marin, she was in the headlands, facing the Golden Gate Bridge. She turned east to the mountains, and she frowned. She always felt the piece of her missing even though she was from Marin, born and raised there. She turned facing south. Had the central coast ever called her this strongly? She turned west and saw the ocean. The mighty Pacific was always with her. It was in her blood. It would be with her wherever she went. She turned to the north and there were the Old Giants, the rains, the ferns, and she smiled.

"El, I'm sorry," a voice said behind her. His voice. She spun around and saw Trev. They both stood in Arcata Community Forest again. It was night. "I never should have kissed you like that. I still would've told Ricky off, though."

"Trev," she said softly. He walked up to her and they hugged. He nuzzled his head into hers. Elodie didn't want to stay mad at him. She didn't have to like him; she shouldn't like him.

Wake up, little one. You are home, but you must turn back.
See him, listen to him. They will all need you. Wake up.

She startled awake, and it took her a second to remember where she was. A chuffing sound behind her made her heart race. She scrambled backwards as she locked eyes with a mountain lion. It froze and then arched its back. She maintained eye contact while trying to unlock her phone. No signal—of course—and no playlist downloads either. The mountain lion stepped toward her with a low growl. Carefully she took a step backward toward the trailhead, and it slowly stalked closer.

Then Elodie realized the striking green of its eyes and tilted her head, until it growled again. She heard a caw above from the raven, and the mountain lion hissed. She backed up more quickly now and brought her phone up trembling. Once she let the alarm sound play she shoved the phone in her pocket and then began clapping. Anything to make a lot of noise, make herself bigger.

The faintest of chuffs slipped out, and it ran off the trail. She let out a sigh of relief for a moment then ran back down the trail to her car.

"Make it to the car, just make it to the car!" she cried out. She finally saw her car. It was the only one in the parking lot. She scrambled inside, locked the doors, and started the ignition.

Elodie heard her phone buzz with a message. She didn't stop to check it until she was home and warmed up from a shower. She laid down in bed and saw it was from Cora.

Please come to the bonfire still. Trev isn't a lousy guy. I did tell him he needs to apologize though and if he doesn't I will uninvite him and Caleb.

Elodie didn't respond. She groaned at the thought of him being uninvited on her account. It would cause unrest. His family would hate her. She just wouldn't go.

Little did she know that mountain lion had watched her the entire way. Had been watching her for some time, while she nodded off. It had also made sure she was okay.

"Clever girl. Let us hope you scared this one enough to stop looking for trouble. She will be in trouble otherwise," Cyrus said. Trevin chirped.

"Thanks, glad you are back in the air."

"Catch ya later, Trevy," Cyrus said, flying off.

Trevin ran home and went straight to his room. He collapsed on his bed and gripped his hair.

"El!" he groaned. He thought about when he was near the boundary line, and he got the faintest whiff of her scent. He had been out with Cyrus to help him get back in the air. Trevin thought it too soon, but Cyrus wanted to anyway. He appeared to be recovering quickly. Usually he circled longer, but Trevin was glad he wasn't overdoing it.

He thought about how Cyrus had spotted her on a trail that paralleled the boundary line. The trees and ferns were brighter around her. The sight of her on the ground, not moving, made his stomach flip. He changed into his fae form and searched for her pulse. It was almost peaceful. *Stupid girl, you fell asleep out here?* he thought to himself. He told her he was sorry and when he changed back into feral, he nuzzled her to try to wake her. Shock grabbed him when his name graced her lips, *Trev*, she'd said, almost with relief? Was she really dreaming about him? He was upset with her for being careless.

She reacted that so fast, faster than he had ever seen a mortal move. The other night she trembled and curled up, but tonight she kept her wits about her. Then she locked onto his eyes. Of course, this odd little mink would get too close to notice his eyes. What on earth was she?

"Fuck. Elodie, you are going to drive me insane if you keep up the stupid night hikes." He groaned and got up for food.

Wednesday came, and she skipped the café. She ended up working later that day anyway, then called her dad when she was home.

"Oh hello, Elodie. How are you doing up there?"

"I'm doing well," she answered, not bothering to mention the last two mountain lion encounters or meeting Trev.

"Work still good? Friends good?" he asked.

"Yeah, work is a lot of fun. The kids love art and nature. Parents seem to like me. Friends are good. I went to a Halloween party and last weekend some of us went camping in Trinidad."

"That sounds like fun. I know how much you missed it up there. I'd have hated for you to miss out on it any longer. Your mom missed it."

"I know, Dad. I miss you, though. I wonder if everyone else in the family is right. I am being selfish."

"You are not being selfish—you are doing exactly what needs to be done. You belong up there. Just come and visit."

"You know I will, in two and a half weeks. I will head down Wednesday morning."

"Okay, sounds good. I'm looking forward to it," he said. "Elodie."

"Yeah?"

"Did you meet anyone special?" he asked with his teasing voice.

"No. No, Dad, I didn't." She laughed. She could feel her face heat again.

"Ricky came by to see if you actually left. When I told him to get lost, he said you were with someone. You told him you moved on."

Elodie sighed. "Seriously, just call the cops if he shows up again."

"I will. I told him I would next time and to leave you the hell alone," he said. She smiled. "Do I get a name or to meet him? To make sure he's keeping my little girl safe?"

"What? No, it was a spur-of-the-moment thing because Ricky wasn't getting the message. He is a friend of a friend. I can't pursue him and he doesn't like me, doesn't have time. His dad is a county seat in Humboldt and I've been told he will take over one day. I don't want to be with a politician." She laughed.

"I know, Elodie. You just want to be in the trees. That's why you can't move back to Marin. You were miserable here."

"I wasn't."

"Stay up there. Visit, but make a home for yourself. I am okay. I love you, hun," he said.

"I love you too, Dad." She hung up and traced the silhouettes of trees through the window.

"Home." She smiled and went to sleep.

On Thursday, she relented and went to the café again. She took a deep breath and scanned the patrons. No Trev. A sigh of relief slipped out. Maybe he wouldn't go. Caleb wouldn't talk to her; she was sure of it.

"Hey, the usual, but make the drink hot."

"It's been chilly," Cora said. "Missed ya last night."

"Work and lesson plans and stuff."

"Missed ya both last night," she said.

Elodie rolled her eyes. "You seem really concerned about a relationship neither of us wants."

"He's a good friend of mine and you are, too. I don't know why he's been so shitty lately. It bothers me. He's usually apathetic, but then he sees you and he behaves differently."

"Well, I'm not sure why my presence here makes him different. I mean, I'm renting a studio, I teach kids the basic state required curriculum, and add in some art and nature activities wherever I can. I'm nothing special or intimidating."

Cora was quiet for a moment. "I don't know that I've ever known him to be with anyone for long. He's mentioned exes, one I know cheated on him and she eventually moved away. Another I heard didn't care for his schedule, but I never met her."

Elodie raised her eyebrows, confused as to why Cora was telling her this. "Is he in the cafe a lot? Are you paying him to take up a seat?" Elodie asked. Cora laughed.

"No, I'm not. I think he just enjoys people watching. I catch him watching interactions a lot. He's always reading about this thing or the history of that thing. Doing research, I assume, for his dad. Plus, he works for State Parks."

"How long have you known him?"

"Oh, we went to school together but didn't talk much. I'd say six years of being friends? He hasn't changed much at all from high school. Then again, neither had Caleb nor Anna. None of them seem to, blessed with good anti-aging genes, I guess." She laughed.

"We will see if he can be bothered to apologize."

"He better."

"Don't uninvite him or his brother. It will only make them hate me more."

"He doesn't hate you, and I want you to come on Saturday."

Elodie exhaled and then took her usual seat. She sat closer to the counter but also so she could see the windows clearly. Elodie pulled out her sketch book and started sketching a mountain lion—they had been at the forefront of her mind since the first encounter with one.

"Know much about the City of Falk?" he asked. She rolled her eyes.

She had heard someone walk in as she sat down, then felt then too near her table. Of course it would be Trev.

"Only that you were doing a lot of research on it, until I showed up." Elodie focused on her sketchbook again. That scent of oakmoss and amber struck her now.

Trevin laughed, greatly amused. "Project for my dad, and State Parks, where I work."

Elodie didn't respond. He watched her draw another fern with some rocks. "It was an old lumber mill town and then abandoned. Bottle hunters started looting the remains and illegal dwellings started up. To remedy the problem, they tore some of the remains of the ghost town down. All that remains is a water tower and not much else. On the surface, at least. There was a lot of underground stuff reported to be there and we are trying to salvage what we can. Before the Old

Giants reclaim what was taken from them," he said. "I am trying to research to find where things might have been."

"Isn't it a historic site? There are records of it." She did not look at him, nor did she seem to be impressed with the history lesson.

"It is, and we have a layout of the town, but not the underground, nor how to access it. The town itself is hard to get to. We are trying to find a way to open the doors, so to speak."

She glanced at her sketches, then the established year she had seen on her own research. 1884. *Any metal would likely be iron, and well rusted over with the fog up here.*

"Ahh, so it is a hidden treasure Humboldt's rulers hope to find? Iron cast in 1884 would not withstand the test of time in the land of the Old Giant's with all the mist and rain. The iron today must be rusted and brittle. Why not just remove it?" she asked, meeting his eyes again. He smirked at her and her way with words.

"It is more complicated than removing some old iron chains, little mink." He leaned forward slightly, his tone sly. "There is one specific treasure that we seek and cannot find. The clues on where to find it are not in Falk and that leads to another mystery: why is this object hidden so well?"

She narrowed her eyes at him. "Is this what you do for your dad? Play detective and treasure hunt? Must be a big boy's dream job."

"Yeah, it is. See, I get to live the stories you read about in your fantasy books," he said with a smirk, then stood up and they locked eyes. She was unamused, and he was not sure why he was even talking to her about this. "Perhaps I will see ya at the bonfire?"

She rolled her eyes.

"Adieu, fortune seeker," she said. He took that as his dismissal and walked out.

Chapter 9

Trevin walked to the waterfront a few blocks down. He listened to the sound of the boats and the water. He heard people walking by as his eyes scanned the darkness of the mighty Pacific beyond his lands. The interaction with her tonight had not gone as intended.

He had hesitated even going to the café tonight. Cora had told him she wasn't planning on going Saturday night and he needed to apologize to her for everything. Observing her order he noticed she had a warm beverage and a muffin. Usually she always had iced. He wasn't planning on staying long and yet seeing her here, he wanted to stay longer. Tomorrow night he would attempt to stay longer, regardless if she was here or not.

When he stepped up next to where she sat and glanced down at her sketchbook, he saw a large angry mountain lion and town ruins with a sign that said 'City of Falk.'

Trevin realized she had been paying attention, and wondered if she was more closely aligned with Nightswift than Greenthistle. Nightswift observed and analyzed. Greenthistle was strength and valor. She drew a lot of mountain lions, probably because they scare her. Greenthistle scares her.

He thought about her words. How ignorant of the world she was. How blissfully unaware of these lands she was and would remain that way, too. Yet the Old Giants and the ferns seemed to respond to her. They were so bright and alive near her. It drove him wild to know why. He thought about her energy tonight.

How closed off it had been. As though she was guarding close and didn't want anyone to see it.

As if the redwoods and her had some kind of tie. The ones here were far older than her home redwoods in Marin. Yet his redwoods, that made his home, made up his bloodline didn't respond to any of the fae here as they did her. It frustrated him that a mere mortal transplant had the power to do this. Trevin knew though he certainly did not want to ignore it, whatever this was inside of her, he did not want to ignore her. He wanted to embrace it, embrace her and find their path out together. His eyes shifted up to stars as his shoulders slumped at the realization she was still pissed at him and rightfully so.

His phone buzzed.

That doesn't count as an apology.

Cora said. He rolled his eyes and leaned his elbows on the railing. His hands became a battle of hot and toasty on the palms and freezing cold on the tops.

Elodie was something baffling to him. She was a riddle he could not solve and a tome warded by magic he did not understand.

His phone buzzed again. This time it was a text from Quinn.

Stop wandering the mortal world, lost cub, come back home and party with us.

Trevin smirked and finished his drink, then headed back home. He walked east away from downtown, to change into feral. Cora's house was a good location for this. There weren't many dense trees but there wasn't any foot traffic or roads either.

As he walked back near the café, the scent of ocean breeze and lavender reeled him as if it snagged him. He followed it two blocks away from the café and he spotted her car. She wasn't in it, yet her scent lingered that much.

He put his hand on the pillar of her hatchback.

"Please no night hikes, El. Please get home safely tonight," he said in a small prayer. He scanned the tops of the Old Giants in the distance, then he ran off.

Once he was out of town, he changed into his mountain lion form and ran swiftly and silently. Up to Sunny Brae and onto the trailhead, he crossed the boundary line between the mortal world and the fae world. He headed to the tavern Q said they were at. He saw Cedar, Quinn and Cyrus there. A female fae with translucent dragonfly wings, light purple skin, and white hair sat on his lap.

Cyrus cut him a smug smile. "Autumn's not here?"

"Nah, she's out with Charles, her mortal lover," Cedar said.

"Oh, she has one of those?" Cyrus asked with some annoyance. He placed a hand on the fairy's thigh as she leaned into him more.

"She found one at the last Halloween party. Seems as though you both have found people?" Cedar said.

"Alena and I are just friends," Cyrus said, licking his lip.

"Only those of high fae nobility are worthy of Master Nightswift. And what business would I have being an estate lady? Too much responsibility. Just let me live my life, away from the dumb mortals. I don't want to integrate," she said, running her finger along Cyrus's ear. His eyes went heavy.

Trevin realized he hadn't felt that sensation in nearly a decade. He remembered Elodie's eyes going heavy. The desire she felt in that moment, and then he remembered her eyes going to his lips.

Why am I thinking about her? he asked himself. *Stupid girl. Maybe the guys were right, maybe it had been too long.* He glanced around the tavern, again all faces in a sea of faces. Taking in those he found attractive, but he could not find the desire to go pursue any of them.

"Dude chill, we got dinner, after the weekend we had can you blame me?" he heard Quinn say.

"Whatever. You are texting her." Cedar said.

"You guys are not the only ones I talk to," Quinn replied.

"Are you talking about Justine?" Cyrus asked. Alena rolled her eyes.

Quinn remained quiet, but Cedar spoke up with a yes.

Trevin got up and went to order a drink. He took the glass with a fizzy beverage in it and scanned over everyone in the tavern. He frowned; he didn't trust anyone in here save for his friends. He didn't trust the fae sitting in Cyrus's lap. He didn't trust a lot of people.

He let out a sigh and wondered if he trusted her. He trusted Cora, and Justine, Charles too. He knew his sister wouldn't be with anyone untrustworthy. That left Elodie. She certainly was sly and observant, he learned.

Then he realized he couldn't even trust her to stay safe from the forests. How could he trust her with anything else? He shook his head and went to take a step when someone bumped into him. He turned and saw a girl a few inches shorter than him. She had porcelain white skin and pastel green hair. Her eyes are also a solid green. She smiled at him and placed a hand on him.

"Oh hi, Trev. Sorry, it's crowded near the bar area. Didn't mean to bump into you." Her coy tone raked over his ears. He saw her hand on his arm, then his eyes traced her pointed ears. She was high fae.

"It's fine," he said, watching her coy smile grow bigger.

"I'm standing close enough to kiss Master Greenthistle. Wow," she crooned with a giggle, moving her hand to his shoulder. He still held his drink and kept his other hand down to the side. "Tell me, what makes a good estate lady?"

"I'm not looking for anything," he said with some hint of annoyance.

"You never seem to be. Might you have a lover in the mortal world? A pathetic little liar?"

He rolled his eyes. "No, I don't have any foolish mortals either." With a scoff, Trevin turned to walk back to his friends. She grabbed him and pulled him in for a kiss. It made his body lock up. He didn't like this, didn't like the tavern, and he hated the fake flirting only for his title. He pulled back quickly.

"I'm certainly not interested in those who cannot listen," he said, annoyed.

"Apathetic doesn't look good on you. It doesn't look good for Greenthistle. There are omens you may want to avoid, predictions, you know."

"I'm not going to let Greenthistle crumble," he said and walked off. Once back at the table, he slumped down in the seat.

"Okay, it looks like you have lost the will to live. What the hell?" Quinn said, rolling his eyes. Cyrus watched with a wicked grin.

"I'm fine. I didn't want to come out."

"You said that at Cora's party too. You say that every time and yet you always do. Seriously, get over the FOMO. What do you think you are missing out on? You could have anyone here and you don't trust any of them." Cedar scoffed.

Trevin rolled his eyes.

"It's no secret you still carry the scars left from losing your mom. We get it. That was a rough time for all of us. My parents hate the Everoak territory for it and want nothing to do with them. Dad avoids them at the council meetings," Quinn said.

"You need to learn to trust at least our own kind again. Hate all the mortals you want. We can stop going to Cora's things," Cedar said. "Mortals are just easier."

"I trust Cora though. I trust Justine and Charles even. They are the type I'm fine with. Even the ones who come and go with the tides, they are interesting that they can just let go so easily of things when they want. Cora's family has had that café forever; it's one of the things that makes Eureka what it is. I don't know. We all need to watch mortals. Fae though, they throw themselves at us, for this title or the chance at being estate lady or lord. It's exhausting. They don't care about me, only what they are granted by being with me, like it's that easy."

"Fine, let the little kitten over there sulk and brood, but Quinn, why are you not flirting with anyone?" Cyrus asked casually, grazing Alena's chest with his hand. She put her fingers through his hair and smiled with heavy eyes. "The long days at work, it's easy to unwind and de-stress from the chaotic nature of mortal politics. You both should try it, especially you, Trev," he crooned out.

"I certainly wouldn't mind seeing what you boys do to unwind and de-stress from your days." Alena laughed, eyeing them.

Trevin rolled his eyes and shook his head.

"Nah, I got a rule. If I ever went for any of Russ or Trev's affections, it'd have to be years after it was well over and done with. I want my own conquest. I don't want to be sampled. We all made a pact, too. No going after each other's affections, fae or mortal," Quinn said.

"It's obvious that a lot of other fae just want into Greenthistle Estate. I can't fault Trev for that. It will all change once I find my person, but I would be pissed if I found them now at this age. Let me live. Then after a few centuries, maybe I will have had enough. It's fun for now," Cedar said with a grin. "And I do enjoy the fun of both mortals and fae."

Quinn looked at Trevin. "You left someone out of Cora's group. Do you not trust the new girl?" Quinn asked. "Pretty sure she is part of that group now. Given the lifestyle of Charles and Justine, Cora is going to want to hang onto her."

Cedar smirked and shook his head. "Oh, she's livid with all of us."

Cyrus stopped kissing Alena, paying attention again.

"What the fuck did I do? She doesn't have to like me anyway. She's Trev's girl now, off my radar," Quinn scoffed.

"Just drop it. Let her hate us. Also, I don't think I'm invited to the bonfire on Saturday night either, because she hates us. Quinn's right, Cora wants her to stick around. They are besties or some shit," Trevin scoffed, rolling his eyes. He thought about their kiss and how it felt. As if it embraced him, entangled him, yet he didn't want to fight it. He wanted to embrace it right back, entangle himself with her, too.

"I told her about our game when they were sitting next to each other at the café. You know what she called him?" Cedar laughed. Trevin rolled his eyes. He didn't want to hear the term. Not about him, not from her.

"Stop," Trevin groaned out.

"She called him a stupid fuckboy, this guy over here, who hasn't gotten laid in five years," Cedar said, laughing. Cyrus and Alena laughed too. Quinn shook his head with a small laugh and looked at Trevin.

Trevin sighed with a glare. "Whatever, she can hate me and all of us."

"That the same one we chased out of Arcata Community?" Cyrus asked.

"Yes. Hopefully, she learned her lesson."

"What? You didn't tell us about that," Quinn said.

"It was a few nights ago. I didn't have time. She was pissed, and she burns off stress with hikes or drawing. I wish she would have just stayed in the café. She fell asleep out there. Like an idiot!" Trevin groaned, running his fingers through his hair.

"Oh yeah, she did. She was real comfy at the base of one of the Old Giants. Stupid mortals. She's lucky Trev was the mountain lion to find her and not the one that attacked me," Cyrus said.

"I don't even want to think about facing it alone," Trevin said with a chill.

Quinn nodded. "Same here. That thing was not right."

"No, it wasn't. It was pure evil ready to rip the world or a raven in half," Cyrus said with a hint of malice.

"I'm glad you recovered from that. I'm glad you are here," Trevin said. Then he watched Cyrus shiver and drop the malice. Exhaustion and defeat washed over Cyrus. He hugged the girl on his lap and pressed his face into her chest.

"I am glad I am too. Thank you guys for that," he said. Exhaustion was heavy in his voice. Trevin and Quinn gave each other a glance. Cedar looked at him as if he was crazy.

Trevin noticed the hold on Alena seemed genuine, seemed soft and kind, like he was reaching for some sort of comfort. It was not the mindless grope of a tryst. His expression looked terrified.

"That sounded terrifying. That was scary. Dad wasn't okay with it, was he?" Cedar asked, turning to Trevin, who just shook his head.

"It scared the shit out of him. He feels responsible for all our injuries, and said he should have been on the chase, not us," Trevin said.

"No! What would've happened if they had gotten injured or your dad did, none of us are ready to take over yet," Quinn said with a shiver. "My dad said he had only ever seen Lord Greenthistle lose it like that once before. Where he was ready to watch everything crumble. My dad pulled it off you, but your dad snapped its neck before mine could react."

"I know. I told him that. I just want to make sure whatever was in that mountain lion doesn't hurt any mortals. They may be reckless in Elodie's case, but none of them deserve that. Not to mention we don't need a manhunt in the woods again. Certainly not one that our dads want to relive."

Cyrus let out a sigh and hugged the girl tighter. She gave him a shocked expression at the embrace, but she smiled uneasily and ran her fingers through his hair.

Trevin watched again and Elodie flashed in his head. He looked down, and in his mind he stood at the gate where that fantasy sat, the one he was tempted to push open, but he usually fought the urges. This time he pushed it open but did not walk down that path. He saw her smile at him, laugh with him. Surrounded by the Old Giants, ferns creating an arch around her, everything bright and alive, she was radiant, like a patron saint. He scoffed and shook his head. *Patron saint of Humboldt. Come on, Trev, you dumbass,* he thought.

"Caleb, what do you say you, Russ, and I enjoy the evening at my place? Let the other two heirs stew in their own moral dilemmas. No need to let past events dampen the mood."

Cyrus trembled with a chill and then that grin was back as Cedar smirked and nodded.

Alena got off Cyrus's lap and pulled him to stand. His body sagged with exhaustion. Cedar stood up, and they walked off.

"Cyrus and Cedar almost act more like brothers sometimes," Quinn said.

"That's weird given what they are about to do, but yeah, they do. He is acting weird." Trevin said with a sigh.

"Probably the recovery. That was a rough night. Don't worry about what happened too much. It's not your fault, or Greenthistle's. Cyrus will be fine.

If you are worried about Cora's friendship, just apologize to the girl. Use those lovely eyes of yours and tell her how dreadfully sorry you are in your smoothest voice." Quinn gave him a gentle shove.

"I know. It's just—there's been a shift. Things are changing faster than I can keep up with and Elodie is getting swallowed up by it. I can't figure out why."

"Yeah, I feel it. There's a shift in the air and the stars," Quinn said. "Let's get outta here. I'm ready to go home."

"No one catching your eye?"

"No. Not here."

Trevin nodded, and they left. They walked off down the street, talking of work and the things their dads all wanted to do. Eventually parting ways to their respective estates for the night.

CHAPTER 10

The next day came and went. Trevin sighed as he sat at the tree line of Eureka, then headed into town. He walked into the café , letting his shoulders slump when he didn't see her.

"I'm serious, Trev. You better apologize to her tonight or I don't want you or Caleb going," Cora said sternly, after taking his drink order.

"I will if she shows up tonight."

"If you don't apologize tonight, then don't come. Simple as that," she said, making his drink.

"You'd really uninvite me from stuff?"

"Yes, I would."

"We've been friends for years, though. What's she have that would override that?" Trevin asked, somewhat put off.

"She comes over, and not just for parties. We go hiking, and camping, and hangs out just to hang out."

"You never asked me to do any of that. Do you want me to come over to hang out in jammies, watch movies and eat ice cream or whatever you two do?"

"No, but I mean you don't talk to me at parties and bonfires much. She does. You just stick mostly to Caleb and Q, and let them ruin any prospects you may have."

Trevin laughed. "You think she's my prospect? Please. You hear the way she talks about the world. The way she sees everything; her imagination is bursting at the seams. Eventually, she will learn all the secrets of the Old Giants and she will move on to the next place. You hear her and Charles talk. Humboldt isn't going to tame her. What makes you think I will? I can't exactly leave."

Cora stared at him, speechless for a moment. She was shocked. "Trev, you do like her. You're enamored with her. Charles said it best, she belongs here, she has a magic that belongs here. You better apologize to her!"

"She's a creative person, and has a way with words, she draws and reads a lot. She is curious. I don't—" He realized he couldn't make himself say he didn't like her; it would be a lie and he couldn't lie, not even to himself. He didn't hate her, she was nice enough, and he had no real reason to hate her. *Yea, that's it. I don't dislike her, as a person,* he thought, then spoke again. "She is no prospect. I will apologize to her if it makes you happy." He rolled his eyes.

"It will. Enjoy your beverage." Cora gave a smug smile, pushing his drink toward him. Taking his usual seat with a sigh, he opened a tablet and scrolled through documents, glancing up often. He had a notebook open to a blank page for notes but fifteen minutes later nothing had been worth writing. He glanced up when the door opened, unintentionally meeting Elodie's gaze as she walked in, ocean breeze & lavender floating in with her.

"Hey, girl. How was work?" Cora said.

"Busy, but worth it," Elodie answered.

"Oh?" Cora asked.

Trevin glanced towards the women, curious about what was worth it for Elodie. They were talking loud enough that anyone could hear them.

"I stayed late to help a student and the superintendent stopped by my classroom." She leaned in, her voice lowering, but Trevin could still hear her thanks to his keen senses. "They gave me a permanent offer! I have a job next year," Elodie beamed with excitement.

Trevin caught Cora's split-second glance at him and promptly cut his eyes down, realizing he was staring. He quickly scanned the café for anyone else who may be listening and noticed a young boy staring at Elodie.

"That's fantastic, congratulations! It's more incentive to stay then," Cora said. "At least for another year?"

Trevin caught himself glancing over. *She was really talking about leaving, making plans to.* He started to think and wondered about what it would be like if she was gone? He'd get more sleep for one. Then he wondered if this shift would still be here. *Did she bring the shift in the air somehow?*

"I can't leave this place yet. I haven't found that thing I left behind when I was little," Elodie laughed, her voice back to a normal volume. "And who knows, I may never leave."

Cora smiled and handed her a drink. Trevin noticed it was iced again. She hadn't glanced in his direction at all, and he went back to his tablet and scrolled.

"Ms. Santi!" he heard the little boy say.

"Oh hi, Konrad. Are you getting a treat?"

"Yeah. My mom said it is good luck for the play tomorrow," Konrad said. Trevin watched her interact with the boy. He saw her eyes light up and her expressions get bigger, how natural she seemed at it. As he watched her excitement and her own curiosity swell, a smile graced his lips. Trevin focused more on her eyes and saw that energy in her. He could see the patron saint of the redwoods and ferns glow even brighter.

What is in you, El? he groaned in his head. *What am I looking at?* A mortal, a transplant, not even born here. Probably hadn't even spent more than a year here in her entire life yet. Her short, fragile life, the patron saint of his lands. He sighed and put his hands to his head and went back to his tablet, confused. *Why is my mind even coming up with these things?*

"Can I see a page of your sketchbook?" Konrad asked. Elodie laughed her self-conscious laugh.

"Okay sure. Let's see," she said, opening to a page.

"Oooh, that mountain lion looks scary," Konrad exclaimed.

Trevin just stared at the tablet, trying to focus.

"They can be scary. They can be regal and majestic too. Maybe they guard the Old Giants in Humboldt. They keep them safe for us, along with the bears and the blackbirds and all the other animals. So we can see their magic too," she laughed.

Trevin tensed, trying his damnedest not to glance over, not to be weird, but she knew too much. Too much for that to be a mere coincidence. *How would she know that? Did she know about the estate lords in Marin, and they told her all about Humboldt? Impossible.*

"What if they act just like house cats?" Konrad asked her.

"I think they do. They laze about in the sun, and chirp at the blackbirds, but I think they don't want anyone to know. They want it to be a secret. They want to be big and fierce, because they are." She glanced at Trevin.

He went still, noticing her in his peripheral vision.

"But you know if you see one, you have to make yourself look as big as you can and scream and shout. Remember, they like their privacy."

"I will remember if I ever see one, Ms. Santi."

"Good," she replied. "We have our home, and they have theirs. We should respect them and their land."

"What's that?" he asked.

"Oh that." Elodie's voice faltered slightly. "Well, it's a silly little mink, with a flower crown."

"Do they really wear flower crowns?" he asked with so much wonder. Elodie laughed.

"Maybe, maybe they wear them and frolic in the forest. But maybe that's enough fairy tales for today. I don't want your mind to be off in dream land tomorrow. Do you remember your lines?" she asked.

"Yes, Ms. Santi. I practiced a lot. I will before bed too," he said. "What are you going to draw tonight?"

"Oh, I don't know. What should I draw?"

"Maybe the mountain lion might want a flower crown too?" he said. She laughed and Trevin couldn't help but notice it was her laugh, not of self-consciousness, but one that made her excited. It made him excited too. He quickly glanced down, sensing her glance was shifting toward him.

"Konrad, let's give Ms. Santiago some time to relax, okay. She will have plenty of stories for you all tomorrow, I'm sure," a lady—clearly Konrad's mom—said. Trevin glanced at her briefly. "Thank you for talking to him, even on your off hours. He loves hearing your stories about your drawings. You should do a children's book," the boy's mom said.

"Oh, thank you," Elodie laughed awkwardly. "Have a good evening!"

"You too," Konrad's mom said.

Elodie smiled and then flipped her sketchbook to a new page and started drawing.

"Fairy tales and make-believe, ruining these kids. A bunch of transplants moving up here speaking nonsense to them," an older man huffed out.

Trevin watched the man glare at her and something inside him was near ready to pounce until he glanced at Elodie. He watched that energy in her fade and the defeat slash her previous excitement down, as though a flame had been snuffed out.

Does she shift through this much emotion every day? No wonder she is restless. She's just aimlessly wandering the planet, searching for somewhere to show her that magic isn't all in her head, Trevin thought. He noticed her glance at him and then put her pencil down with a sigh of defeat. She closed her sketchbook.

Trevin usually kept to himself during these observations, even if people were being rude to each other. He'd make notes, draw his conclusions, and let it be. The Nightswift method. Tonight he would let that Greenthistle sigil of strength and valor ring loud. He gathered his things, stood up, and walked toward her, exchanging a glance with Cora, who watched with great interest.

Elodie flinched when he sat down next to her.

"Draw the mountain lion, Elodie. I want to know what it would look like wearing a flower crown. Maybe it befriended the little mink," he said with a warm smile. She scowled at him.

"Why bother? Mountain lions eat minks and martens."

"They don't actually," he said. She narrowed her eyes at him. He smiled, waiting for a 'how would you know?' question. She cut her eyes back down and Trevin sighed. "I'm sorry for what I did at the party, Elodie, and I'm sorry my brother is a huge asshole sometimes."

"Okay."

"I'm sorry I eavesdropped on your conversation and I'm sorry I've made you uncomfortable. It was wrong of me and I understand if you hate me. I just have never wanted the same reputation as my brother. I don't hate you or think you are foolish at all," he said, meeting her stunned expression.

"Why not? I'm some dumb transplant here to ruin your lands, as if they are not important to me too," she said with a frown.

"That is exactly why I don't want you to hate me or this place either. I know I fucked up. Hearing you speak of the magic in the Old Giants, hearing your words is lovely and your curiosity is pretty inspiring. Watching you interact with your student, seeing the excitement in him, makes me glad you chose Humboldt. It makes me laugh at how foolish Marin was to let you go," he said.

Trevin watched her glance at his lips briefly then back at him causing him to smirk.

"Stop. This is another game," she said, glancing around—likely for Cedar or someone watching them. No one was.

"It's not. It's entirely the truth. I swear I'm not lying. I will never lie to you," he said, locking eyes with her.

"How's your treasure hunt going?" she asked, then frowned. "Sorry, how is your work with State Parks on archiving the things left behind in Falk?"

"Take a walk with me and I will tell you about it?" Trevin smirked, seeing the energy in her boil. She was stewing in a lot of emotion.

She narrowed her eyes and glanced at Cora, who looked confused as well as she eavesdropped on their conversation.

"I will make sure you get back to your car at a reasonable hour. I swear that too. Give Cora a text when you get into your car," he added.

"I'm not stupid enough to walk off with some guy whose dad could probably sweep any unsavory acts under the rug. No offense."

Damn, I have my work cut out for me. I probably shouldn't even care about earning her trust though. Why is this energy any of my concern, really?

He let out a sigh of resolution, acceptance.

"Okay, Elodie. I understand and I certainly don't want you to have that impression of me either. Will you at least accept my apology for being so shitty before?" he asked. She slowly met his eyes. He could hear her heart pounding, and he didn't know what caused it.

Elodie met his eyes with some confusion at his sincerity. He had come off so confident and smooth before, but she was seeing him stumble. "Yes. I accept your apology," she said, and he grinned wide at her.

"I think you should go to the bonfire. I'll leave it up to you. If you'd prefer me not to go or Caleb, we will not be there," he said.

She glanced over to Cora, who had long set down the mug she had been wiping and now leaned on the counter listening.

"I don't want to be known as the one who disrupts everyone's way of life. I don't even want to be the talk of the town or have a spotlight on me. I kind of hate it. I come here because I enjoy being around people, but I hate being the center of attention. I worry every time I open this sketchbook that it might make people question things about me. So I certainly don't want to be known as the new girl who had a falling out with one of the estate kids. Or be a disruption in their lives. I am no princess, nor am I anything rare or special. I'm just ordinary. Please go on Saturday. Caleb too," she said in a quiet tone. He felt confused as he processed what she told him, unsure how he felt about everything.

"You want to be here but not be seen. You want to blend in till the wind catches you and pulls you somewhere new. While I have seen plenty of transplants pass through here with that same desire, I must say, I do think there is something special in you. Something I have not seen before, something new, foreign, like your namesake, Alodia." He met her scowl.

"You have an odd way of flirting. Do you do this with everyone you play the kissing game with?" she asked with an inquisitive glance.

"No, I don't, I'm not—" His words faltered yet again. He wasn't flirting, was he? He didn't want to. He tried to cover up his inability to speak the words, but she spared him the trouble.

"In your research of my name's meaning, did you see there was a ninth century Spanish martyr? A young girl who was killed for her beliefs alongside her sister. They were deemed saints by the church, Saint Nunilo and Saint Alodia," she said, and a smile graced his lips.

"Saint Elodie of Humboldt, with such a strong conviction of the magic in the Old Giants. Never to become a martyr for it. You have my word." The confident tone was back in his voice "You have Greenthistle's word."

An odd sensation occurred in Trevin with those words. Almost a tap or a tug on something in him.

"Saint of ruining the kids of Humboldt, one fairy tale at a time," she said with a feigned attempt at sarcasm. He could hear the dread in her voice. He hated that her own wonder and curiosity had dampened, that she had been made to feel as though she had to hide it. If more people were like her, he may not have to hide as much about himself as he did.

"No, you are giving them brighter eyes to see more, to create and dream more. When they see the emeralds on those ferns and history lessons on the redwoods, they will want to keep the Old Giants safe." He placed a hand on her upper arm gently. "I will see you Saturday night, I hope. No night hikes either, Lady Elodie." How that title excited him.

She frowned and watched him stand up.

"Trev," she said, meeting his eyes. He turned to her, noting how his name sounded when she spoke it. "You can still call me El, if you want."

Trevin beamed widely at her. "Well then, El, I bid you a good evening."

Some odd sensation of curiosity towards him formed in Elodie. A sensation of tapping on something in her as if it were getting ready to pull a thread tight. She refocused on the scent of oakmoss and amber, now fading as her eyes followed him till he walked out. She could see eyes shifting toward her, including the old man from earlier. He shook his head in disappointment. She snapped back too when someone sat across from her and met Cora's grin.

"Girl! He is being so weird and I am not going to lie. I kind of love watching you two work through this," Cora said with a laugh.

Elodie shook her head with a sigh. "I'm glad it's amusing for you. Seriously though, why me? I'm sure there's some other transplant that moved here recently. I'm sure the university in Arcata has some too," she groaned.

"As I said, I haven't seen him pursue anyone in years. If you are seriously not looking or don't want that kind of attention, he will listen. I know you got out of a bad situation and I can imagine his odd behavior might be overwhelming. And before you say you don't want to be seen as the disruption to our lives, you are not. You are a welcome presence. You are allowed to put boundaries down and have them respected. Regardless of what their last names are or what their families do. But I must say. I do want to see what a mountain lion with a flower crown would look like too," she laughed.

"I know. I guess I've always been too curious, not even naïve, just foolish, because I know better. He is so stupidly attractive, even Caleb isn't bad on the eyes and Anna is gorgeous. I hope Charles sticks around for some time. I don't want to set a boundary that I may not keep. I will be okay. I mean, I don't think anyone is as much of an ass as my ex. I can handle Trev's glances and grins."

"You'd miss those emerald eyes of his," Cora laughed. "See ya on Saturday?" Cora got up as the door opened.

"Yes, I will be there," Elodie said with a smirk and a sigh of acceptance. She glanced at her closed sketch book and then at the seat he was in when she walked in. She thought about the things he said. He sensed something in her, something she too had not been able to explain in her. She wondered what he saw.

She thought of his eyes and smiled to herself. With a goodbye to Cora, Elodie headed home. Before she went to bed, Elodie leaned toward her window and watched the tree line.

Elodie. Keep searching.
They will need you.
El. Wake up. We need you.
Come home.

She narrowed her eyes and grabbed her sketchbook, then continued drawing the mountain lion.

Chapter 11

On Saturday morning, Elodie helped with the fall play. Afterward she had lunch overlooking the ocean from the hatch, then headed south to Ferndale. She stopped in a used bookstore. Browsing the entire store with no particular book in mind, a title caught her eye: '*The Town of Falk*'. Eager to see how old the book was, she turned to the publication page, seeing the year 1885. That was one year after Falk was founded. The pages full of drawings, maps, history, and plans for expansion enraptured her. She flipped back to the first map of the town layout, then to the planned expansion, noting the changes.

One page titled 'Map to underground' had a box with lots of lines, reminding Elodie of a maze. Underneath the box read 'King' with the letters Fe and 26. *Iron element? On the periodic table? This is weird.* Elodie remembered the conversation about Trev's treasure hunting. Her eyes scanned for a price, finding the five-dollar tag.

"Why is this so cheap?" she asked herself and went to pay for it. The woman behind the counter looked over it.

"This has been sitting here for ages. I found it in the back, buried and forgotten under stuff. I knew someone would buy it, eventually. Planning to go see the remains?"

"Yes. I heard the hike was somewhat challenging, but I want to try it. Plus, I love old maps and stuff," Elodie responded.

"Ahh, this is a good book then," the woman said, ringing up the book. Elodie handed her cash and took the book. "I suggest you go see it soon. What's left of it, anyway. I don't have a lot of faith in any of our county seats to not just rip everything up over there, even with State Parks working with it. I hear Greenthistle has his oldest working on it, but those estate kids can be reckless. I know Mr. Greenthistle thinks it will be good for his son, but it's such a sensitive area. I'm worried they will just bulldoze it all up. For what? To archive things? Maybe stones ought not to be turned, ya know?"

Elodie thought about her words and then about Trev's. He had said he nor his dad wanted to go and rip things up. He seemed to want to preserve the area, too.

"I will be sure to go soon, then. Thank you," Elodie said with a nod.

"Have a good day and be safe out there."

Once Elodie got to her car, she drove to Russ Park trailhead. Relief hit her when she noticed a few cars parked. Her mind went back to the mountain lion. The one with striking emerald green eyes. She wasn't sure mountain lions had green eyes.

With her trekking poles clipped to her pack and her phone volume set to high just in case, she began the hike up to the pond. She hurried to the top, wanting to see the view she had seen pictures of. The sun would be setting soon. *No night hikes.* Trev's words played in her head. "If you insist, Prince Greenthistle." Words intended for her and the trees. Once she found the bench and took in the jaw dropping view, she had a snack and pulled the book out.

As she flipped through the pages, Elodie noticed imprinting on some pages. She ran light fingers over some of them, feeling small ridges and bumps in the paper. Then she noticed some of the illustrations even had imprinting in them too.

One image caught her eye, her fingers glided over it, searching for any imprint.

Wake up.

A voice whispered as soon as she felt the lines, but she couldn't make out what it said. The overcast sky didn't help much when she held it up for more light, either. She searched for any reference number or footnote, but found none.

A crescent moon facing up, points growing thin and sharp, with a tall redwood shooting out from the center. Three ferns surrounded the tree. Atop it sat a sun with eight points.

Elodie thought it would make for a good tattoo, then realized it might be offensive for a transplant to get something that may be sacred to the area.

"I wonder what it says. Maybe I just need better lighting? Or get a rubbing of it if I was careful enough." She hadn't used charcoal in ages but could pick some up.

She started reading the page, which had a section about binding things to an anchor. It spoke of things old and new all at once, timeless, ageless, and things that could be sealed away or released. She flipped the page before and it spoke of spirits, some good, some bad. The following page had a section on types of stone and sediment to use as anchors; layers of limestone, quartz, and bedrock.

On the next page, a blueprint for the logging mill in Falk. Along the edge of the page were illustrations of a mountain lion, a bear, a raven, and an elk with the word *inanis* below them. Her fingers searched for any imprinting but found none.

Wake up.
We need you, El.

Elodie realized these were all animals native to the area. She squinted her eyes, wondering what the word meant, then pulled her phone. She paused, reading the meaning. *Inanis* was Latin for foolish, void, vain, and empty. Confusion took over, as she stared at the image of the native animals. A frown crossed her face in defeat, then she realized the time and how dark it was getting.

She heard a caw and spotted a raven flying off that she hadn't noticed. Her heart tensed and listened for any sort of groan or growl from a mountain lion remembering the last time. Taking this as her sign to go, she shoved the book back in her pack and hurried to her car, not completing the loop. Her eyes and steps watching for the banana slugs.

Soon.
She will wake up

Soon. Soon. She will come home.
We need you, El.

The voices whispered. She thought about the symbol upon hearing these voices. How much she wanted to know what had been pressed into the page. Over time, the Old Giants started to call her El, and she grew uneasy at the thought. They hadn't called her that until she had met Trev. It was a secret she would keep guarded until she could figure out what he had to do with it. It was why she didn't want to avoid him entirely.

"Why do I think of him?" she asked herself. "Why does he linger in my mind? He's not the first guy to kiss me randomly or even the first one to do it on a stupid dare or bet."

There was something about him that intrigued her. She had a hunch; something about her intrigued him. Yet Elodie knew she had to be cautious, for being on his radar with his last name was not a wise idea. The way the butterflies danced in her at the thought of that kiss, though. That kiss was a game for them all. "Why do I even care? They can play their games; doesn't mean I need to."

She reached her car with a relieved sigh, then drove home so she could change before going to the bonfire.

Chapter 12

When Elodie arrived, she saw Charles's adventure van, then noticed Cora and Justine at the fire pit. With a small bout of relief, she walked over to them.

"Hey! How was the kids' show?" Cora asked.

"Oh, they did great. They were proud of themselves and the parents were all happy. But it was a long day." She laughed.

"I'm glad you're here. Glad someone apologized too," she said, nodding over to her left. Elodie glanced over and noticed Trev standing with Caleb, and a tall stockier male. She noticed Justine's glance at them too.

"Has Q started chatting with you yet?" Cora asked, turning to Justine.

"Maybe," she said with a bashful grin.

"I thought so. I've caught him glancing over a few times. Why do you guys play like you aren't a thing? You don't have to lie. Charles and Anna are not serious but they don't hide that they are into each other," Cora said, looking past Elodie, who turned around and saw Charles resting his head on the girl. Anna was strikingly beautiful, just as she remembered her from the Halloween party. She had a green beanie on with a thistle plant that was similar to the one she had seen on Trev's shirt. Her eyes and smile were just as sly as Trev's were. They had different features, but she could certainly tell they were related. Elodie wondered if she took after her mom or dad more.

"I know, I just, he's got his reputation. If I let myself act normal with him, if I let myself act like Charles does with Anna, I'm gonna get stuck here. I'm going to want something more serious and then this is it," Justine said, then turned toward Elodie. "So where does that leave you and Trev?"

"Nowhere. We, umm, we can talk for now without me calling him a fuckboy. I guess he doesn't like that term, but what else was I supposed to think?" she asked, somewhat defensively.

"He really doesn't like it. He does try to avoid the games. I have heard the guys make fun of him a good bit. They make it sound as though it's been a while for him. He just shrugs it off, though," Cora said. "I heard what that old guy said after your student left. The glare Trev shot at him could have set that man ablaze," Cora said with a laugh.

"Just say hi to him at some point tonight, yea? Cora insists we all need to be paired with the estate kids for whatever reason. Probably to keep us here, since we know they are never leaving," Justine laughed. Cora laughed too.

"Okay, I will. I do want to tell him about a book I found in Ferndale today. Oh, and I might have finished the mountain lion with the flower crown drawing when I got home that night." She laughed.

"Aww, let me see it," Cora said. Justine asked what the story was behind it. As Elodie explained, she glanced at the trees. She thought about the symbol in the book again.

Soon. Soon. El.
Keep alert.
Wake up. Soon.

There it was again, *El*. She glanced over at Trev. He turned his attention to her and nodded with a curious smile, then turned back to Q.

"I'm going to go to the restroom quickly," she said. Cora and Justine nodded.

"We will be talking to Charles and Anna. You should meet her," Cora said.

She walked into the sandy public bathrooms. They were messy, but at least didn't have the usual smell public bathrooms always tended to have. They were also freezing. She wasn't in need of using it, she just needed a moment to sort through everything she had learned today. A sigh escaped her as she glanced at herself in the mirror. Her hand grew warm, as though it pulsed with a pump of blood and she lifted her hand to examine it. There and gone in the blink of an eye. That sigil again came to mind for some reason.

Walking back from the bathroom toward the fire pit, Elodie watched her steps wade through the shadows. The air was chilly, causing her to put her hands in her pockets as she made her way back toward the light of the bonfire.

"Hey, wait up," she heard someone say. Elodie took in this new stranger approaching her. He was a few inches taller than her, with short blond hair, shaved on the sides and longer on top. Elodie noted his fair skin, a slimmer but still tone frame, a sly smile and sky blue eyes. Unease crept over her. With all the oddness of Trev, she wasn't sure she needed any more random people introducing themselves.

"Hello," she said, holding her ground.

"I haven't seen you at the bonfires before," he said, walking closer and holding her gaze.

"I'm here and there," she answered, feeling uneasy.

"Are you new to the area?" he asked with a wry grin.

"I've been here for a bit," Elodie said, hearing people around the bonfire. She wanted to be near anyone else right now, even Trev despite their odd interactions thus far.

"Well, you are here now and so am I. Maybe we can become good friends. Name's Russ," he said, leaning in closer to speak into her ear. She glanced at the trees in the distance.

Turn around. Turn around. Too dark. Too fast.

She heard in her head, then saw him grin wider as though he too heard the warnings.

She went to turn away, then went rigid when his hand came to the small of her back. His sly little laugh felt like tiny pinpricks.

"You are a lovely little creature. Care for a stroll along the beach?" he crooned near her ear.

"I should get back to the group." She swallowed hard and stepped away from him. Another mischievous laugh sent a chill down her spine.

"If you insist. I will see you around here and there, I'm sure." His sly tone echoed in her ears as she walked away and back towards her friends.

Humboldt sure had a lot of creepers. She could handle the awkward banter with Trevor and even his brother flat out not liking her, but the feeling this guy gave her was not one she enjoyed. She hurried to the bonfire and sat down on one of the logs where many people were, and there was light.

Trevin sat next to her, and she jumped. "You okay?" he asked.

She looked at him wide eyed and nodded her head. She had spotted her friends standing not too far from where she had sat down. "I'm fine, thanks," she answered bluntly.

"Your ex leaving you alone? Does he need more proof you've moved on?" Trev asked with a playful smirk. She compared the grin to Russ's, noting the difference. Trev's eyes were friendly, his smile more relaxed. Russ seemed intent on a conquest, not curiosity.

"I'm fine," she said, getting up and walking towards Cora, Charles, and Justine. Anna had an arm around Charles. Elodie wanted to talk to Trev, but Russ had made her uneasy. She wondered if Trev would step in to help again, but also didn't want to rely on him. She felt safer with Cora and her other friends.

Trevin watched her carefully, knowing something or someone had upset her. Quinn sat beside him in her spot.

"Getting mighty possessive there. Want to have another round of the kissing game?" He laughed. Trevin gave Quinn a shove.

"Shut up. I'm just refusing to play from here on out," he said. Quinn laughed and shook his head. Trevin tuned out Quinn and listened in to the conversation happening close by.

"Elodie, meet Anna," Charles beamed. Autumn smiled warmly.

"Hi! It's nice to meet you! Cora told me you love hiking and the big trees," she said. Elodie nodded.

"Yes, I do. I enjoy being here. Humboldt is magical," Elodie answered.

Autumn smiled widely. "It is! I hope it treats you well."

"I hope so too. Your family has been here for a while?" Elodie asked.

"Yeah, Greenthistle is an old name here. We can trace our line back generations. Where are you from?"

"Marin," Elodie said shortly.

"Ahh, lots to see and do there, yes? I've been a few times—I have friends down there."

"Yea, there is a lot going on there, but I am not sure it's for me sometimes. I don't know, I guess it's where I grew up though, so it is home too?"

"Maybe Humboldt will become a home of sorts, too," Autumn replied with a genuine tone.

"Oh, Elodie fits in here much more than Marin. She's felt the pull of the Old Giants for some time, her words not mine," Charles said. Elodie nervously shook her head.

"I feel the magic from them too!" Autumn said. "Seems they may have settled in your heart already," Autumn continued.

Elodie let out a nervous laugh, then glanced towards him and Quinn. Trevin realized Quinn was staring at Justine, and he shoved his friend playfully.

"Do you have a favorite hiking trail, Anna?" Elodie asked. Trevin focused on their conversation again.

"Yeah, there's a few I love to do. The Sunny Brae trail is nice, just south of Arcata, and it connects to the forest. I'd love to show you sometime if you want," Anna answered.

Quinn nudged Trevin's shoulder. "She totally looked at you, you sly dog. Trev, are you going to get a mortal to fawn over you? Damn. Are you sure you don't like her?" He patted Trevin on the shoulder.

"No, I'm not trying to get anyone to fawn over me. She's just foolish and needs to be watched over," Trevin scoffed. Quinn glanced past him.

"Caleb's got one already," Quinn said, and Trevin turned to find his brother holding hands with a girl who leaned into him.

"Does that mean you are going to go get Justine?" Trev asked, rolling his eyes.

"Maybe."

"I noticed you haven't flirted with anyone here. Have you gotten back with her?"

Quinn laughed and shook his head with a grin.

Trevin laughed. "Not even two weeks. We knew it!"

"Damn near about," Quinn said, still laughing. Cyrus sat down next to them, and slumped over.

"Glad to see you made it!" Trevin said. Cyrus looked at him, defeated.

"Yea," he said with a frown.

"What's wrong? Are you okay?" Quinn asked.

"Yes, I'm fine. It is taking a while to recover," he said quietly, making sure no one would overhear them.

"Trust me, whatever that was, it was pure evil. Lord Greenthistle had the right idea to kill it," Quinn whispered. "It took me a few days to recover."

"It took me a while. That mountain lion busted open my lip real good. I was lucky it missed my eyes," Trevin followed up.

"Yea, I'm glad you are all okay," Cyrus said, looking even more defeated.

Trevin watched him closely; this was not the Cyrus he knew. Cedar was acting more like Cyrus had before the accident. He saw Cyrus glance in Elodie's direction and pause before turning back to them.

"Did I hear you were back with Justine?" Cyrus asked, now back in his sly tone. His demeanor kept shifting between near malicious and then complete exhaustion and defeat. Trevin wondered if his recovery was draining him. He wasn't sure what was happening. Even if he had gotten something from the attack, Quinn nor himself were showing any signs.

"Yes," Quinn said bashfully. "She's fun. I think she's talking about moving somewhere else. Charles isn't good for these girls to stay with his stories." He laughed.

"Q isn't getting attached to the annoying mortal, is he?"

"She's not annoying, but no, I'm not getting attached. We said no strings attached," Quinn said with a laugh. "She'd probably be pissed if I walked over there and did what Charles is doing with Anna." He followed up with another laugh.

"Do you want to?" Trev asked him. He had not known Quinn to be clingy, or even that affectionate when he was in a relationship. There seemed to be a shift in the air affecting them all.

"It might be fun." He smirked.

"You missed her, huh?" Trev asked with a grin.

"Maybe. You know how it goes, though. She'd be better off just moving in the next year or two."

"You know Justine will be a problem. You ought to keep better tabs on her while she is away," Cyrus said.

"I know. I will," Quinn said.

This was one of the problems they had that the bigger cities didn't. So many people coming and going, the estate families could be more elusive, blend in easier. The population was smaller up here. Even if a good percent were the ebb and flow type.

"And Anna has found a mortal, too. She is still hot. I remember how she was, her body pressed against mine." Cyrus bit his bottom lip in a lustful manner.

"Okay. Enough of that," Trevin said as Cyrus and Quinn laughed.

"Nah, don't worry. I'm sure I can find someone new." Cyrus locked his eyes on Elodie. She glanced up and tensed, wide eyed, then quickly looked away. Trevin turned back to Cyrus, who had a gleam in his eye. A newfound rage brewed inside Trevin.

"Don't," Trevin said with clear intent. Cyrus fixed on Trevin now with a challenging smile. "Cyrus."

"Yeah, I wouldn't. He's got a claim on her. They kissed on Halloween," Quinn said.

"I don't have a claim on her, but she doesn't need that."

"Ahhh, Trev, nice to see you writhe," Cyrus said. Trevin stared at him, confused, as did Quinn. Cyrus smiled, dropping the challenge in his eyes, and laughed. "Lighten up, I'm kidding. You act as though you are vowed and waiting for the right moment to swap blood," he said with a nervous laugh.

"No. I'm not vowed to anyone, certainly not a mortal, but honestly, don't play your games, Russ," Trevin said.

"Of course. I'm going to get another beer—do either of you want anything?" Cyrus asked. Trevin shook his head and Quinn held up his nearly full one. Cyrus nodded and walked toward the cooler.

"Elodie, you are really going to leave so soon? You haven't even been here for two hours." Trevin heard Cora say and turned his gaze in Elodie's direction.

Quinn laughed. "Come on, I want to see Justine's reaction anyway. At least stand next to your girl," he said, giving him a shove.

"She's not my girl," Trevin groaned, but followed Quinn.

Trevin saw Elodie's eyes flicker over him, then to Quinn. He also watched Quinn walk up to Justine and put his arm around her.

"Q! Hi!" Justine was stunned. Autumn smirked then glanced at her brother, who stood next to Elodie. He heard Elodie's heart rate increase then met his sister's eyes, and subtly shook his head. Trevin could see Autumn's inquisitive expression, wondering if he was going to do that to Elodie.

"Have you met Q, Elodie?" Justine asked.

Elodie shook her head as she took in the sight of him. He was probably five inches taller than Trevin and had a ton more muscle. His eyes were a warm amber with hints of gold. He had tan skin similar to her own and black hair shaved short and a goatee and mustache.

Trevin glared at Quinn watching him give his wooing smile at Elodie. When Quinn had met his glare he just laughed.

"Hi," Elodie finally said in a small voice. *At least he was introduced to you, the same way that Justine and Anna had been.* She didn't get any sense of unease with Anna. In fact, Anna put her at ease; she seemed like someone she wanted to be friends with. She noticed Q seemed to put her at ease too.

"Hello, Elodie. It's nice to finally meet you. I've heard plenty about you," Q said with a sly little laugh.

Elodie heard Trevor sigh.

"I really hate going places with you and Caleb sometimes. El, please," Trevor said. His tone dropped into a hint of plead that she wouldn't yell at him, use that word on him again.

"It's okay. I forget what small towns are like. Marin was a lot easier to become a nobody in," she laughed nervously. "Glad you all got amusement out of it though," she said, feeling self-conscious and defeated.

"I assure you, nothing bad has been said about you. It's rather interesting to see Trev act this way. I can't recall the last time he did," Q said with a laugh. Anna and Cora laughed too, and Trevor sighed again.

Elodie was trying to force herself to say what was on the tip of her tongue. She turned to face Trev. "Take a walk with me, yeah?" she asked.

Their eyes met, and he nodded. They walked side by side, toward the water.

They were quiet as they walked along the dark and chilly stretch of beach. Trevor finally broke the silence. "I'm sorry for Q and Caleb. And what I did."

"It's okay. I'm sorry I made such a big scene at the café," she said.

He shrugged. "Ehh, I deserved it," he said, then glanced at her.

Elodie listened to the waves, then glanced over toward the trees in the distance.

It cannot be undone.
Home. Home.
He will see soon. They all will.

She shook her head and then met his curious eyes.

"Did you want to talk about anything in particular or just need a witness when you fight the krakens and sea sirens?" he asked.

"What if I am a sea siren, luring the treasure hunter to the murky ocean depths?" she asked, looking up at him.

He glanced at her and let out a warm laugh. "I'd certainly be impressed with your glamour and I suppose I could go willingly if such a beauty was the last I ever saw."

She laughed. "Ahh, young estate prince, eloquently spoken," she said, and he laughed again.

"I am no prince, my dear little mink. However, you are a great many things. Both new and foreign."

"I wanted to ask you about the City of Falk. I think you were going to talk to me about it on Thursday?" she asked. He eyed her.

"I was. You seem very observant, and your way with words is fascinating. The kids are lucky to have you as a teacher. It excites them. You were onto something with iron. I was going to ask your thoughts on things, but I didn't want to do it with so many ears listening."

She stared at him for a moment. "Oh. So there really is treasure? Like an old untapped vein of gold?" she asked, brimming curiosity.

"Maybe, but it's not a literal treasure chest overflowing with gold and jewels."

"What is it then?"

"We aren't sure yet exactly. We just know it was last recorded in Falk, and it contains a lot of knowledge," he said.

"Like a book? Some kind of magical tome?"

Trevin laughed. "You and your fantasy books."

She smirked and eyed him. "You want me to help you brainstorm on where it might be in Falk?"

"I don't know. We were having a good conversation on it and I figured since you are a fresh set of eyes, maybe you could figure out something I'm missing."

Elodie remained quiet. She thought about what she had seen in the book, and what the lady in Ferndale had said.

"Your dad doesn't want to bulldoze it all down and dig trenches, right? You want to see it preserved?" she asked, glancing at him, then back to the sea.

"We want to be as minimally invasive as possible," he said. She nodded and inhaled. "The last thing we want to do is disrupt the earth, reclaiming the land that was taken."

"I went to Ferndale earlier today and found an interesting old book on Falk." She told him about the year it was published and the things she saw in it.

"What language is the book in?"

"English. I went on a hike in Russ Park afterward. It was later in the day and I remembered you said no more night hikes. So I stopped and sat down and flipped through it. There's stuff pressed on the margins, but given the age of the book, it's hard to tell what it says. I meant to get a rubbing of it, but I need vine charcoal. I think a pencil or pen will ruin the pages."

"A rubbing?" Trevor tilted his head in confusion.

"Yeah, you can use a crayon, but charcoal works better. Vine charcoal is really lightweight but has a lot of pigment, so it's easy to get rubbings."

"I know, I just didn't think people still did that," he said.

She rolled her eyes then sighed. "Yes, people still do that, or at least us odd ones do."

"El, what I meant was I wouldn't have thought to do that. Can you tell me anything about what's on the sides of the pages?" Trevor asked, clearly intrigued.

"There are images, words, maybe town names. I saw Sunny Brae and I know that's not far outside of Arcata, but I've never stopped there," Elodie said, noting his inquisitive expression. "One page has a box, with the Fe 26. The element for iron, if I recall my science classes. Under that was the word 'King.' Trevin narrowed his eyes processing the information. "King, king? King Range? Iron?"

"I don't know. It's hard to make anything else out on it. The Lost Coast Trail is there."

"Iron in King Range, I wonder what the significance is?" he said.

Elodie shrugged. "There was a symbol. Sigil? I dunno what you'd call it. It was in black ink but there's something pressed into the page, a word. I can't tell what it says. So that's what made me think of doing a rubbing." Her eyes traveled down to his lips then his neck and chest. "I, uhh, the symbol, sigil, whatever it is," she said, getting embarrassed and trying to recover. He smiled at her as she described the sigil. "It would be a neat tattoo, but I don't know what it meant. It just reminded me of the Old Giants and the ferns with the moon and sun. I don't know," she said, finally recollecting herself.

"Interesting. I haven't seen a symbol like that before. Would you be willing to let me borrow the book?" he asked. "I promise to be careful with it, and will return it when I'm done.".

"Yeah, sure. I have it in my car," she said, turning to head back toward the bonfire.

He put his hand lightly on her upper arm. "El, stay longer. We don't have to stay down here, but we can go back to Cora and everyone, hang out and relax. I can walk you to your car when you do leave?"

"When you say I can leave?" She scowled. He sighed and dropped his hand.

"No, I just don't want you to be uncomfortable at things I might be at. I don't want to be a disruption to your life. You said you didn't want to be a disruption to us. I don't want the little mink to not experience life here because I messed up." Trevor met her eyes.

"Sorry, it's just residual baggage from my ex. He would say he would walk me to my car then act almost irritated when he actually did. Usually he just wouldn't. Plus if you can't tell I am awkward and somehow I have found myself on your radar. Your dad is a county seat and your brother is a cop. I shouldn't have yelled at you that day, especially after you were injured. I got overwhelmed." Elodie sighed, feeling even dumber for admitting that to him.

"People will draw their own conclusions. I certainly got some glares after you left that day. For the record, I don't think you messed up though, at all. It certainly has been interesting, little mink."

She realized she felt at ease instead of mortified. Something about him felt almost comforting. Secure.

"Hey, El? Earlier when I sat next to you, you seemed tense. What had you like that?"

"Nothing." Her answer was short and she cut her eyes down, not wanting to talk about it.

"If someone made you uncomfortable, other than me, that is, please tell me," Trevor said. "You are safe up here. This area is safe."

She met his eyes again and furrowed her brow in confusion. "I'm okay. If you want to be the only one who makes me uncomfortable, I hate to break this to you, but I make myself uncomfortable. A lot. So good luck." She lowered her gaze.

"Little mink," he said softly. "We can get back to walking, or rejoin the others if you'd like?"

They walked back to the group to find Q and Justine were gone and Anna and Charles still stood with their arms around each other. She was wearing his flannel now. She smiled warmly and glanced at her brother then to Elodie.

"Have a nice walk?" Cora asked.

"Yes, we did." Elodie nodded.

"It was a pleasant chat. No sea sirens or krakens though." Trevor gave Elodie a nudge and her cheeks heated.

"Q and Justine decided to head off somewhere. Hopefully you didn't need a ride," Cora said, looking at Trevor and Anna. They both shook their heads.

"Nah, we got one," Trevor said.

Elodie wondered what kind of car he drove. She figured she could save the question for another night.

"They like each other a lot. Q seems like he has some good pranks up his sleeve. The mostly fun kind," Charles said, holding Anna close.

"Oh, he does, and they are good for each other," Anna said.

"Q and his stupid ideas sometimes." Trevin rolled his eyes. He gave Elodie a small grin, and she returned it. "I'm going to go find Caleb and Russ, make sure they didn't get into too much trouble, I will be back though, okay?" Trevor said softly to Elodie. She nodded.

"Okay," she said, then realized that Russ might see his friend walk her to her car. She was uneasy with that thought and debated on slipping off to her car; it was a clear shot from where she stood. Then she watched Trev walk over to his brother and let out a small sigh as her shoulders slumped.

Anna glanced over to where Trevor was standing with Caleb and Cyrus, whose eyes met hers with a wry smile. Anna narrowed her eyes and looked away with an audible exhale.

Elodie had also watched the exchange wondering what Anna's relationship was with Russ. If she had the same feeling. She glanced at Charles who seemed unaware but certainly had a firm grip on her. Her eyes shifted to Trevor again and wondered if he would step in to protect her, from his own friend. She smirked to herself at the thought. *Why do I even care about that? I don't need his protection. I don't need to be in a place where I need protection.*

She scanned the tree line again.

Home. Home.
It cannot be undone.
They will need you. Wake up.

It was always the same messages, but she didn't know what it meant. She didn't know who would need her. Surely, Trev didn't need her. Q and Caleb seemed plenty capable of taking care of themselves. Russ too. Anna maybe? Cora, Justine, and Charles?

She sighed and saw Anna give her a curious glance then turn back to Charles. Elodie then noticed Trev, Caleb, and Russ looking at her too. Caleb as expected was annoyed and already had turned away. Trevor gave her a curious warm smile. Something with Russ's gaze left her uneasy as though he were waiting for the right time to strike.

Cyrus held his grin watching her. "I will say that new girl certainly is interesting, no?"

Trevin observed the grin. "Why do you say that?"

"Something is in her. She is not normal."

"It's a coincidence. I mean come on, there are a ton of people here. The energy surges may not even be linked to anyone, certainly not a dumb mortal," Cedar said.

"Oh, it's her alright. I'm willing to bet that's why Trev here wants her in particular as his new plaything," Cyrus said, his grin growing wider watching as Trevin's glare formed.

"I'm warning you, do not pursue her."

"Are you going to sleep with her?" Cyrus asked him. Trevin didn't change his expression.

"Leave her alone. What about Alena?"

Cyrus laughed nonchalantly, causing Cedar to look at him now. "What happens over there stays over there, the mortal is not over there," he said.

"Cyrus," Trevin hissed in a low voice.

"Don't waste your time, she's way too emotional and a prude. She almost cried after Trev kissed her. And she cussed us both out when I told her about the kissing game. Besides, if he wants to get laid finally let him, he will just reek of mortal for a few days. Alena is way hotter and way better."

Trevin remained quiet but held his glare on Cyrus who grinned back at him deviously.

Fucking Cyrus, what's gotten into him? He eyes her with malice. How did he get me against a wall like this?

"Leave her alone," Trevin growled.

"I can see you have your claws out. You act differently with her, shame you got stuck with something like that." Cyrus's grin was unnerving.

"Yes, I did, so you don't have to worry about it." Trevin resisted the urge to snap back. He knew this was the bait, and he refused to take it.

"Not worried in the least, kitty cat," he said.

"It's all in good banter," Cedar said, sensing the tension.

"Whatever. Behave yourselves tonight. Try not to break any hearts," Trevin scoffed then walked back over to where Elodie was. He stood near her and did not glance back over at Cyrus. He noticed Elodie's nerves, but he also saw her smiling. He savored the way she smelled, listening to the conversation.

When Elodie decided to go, he followed her, excited to see what was in the book.

"Us walking off together twice now is going to set a precedent, people are going to talk," Elodie said as they walked towards her car.

"So, it sets a precedent. People make assumptions all the time, don't worry about them," Trevin said, walking next to her.

"I don't want to set the wrong precedent. Elementary school teacher and all." She sighed. "Or for your dad to get me fired or something."

"Why would he do that? He didn't do it to Charles. He hasn't done it to any of Caleb's conquests, and some have grown obsessed with him." Trevin laughed.

"Yea, but aren't you going to try to take over the county seat? Do you think Caleb or Anna would go for it?" she asked, noting his confidence now.

"Well, as it has been for the last two generations, it's the first born. Some call it tradition, some might call it nepotism. The firstborn Greenthistle has just ended up with a seat though. Same with Nightswift and Ashdale. My siblings said they don't want it," he said.

"Do you want it?" Elodie asked, noticing him sigh.

"Yes and no. I want to make my father proud, and do Greenthistle proud. Yet at that same time I question if I am the best suited for it. I mean Anna and Caleb have some strong qualities. I feel I need to do it though. Ya know, like something is calling to me, telling me I need to."

"I know the feeling," Elodie said as they arrived at her car.

"You do?"

"Maybe not exactly, but sometimes it's almost as though I feel these trees, the Old Giants. I know it sounds like I'm high but I'm not. They have always had this strong hold over my heart. At first, I thought it might just be nature being beautiful. The Joshua Trees in SoCal, as much as I love them and that place, didn't have this pull. Olympic National Park is amazing, but I never felt like I did in the redwoods. Every trip up here was four days at most and it never was enough. I finally decided to try living here with them, as though something told me this was what I needed to do." Elodie laughed and shook her head, fidgeting with her keys. "I'm sorry, I sound crazy or high."

He eyed her closely, seeing her nerves, and her energy. It was swirling in her. Trevin could see she was embarrassed. *Curious little mink.*

"I don't think that's anything to be embarrassed about or feel crazy about. I feel them too. A lot. The Old Giants hold a lot of magic and it takes a special person to actually see it," he said. Her eyes widened. "Maybe that's the reason why I keep acting weird around you. You are different in a rare way I haven't encountered before and I don't know how to react to it," he said, leaning nearer to her.

"New and foreign?"

"The Patron Saint Elodie of Humboldt. Has a ring to it, no?" He smiled, seeing everything shift in her eyes. He then realized he was feeling a desire he hadn't felt before.

Elodie swallowed hard before speaking. "I don't want to end up a martyr, so how about sticking with little mink," she said.

Trevin laughed and placed his hand on her shoulder. Their eyes locked. *Why do I want to kiss her again, a mortal, Trev?* "No no, dearest little mink. No becoming a martyr. I will see to it. If the Old Giants connect with you, you're special," he said.

She sighed and shook her head. With the beep of her key fob, she opened the door and grabbed her pack. He noticed the patches on it. A day pack with a blue hose coming out for water. She pulled out an old book and handed it to him.

"I guess, keep it as long as you need it. It wasn't that expensive but at some point, I do want it back," she said.

"Of course. I will read through it this week and see if there's anything new. Get home safely okay and no night hikes either." He took the book and eyed the cover for a moment.

"I know, Prince Greenthistle has forbidden it." She sighed, he laughed again and shook his head.

He fought the urge to hug her, to kiss her. Every second was a new battle he didn't want to be fighting. *What is wrong with me?*

"It's dangerous out there. Prince Greenthistle wants the patron saint of Humboldt to live, not become a martyr," Trevin said, now feigning confidence.

Elodie shook her head and laughed. "You are pretty odd yourself, Trev, but you get home safely too, okay?"

He nodded and closed her door for her, then flipped through the book and watched her car pull out of the spot then drive off. His eyes scanned all the new maps and information. He started to get sucked into a passage, but knew better and put it in his jacket pocket before going back to Cora's group.

She gave him a grin. He shook his head and laughed. After a few minutes, he felt no desire to be here and said his goodbyes. For a split-second he debated on running by Elodie's place to make sure she was there but he knew that was turning borderline weird. He just told himself she was safe.

Chapter 13

Over the next week, they both glanced at each other across from the café. He would be buried in notes or his tablet, and she would usually be between lesson plans and drawing. They would steal glances at each other, but didn't talk. Elodie didn't know what to say to him. She could not deny the attraction to him, but she also knew pursuing him was asking for attention she did not want.

On Wednesday, Elodie saw him when she walked in and took her usual seat. She glanced over at him and took a deep inhale, recalling Saturday night.

What if Anna is hoping something happens? No, that's dumb. That's weird, she thought. Her eyes fixed on the corner of an envelope sticking out of her sketchbook. She focused on the open page filled with various doodles.

There were two more work days before the November break and Elodie thought about what she needed to do. Then she would be off for a week and going back to Marin to see her dad for the holiday. It filled her with an odd mix of unease and happiness. She had missed her dad and other things about Marin, but she knew she would miss Humboldt a lot.

She sat back and glanced at the page of things that reminded her of Humboldt. The thought of driving south on Avenue made her frown. Highway 101 would take her inland and the land would fade from greens and deep browns to golden fields and bigger cities. Sure, there were Redwoods and ferns along the way and back in Marin, but it wasn't Humboldt. She would see those ferns and know he was in Humboldt and she was not. A sigh escaped her.

Then she realized how stupid that was. Her eyes roved up the brick wall as the realization hit her. How utterly stupid it was to think of Trev this much. As though he was in everything that made Humboldt a place she loved. She sighed again.

She glanced at him for a moment, taking him in, before looking at the envelope again. *I need the drive south to know if I am home or I left home.* An exhale of acceptance, in affirmation to rationalize her thoughts. She needed space, so she packed up her things and stood up.

"See ya, Cora," Elodie said. Her heart was beating faster.

"Later, have a good evening," Cora responded. Elodie took an inhale and walked toward the door, knowing she'd have to pass him.

A small nervous smile crept over her lips as she set the dark green envelope down. 'Trev' was written neatly on it in an almost emerald green tone. She smiled a hint wider and then headed for the door before he could react.

His eyes shifted back to the envelope on the table. He flipped it over and saw one small piece of tape with a fern pattern holding it closed. Carefully he opened it and pulled out a piece of nice, heavy paper. A short note written neatly in green ink.

'I didn't get a chance to show you Saturday, but you said you wanted to know,' was all it said. He narrowed his eyes then flipped it over.

A smile formed that reached his eyes. He saw a mountain lion and a mink both wearing flower crowns sitting in front of a redwood and ferns. Done in black ink, the flowers were golden poppies and purple lupines. He just stared at it with such glee.

She had drawn this just for me? This wasn't just a sketch in her book she showed me a picture of.

He knew she was good. Had known she was someone kind and who cared a lot about his home because it was her home too. Her home that had for whatever reason called her and her energy to this place. He didn't trust easily, mortal and fae alike, but he wanted to learn to trust her. This small token of acceptance, this small thing between them that they would share. Trevin realized everything this drawing represented. Him and her, bright and curious at this newness in his home.

Elodie let out a huge exhale when she got to her car.

"Why am I so awkward? Why is he so weird? He acts as though he's so smooth and sly, but then I catch him off guard. As if he's never been given anything like that before?" she said to herself. She drove to the store for supplies and her phone buzzed.

Elodie laughed while reading the messages from Cora, who wanted to know what she gave him. Commenting on the awestruck look he gave her and how weird their methods of flirting were.

She grinned bashfully and responded by insisting they were not flirting and telling her about the artwork, she would be surprised if it didn't end up forgotten in a notebook eventually.

Cora's next response pulled an audible laugh out of Elodie and she replied informing Cora she was sorry to disappoint but they did not make out on the beach.

Elodie was too nervous for the café the rest of the week so she skipped it. Opting to have dinner in her hatch overlooking the beach instead.

Once again she found herself bashful at the thought that he was watching the door frequently. She wasn't sure why she was so embarrassed to see him again. It was not that she didn't want to, rather quite the opposite.

Elodie felt the urge to explore this place more, and realized she hadn't explored much of it. After snapping a picture of the sunset, she climbed out of the hatch and drove home. Settling on camping in redwoods, she booked a campsite.

The next night Trevin sat in the café trying to focus on work while also thinking about her and her power. If Cyrus sensed that energy in her as much as he did, then he knew it was there. The rest of their friend circle was no help. He also found himself still trying to fight the urge to want to kiss her again. Craving the scent of sea breeze and lavender now, he liked seeing her, knowing she was near and safe.

He thought about last night. How her emotions change from worry to sadness to confusion then realization, though he could not figure out what. And as she packed her things she missed his shoulders slump.

Elodie had missed the unease and nerves in Trevin's expression. If she could hear his heartbeat, as well as he could hers, she would have caught it.

He was learning the sound of her walk and last night as she walked toward the door, she walked toward him instead. His eyes traveled up to her almost transfixed. That scent nearly suffocated him, and he was entirely okay with the sea breeze and lavender snuffing him out. The heat in her cheeks and that energy in her was almost cascading over him. He wanted to embrace it.

Trevin glanced at the door again anxiously tonight.

"She said to tell you she's not planning on doing any night hikes, and is safe from the sea sirens and krakens," Cora said walking by, watching Trevin deflate. "Honestly Trev, you are worse than a love-struck puppy."

"I'm not love-struck. I just, I enjoy the banter with her when she doesn't hate me. I'm tired of staring at work stuff, I'm stumped and I wanted to see if she had any ideas."

"If you insist," Cora said, shaking her head and walking off.

Trevin sighed and finished off his drink. He got up and bussed his glass.

"Want me to ask if she will be here tomorrow?" Cora asked.

"No, I'm sure I will figure out this work thing," he said. Cora nodded and watched him leave.

Once back at home, he dragged himself to his room. A smile formed as soon as he saw the drawing. "I hope you are safe, little mink." Unable to focus, he went downstairs to workout. When he was finished, he headed back to his bedroom to look at the book.

CHAPTER 14

It was the first official day of Elodie's holiday break. Despite having the week off, her internal clock told her to get up. After spending the weekend in Redwoods National Park, she felt almost euphoric from the last few days there. In two days, she would make the trek back to Marin for the holiday. Her only real plans today were to meet up with Cora and Justine in the afternoon. Since the café was closed on Mondays, they decided to hang out at Cora's place. Until then though, she was going to grab a bite at the bagel shop and enjoy the early morning air on the beach.

Walking down one of the less populated streets, she smiled to herself at how quiet it was even for a Monday. If this was the city or even Marin County, brunch spots would have a line out the door at 7 a.m. As she walked down the slight hill past closed shops, a mural in an alcove caught her eye. She had seen it dozens of times, but it was another reminder how much she liked being here. There was a tin planter blooming with life, and behind it lay a person slumped against the wall. Her eyes fixed on that person and she froze.

She didn't know what to do upon seeing Trev passed out. The last time she saw him was when she gave him the drawing. She hadn't been avoiding him exactly, but she also wasn't sure she would consider him a friend yet either. It was freezing this morning, and he only had a hoodie. His skin looked cold to the touch. His face scuffed and his clothes were dirty.

Had he fallen? With how in shape he was, it was doubtful he tripped and fell. She shrugged and figured it could still be possible. Then she wondered if he tried his pretty words and coy smiles on the wrong girl and she or her partner put him in his place. Still though, to leave him like this didn't sit well with her.

Her thoughts raced as she debated on nudging to wake him up. *What if he wakes up swinging? Or wakes up pissed, or his dad shows up? No doubt with his dad in the local government he could get me fired at work.* She shook her head.

"He's smart. He grew up here. I doubt he's never been in trouble before. What can I do?" she said quietly to herself with a shrug and turned to keep walking, then stopped. Her eyes assessed him again, and something in her tugged as a thought crossed her mind. "How often has this happened to you?"

Would she really leave someone, friend or odd, weird acquaintance thing they were like this? Just out? What if someone else had seen him? This was not going to look good for his family. For the estate, or whatever. She sighed and realized what she was doing. She was trying to help someone who could suck her dry if she wasn't careful. Kind of like Ricky had done.

Another sigh slipped out. She hated how much she was debating on what to do. She thought back to her friend in the city. She'd have left his ass here. Then she thought about Cora and Justine '*People tend to look out for each other here.*' He called her an array of nicknames and watched her a lot for some reason and yet she couldn't bring herself to ignore him, either. He made her smile sometimes. Cora said he liked the drawing, liked her and he had been sincere in his apology, didn't find her weird for this thing in her. He was already a part of her life here.

She nudged his shoe with hers, but he didn't respond. Her heart rate quickened, and she nudged him again. Still no response.

"Trev," she said softly. "Trevor." Kneeling down, she gripped his hand. Then flung her hand away. His skin was burning, yet appeared normal, not even red. "Trev!" she said, putting her hand on his shoulder, cold as ice. Yet his hand was so hot. "Trevor!" she said, placing the back of her hand on his cheek. His skin was freezing, and she noted the tribal design across his cheekbones. *Did he get drunk and get tattoos on his face?* She pressed two fingers to his neck, his pulse slow. He groaned. "Trev, wake up!" she said, noticing the markings on his face were not smudged. Elodie wondered if the markings had to do with part of his heritage given how long his family had been in the area. She made a mental note to research the symbolism when she got home. They hadn't appeared puffy or fresh as she would expect.

"Weak," he groaned. He lifted his hand, then dropped it as though it was too heavy to hold up. The sound of metal hitting the ground made her head tilt in confusion. "Burning, so weak. Help." His speech slurred. He didn't open his eyes.

She fixed on him then his arm. Impulse took over her as she grabbed his hand and slid his sleeve up, searching for burns further up his arm, but there was nothing. No burn marks. She slid the bracelet up and he whimpered weakly, trying to pull his arm away. It was not tight or cutting off circulation, but it was not going to slide off either. She turned it, realizing there was no clasp. Upon closer inspection, she noticed a seam as if it was welded on him. She hadn't noticed him wearing it before. *Odd choice but okay,* she thought to herself.

Then she realized the bracelet was cold, yet his skin burned.

"Impossible," she said.

As she ran her fingers over the ridges and bumps of the metal, she noticed the weight and texture of it. She was no expert at minerals, but she did recognize this metal.

"Is this iron?" she asked, fixed on the bracelet as though it would answer. Her mind was already fitting the puzzle pieces together. His sly grin, his gentle touch, the iron element at King Range, the thing they were seeking in Falk, how well he dressed at the Halloween party. Her eyes scanned his face, tracing the lines. She dropped his hand and scooted back, stumbling backward flat on her ass dumbfounded, staring at his face. *His ears, are they pointed?* She couldn't see them with his hood up, and then her eyes widened, confirming what the puzzle revealed.

"No!" she gasped, remembering that first night how he had traced her ear. How soft his touch was, how good his hearing always seemed. Her mind raced. "Oh no!"

Three estates that everyone knew had a lot of power in the county, yet could not be located on the map. If they lived in the forests, to govern more than just the towns and ordinances said towns bitched about, they governed the lands, the forests.

He was fae! This iron was hurting him.

How had no one mentioned this? Did they all assume it was common knowledge? *Trev was that his name? Trevor or? Fae never gave their real name;*

it could be used to make them do things. She never had asked him for his. What if Cora only knew him as Trevor? She had just assumed it was. That would mean Caleb, Anna, Q, Russ were all just variations of their real names.

Staring at the realization that sat in front of her, ferns seemed to grow out of the concrete and she gasped.

Elodie. Help him.

A whisper of wind passed through her, causing her body to tense. She looked around, then at Trev.

"Oh dear, are you okay?" a man asked. He was wearing a green and blue flannel over a T-shirt and jeans. A black trucker hat with a Highway 1 patch atop his head.

It took her a moment to realize how weird this would look to the man: sitting on the ground, shock clearly all over her face. Her heart was racing with a million thoughts.

"Are you hurt?" he asked, offering a hand. She shook her head and jumped up to her feet.

Elodie looked at Trev, his hand laying where it had fallen.

"Oh bother, it seems like he got into a scrap. These estate boys can get so rowdy. Usually Trevor keeps out of trouble though."

Elodie glanced at the man, then back at Trev. *Trevor. He called him Trevor. He doesn't know he's looking at a fae.* She couldn't leave him here. Not when he was being drained of his life. Not when this could potentially wreak havoc on Eureka, on Greenthistle.

"I...we were at a party with friends last night and he left. We couldn't get ahold of him. Can you help me get him into my car? Anna is still at my friend's house, spent the night!" she said, hoping her lie was believable. Then the thought struck her. *If he was fae, he couldn't lie, everything he had said had to be true or a manipulation of words.*

"I guess the party explains his weird makeup. I do not understand these boys sometimes. I may not always agree with his father, but he is an honest man, at least." He sighed. "Where's your car, hun?" the man asked.

"Round the corner, purple hatchback with the Thule Box on top," she said, grabbing her keys. He nodded and headed toward Trev. Elodie grabbed the hand that was hot in an attempt to help, her sleeve pulled down over her hand for another buffer. The man knelt down and took Trev's other arm, lifting him to his feet. Trev's head dropped to the side. She winced and pushed his head up to avoid further injury and to keep the hood up. The urge to feel his ear was nagging at her, but she was also terrified to confirm it was true. A short walk later, they were up the hill and next to her car. She opened the door, and he set Trev in the seat. Elodie quickly closed the passenger side door.

"Thank you, sir! So much! I'm sure Anna is worried about him. I will take him right to her!"

"Okay. Umm, see to it he gets home. I do not want to be on the wrong end of his father's wrath for this," the man said, shaking his head.

"Of course! I will make sure he knows you helped me. I will tell Anna!" Elodie said, lying through her teeth but pulling out her cell phone anyway. She wouldn't tell Anna, because she didn't have Anna's number. She had no way of contacting her unless she went through Charles, but how would she cover this up? The man nodded and walked off. She jumped in her car and stared at him. His head sagged forward.

She supposed she could go to city hall, but what if they accused her of doing it? "What would they do to me? What are they going to do to me?" Her eyes looked up to the sky, then at him. He was still unresponsive.

"I swear if you wake up right now." Elodie gritted her teeth and reached over his lap to recline his seat back slightly. She pressed into him, his scent engulfing her senses. *Damn, whatever he uses smells really good,* she thought, taking a deeper inhale.

"Weak," he groaned, reaching his hand up. The back of his hand weakly met her stomach, and she went still feeling his hand turn and his fingers rest there. They were hot through her shirt, burning almost. The only confirming factor was that he was in trouble.

"Trev," she said, backing up.

"It burns," He slurred a whimper and dropped his hand again. "Please." He still hadn't opened his eyes or lifted his head.

She took a deep inhale and threw her car in reverse, then drove the few miles home. Her small studio was a rented room above a garage on a large property nearby. Luckily, the owners were away for the week. She parked and jumped out of the car, then opened the garage, searching for anything she could use. Her eyes fixed on the large stainless steel lock cutters.

Grabbing the tool, she ran back to the passenger side door. Once the door was opened, she took one split-second pause to think about what she had to do. Carefully slipping part under the iron, she squeezed the handles, leaning her back against him. She struggled to get a good angle with his arm limp.

"Damn it!" She gritted her teeth. Her heart pounded as she undid his seatbelt and pulled him to the ground. He groaned faintly. "Come on, Trev," she hissed as she pressed his arm and hand down with her knees.

She squeezed the handles but still wasn't able to get it. A gust of air passed through her nose in frustration and then once more she gripped the handles, ready to try again. She trembled as she put all of her weight into squeezing the handles together. "Come on," she whimpered, trying to find more strength. Finally, it snapped, and the momentum nearly caused her to fall on top of him. A moment of terror filled her as her eyes traveled down to the band, worried she had snapped bone and not metal.

To her relief, the tool had broken the band and it lay on the ground beside his wrist. He whimpered again, and she backed up, scanning his face and noting the markings and then his ears.

Trevin's breathing picked up and his eyes fluttered open, confused when he found Elodie next to him. His eyes shot wide, and he sat up. The sea breeze and lavender he was inhaling hadn't been a dream. *Does she always wear this? It must be body spray or something,* he thought. Then he realized he wasn't glamoured. She was seeing him as he really was—fae.

She met his gaze for a moment, before her eyes traveled over his face. Then to his ears. She backed away, now terrified.

Trevin watched her as though he were the prey. Still in a haze from sitting up too fast, he examined his wrist, and the wrecked iron bracelet, then to the lock cutters. His eyes saw her car. The passenger side door opened and took in the surroundings.

"Elodie?" he said in shock, piecing everything together as he rubbed his wrist. Then something warmed in his core. "El?" He smiled at her warmly.

She was frozen stiff. Her face was pure terror. "You're not mortal, you're fae!"

He nodded, admitting it. "I glamour myself when I'm in town. I have to. How do you know what I am? Who told you?" he asked, now growing worried. His voice was still calm despite the pounding of his heart as he realized the weight of the situation.

"No one. I saw you passed out, and I tried to wake you, but you didn't move. I freaked out and grabbed your hand but it burned," she told him the events that followed.

He shifted his gaze to his wrist again, now rubbing the skin, feeling the relief from the burn, then looked at her. *She saved me? She helped me?* His expression shifted into an endearing grin. "You helped me?"

Elodie watched him still terrified. "I did," she said quietly, then covered her mouth with her hands. He could hear her heart pound wildly. "You're fae," she said again, this time her tone more in awe of the realization.

"I am. We are not allowed to tell anyone. No one's guessed before. No one talks about them. Just folktales and myths. You are the first in my forty-five years of existence to figure it out."

"Your estate? Family? Trev, Trevor isn't your name, is it?"

"All high fae and Trev is a variation of my name that I go by. Asking questions I suppose I'm bound to answer. This is your place—can we go inside?"

Her eyes widened, and a gasp escaped her. She had led him straight to her place. A fae right to her door. She scooted back and shook her head.

"El, let's talk. I had a hunch you were different. I am not going to harm you. I promise. If anything, I'm bound to you."

"I don't want to be bound to you! You will whisk me away to your estate that is on no map and make me your servant, or your—" She cut off with a gasp and scooted back more. He shook his head, and watched her eyes water. "This isn't happening." Her breathing became more frantic.

"No Elodie, I will not hurt you," his voice was soft, trying to console her. "I will not hurt someone who helped me, saved me. We both need to get cleaned up and warm. Plus, it is going to rain soon, and I'd rather not answer such questions where someone could see or hear," Trevin said, glancing at the trees.

Her blurry eyes took in the dark clouds and then fixed on him again. He watched her struggle through her thoughts as a whimper slipped out.

"Do you plan to force yourself on me?"

"No. I do not," he said, locking eyes with her.

"Ever? Or just not right now?" Trevin knew she understood he couldn't lie, but a lie of omission was possible—he hadn't told her his name, just that what he went by with mortals was a variation of it. She was smartly watching her words.

"No. I never intend to force myself on you. I've never forced myself on anyone."

"So you glamoured them to get your way instead of forcing yourself on them?"

"I've never once done that either. I will not glamour you, or anyone else, ever. I'm not a fan of most mortals. You can all lie. Mortals are fickle and I just don't care much for pursuing them."

"Yet you want into a stupid mortal girl's house?" Elodie pressed against her car.

He sighed and let his shoulders slump. *Please, little mink. Don't be frightened.* Trevin said in his mind.

"We shouldn't sit outside." He glanced up. "I think it is far safer inside, behind closed doors. Fae have a lot of rules and we need to be very careful now. Please?" Trevin asked.

"Are you going to call your friends over here now because you hate mortals, and you hate me? Think toying with us is fun? Q, Caleb, Russ! Anna!" She shook her head and rubbed her eyes. "Wake up! Wake up," she whimpered.

He sighed again and an odd pain formed inside him. He knew he was hurting her, but he also couldn't just leave. He could not let word get out, or let her face the other side of the boundary alone.

"Never. I'd never let them or anyone hurt you. They wouldn't and they won't. We do not harm mortals." He eyed the broken cuff and nudged it toward her with the lock cutters. "Put this back on me if you don't trust me," he said.

Concern washed over her face. "No, that could have killed you!"

"After a week, maybe?"

"A week?! Like that? You were hardly responsive!"

"El, please," he pleaded. "I will come clean. I promise. Just not outside." His eyes glanced up to the trees, worried at any second he would see or hear a raven and sentries would surround her.

Elodie swallowed hard and nodded. Slowly, she got up to her feet and watched him, her eyes scanning his face, taking in everything he was.

"You can ask me anything. I have to answer truthfully. You know this?"

With a nod, Elodie closed her car door, tossed the bolt cutters and the cuff in the garage, and went upstairs. He watched, then followed. They sat at opposite ends of her couch and looked at each other closely. Trevin felt cautious and worried, he could only guess Elodie felt shocked and maybe a little fearful.

Elodie had let a fae into her house. What defense did she have? *I have wandered out on those trails at night. I could have been whisked away by any of them. Sea sirens and krakens are not the most dangerous thing in the forest. He was. Russ was.* An uneasy breath escaped her.

Her eyes traced the markings on his face, a thin line on either cheekbone, another shorter line underneath, three-quarters of the length as the one above it. Three dots under that. A line down his bottom lip, chin, and the center of his throat, disappearing under his hoodie. Then she fixed on his pointed ears and dazzling eyes.

"You really glamour yourself every time you go out?"

"Beyond the boundary line, yes. I have to."

"Anna and Caleb?" she asked, her eyes wide. "Your dad? Mom?"

"All pure blood high fae," he said.

"You, you can't rub the markings off your face? It's not makeup? A tattoo?"

He rubbed his thumb down the lines on his cheekbone and they moved with the skin, scuffs and all, not smudging. "No, I can't. Born with them. We all have them, just different markings, though Caleb, Anna, and I have similar ones. Anna has one line, and more dots, Caleb has fewer dots," he said.

"Are they, do they appear anywhere else on you?" she asked. He smirked slightly and nodded.

"Down my chest and outlining my ribs, wrapping around to either flank. Two bands above and below my knees, I can show you if you like?" he said. She blushed and shook her head.

"No, I will take your word for it. Your dad has a lot of pull in this county, because he's fae?" Elodie swallowed hard. "Russ and Q, their dads too?" she asked. He nodded.

"Lord Greenthistle, Lord Nightswift, and Lord Ashdale. Greenthistle is the oldest line, followed by Nightswift, then Ashdale. Then there are the estate kids. The rich fuckboys who live out in the forests. Well, Russ is, Q isn't as bad. And me—I tend to be the loner of the group. I don't talk to too many people if I can help it," he said.

She looked at his ears again. "You, you probably think I'm stupid," she said, blushing slightly.

"Why would I think that? It is rather the opposite actually, you figured me out. Not only that, you saved me. I'd say you are clever, observant, loyal, kind, strong, and brave, little mink. Not stupid at all."

"Cora's Halloween party—you ran your finger along my ear, my wire frames, and then I asked if you'd ever seen a fae before." She covered her face and groaned. He let out a soft laugh. "Why did I say that?"

"As I said before, I knew there was something different about you, and you make a pretty fae. You are very pretty." Trevin smiled. She still wasn't looking at him.

"Stop," she said, taking a deep inhale and removing her hands from her face, then sighing it out. He smirked to himself. "What is your real name?" she asked.

He dropped his grin. "You know what power you'd hold, I assume?"

"I do. I'm not going to use it, I promise. Just, I want to know. Trev? Trevor?"

He took a deep inhale.

"Trevin Greenthistle, young master of and heir to Greenthistle Estate, when my dad, Lord Greenthistle, decides to hand it over to me. When hell freezes over," he said with a small laugh.

"Trevin," she said. He smiled.

"What, what is your power, what can you do?" she asked. "What can Anna do? Caleb? Those are not their real names, are they?"

"One question at a time, El. My power or gift is what they call an empathic seeker and receiver. I can see the emotions of others. I know what they are feeling. I can, in dire situations, pull them off an individual, but I don't do it often because it's not always best. It's how I was able to read so much about you the night we met. As far as my siblings' names, Anna and Caleb are a variation. May I ask you to allow me to omit theirs as it is not mine to give? I promise I will confirm if you choose to guess correctly," Trevin explained.

"Okay."

"Thank you, Elodie. I love my siblings, a lot. I don't want them hurt or to unknowingly bind them to anyone. I am fine being bound to you. I trust you. Caleb is unearthly strong and fast, what I lack in muscle mass he got double of. Anna is very clever with the tongue and she can sway people to do things in her favor. And before you ask, no, she has never done that to you or Charles, or any of our friends. She won't either," he said and watched her head nod.

"What does being bound mean?"

"It simply means I will look out for you. If anyone tries to harm you, I intervene. A favor for a favor."

"We are even. You helped me with Ricky," she said nervously. "I'm fine."

He smiled again. "There are people to watch for, things to watch for. As master of and heir to Greenthistle, the three estates watch out for the mortals in these lands. So, I would keep an eye out for you anyway, but now I can act much quicker and without restraint. You are under an estate master's watch."

She swallowed hard. "You helped me before being bound to me?"

"I did."

"Why?"

"Something about you intrigues me. I can't pinpoint what, and I don't want anyone else snaking in before I figure it out."

"Then what? You will whisk me away when you find out what is intriguing about me? Use me for things?"

He sighed and shook his head. "No. I am not going to whisk you away or use you for anything. I wouldn't use anyone. I just want to see to it that you are safe here in Humboldt. What if we agreed to be friends now?" he asked.

She snapped her head back. "What?"

"You know, like you and Cora, or you and Justine? Or Charles? You and I?" A smile crept over his face. "El and Trev."

"So you wouldn't just glance at me in the café or at gatherings, then look away with your coy little smiles." She paused and tensed abruptly.

"What sudden realization did you come to, El?"

"You've been stalking me or flirting with me this entire time?" She stared at him, confused.

"I mean, I wouldn't say flirting the entire time, and stalking was not my intent, please do not feel it was with any malice. It's hard to explain though. So instead of trying to explain it, why not be friends to start? So it doesn't have to be awkward at the café or at gatherings?" he asked, watching her eyes narrow.

"You are really going to live forever? And look like that?" she said, eyeing him up and down. He smirked.

"I will show some age, but for the most part, yes."

"Forty-five years old?" she asked. He nodded. "And you never pursued a mortal?"

"A few. I kept my distance usually."

"But you've slept with them?" she asked, eyes darting away from him.

"Russ and Caleb laugh at my number, but I've had a few of each. Some here, some from Del Norte, Trinity, Mendocino. Even one in Marin, though it was more of a fling," he said. She nodded.

"Do you play kissing games often?" she asked.

"Russ, Q, and Caleb do. I don't. I don't want to lead people on. I've helped them chase a guy around a few times, but mortals tend to fawn over us unless we establish the reputation as a fuckboy. Regardless of my distrust of most people, I do not like when people are hurt."

"How many are a few?" she asked. "Mortal and fae?"

She was beginning to panic. *He is going to say over a hundred of each, probably. Why are you even asking? Why are you curious? You don't want to date a fae, you can't date him! He said friends. Do I even want to be friends with a fae? Anna?*

"Nooo, never mind. It's not my business. I should not be asking questions like that. I am sorry," she stuttered out. He smirked.

"Three and six," he said. She looked at him shocked. "That number is the lowest of all of us, save for Russ's younger sister," he said. "I'd imagine though, it might seem like a lot. Fae kind do that a fair amount. Russ and Anna used to have a thing, and I hated it," he said with a laugh.

"Russ and Anna? Was it some kind of house alliance thing?" she asked, confused. "He was at the bonfire? Blond hair and blue eyes. Fae." A chill shot through her.

Trevin watched carefully. "He acts pretty arrogant and pompous but I assure you he is good. He will not harm you. I saw the looks he gave you and told him to knock it off." Trevin placed his hand on her knee. "But I was certainly relieved when Anna and him ended it."

Elodie nodded still tense. "So, if you are forty-five, and look in your mid-twenties, how old is your dad? I take it he's a little older than he looks?" she asked.

Trevin nodded with a grin. "He is four hundred."

"I see, so when I saved or helped you with the iron bracelet thing, did that bind me to you or your estate? To your dad somehow? I don't know the rules."

"No, you do not owe us or me anything aside from keeping quiet about what we are. I do need to tell them though." Confusion came over him and his brow furrowed.

"What is it?" she asked, placing her hand on his arm bringing him back to the present.

"Attacks on the estate lords are a death wish. An attack on the heirs or estate masters as we are called is another matter entirely. It cannot be ignored because it's a threat to the entire estate, maybe the territory too. Attacks or threats toward the heirs are a sign that another estate wants to challenge for the position. If mortals know of us it's one thing. But it would be just like a fae to take down the heir to inherit the largest hold on the territory. Greenthistle is the oldest too. But Ashdale is the newest to power, why would they attempt to overthrow Greenthistle by a direct attack?"

Worry cascaded over her face with a frown. "I just put myself in the crossfire, didn't I?" she asked. He looked at her tilting his head in thought.

"No. I will make sure of it. I have to tell my dad that you know about us, I have to tell him about this entire thing. I will tell him Greenthistle has to keep you protected. Anna already wants to be your friend. Caleb isn't going to like it, but I will see to it you are safe. Anna is strong and can hold her own, between her and me you are safe. I promise," he said, taking her hand. She blushed.

"It's really okay. I can just get rid of the bracelet. Bury it or throw it in the ocean? No one saw it. I kept your hood over your head and held your sleeve down," she said.

"Someone might have seen it at any point. We watch a lot. We have to. The estates' watch out for their lands, that includes its residents too. They can make or break us. It's a delicate balance for everyone. You protect the Old Giants—we protect their secrets. Either way, don't be scared, okay?" he said. She nodded and looked at him. "Can you agree to a set of terms?"

Elodie swallowed hard. "A bargain? With a fae?"

Trevin nodded, still holding her hand. "Do not speak of what we are, ever to anyone, never use my real name to anyone but me and only when we are alone. If you speak, we have holding cells on our side of the boundary. I do not want to see you in one, ever. I will see to it you are safe, but if you speak of us, I can only do so much."

Elodie looked worried.

"Never speak of what we are and you will not end up in one. Please?" His voice nearly pleading.

She nodded. "Trevin. I agree, to never speak of what you are."

Trevin sighed in relief. "You will be safe, I promise you, El."

"What happened? How did you end up with it on you? Who did that?" she asked. He sighed.

"I can't remember." His tone contemplated as he began to retrace his steps. "I was out with Q and Russ at Ashdale Estate, and on my way home from Q's." His expression grew bewildered. "I can't remember any of it. I was running and then I—" He rubbed the back of his head. "I fell forward? Hit the ground and felt the iron. It's hazy. I woke up on the ground and I saw you recoil, I saw your face riddled with fear and panic. I was the exact thing your fairy tales warn you about, and I don't want to be."

"I'm sorry. It's just that fae aren't real, weren't real. Now one is sitting on my couch."

He met her eyes. "El, you will be watched over. I give you my word. I will always keep you safe as long as you remain in Humboldt," he said, placing a hand on her knee again.

Something tugged inside Elodie. Tugged toward him. Elodie wondered if he did in fact bind himself to her with those words.

"And again, I am sorry about every weird and creepy thing I've done," Trevin said with a hint of a bashful laugh.

She nodded.

"We are friends now, right?" he asked

"Yes." She nodded.

"You won't tell anyone about me, what I am? Not Cora, Charles, or Justine? Your coworkers? Not even friends in Marin?" he asked uneasily.

She found him being genuine, and something in her wanted to prove him wrong about mortals. She had a dozen more questions, but she'd likely pass out before she could ask them all, say all the things she wanted too.

"I won't tell anyone about this. I promise. I know mortal promises mean little but I promise you, Trev," she said with a small sigh. "The redwoods are important to me in a way I don't think I understand yet. If anything happened to them, I don't know if I'd be whole ever again. I trust your kind with them a whole lot more than I trust my kind. Humans can be complete trash to their environments so I don't blame you or Caleb for hating us. Your secret is safe with me."

"I can see the sincerity in you. One of the benefits of being an empathic seeker, I can tell when people are lying or being true. I can see you being true and honestly El, I don't think it takes an empath to see you are nothing like other mortals."

"What was it about me you found different, odd?"

"There is an energy in you. A power I've never seen in either mortal or fae before. I watch because your emotions cause it to surge sometimes, causing the Old Giants to react to it."

"React? How?" she asked, confused but in awe.

"More alive?" he said, gazing into her eyes. "I think what caught my attention might have been your perfume or body spray that flooded my senses. Our senses are stronger being fae. Then I felt that power and I wanted to see it closer. The eyes are the easiest way to see a person's emotions so I grabbed your chin like a creep and once I was past your emotions, I saw it simmering. I've seen your fear mask it, and I've seen it spent and reduced to a trickle. I saw it simmer after you told Caleb and me off. When you were on the phone with that asshole, it boiled over and I could see the trees tremble, almost. I glanced at Caleb who also noticed it. I only came back to my senses when I heard you talk and you were looking right at me. It takes a lot for someone to catch me off guard and yet you do it often, little mink," he said with a laugh.

"You always know what I'm feeling? Should I never make eye contact with you again?" she asked with a frown, cutting her eyes down.

Trevin laughed again. "I may know what you are feeling but I do not know what fuels it. I can't turn it off."

She swallowed hard and nodded. "So the scent that drew you in was cherry blossom?" she asked.

Confusion cascaded over him. "No, ocean breeze and lavender. I smell it now. It's all over." He froze for a second. His eyes widened. "You don't wear that scent much do you?"

"I might have lavender body spray but I don't think I've used it up here yet. Ocean breeze, it's in the air," she said, he swallowed hard and nodded.

She had always noticed the smell of oakmoss and amber on him. It smelled of earth, and warmth and spice. It was alluring to her which she found odd since she hadn't ever noticed that scent on anyone before. It must be a fae soap he used.

"Maybe it was someone nearby," he said with unease. "Let me give you my number. Call me any time, call me if you ever feel in danger, I give you my word I will come. Or you know, call me if you just want to talk, or hang out, dinner, hike, coffee, redwoods, whatever. Text me if you have any questions too," he said with that endearing gaze.

She nodded and handed him her phone. He entered his number and then sent a text from hers.

"El, I didn't lie, you know. You are beautiful," he said.

She blushed, and he smiled. "Thank you." She glanced down and then back up at him. "You are very handsome, breathtaking even." A nervous laugh to match the heat in her cheeks.

His grin grew wide. "I know I said I wanted to start as friends, but may I kiss you again, to make up for last time. I should have asked before I ever touched you," he said.

Her eyes traveled to his lip, the line that traveled under his hoodie.

Elodie certainly hadn't hated their first kiss. She certainly didn't hate him either, despite everything that had happened between them the last few weeks. Rather it was quite the opposite.

"This isn't some other game or bet between your friends or brother?" She frowned.

"No, it's not. I promise."

She looked at his eyes and then nodded slightly. "Okay."

Her heart thudded in anticipation as she leaned in.

Placing his fingertips under her chin, he lifted her head and pressed his lips to hers. His fingers ran along her ear and her breath hitched slightly at the sensation. Trevin pressed into the kiss, cupping her jaw lightly. She brought her hand up to trace his ear, running up to the point as he had done to her. He trembled and a slight moan escaped him. Instantly he pulled away. Elodie's eyes went wide in shock about his reaction but also how it felt for her.

"Ears are sensitive to us," he said with a bashful laugh.

A laugh escaped her too as her eyes traveled down that line. "Us too."

Her eyes traveled down his body and she felt her desire build. That kiss felt as though something in her was reaching for him. She wanted it and was far too stunned how much she had wanted it, wanted him.

"I have to get home. My family is probably worried," he said, regaining his composure. She watched him not moving, her eyes widened, assessing everything she could.

"Okay," she said, finally standing up too. "Do you need the iron bracelet thing? Does your dad or the other estate lords?"

"No. It is a known thing in our world, I'd need to carry it in a bag or something. Even if I put it in my pocket, it could still hurt me. It's safest where you tossed it," Trevin said. She nodded and walked him to the door. He turned and faced her. "Sorry if I ruined your day, you looked like you were going to go hiking?"

"It's Thanksgiving week, so schools are closed. I was just going to hang out in my hatch with breakfast from the bagel shop then meet up with Cora. I camped in the redwoods Saturday and Sunday."

"You camped, solo?" he asked.

"Yeah, I do it often, I have a bed and stuff in my hatch. It's pretty easy to set up and take down. Nothing like Charles's van, but I've done it a lot of places."

He glanced around noticing her Camelbak and hiking boots.

"Sounds like you know about the great outdoors, that's good," he said.

"You could say that."

"By the way, thanks for the drawing. It is amazing, little mink," he said. She laughed bashfully. "Be safe, I will see you soon," he said with a smile. It was not coy like before, but warm and happy. "Thank you again, I owe you my life, Elodie."

She watched him open the door and then she tensed for a moment. "Trev, get home safely, okay?"

"I will." He smiled and rubbed her arm. "Remember, not a word of this, of me, to anyone." She nodded and watched him slip his glamour back on. His ears were normal, his facial markings gone, he appeared mortal. He walked out and headed down the stairs and off the property toward the trail she often walked. Just before he went out of view he glanced back with a smile.

Elodie quickly slipped back into her house and locked the doors. She let out the biggest sigh and fell back on the couch.

"I saved a fae, I kissed a fae twice, a young master and heir to one of the estates!" Stunned hardly described her right now. "Do other counties have them? Does Marin? I have so many questions!"

Glancing at her phone she thought about her friends in Marin, then thought about Cora. *She'd probably want to know that we were friends? That kiss? What were we? He is bound to me?* She didn't even know what they were or what to say.

Then she sat up and wondered where he lived, how was he getting home? In the forest? On those trails? Did he live near her?

Taking a deep inhale, she grabbed her backpack and drove back to town. Elodie went about her original plan for the day. She watched every person she encountered much closer. Stopping to glance at newspapers and bulletin boards dealing with city things. When she got to the beach and laid in her hatch, she processed this knowledge. No one knew what she did. Trev had two lives he lived, and she had found a way into both. She focused on the tree line and wondered if this was a coincidence or if there was a reason for all of this. That thing she was searching for, was Trev supposed to help her find it?

# Chapter 15

After leaving Elodie's, Trevin ran to the estate. His heart thudded as he thought about these feelings he had been feeling and the reason for them. The anticipation as he leaned in to kiss her again swirled in his mind. When he pressed his lips to hers, the feeling from that first kiss was so much stronger. His fingers ran along her ear and her breath hitched slightly at the sensation. He forced himself to pull back and hated the absence of her lips on his. Yet he was terrified he was going to lose that battle of self control, worried she might say something she would be sure to regret one day. So he knew he had to go.

Once he ran inside the doors, he skidded to a halt, seeing his dad, Cedar, and Autumn all worried.

"Change and sit down! Start talking. You went rogue. Why?" his dad demanded. Trevin changed and started to explain.

"I don't know how much time had passed, but I heard someone call my name 'Trev, Trevor,' but I couldn't respond. I could hardly move and the conversation was muffled. Someone lifted me." He paused, realizing how lucky he had been.

"Trevin! Who saw you? Did they see you like this?" His dad demanded again. Stress and worry plastered Autumn's and Cedar's faces. Trevin looked at his wrist and shook his head.

"I woke up on the ground, and I saw—" He laughed at the absurdity of this situation. "Elodie."

"The stupid mortal girl who yelled at us?" Cedar groaned. "She knows about us, great!"

His dad nearly snarled. "Fetch her! Now," he said to nearby guards. They nodded, then froze hearing Trevin's shout.

"No! Let me finish! She's not stupid! She was sitting there in the dirt, petrified. I saw the bolt cutters and the iron cuff. She cut it off me!" Trevin said with a raised voice.

Terror now took hold of Autumn's expression. Lord Greenthistle had a moment of worry and then quickly masked it and narrowed his eyes at his eldest.

"She saved me! She found me across from the state department and dragged me to her car, kept my hood up, and saved me. She's good. She's different! She tried to wake me and grabbed my hand, only for it to burn hers. Then identified the metal and saved me, Dad! What would you have done to get it off me?"

Trevin caught Autumn's expression shift from worry to gratefulness and he knew his sister would watch out for Elodie, too. Her eyes rose to meet him, and he quickly went back to his dad.

"She knows about us." His dad's tone was stern. "The first to ever know about us in my lifetime that wasn't already in the hold. Trevin, first that mountain lion could have killed Cyrus, then the iron cuff? And a little mortal girl now knows about us? Things are changing too rapidly. We cannot brush any of this off. This mortal cannot be left unattended."

Trevin now noticed Cedar's face change. His expression was different from their sister's. Cedar had one of disgust and anger growing. Trevin guessed Cedar too knew what this meant. Like it or not, Elodie would be a constant in their lives now. Elodie was no longer able to be out of sight and mind of Greenthistle Estate. Trevin swallowed before he spoke, his voice calm and clear. He would not let her suffer. He met his dad's gaze.

"El saved me. If I was still in that alley at this hour, what would have happened? She said my skin was freezing, and I appeared roughed up. Look how dirty my clothes are! She could have left me, or called 911, dropped me at a hospital but she didn't. She took me to a secluded place, her place, and cut it off me. I've been nothing but weird to her ever since I met her. She didn't have to do any of that, but she did. I made sure she understands that she cannot speak a single word of this to anyone. She agreed to the bargain, if she speaks, she goes in the hold." Trevin's eyes locked with his dad's in defiance.

His dad sat back and sighed. He stared up and thought about this.

"I can't explain what it is about her, but there is something in her. I've tried my damnedest to figure it out, but I don't want anyone else to hurt her if it is something. I bind myself to be her overseer. As Greenthistle's heir, Greenthistle is to protect her." Trevin turned to his siblings. "You both feel it. Quinn did too, so did Cyrus. I know you do. Cedar, you reacted to that shift at the Halloween party. She caused that."

"Shut up, bro. You don't know that was her. It was a split-second surge. It could have been anything or anyone. I'm not babysitting her. Throw her in the hold!"

"No! It was her. I sensed something in her before that. I see it swell in her when she's upset, angry, or scared. When she's relaxed or happy, it's different. It's comforting, soothing."

"It's called you needing to get laid. Take her to bed and get it out of your system finally. She's cute, good job, just bed her already," Cedar said. "Mortals don't have power."

"Shut up!" Trevin yelled back.

"Enough!" their dad demanded, followed by a sigh. "Fine. The second she's out of line, Trevin, the second she opens her mouth, you bring her to me. She is your responsibility. You are to babysit the mortal girl. You still have your duties, and this is another task. Understood?"

"Yes, sir." Relief lined Trevin's voice.

"That's hardly a new task. He's been stalking her, chasing mountain lions off her ass, and pissing all over her since Halloween, anyway. I saw you at the bonfire with Cyrus. I was right there," Cedar scoffed. Trevin glared at him.

Lord Greenthistle narrowed his eyes. "What was Cyrus's interest in the girl? What was yours, Cedar? And Quinn's? You don't tend to go after the same ones on the same night."

"She's cute, a new face. Nothing more than that. Nothing special. Clearly, she's been claimed by Master Greenthistle. So I backed off." Cedar crossed his arms.

"Quinn doesn't seem to have an opinion of her. He's back with Justine, anyway. Cyrus though." Trevin paused.

"He watches her, but not like Trev does. He gets that gleam in his eye like he senses something in her, too. He makes Elodie uneasy. Her reactions to Trev and Quinn are different. Tense and unsure, but curious. She shudders away from Cyrus," Autumn said.

Lord Greenthistle sighed again. "Do either of you two sense something in her?"

"It's faint. Sometimes it's hard to sense, but it is there. It did surge after Cyrus and she looked at each other. The trees almost shivered, but that was my only interaction with her," Autumn said.

"I guess I felt something, but I didn't get close to her with this horn dog ready to strike around her," Cedar responded.

"Okay, Trevin. I cannot deny we got lucky, she thought quickly and correctly. She has my gratitude for what she did. You will watch her very closely. If she speaks of anything to anyone at all, you bring her to me. Autumn, Cedar, she is under Greenthistle's protection for now. If anyone fae or mortal tries to hurt her, you act," he said.

"I don't want to babysit her. What the hell? A mortal?" Cedar groaned.

"Yes, sir." Autumn nodded.

"Cedar?" Lord Greenthistle said. Cedar sighed and rolled his eyes.

"Understood," he said with a groan. "Stupid girl."

"I didn't give her anyone's names. I promise," Trevin said with a sigh of relief.

"Does she know yours?" His dad eyed him.

"Yes."

His dad leaned forward and rested his fingers on his head. "Walking a dangerous line, Trevin, a dangerous line."

"I promise this will be okay. I promise she will not betray us. Greenthistle will be safe, Nightswift and Ashdale will be safe. I will ensure it," Trevin said with determination.

"She better not. She will be dealt with otherwise."

"Understood, sir. Thank you." Trevin bowed his head.

"You are excused." Lord Greenthistle sighed.

Trevin ran upstairs and let out the biggest sigh. He flopped in his bed and ran his hands through his hair. "El. What am I going to do?"

A knock sounded at the door. Trevin sighed and pushed himself off his bed. He glanced at the drawing Elodie had done for him as he called, "come in."

His sister walked in, closed the door. "You like this one, don't you? I noticed you at the bonfire. I've never seen you act this way over anyone before."

"Autumn, I don't know what is happening. I don't know what she is or why she showed up, but now she knows about us." Trevin's heart was pounding.

"Enjoy the ride with her. I know you haven't had the best luck with mortals, but as long as you don't get attached to them, it's fun. Charles is great. Elodie seems lovely. She really figured this all out? No one told her?"

"Yes." He sighed and leaned against his dresser. "She reads a lot of fantasy books, take your pick on a title or lore and I'm sure she will ask if it's true. Her questions are endless. If you want to take over answering, feel free," he groaned.

Autumn laughed. "She was looking for us, wasn't she?"

"I don't know what happened. I don't know who put the iron on me. Things could have been really bad and her, of all people. The one who walks head first into the shadows and trembles the entire time," he said, mindlessly rubbing his wrist.

"I will keep an eye out for her. She will be safe."

"Help me ward her place later, yeah?"

"Of course," Autumn said. "Don't get attached to her. It will only hurt later. You know this. But it is good to see you trust someone new again," she said, standing up. Then her eyes noticed the drawing on Trevin's mirror. She tilted her head at the mountain lion and the mink with flower crowns.

"What is that?" Autumn asked, confused. Trevin sighed.

"It's a long story. Elodie is different. She sees so much and her imagination will get the better of her one of these days. I'm worried it will lead her into danger. Please look out for her when you can. I'm not going to ask you to babysit her when I can't be there, but if you notice her, just make sure she doesn't wander off a cliff or something?" Trevin asked with a hint of pleading.

Autumn laughed. "Of course, I will. Charles and Cora speak highly of her," she said, then left the room.

He waited until the door was closed and sighed, bringing his hands to his face. Trevin thought about the longing he had felt to be near her, to be better for her. To keep her safe and how territorial he was over her with anyone. Then the scent that drove him wild. He knew he couldn't ask anyone about it without them knowing.

He was vowed to a mortal. To her.

"Little mink, you cannot be my vowed, but I don't think I have it in me to reject you. I never did and now I can't."

He stared at the drawing of the mink and the mountain lion. It was them, him and her—Trev and El, the bonded pair—doomed from the beginning.

With a huge sigh, Trevin dragged himself into the shower.

Chapter 16

At Cora's that evening, Elodie casually asked questions about Trev. Cora answered them all with glee as they made dinner and sipped wine, allowing Elodie to learn more about Trev. The more she learned, the more she understood about why she had to hold his secret close.

Cora had shown her pictures of Q and Russ's parents. She learned Q had a job with CALFire as a firefighter and Russ worked for Caltrans—California's Department of Transportation—as a maintenance supervisor. She had known Trevin was a senior park ranger. Their parents usually all made appearances in town for 4th of July, Thanksgiving and Christmas. She had learned Trev had lost his mom shortly after they had all graduated from high school. The Greenthistle family was devastated. It was a sad day in town too. Elodie felt something in her heart tug learning that Trevin always seemed to hold his mother's passing close to him. He hadn't bounced back as his siblings had. Then she remembered his abilities, to see emotion, to bear the burden. With how kind he was and his empathic abilities, she wondered if he took on more of his siblings' emotions after their mom passed, wanting them to be okay even if it cost him. And now he wanted her to be safe too, he said he'd protect her and took on another responsibility in doing so.

On Tuesday Elodie managed to sleep in, then wandered around town again. Curiosity led her to the bookstore to just see what books they had gotten in. She went upstairs to the fantasy section and was interrupted as she reached up to grab a book with a green spine that had caught her eye.

"Oh hi, Elodie."

Elodie's head turned.

"Hi Ann...a," she said, pausing, wondering what the girl's name actually was. Her curious nature always got the best of her. She often felt like it put people on edge. It had to put Trevin on edge. Her eyes darted to the girl's ears, then to her eyes. Anna laughed.

"Have you read a lot of fantasy books?" she asked curiously, eyeing the title in Elodie's hands.

Elodie blushed. "Yea, it's kind of always been my guilty pleasure. I have a collection in Marin—at my dad's," Elodie said bashfully, pausing awkwardly. Anna gave her a coy smile that was similar to Trevin's.

"What about fantasy romances?" Anna asked. Elodie shifted nervously.

Elodie shifted, hesitant to answer. "Yes, those too." Elodie let out a little laugh, but it was shaky, nerves high.

Anna laughed while picking up a book on the shelf. Elodie's eyes shifted from one staircase to the first floor and the store exit. Trev said Anna wanted to be friends, but Elodie was nervous. She hadn't spoken to him since she helped him, except for a good morning text from him.

"It's such a fun world these authors create, isn't it? With dragons, blood-sucking vampires, and dashing fae princes, no?" Anna crooned.

Elodie felt her cheeks and ears heat. "Yes, fae princesses too," she said meekly, glancing at the girl, who laughed jovially. She tensed when Anna placed a hand on her shoulder.

"Thank you, by the way, for what you did for him. I was so worried when I couldn't sense him that morning. His room was empty. It means a lot to my family," she said quietly. "Even to Caleb and Dad."

Elodie nodded. "People tend to look out for each other here, right?" Elodie said.

"They do and we will. You have my word." Anna gave a sincere smile.

"Hey, Elodie," Charles said, walking up to stand next to Anna, who gave him a wide grin.

"Hi," Elodie responded with some unease, her eyes shifting from Charles to Anna.

"Anna and I were just going to grab a bite at the café. Are you free to join us? I mentioned how well you draw, and she was saying we should all get together."

"Yes! We should double date sometime, with Trev! Leave Caleb to his silly games," Anna beamed. Elodie felt her ears heat.

"Where is Trev anyway? At work or?" Charles asked.

"Yea. He, Russ, and Q have a few days a month they have to all be out in the field. Doing a bunch of running around and errands and sorts, if you will. They are all so dedicated to following in their dad's footsteps," Anna said, looking at Elodie. "Usually it's Mondays, but they moved it to today this week due to some unexpected circumstances."

Elodie met her gaze, wondering if it meant mortal world stuff, or fae stuff. She noticed Charles linking hands with Anna. She had known they were a thing and wondered if Charles knew the truth about her, if he knew her real name.

"I don't want to intrude if it was a date or something," Elodie said nervously.

"No, not at all. We were spending time together after I got off work. He has a lesson later and then I'm heading to his place," Anna responded with a sly grin. Charles nodded with a goofy smile. Elodie realized what was likely going to happen.

"Okay." Elodie put the book back on the shelf.

At the café, Cora greeted the three before making their drinks. They found a table, and spent the time chatting about hikes and places they had traveled. Anna listened with glee. After an hour, Charles headed off, giving Anna a long passionate kiss.

"See you later tonight, yes?" he said. She smiled up at him.

"Of course. Let me know when you are home."

"See ya, Elodie," he said and nodded. Elodie waved and nodded, watching him leave then shifted her eyes to Anna's, noticing her smile turn sly.

"So, what does that expression mean?"

"Whatever do you mean?" Anna asked, giving Elodie the same gaze.

"That one, that you are directing at me. I've watched Trev enough to know, especially now that those smiles mean things."

"How often do you watch him?" Anna asked with curiosity.

"I notice it on occasion, when he is at this very café."

Anna laughed. "What are your plans tonight?"

"I have none. Go home and read or draw? I'm off all week for the holiday. I'm heading down to Marin tomorrow. I will be there till the weekend to see my dad." Elodie noticed Anna's expression changed to inquisitive.

"Oh. It's been a while since I have been to Marin. I have some friends there," she said.

"Do you want to come? I'm sure my dad wouldn't mind. There will be a few relatives I don't really talk to. I'm kind of estranged from my extended family," Elodie said. "Does your family do anything for Thanksgiving?"

"No, I can't go on such short notice. And we normally don't, but Dad and Trev usually make appearances. I am sure they will be busy Thursday morning." Anna leaned in closer and spoke quieter. "We did celebrate our equinox ball in September. Nightswift Estate hosted it."

"Do you celebrate Christmas? No, solstice right?" Elodie asked, noting the hushed tone. Anna nodded. "What are they like? The Equinox and solstice celebrations?"

"Oh, they are so much fun. Such a grand revelry. One of the three estates hosts. There's food and wine, and everyone wears attire to reflect the season. Lots of red, orange, and yellow dresses and gowns, leaves and feathers braided into our hair. I love doing hair. The guys wear outfits too. Most had black or red with the trim and accents, tunics, corsets, and the sort, you know," Autumn gushed. "Dancing and performances all evening, mulled wine and fire pits for this one."

"That sounds magical. Were yours and Trev's Halloween costumes from that?" Elodie's curiosity brimmed.

"He wore his Spring Equinox outfit from last year, since he was too lazy to put any effort into his Halloween costume. Mine was clothes I got for promo. Russ's two sisters and I get a lot of clothes for free to model."

Elodie nodded. "What is the winter solstice celebration like?"

"Winter solstice will have ice sculptures and hot cocoa. Everyone in shimmering gowns of whites, silvers, blue, purples, and grays. We have ear cuffs we like to wear and jewels braided into hair. I'd love to do yours sometime," she said, then her eyes grew wide. "You should come to the Winter Solstice—Greenthistle is hosting it!"

Elodie gasped. "I can't. I'm—sure I'm not allowed. What would I even wear? I'd have to go to the Bay Area to find something worthy enough."

Anna leaned in and whispered, "At Trevin's estate, and please, our tailors would make your gown. They are making mine," she said with a wink. Elodie looked away bashfully. "Would you like to come over tonight for dinner?"

"With your family? Your dad?" she asked, suddenly going rigid.

"Yes."

"Am I even allowed? It's all forbidden. Isn't your dad not fond of me? Caleb is not fond of me?"

"They are fine, Trev ensured you would be safe. The bargain, remember?" Anna said so softly it was a whisper

She shook her head. "But I'm going to a place that's hidden," Elodie said uneasily. "Is this a trap?"

"No, it's not. It's me wanting to show you things you know about because you figured it out and you saved my brother's life. Besides, I have to meet up with Charles at his place." Her voice was hushed.

"And you want the ride home and back to town, I assume."

"At least the part of the way cars can go."

Elodie frowned and the unease settled in. "Are you going to Charles's place later?"

"Yes, I am."

"Okay," Elodie said with a huge sigh of nerves. "I need to see my dad tomorrow, though. I want to see him." Her sad eyes met Anna's.

She took Elodie's hand. "You will. You will get home safe tonight. I will see to it," Autumn said. "I promise."

"Okay."

"Great," Anna said, getting up. Elodie followed. They waved bye to Cora, then walked to Elodie's car and Anna noticed the back setup for camping. She laughed.

"Charles mentioned you have a nice set up. He wasn't wrong."

Elodie nodded and followed Anna's directions, realizing she was in Sunny Brae.

"You don't have a car? Trev doesn't either, does he? You run this every time? You run to Charles's place? Trev ran home from my place? Twenty miles? One way?" Elodie asked, realizing how far this run would be. She knew fae were faster and stronger, but just how fast was mind blowing.

"He didn't show you?"

"Didn't show me what?"

"Oh, we all just assumed he did. Even Dad, that picture you drew him? You don't know?"

"Know what?" Elodie asked, confused.

"I guess I got this one. I will show you when you park the car," she said, continuing to give directions through the neighborhood. They stopped at a trail head.

"We are hiking? You hike this trail then hike to Eureka?"

Anna laughed. "Just wait and see," she said and got out.

"How far is the hike? I have to hike back, too. I'm going to hike back, right?" Elodie felt her heart pound and her throat hurt.

"Yes, Elodie. I promise you. It's a four-mile round trip. Just stay close to me and I will help you through the boundary."

They began walking along the trail. "I'm going to show you how we get from Eureka to home without breaking a sweat. Don't scream, okay? I'm not going to hurt you. I am still me and you will still be able to talk to me once you align your headspace," she said. "If I hear anyone coming, I will change back. It would raise too many alarms to be seen hiking with me in feral."

"In feral? What?"

Anna smiled and changed into a mountain lion. Elodie backed up with a gasp bringing her hands to her mouth.

"What!" she gasped out. "Anna?" The mountain lion chuffed and nuzzled her hand.

"Can you see it's me? Can you hear me?" Anna's voice flowed in her head. She stared into the mountain lion's eyes. She was an average size for a mountain lion and Elodie realized she felt no threats and wasn't scared of this one. She could see Anna's blue-gray eyes through the amber colored ones.

"Can—Trev, Caleb, Q? All mountain lions?" Elodie gasped.

"Let's walk. I cannot believe he didn't show you this. What an ass," she said with a small push of air through her nose. "Each high estate is aligned with an animal native to the area. Greenthistle is a mountain lion. Ashdale or Q's estate is a bear, and Nightswift or Russ's is a raven."

Elodie's body froze, and another gasp slipped out with realization. Anna turned and looked at her.

"Trev!"

"What is it? What about him?"

"The day I met Caleb. He told me about the kissing game they had. I was pissed at them both. I needed to burn off steam," she said, speaking of the experience in Arcata Community Forest. "But when I saw that mountain lion's eyes, they were as green as emeralds. It was Trev, he watched over me even before the iron cuff, before he was bound to me."

"He has." A small purr from the mountain lion.

"How does he not find me the stupidest mortal he's ever had the displeasure of meeting? Do you think I'm stupid?" She gasped.

Anna laughed. "No, I don't. I thought you sounded like a wonderful person full of great stories, like Charles. I wanted to get to know you more. Once I heard Trev tell the story yesterday, what you did for him. I knew you were someone important, someone I would become friends with, for a long time," she said, and let out another purr.

Keep going, Elodie. Elodie. Soon.

Elodie stopped and gazed up at a nearby redwood. Her eyes traveled down and felt the ferns shift toward her. She looked over at Anna who slowed and turned to face her.

"Oh," Anna said, watching the plants sway toward Elodie. "That is odd." Anna tilted her head.

That word again. Odd. Trev found me odd, and now Anna does, whatever her name is. The trees talked to her, called to her from two hundred miles away. She didn't want to tell them lest they find her even odder that some silly mortal hears voices in the trees. She shook her head at the thought. They'd all laugh at her.

"Would you like to guess my name?" Anna asked.

"You're okay with me knowing? I will never abuse that, I swear," Elodie said following the mountain lion when it walked again.

"I trust you, Elodie. You saved my brother's life, I am grateful for you."

Elodie nodded. "Okay, Anna."

"Think of nature. Think of time. Think of color passing by," she said. Elodie's mind repeated the clues as they walked.

Elodie. You will see. Soon you will see.
Others will too. Elodie. You are home.

Elodie's eyes traveled to the tops of these Old Giants she walked among. A small warmth in the air, an embrace of the warm breeze welcoming her. With a hand out to lightly caress the ferns and the water drops, Elodie took in the sensation, as though they yielded her the magic they held.

"Trevin is right. Something is different about you."

Elodie looked at her with her jaw agape. "What?"

"I sensed it at the Halloween party, along with Trev and Q. Trev told us about it and now that I'm seeing the way these ferns and Old Giants respond to you, I know why he made Dad swear Greenthistle to you. I've run my hands through hundreds of ferns and they're in my blood, but I've never seen them respond to anyone like this before."

"An odd and foolish mortal." Elodie frowned watching her steps.

"If you'd rather us not be present in your life we don't have to be, but umm, we do need to keep an eye on you. You are the first to find out about us, to rescue one of us and you got that iron off him. I don't know what Dad would have done to get it off him. It's no light matter what you did. He is grateful for you." There was remorse in Anna's tone.

"No, it's not that. I do want you and him in my life. It makes sense that I have to be watched, I figured out you all exist. I just, I feel bad that he has to be the one to watch. I feel bad that any of you have to watch over me, you are all busy with two lives." A defeated sigh escaped Elodie. Anna let out a chuff.

"Trevin was eager to accept the responsibility. I don't think he minds at all. In fact, I have never seen him so quick to take on the task. He trusts you and he does not give trust easily, to mortals or fae."

"Oh."

"You are good for him, you bring a drive out of him we haven't seen in some time, and I think Dad noticed it too. He did eye you at the Halloween party too. I heard about the kiss you two shared," Anna said with a hint of a smile. "It's been a while since he's kissed anyone, certainly like that. I think it had little to do with Caleb's game."

"I'm just a mortal who wanders into foolish situations. Trev could have anyone."

"I saw you talking with Charles and was worried you were interested in him. Trevin certainly had an interest in you, he snapped back at Q for eyeing you that night. Funny you and Charles are friends—how did you meet him?"

"We met at Cora's. He must have moved here around when I did and he overheard me talking to Cora about where I worked. He introduced himself as the music instructor. We talked about our vehicles and I just got used to seeing him at Cora's or at the café. Now that he's busy with lessons, I don't see him there. I see Trev instead at the café." She laughed nervously.

"Trev isn't going to hurt you, or make you serve us, we don't do that, Dad doesn't do that. Dad says there was one human bound to serve Greenthistle when he was younger. He said he just couldn't get over the void in their eyes. Swore he would never do that and took every precaution to prevent the option from even occurring."

"Until me? I messed it up because I'm odd." She frowned again.

"Elodie, I didn't just ask you to come over for the ride. It makes little difference to me if I run the whole way back to Eureka. I asked you to come because I do want to be your friend. I do want to get to know you. Having someone you know means we don't have to shut our life down for a few years and say goodbye."

"Yet," Elodie followed up.

Shhh little one. You will see. You will help them.
The little mink has a wisdom many have not seen.

The voices whispered again and Elodie's eyes traveled up the trees.

She heard Autumn groan.

"No. You have a long life. I know you do. Greenthistle will ensure it."

Elodie listened and kept walking.

"And as I said, I like what you brought out in my brother too. The last few weeks, he's been different, more alive."

Elodie thought and listened again.

Elodie. Home. You are home.

She frowned. "He is Greenthistle's heir. Not sure I can wrap my head around that yet." She paused, assessing her next step in the dark. "He is even more beautiful in fae form. His eyes are as bright as these ferns after rain and kissed by the sun. Plus I'm sure there are alliances and pacts and things to be made with nearby territories," Elodie said, sighing.

"He speaks fondly of you. Enjoy it, okay?" Anna stopped and changed into a human, a fae.

Elodie saw five dots above each eyebrow, five dots along her cheekbones and one line under. Her lip had one line and ended at her chin with one dot. Then Elodie's eyes moved to her ears, pointed just like Trevin's. Chestnut hair, blue eyes, tan skin, she was strikingly beautiful too.

Anna held out her hand for Elodie. "Take my hand. I have to bring you through the boundary."

Elodie nodded and took it.

Home. Home. Soon. You will be home.

The trees said as she passed through. A moment of pressure on her body and a small teal flash of light made her pause to take in her surroundings. The greens of the foliage were brighter even though it was after dark.

"Any guesses on my name?" Anna asked, smiling and letting go of her hand.

"I'm still thinking," she said, looking around observing bioluminescence on the plants and hearing various animals. She paused seeing some fae pass by, as though this were a well traveled footpath. Some lights and structures nestled between the trees were to her right.

Home. Soon.

She heard the trees say, embracing her again with a warm swaddle of air. Elodie looked at Autumn.

"Nature, time, colors passing," Elodie recited Autumn's clues aloud.

"Keep going," Autumn encouraged.

Nature, time, colors passing. Imagining the clues as she said them in her mind.

Elodie noted the surroundings become more secluded, fewer buildings spread further apart. This place was the stuff in her daydreams and imagination, beyond it all really. Yet she did not let herself fall into the notion that fairy tales could not turn into a nightmare. Trevin had told her as much when he swore his protection. The thought of him excited her, the sensation she felt when they kissed. That too brought its own unease for a few reasons.

She also thought about how they had to say goodbye to their lives, to the people and bonds they formed, and Trevin spent most of his life avoiding mortals, yet somehow she caught his eye. The trees always called to her regardless of where Elodie had traveled. When she did travel here, it never felt like enough time here. She wasn't sure she would ever have enough time here now even if she never left. What was time for her? To them? All of them lost things, the only difference was her time would end one day. They would all keep on living to see new people come and go. They would lose parts of them, pieces of them. She thought of Trevin one again and now Anna. Time, nature, range of colors, you see the fall colors.

"Autumn," Elodie said. The girl walking beside her laughed and smiled warmly.

Welcome home. Little one, Soon.

"The lands welcome you. It is said the rare ones, the special ones, are welcomed with glee," Autumn said.

They kept walking and Elodie could see a large house ahead, framed by redwoods.

Trevin let the warm water of the shower fall on him. He had spent the day in training drills with Lord Nightswift, Cyrus, and Quinn. The heat soothed his muscles, and he knew his body would heal by the end of the night. It was part of the conditioning to change a bunch between feral and fae. It always took them longer to recover when they did that.

As the warm water ran down his body, she flashed in his mind. He closed his eyes and pushed the mental gate open, letting himself wander down that path. Thoughts of their kiss filled his mind, what it might feel like to hold it longer. To press himself against her. He sucked in a breath and let his hands wander.

He imagined what her hands might feel like. Stroking him, her gasps, her moans, her eyes going heavy.

"Elodie," he moaned, imagining her hands on him, kissing him. He thought about hearing his real name moaned from her lips. "Fuck." He moaned again and kept stroking, thinking about what it might feel like with her. Wanting her was wrong, but he loved the way he felt kissing her and the way she looked at him with desire. *The way her gasps sounded, her round ears—mortal ears*, he thought. *She's a mortal.* He couldn't, but some part of him could and did want her. She was forbidden to him; she was a ship passing by the rock he was bound to forever.

"Elodie," he moaned, imagining kissing down her neck as she moaned his name, he released with a grunt. A sigh escaped him and he rested his head on the wall, still holding himself with the other. "Fuck." Another sigh, then he finished washing himself. He got dressed and put on a black T-shirt and green athletic shorts. After a full day of activity, he wasn't shocked when his stomach started making noise. He knew dinner would be soon, so he could settle on a quick snack to hold him over.

He eyed his phone, wanting to text her, but not sure what to even say. He sighed. "Elodie, you silly little mink, how did you sneak onto my radar? Am I even on yours?"

When he opened his door, he inhaled ocean breeze and lavender. He craved it, and knew he couldn't have it but he wanted it. The scent only grew stronger as he walked down the stairs; he turned the corner and his jaw dropped, his body tensed up.

Elodie's eyes went wide and her cheeks heated. Trevin watched her eye his body up and down, eye his ears and his face. *That damn look of lust in her. Mother above.*

Neither one said anything for a moment.

"Hi," she said nervously.

He couldn't muster a word. His mind was trying to figure out if he was seeing things. Was he that hungry he was hallucinating? He heard Autumn's laugh and finally snapped out of it.

"Hey," he said uneasily, then turned to Autumn. "You brought her here? Why?" he asked.

"Why not? We ran into each other at the bookstore. I was with Charles and I had some time to kill between meeting back up with him. I figured why not, since she knows about us and all. Knew most things about us," she said, eyeing her brother.

"What? I told her everything about the estates and let her see me like this." He waved his hand around his face and pointed to his ears.

"You didn't show her our feral, or even tell her about it. She just thought we trekked all the way to Eureka every time we went into town," Autumn scolded.

He swallowed hard and glanced at Elodie, who cut her eyes down. "She didn't ask?" Trevin said, not sure what else to say.

Autumn sighed in disappointment and rolled her eyes. "Really, Trev? You idiot. I wonder why she didn't ask if we could change into mountain lions?"

He looked at Elodie, worried.

"It's okay. It was a stressful morning. It has been an interesting few days," Elodie said nervously. "I hope I'm not intruding too much. I was curious when Autumn mentioned it," she said, noticing Trevin turned at his sister with shock.

"I didn't give her your name or Caleb's. Only mine," he said. Autumn remained smiling.

"I know you didn't. I told her to guess with a few clues. She's clever."

Trevin watched Autumn take Elodie's hand and saw both girls' eyes gaze past him. Elodie's eyes wide with fear as Trevin heard footsteps, his dad's. He spun around and locked eyes with him. His heart pounded as Lord Greenthistle narrowed his eyes at the three.

"We have company? Might the two of you care to explain why you doomed a mortal to the appropriate fate?" Lord Greenthistle was clearly unamused, Elodie gasped.

"I brought her. Trevin was unaware, caught off guard. I ran into her in town and had some time before meeting back up with Charles. Dad, this is Elodie Santiago. I only felt it was safe because of what she did for Trevin and wanted to befriend her."

Trevin felt his protectiveness flare, and he didn't know why. He had never once wanted to defy his dad.

Lord Greenthistle focused on Trevin for a moment, then sighed with an eye roll. "I must say Trevin, this new fire in you is delightful, but you know better than to direct it at me, boy. Save it for real threats," Lord Greenthistle said. Trevin bowed his head in apology.

Lord Greenthistle walked past Trevin, who spun around to see pure fear pulsing through Elodie's veins. Her energy pulsed with every heartbeat.

"Lady Santiago, I appreciate your formalities. They are most commendable. Please be at ease," he said. They looked at each other for a few moments, each clearly taking the other in. "I thank you, as does all Greenthistle Estate, for helping Trevin. Know that this matter is being investigated and taken seriously. Know that Master Greenthistle has sworn the estate to look out for your safety and sworn himself as your personal overseer."

Elodie gasped and Trevin wished he knew what her thoughts about everything were.

"I suppose Autumn at least informed you that dinner will be served shortly. You are a guest, after all. Lest you think we are ungrateful for your actions," he said, still watching. Her mouth gaped open.

"No Mr. Lord Greenthistle, Sir. Never. I thank you for dinner and hope I am not a bother or disruption. I promise I will not speak of this to anyone ever," she stuttered, clearly unsure how to address him.

"Lady Santiago, eyes on mine."

She swallowed hard and Trevin watched her throat bob as she slowly lifted her head to meet Lord Greenthistle's intensely focused gaze. He watched his dad's head tilt as he studied Elodie as if he were trying to puzzle out what he was seeing in her.

Come on, see it, Trevin said silently. His heart pounded. *Would I really fight Dad over her? My vowed. El.*

Trevin watched her, and for a moment he was taken back to the Halloween party after the phone call when he wanted to comfort her. He wanted to now, but he remained where he was, knowing his dad would not appreciate it.

Lord Greenthistle turned to Trevin with narrowed eyes before walking off to the kitchen.

"Let's go upstairs. I can show you around," Autumn said, taking her hand. Elodie nodded and followed, glancing at Trevin as she walked by.

He stood there as they headed upstairs. His stomach was in knots, and it wasn't just his hunger. He slumped his shoulders and dragged himself back to his room and paced.

"Great, she's here and I don't know what to do." The realization of what he had done in the shower—when she was on the way to his house or already in his house—hit him hard and he physically cringed. "She'd be disgusted. She probably thinks I'm weird now." She was here. His dad offered to protect her. She was a few doors down with Autumn, and unless he wanted to act like a fool, all he could do was pace until dinner.

Chapter 18

"Wow, your room is huge and your bathroom alone is like half the size of my entire studio," Elodie exclaimed.

"It's comfortable, to say the least. You mentioned you liked to hike," Autumn asked.

"I do," Elodie replied, looking at Autumn.

"There are lots of trails nearby. You should stay some night, maybe a long weekend?"

"I couldn't even imagine staying here. This house is amazing. The Bay Area has nice big houses but this, it's a literal estate or château. Everything is so beautiful. I hope I'm not intruding too much," Elodie said, feeling stressed and worried she was overstepping.

"You are not at all. Dad just isn't one for surprises, but I tend to get away with a lot more than Trev and Caleb do. Daddy's little girl and all."

Elodie laughed. "I know the feeling. Only child, though."

Autumn showed her around upstairs noting Trevin's door was closed. Cedar's was open but empty. As they continued downstairs Elodie noticed the artwork was from all time periods and various styles. She noticed family portraits of them all, including a fae woman who she could assume was Trevin's mom, Lady Greenthistle.

They had an indoor pool and training ring. The room opened up to the outside, where there was an even bigger pool, a deck, and fire pit. It was everything a multimillion-dollar property had in Marin or Sonoma, but more. She imagined a seasonal themed revelry in this yard and the house, how grand it must have been. They literally lived like royalty and yet acted so normal when they were in Eureka.

Eventually, Autumn led Elodie through the kitchen. The scents of various dishes and spices permeated the air. Pans simmered as the kitchen staff worked, paying them no mind.

"You have staff. At your house?" Elodie asked.

"We do. They swore their allegiance to Greenthistle and to some it is a great honor to work in a high estate. Some have quarters here, some don't, but all get paid very well. Dad sees to it. And no, it's not from Eureka's taxes either. Dad has the job on the county seat, but also on the fae council of honors for Greenthistle's lands here in Humboldt. It's a big tree similar to the US government, but we tend to work more in unison than the mortal governments."

"I can imagine; we can be trash sometimes," Elodie said. Some staff glanced over with a gasp to hear a mortal say that about her own kind.

"That's not to say it's peaceful all the time. Sometimes, estates will try to overthrow the ones in power. It's always an odd number of estates in power. There is some contention in Everoak County, but Humboldt has been peaceful for centuries. Same with the Del Norte, Mendocino and Trinity counties too. Marin's five estates have been peacefully in power for centuries too."

"Marin has them? Five?" Elodie asked, shocked. Autumn laughed.

"Yes. They do. I'm friends with the heirs, some older than us, some younger. Trev and Caleb are friends with them, too. If we go into another territory, it is required that you request permission in advance. It's frowned upon to just cross the lines without notice. It could lead to an altercation. The number of high estates depends on people to land mass ratio. Los Angeles has nine, San Diego seven. They are the biggest. San Francisco and most of the Bay Area counties have five."

"Oh," she said, "Can all fae cross to the mortal side? Do they?"

"No, high estates of a territory are expected to integrate into the mortal world. So that's why Trev, Caleb, and I have jobs in town. We all have to maintain the balance between worlds and our responsibility as high estate members. Others who wish to integrate have to apply and go through a number of tests and certifications; it's a two year process. Even us estate kids have to go through training and stuff before we can start going to mortal school. Then we have to continue school here in the summer," she said, leading Elodie to the dining room, which was just as lavish as expected. The table had been set for five. It could easily fit twenty. The place settings were all at one end. Autumn motioned toward a seat and took the one near the head for herself. Elodie assumed the rest of the family would join.

"Wine, Lady Santiago?" a woman asked, pouring some water into the goblet. Elodie noted the fae's ears and pale blue wings. White hair pulled nice and clean back in a bun.

"Oh, no thank you. I have to drive."

"Of course, Lady Santiago," she said, bowing and tending to Autumn.

"You will be fine with one glass. It's just a regular red, not fae wine. Don't worry, we will save that for when you stay the night," she said with a smirk. Elodie got nervous. "Thanks, Ms. Candytuft," Autumn said, taking a sip. The fae looked at Elodie holding the bottle up as an offering, and Elodie nodded and held her glass up. Once it was poured, Ms. Candytuft walked away.

They heard a sigh and a groan. Elodie kept her eyes down.

"The little mortal, so enraptured with the fae now sits at their table. We meet again, El," Caleb said, followed by a laugh. "Perhaps she's been brought here to be spirited away."

"Caleb, knock it off," Autumn snapped back. "Maybe no one in Eureka even thinks of you as they do Trev and me. No one will miss you when you go," she said.

Elodie went wide eyed and hoped Caleb did not take the seat across from her.

Autumn glared at him as he glanced at the seat facing Elodie, smirked, and took the one across from Autumn. Caleb laughed again, watching relief cascade over her body as he sat down.

"It is fun to see her tremble. She should." A sly tone lined his words.

"Caleb!" Trevin growled, walking in. "Stop."

Autumn watched her brothers lock eyes as Trevin towered over Caleb. Elodie still hadn't looked up.

"We can take it outside in feral? Hell, you in feral and me like this, I'd still pin you," Caleb said, not at all intimidated.

"After dinner, you two can go spar. Trevin can channel his newfound fight correctly," Lord Greenthistle said, causing everyone to straighten. "Sit, Trevin."

"Like a good little doggy, in front of his little plaything," Caleb said with a laugh.

Trevin gripped the fork, growling in anger. Elodie gasped, causing him to freeze. Caleb laughed harder.

"Silence, Caleb. You ought to take a lesson from your sister if you wish to use your words instead of your brute force for once," Lord Greenthistle said, unamused. He watched Trevin closely.

"Ahh, he certainly could benefit from some thought once in a while," Autumn said. Caleb narrowed his eyes at Autumn and she smirked. Elodie swallowed hard.

"Please, Ms. Santiago, forgive my children's poor manners. I did raise them to behave. Get them around a mortal and you'd think they are all wild animals," Lord Greenthistle said, still unamused.

"No. I, I—" Elodie stuttered, not even sure what she was supposed to say. "I know this is not normal. Or even right for me to be here. but I do thank you from the bottom of my heart for your hospitality tonight." Her words tumbled out in one breath.

"While I will say it is rare, it is even more uncommon to hear of a mortal saving a fae. Especially a high estate master. It is I, Ms. Santiago, who thanks you from the bottom of my heart. It was a wise choice to take him somewhere more secluded so quickly. Tell me, what compelled you to do so?"

Elodie explained her initial thoughts upon seeing him, and his reputation, and how she feared the worst when he didn't wake. How she started to piece everything together and that the iron was burning him. Trevin smiled slightly, listening to her talk.

"When I connected the iron, and all our encounters, I fell back on my ass, startled. I looked around and knew I had to get him to the car," she said. "The studio I rent in Cutten is tucked away. The property owners are away in Truckee this week."

"Well, again, I do thank you. My children all mean the world to me, and Trevin is important. We have a way of sensing each other, but when he had the iron cuff on none of us could find him. It must have happened when we were asleep. When he wasn't in his room, we were concerned. The iron cuff is a battle cry of sorts for fae, but the fact that it was used on a high estate heir has us on edge."

"Who might have sent the battle cry? Do you think it's mortals?" she asked.

"Doubtful. It is very hard for mortals to sneak up on us. He was on his way home from Ashdale Estate. On this side of the boundary. Where you are the first human in centuries to cross over. There are halflings here, even those who are a quarter or an eighth fae, but you are the first full mortal I've ever seen over here. Consider yourself extremely lucky. Whoever put it on him was fae and dragged him to Eureka. May the Great Mother help them when I find out who."

"Trev said even if it was in his pocket, it could hurt him. How could it be put on him and welded on?" she said, her emotions more distraught.

"The only conclusion the estate lords could come up with was someone here used a sedative and dragged him out, and a mortal or a glamoured one did the welding. We are inspecting any machine shops in the area for leads."

"Sure are asking a lot of questions." Caleb narrowed his eyes. Elodie narrowed her eyes back at him. She may be intimidated by everyone at this table, but she did not like the accusation in his tone.

"You may not care about me or my kind, but I do care about your kind. A lot. It is a fearful respect, but I trust you to defend these Old Giants against the plight of my kind long after me. They mean a lot to me. So I don't want any of you getting hurt," she said with reverence. Autumn and Lord Greenthistle gave her smiles of approval.

Caleb locked eyes with her and a slight grin formed. "Touché, El," he said, sitting back.

Plates of food were brought to the table—salad, bread, a main course with lots of meat. A prime rib that had been sliced. The smell and presentation made her eyes go wide. She noticed Trevin watching her, causing her to blush and look down.

"Well said, Ms. Santiago. Know that the situation is being monitored and know that you will be safe. Trevin and Autumn will ward your dwelling later. No one but you may enter, not even them. You will need to allow them inside. They will explain everything later," he said, sipping his wine. "Onto more pleasant conversation. The holiday is coming up, the elementary school is on a break, are you celebrating?" Lord Greenthistle asked.

Like the switch was flipped when it came to Lord Greenthistle, she was on edge. She kept her eyes down. Caleb and Autumn dug in.

"I'm driving to Marin County tomorrow morning," she said, and saw the worry wash over Trevin's face. "To see my dad, spend the holiday with him and some extended family. It's been a while since I've seen them," she followed up.

"When are you coming back?" Trevin asked.

"Saturday or Sunday. I'm not sure yet." She glanced at him, somewhat confused as it was the first thing he had said to her at dinner. She glanced at Autumn, who had her smug little smile plastered on her face.

"Does your extended family live far?" Lord Greenthistle asked.

Elodie looked down and inhaled before answering. "No. They live In Stinson Beach, and Dad lives in Novato, where I grew up. I spent a lot of time in Point Reyes when holidays were at their place."

"Lovely area. Are you not close with your extended family?" Lord Greenthistle asked.

"Um, it's, it's been a strained relationship since my mom passed," she said, her face heated. "It feels as though we get along just for my dad's sake. So I usually go hiking when I'm home. Point Reyes is technically closed and I don't want to be on a National Parks blacklist for trespassing, especially with work, but lots of other areas are open. Some nights I car camp and I have a sleeper setup, so it isn't as bad as it sounds." Elodie realized she was starting to ramble.

"Sounds as if you fit in well here, then," Lord Greenthistle said with a warm smile. She nodded.

"Why not just get a van then? Your little hatch can't be that comfortable?" Caleb asked.

"It's not so bad. I mean, it's easier to maneuver, and better on gas. I don't know if I fit the adventure van life."

Caleb looked at her dumbfounded, then glanced at Autumn.

"Yea, I dunno that Charles fits that life either, but look at him," he said in jest. Autumn rolled her eyes.

"Shut up. He does. Elodie too, obviously, or she wouldn't be up here."

"I'd say she fits in well up here. She helped the estate yesterday," Lord Greenthistle said, still straight faced, taking another bite of his food.

"Of course. People here tend to watch out for each other," she said.

Lord Greenthistle set his fork down and fixed his gaze on Elodie. He titled his head. She swallowed hard and slowly her eyes rose to meet him.

"Please do tell me, Lady Santiago, what was it that made you pick Humboldt? I do wonder what might we be graced with. What presence might have graced my eldest son," he said, bringing his hands to rest his chin upon.

"I..." She hesitated and glanced down, then back up. "I know it sounds silly but, ever since my last camping trip up here with my parents, I've felt these Old Giants calling to me. Even when I was abroad, across the Pacific Ocean, I felt it. It was faint, but still there. I'm not from here, and never lived here before now. They always called me, and I wanted out of Marin, away from the city. I lived in the city for one year and aside from being broke, I was suffocated. Golden Gate Park or Lands End was never enough. After a year, I went back to Marin. Always the Old Giants in the north though, calling to me. I feel as though I left something here on that trip, as if part of me got left behind when I was little. Maybe it's that my mom never got to come back, and she wanted to. She spoke of the magic here often and our last trip together as a family when I was eight. Ever since then I have thought of these trees, the ferns, and the ocean often. The mist and the rain—all feel like I am part of it, or I guess I want to be." She avoided eye contact with all of them, somewhat shocked she just admitted that.

"Now you are sitting in a fae family's house, eating dinner with a high estate lord. Count your blessings. You certainly weaseled your way here, didn't you?" Caleb said with a laugh.

Elodie nodded nervously. She had caught both the lord and his heirs' gaze, though.

"Caleb," Trevin hissed out.

"I must say you are a very odd mortal," Lord Greenthistle said, with an inquisitive tone that caused her to visibly flinch. "Very well. Greenthistle will protect you, all three of them will. Do not speak of anything here to anyone. You make no mention of having visited our home to anyone ever. Should you do so, we have a holding facility you will be put in until you and the high estate lords reach an agreement. Your life will not be what it is now. Is that clear?"

"Yes sir, Lord Greenthistle. I'll give you my word," Elodie said in a small voice.

"Mortal words mean very little," Caleb scoffed.

"Caleb!" Trevin snapped.

She picked up the steak knife and looked at her palm, unsure. "Blood? I don't know what exactly is true and what's not about bargains. Forgive me."

"El, please put that down," Trevin said, and she noticed the worry in his tone.

"There is no need to spill blood at my table. I see your emotions—they tell your thoughts and show your heart clear as day. The lands like you. Do not abuse it," Lord Greenthistle emphasized. She nodded and set the knife down.

"Thank you, Lord Greenthistle, sir." Elodie looked down.

"I also advise you to be mindful of what bonds you form. Your attachment to mortals and fae alike can alter at any second," he added. She tensed and took a deep inhale, then nodded.

"Of course, sir. I know my time is finite. I know I have an expiration date."

"You are a smart girl," Lord Greenthistle followed up.

Chapter 19

After dinner finished, Lord Greenthistle insisted Trevin and Caleb get some of their energy out and scrap. Trevin walked outside with Caleb.

"We might get a little rough, but we never actually hurt each other, plus we heal quickly," Trevin said. Elodie sat on the bench and watched as Caleb changed. He was massive. A low little growl slipped as he stretched his front paws out, extending the massive claws.

"Make sure you can recognize each of us okay? It will help if we ever need to intervene in this form," Trevin said. She nodded again. When he changed, her mouth fell agape.

"Trevin." Her voice was full of awe; he looked at her and purred loudly. She was fixed on the green eyes; on this animal she had seen before. Her eyes went wide as she focused on Caleb pouncing toward Trevin, coming right at her.

Trevin spun around and tackled Caleb down with fury. Caleb pushed up with a growl and then pinned Trevin, letting out a snort.

"Gonna impress your new plaything or just keel over?" Caleb's voice said in her headspace.

"Shut up!" Trevin growled, kicking Caleb off him.

Elodie watched, worry formed on her face.

"This is their usual. It's been a real treat to see Trev fight back so hard though," Autumn said in a hushed tone.

"Aww come on, Trevy. Greenthistle is strength and valor, all you do is sulk," Caleb taunted. Trevin growled and kicked him off then lunged. Caleb fought back hard. Elodie grew worried.

Caleb slammed his paw into Trevin's head. Trevin growled, latching onto Caleb's scruff and slammed him down. Caleb roared back angrily. Elodie put her hands to her mouth, watching their fight unfold in front of her.

"You are getting feisty," Caleb laughed. Trevin growled again.

"They are fine. They always make a big spectacle of it," Autumn said. "And now they both want to show off."

Caleb now kicked Trevin, and they scuffled more until Caleb pinned him again.

"Young Master Greenthistle, so easy to pin down," Caleb taunted, getting right in Trevin's face. Trevin growled low and flipped Caleb on his back causing him to gasp in shock.

"So are you, little brother," he growled right in Caleb's face.

"Truce till next time, keep up the fight. You should have had this fire all along," Caleb said, pushing Trevin off him and stalking off. He let out a low growl in Elodie's direction, and she frowned. Trevin roared at him.

She knew she did not belong with them. This was a world she could never be part of. Yet she wanted it, felt it calling to her. Part of her wondered if it was selfish to want it. Her thoughts trailed to what her life would be like here.

Trevin walked up to her, still in mountain lion form. "Come sit with me?" he asked. She nodded and followed him to the grass where he flopped down, then sat next to him.

"You can sit closer if you'd like, or feel my fur. I'm not going to bite." He laughed.

She nodded and ran her hand down his back as he purred. He was softer than she expected. "You are stunning," she said softly. Her fingers traced the round shape of his soft velvety ears and he purred louder.

"Still sensitive?" she asked with a laugh, leaning more against him.

"Yes." He nuzzled into her.

"Trevin?"

"Yes?"

"That night I met Caleb, I was so flustered that I went on a night hike in Arcata Community Forest. But you knew that, didn't you?" she asked and felt him deflate with a sigh.

"I did. The boundary line is near there too and I was helping Russ with something but I sensed someone on the trail. We investigated since it was too late and too far out on the trail for an evening stroll. Russ was the raven. We make sure our fellow animals do not hurt mortals. It's part of all our jobs. I communicate with mountain lions but I can talk to other animals if I need to, just in different ways.

"I saw you on the ground and I too feared the worst. To keep watch for any danger, I sat with you, like I am doing now. You said my name in your sleep and I was confused because you were so upset with me earlier. Then as if someone snapped their fingers, you moved so fast. I was shocked. I knew I had to play the part and act aggressively to get you to go back to your car. You maintained that eye contact as you were taught to but then you noticed my eyes, didn't you?" he asked, with a hint of a grin.

"I wasn't sure why I thought of you, but I did," she said.

"When I saw you make yourself look bigger, I knew that was my cue to run off."

"But not before you let the chuff slip out?"

"I watched you get back to your car and back out. You are an interesting little mink," he laughed and she leaned back against him. She brought her knees up, and he wrapped his tail around her waist and purred.

"That feels nice," she said, enjoying the rhythm of his purr against her back. "This is nice."

"That first night I noticed you at the café, that night hike, was that you too?"

"It was. But there was an actual mountain lion tailing you."

"Your chirps were telling it no?" she asked.

"Yes," he said. "I've been nothing but weird to you since we met, and I'm sorry, Elodie. I'm don't normal act like a dumbass."

She laughed. "You watched over me and maybe, part of me had a feeling so when I saw you yesterday, I knew I needed to help you." Elodie rubbed his tail. "But you don't need to bind yourself to me, I think if anything I owe you a lot more than you owe me. Three times now you've come to my aid and I've only helped you once."

"El, the iron cuff is no light matter, and I'd keep watching out for you even if I'd never had it on me. I wanted to be the one to oversee you. I want to make this place safe for you. It's important to you. You are under our protection, a threat to you is the same as a threat to any of us. I'd act without hesitation if someone threatened you. I didn't like you recoiling from me and I knew you were scared. I didn't like it."

"Thanks, Trevin. I will stop being stupid. Sometimes I feel this urge to be near the Old Giants, more near than my place. To actually be out there," she looked down at his tail. "And I struggle with if it is wise for me to be here in Humboldt because that urge puts me in dangerous situations. I got so lucky you were there, you cared about a stupid mortal. The urge to be with them though is so strong. I don't know what's right."

"They do have their magic, I'm glad you can feel it. And you're not stupid. You need to find something, we are here to make it safe for you now. I'm happy to help you any day or night you want to go out there. I promise I won't be overbearing as your overseer," Trevin said.

"Thank you. I feel them calling to me," she said, he turned and laid on his side looking at her. She was pressed against his stomach now.

"They call out to you often?"

She blushed and looked down. "Yes. So much more now that I'm here. As though I was too far away before, now I feel it when I hike, or brush my hand along the ferns."

"Well that is interesting that they tell you that, and you have that energy in you. My curious little mink," he said. She blushed and glanced at him.

"Mom spoke about magic up here a lot. She loved all of the North Coast. My dad said his world felt brighter when he saw us holding hands and walking with these giants. The last time we were up here together, we were on a trail, in Arcata Community Forest. We walked a good bit and I was so entranced by the trees like usual. I wasn't watching my footing and tripped and fell right into a small stream. I sliced my hand open on a sharp rock. Mom and Dad were worried, they had a first aid kit, but we went to the hospital since the cut had been in the water. I ended up getting stitches. I told them I didn't want to cut the trip short.

"We stayed closer to town. Sequoia Community Park, trails on Avenue, that sort of thing before heading back. We stopped along the way and did a night in Fort Bragg too. Mendocino would have been my second choice if Humboldt hadn't worked out," she said.

As Trevin listened, he wondered how close she had been to the boundary. He would have been seventeen at the time. Mom still would have been with him.

"We never made it back up here after that. I'd come up with friends and stuff but it was a short trip. I'd spend evenings in my tent or a cabin debating if I should go out but thinking it'd be foolish. My dad and I went more east, and south. Sierras, Yosemite, Big Sur. After Mom, we still made a point to travel together as a family just him and me, but he lost some of the thrill. I couldn't sit still and I needed to travel, so I would go often. Even to other countries. The redwoods are always in me, as though if I really did lose a piece of me that day, they filled it. When we lost Mom, it was rough. It was a stupid car accident too, the wrong place at the wrong time. She was coming back from errands and I stayed home with Dad. It was a long time until I made it back up here. Despite longing to be here, I was worried it'd hurt. I felt guilty when I moved down south for school and when I went abroad. Eventually it ran its course, and I came back up to the Bay Area.

"I moved back to Marin County and met Ricky shortly after. We were good for about a year. Then he started cheating, doing harder drugs, and making nights in the city a priority. Sometimes leaving me high and dry in the city if I was going to meet him for a weekend. I put up with it for another year and I guess me walking in on him cheating was the final straw. I told like four people I was leaving. I packed my hatch up and drove up Highway 1 in August and never really looked back. Tomorrow will be my first time back." She laughed to herself "Ricky didn't even realize I moved so far. I still don't know if he knows where I went. Idiot."

"I'm glad he doesn't know. He should be glad he doesn't either. If I saw him here, I'd definitely spook him out," he said letting out a low growl.

Elodie smiled. "Thanks, but he's not worth your time," she said. "I was grateful you did what you did that night, even if it was a game for you. I just saw you standing there. I realized you probably heard the entire conversation and hoped you'd play along. I figured Cora didn't really allow creeps in her house so I took a chance. I wasn't expecting you to kiss me, or to tell him off. I guess, I was out of line too to use you like that."

Trevin laughed. "You didn't use me at all. And I'm sorry everything got so confusing. I should have come clean, but I didn't know how to. I thought about kissing you before Caleb made the stupid game. You caught my eye when you walked in, that energy in you. Then I noticed your ears, and the more you spoke the more curiosity sparked in me."

"I'm glad the five hundred-year-old fae were all busy and the forty-five-year-old was not," she teased. Trevin let out a chuff.

"I'm glad you're here tonight," he said, letting out a sigh as he glanced at her then turned his gaze to the sky. "We lost Mom when I was twenty. It happened while she was visiting friends in her home territory of Everoak. She hadn't mentioned to me she was going that evening. Dad forbids us from going there. It was a strange accident. An animal trap snagged her leg, but it was lined with floss flower oil which will kill us. It stops our ability to heal, and then prevents the blood from congealing, so we don't even have that. It bleeds us dry. She cleared the travel with Everoak before she went too, and stuck to trails at night. The Everoak estate lords were mortified when they heard. They knew they'd not only hurt one of their own, but she was a high estate lady of Greenthistle Estate. Dad was ready to wage war until Ashdale and Nightswift stepped in. Dad refuses any contact with Everoak, and they've made no amends. It was rough, and he pushed all three of us hard.

"I think I lost part of me that day and I wasn't sure I'd ever get it back. I wasn't sure I was cut out to be the heir when I lost her. It's always the first born though. Mortals had to be glamoured to set that trap. It was iron and floss flower, neither has an effect on mortals, it's just an oil with a pink shimmer for you. I started to despise mortals and formed a distrust of fae too, for setting the snares. Eventually I grew to admire what mortals had done up here though. Your government parties aside, people come together to protect the lands, the Old Giants. To further hone my empath gifts, I would watch people at the café and I reconnected with Cora.

"She invited me to her parties, and eventually we all started using it as another chance to practice our gifts on mortals. That included flirting and dating. The last mortal for me was so good at masking her feelings. We had a lot of fun and we knew it would be temporary. She took some job offer in LA, but she cheated on me and said it was because she was bored with me, that I was just a pretty face and nothing more. It was a new kind of hurt, that she could disregard me like that. The fae I'd date were not much better, just in it for the title I had. A lot of families push their sons or daughters toward me. It all kind of just sat wrong with me, and it felt like no one had my best interest in mind, they all wanted something.

I didn't trust anyone save for my family, Nightswift, and Ashdale estates. I trust Cora, and Justine as much energy as she can be. Charles is nice, Autumn is crazy about him." He laughed. "I trust you too obviously."

"Getting cheated on sucks. I've been there. I'm sorry about your mom. That has to be hard. To know, it was both, I see why your dad was so worried about the iron cuff. Autumn said Everoak is kind of in disarray, there's such a small population there too."

"It's a mess. I've never been, probably never will go."

"It's pretty. Fall colors just explode there against the mountains, but it's far, even for the kitty cat." Elodie ran her hand up his chest, her fingers through his fur feeling him start to purr.

"You know, maybe our moms met wherever they are and became friends too. I think my mom is proud of me, and I know your mom would be proud of you. You are brave and take your job seriously. You will make Greenthistle proud, I know you will." Her words trailed off, realizing he would be estate lord for a long time, long after her. She frowned for a moment and then let it go, realizing he would find a fae, and they'd have kids of their own. Elodie hoped they would be kind and treat him well and that his heir would look out for the stupid mortals who wander off into the woods. She felt a small pain in her throat and swallowed it. This was not her place. They were friends, even if they got to the level that Autumn had with Charles and Q had with Justine, could she do that?

"El?" he said softly, turning back from looking at the sky to look at her.

"Yeah?"

"You're coming back from Marin, right?"

She laughed softly. "Of course I am, I'm not abandoning my job. Moving around a lot means I need good references and leaving mid-school year would not be wise. Besides, I like my job a lot, and I like it here. I'm coming back Sunday, Saturday if Marin sucks."

He purred. "Are you going to be okay, if Ricky shows up?"

"Yeah, I will. I've dealt with him before."

Autumn approached in feral, causing Elodie tense. For a moment, she relaxed back against Trevin and then she pushed herself up bashfully.

"We should get back, plus Trevy over there probably needs another shower. I'm sure that's why he hasn't changed back to fae."

Trevin let out a groan. "Do you want me to go with you?" Trevin asked.

Elodie looked at him and then at Autumn. She felt closer to him after tonight and yet knew she should keep her distance.

"I will be okay. Besides, you weren't expecting any of this tonight. How about I message you when I'm home?" she said. He nodded and dropped his tail.

"Okay. Be safe. Message me anytime," he said to Elodie and then turned to Autumn. "Keep her safe," he insisted.

"Of course, you know I will." Autumn smiled.

When they got to the stairs, she glanced back at him. There was a hint of longing in his smile as he watched them head out the door.

Chapter 20

Autumn and Elodie walked in silence. Elodie looked around at everything she saw and wondered what it must be like living here. Crossing over as the estate families did. She thought about Lord Greenthistle and the amount of power he must have. How long he had that power, how long the bloodline had that power, imagined Trevin in that position. He would assume the role of county seat. He would be the one to decide on silly mortals that got too curious. She wondered if he'd remember her. Wondered how things would be in twenty years, in forty years. Would she still be here? She knew Lord Greenthistle was just trying to protect them both when he warned her about bonds. She swallowed and put her hand on the redwood.

Wake up. Wake up.
Do not push him away. Do not push him out.
This cannot be changed. You will see.
He will need you, she will need you, they all will.

Elodie stumbled back and felt the support of the mountain lion.

"Careful. I'm sure Trevin would be upset if you skinned a knee or got your pants dirty," Autumn laughed softly.

"I don't know about that," Elodie answered. "I'm sure he's going to get tired of having to follow me on trails. At least now he doesn't have to hide," she said with a laugh.

"He looks out for people he cares about. That isn't going to change," she said. "Take my hand. We are at the boundary," Autumn said, holding her hand out. She had changed into fae. Elodie took it and they walked through the boundary. Autumn stood still for a moment, listening, and then changed back into the mountain lion.

Elodie walked, noticing her senses slightly heightened. Something in her was telling her she needed to be here. She watched Autumn walk, her tail sway with her steps. Her ears move, listening, ever alert.

Wake up. Wake up.
He is bound to you. It cannot be changed.
They will need you. Elodie. El.

Elodie looked up at the trees, feeling the mist on her face. She thought about their words, *bound*. He said he wasn't, but the Old Giants knew things. They would know things long after the last human walked these lands, maybe even the last fae.

"Elodie, I'm sorry if tonight was too much. I just got excited that someone had figured us out, and you saved my brother. I'm sorry about Caleb, too. He can be such an ass, too. He will not hurt you. He is no threat," Autumn said.

"I know he will not hurt me. I don't even need him to like me. I should have expected some resistance. I'm something new, and I can't expect everyone to welcome me with open arms."

"I forget how intimidating Dad can be, too."

"When I saw him behind Trevin, I thought my best-case scenario would be losing my job at the school. I was sure I would be forced to serve tea to the estate lords forever."

"Dad doesn't do those things. You are safe," she answered with a laugh.

"What happens if humans find out? I guess the ones who don't save young masters of the estate?"

"One hasn't in so long. Not that I've known. The high estate lords give them a choice. Scramble their brain and drop them at a predetermined location. Or they are forced to work for us, odd jobs on our side of the boundary till they pass on. They are housed and fed, of course, but they live rather solitary lives. Class hierarchy unfortunately. At least that's what I've heard. I think the last one might have been over three hundred years ago from what I saw in records. Dad said he was really young when they last had one."

"Scramble Brains? Like brain dead or just a memory lapse?" Elodie asked somewhat surprised with her curiosity over terror.

"According to records, it's different for everyone. Some are reported to have amnesia and have to learn how to walk and talk all over again. Others wake up and feel as though they just blacked out for a night. So all the high estate rulers of a territory are there to document the subject's desired drop off location. Consider it malpractice insurance," Autumn said calmly.

"Oh," Elodie said with a shiver. "I think I'd take working in servitude over my brain being scrambled."

"Are you upset at that? That I brought you over here? Trevin made Dad promise you'd be safe, that he would not lock you up or wipe your memory. He agreed. What you did for us was no light matter."

"That I laid him down in the dirt and had to force all my weight on those bolt cutters? Like some weakling?" She laughed again. "And no, I'm not upset. I wasn't sure what to expect, but I didn't think you'd lead me into danger. Even if it had turned out to be a horrible demise, at least I'd have known it's all real."

"I'm glad. You are good for us. You are good for him," she said. "I've never seen him let anyone lay on him like you did tonight. Mortal or fae."

"Oh."

"I've never seen him tower over Caleb, either." Elodie smiled and looked at Autumn with her glamour on. "It's almost weird seeing you like this now," she laughed, changing the subject.

"You are one of the lucky ones that gets to see us in all our forms," Autumn said.

"You and Trevin are breathtaking. I think both your eyes are striking, they are like emeralds or sapphires," she said, unlocking her car and walking to the driver's side door.

"Thank you for the compliments. You are really pretty yourself. I see why you caught Trevin's eye," Autumn answered as she buckled her seatbelt in the passenger seat.

Elodie blushed. "Please, with everyone I saw tonight, all the families pushing their daughters on him. The dashing fae prince has no time for a silly mortal."

"So far, he has a lot of time for you." Autumn smiled. "Just like I have a lot of time for Charles. It didn't sound like you lived far from him. I think I can walk from your place."

Elodie nodded quietly as she drove down the road from the trailhead, and pulled her car under the carport.

"I am sure I will see ya when you get back from Marin. Do you want my number? Maybe if you change your mind about the solstice ball. Or something," Autumn asked.

"Sure," Elodie said, entering Autumn's number. "Thanks." She watched Autumn head down the road towards Charles's house.

Elodie went upstairs and took her shoes off, messaged Trevin that she was home safe, and got ready for bed. She sighed.

"What a few days this has been," she said to herself and started packing. She talked to her dad and then laid down.

When a notification popped up on her phone, she smiled seeing it was from Trevin. He told her it was nice to see her tonight and then wanted to know what time she was leaving tomorrow. Elodie laughed when he told her no night hikes either. A giddy feeling came over her at his response.

Seriously, if you insist on night hikes now, let me know please. I will be there.

Of course, Master Greenthistle. Good night.

Sleep well, little mink.

"I'm a fool. This is a just silly crush and I'm not fifteen. I should just enjoy it. I envy Autumn and Charles. Maybe sometime in Marin will settle these feelings." She sighed and put her phone on the charger. "Sleep well yourself, Overseer." She laughed to herself again.

Chapter 21

The next morning, Elodie heard a knock at her door. She opened it to see Trevin standing there with an iced coffee and a brown bag with the bagel shop logo. She looked at him and felt her jaw fall slightly agape. He smirked at her reaction.

"Hey. Not sure if you were hungry, but I figured you might want a bite before you headed south."

Her face lit up as she took him in. He was wearing a black and green plaid type button-up shirt under a hunter green v-neck sweater with dark gray fitted slacks. She was in teal leggings and a gray and goldenrod hoodie, and still barefoot. Her eyes lingered on the fitted area of his pants, then looked up to meet his eyes. Trevin watched her and grinned wider.

"Thank you. Please, come in if you have time. You are not late, are you? I'm sorry. I look like I just rolled out of bed."

"No, just some time by nine. We have a big meeting at ten. Q and Russ will be there too, plus our dads, of course. And you look comfortable. Like you could crawl back into bed where it's warm and safe," he said with a laugh.

She narrowed her eyes.

"You think I can't do much when it comes to hiking and backpacking, huh?" She smirked.

"I'm pretty sure you know how to scare a mountain lion off. Plus, listening to you talk about the hikes in places I've never been, I think you know a few things. But I know this area really well," he said with a laugh.

"Honestly, I think we are even. Besides, you are busy being an heir, don't worry about me," Elodie said, expecting him to say he wasn't.

They sat down and ate, awkwardly quiet for some time, but neither broke the silence. She noted his round ears, the eyes slightly dulled.

"Is it hard to keep the glamour up? You do this all day?" she asked, finally breaking the silence.

"No. It doesn't take much—we are all so used to it by now. The boundary line has a reminder, similar to a pinch. We learn when we are little and practice a lot. I would only drop it here honestly. Dad and I keep it up in the office all day," Trevin said, finishing off the last of his food.

"Oh. It seems like one more thing to remember." She noted, "I guess it's no different from my keys or phone, though."

"Yeah. Just one more thing. Though I usually don't have keys on me. The estate is warded to only open for us, or those we bring in," he said with a smile. "What did it feel like for you, crossing over the boundary line? I've never heard of a mortal crossing over—it hasn't happened in my lifetime."

Elodie told him about the small bit of pressure. About her sharper senses, but that it had faded by the time she got home. How the air almost seemed to give her a warm hug. She beamed remembering.

"Interesting. I am glad that the land likes you."

"Is your dad pissed at me?" she asked. "He's not going to get me fired, is he?" she asked. Trevin looked at her, confused.

"Why would he do that? He's not the King of Humboldt, El. Estate lords don't get to just run people out of the lands. He wasn't pleased, but I think he can see you will not betray us. He is not one for surprises,and he was impressed you talked back to Caleb." He laughed.

"Caleb probably still hates me?"

"He's just jealous that he can't play the kissing game with you," Trevin replied with a smug tone.

"Is that some rule of the dumb game?" she asked, keeping her tone curious, not irritated or spiteful.

"No, not exactly but we made a bargain, not going after the same ones until it's well done and over with." He laughed, then met her eyes. "That said, if you want to pursue anyone, kiss whoever, do whatever, then of course you can do as you please," he said, still watching her. Elodie shook her head.

"I couldn't even imagine walking up to any of them, even before I knew what you were."

"You walked up to me. We put on quite the show, apparently." He smirked.

"That the new girl just insisted she was the girlfriend of a county seat's son?" Her face heated as she said the words, feeling a rush of nerves realizing what she had said.

Trevin smiled and shook his head. "Then she ended up saving me."

"Then you got stuck on babysitting duty," she said with a sigh, deflating.

"El, I wanted to. It'd be me or a random Greenthistle sentry. And I was keeping an eye out for you before then, anyway."

Their eyes met, and something inside her tugged. She wanted to know what he was thinking and feeling, and she wanted to kiss him again. However she knew she would not voice any of that right now.

"I should get on the road. I don't want you to be late."

He held her gaze for a moment, then nodded. "Text me when you get there? And feel free to message me any time," he said, standing up.

She remained seated, now nearly eye level with his hips, and she quickly looked away. "Hope you have a good day, and that the meeting isn't too boring," she said as she finally stood up, avoiding his gaze. "Thank you for breakfast. That was really nice of you."

He grinned ear to ear and shook his head. "I'm no fuckboy, El."

"Good, you are too old to be one." She laughed and gave him a soft shove on the arm.

He watched her grab a backpack and canvas bag. "Do you need help getting stuff in the car?"

"No, I pack light. I still have stuff at my dad's anyway, so if I forget something I probably have it back home."

"Right," he said, and she noticed some unease. "I will see you when you get back, maybe at the café or something?" he asked.

She nodded and eyed him up and down. "Do you want a ride? You are not walking in that, are you? And you can't be in feral in town."

"If you are offering. Sure."

They got in her car and she dropped him off. Her cheeks flushed when he smiled at her and glanced at her lips.

"Do you actually want to do this?" she asked quietly, as she watched him walk into the building. A sigh escaped her as she shook her head.

Elodie got on 101 South and turned off at Avenue of the Giants. She pulled off at a turn out and walked a trail for a few yards, yielding her senses to the environment. She had known she would do this, knew it'd probably take her closer to five hours with the stops she'd make. Even longer if she did Highway 1 as well.

Come back. Come back.
Bonds cannot be broken.
Wake up, wake up.

Elodie listened, then pressed her hand to the base of the redwood and her eyes followed the trunk up to the sky. The sounds of the earth seemed to grow louder.

All will be well, little one, return to us and awaken.
You are needed. You are important.
He will see, they will all see.

It was overcast and a light rain had washed over the lands. She noticed the green of the ferns. How bright they were.

"Trevin," she whispered, holding the fern gently. He was made of these lands. His family was. Greenthistle, Nightswift, and Ashdale kept these lands safe, and she felt blessed enough to know it.

Yes. Awaken.

She let out a small sigh and went back to her car, continuing south.

As the miles and redwoods passed, she came to the last stop before the county line. The One Log Cabin and The Grandfather Tree. She parked and got out, realizing she hadn't made it very far in the time she was driving. Elodie shook her head and glanced back north.

Come back home. Soon.
We need you. He will need you. El.

It called to her, and she felt sadness creep in as she looked north. With a sigh, she got back in her car and continued south, feeling the sadness grow. She took a picture of the Mendocino County sign and pulled over on the next turn out.

"Soon," she said, continuing south.

Over in Eureka, Trevin was sitting in the morning meeting, along with his dad, the other estate lords, Quinn, and Cyrus—they were all zoned out, Trevin coming back to the present when he felt an unusual chill. Trevin glanced at his dad, who had turned from the window to him. It almost felt as if the Old Giants let out a collective sigh. He narrowed his eyes, then his phone buzzed. He noticed his dad put his phone away and Trevin saw two messages on his.

Momentary shift; Autumn and Cedar are checking. Nightswift has the ravens out.

His dad's message read.

Trevin nodded, then opened the second one. It was a picture of the county line sign from Elodie.

I miss the Old Giants already.

Trevin looked at her name and then to the trees. He tilted his head.

Was this you, El? He asked himself. He glanced at his dad again, who nodded at the presentation. Trevin put his phone down and tried to focus on the meeting, then went on with the rest of his work for the day.

Trevin was with his dad in the office, finishing up for the day.

"Any word on what that was?" he asked.

"Autumn and Cedar couldn't find anything. They did feel it, but it was as though it passed as soon as it occurred. Nightswift said the ravens reported nothing out of the ordinary."

Trevin nodded and couldn't help but think of the coincidence as to when Elodie had sent that picture and he felt the shift. *She couldn't have caused that. There is no way.* He messaged her anyway.

Where might you be now, little mink?

                                    Sebastopol. Almost home.

Trevin frowned. *Home. Her home.* He let out a sigh. She was temporary, in every sense. Regardless if she was a transplant here for a year or she made a long happy life up there, she was temporary. Passing just as soon as it had begun.

Vowed? Impossible.

His dad looked at him. "What?"

"Nothing," Trevin responded, watching his dad set down a very full file.

"I did some digging on your little mortal. Did you know she lived abroad for two years? Very well-traveled," Lord Greenthistle said, "Attended school in Southern California. She is probably well versed in all matters of the state at this rate. Maybe the West Coast."

"Dad! What the hell?"

"Her father is retired from the Utilities Commission. Her mother was a CPA before she was in a car accident. Unfortunate. She was eleven when it happened. Such a little cub."

"Dad!" Trevin snapped.

"Come on, did you really think I wasn't going to do my research on this? She is a liability. Be sure you keep an eye on her."

"Sounds like you are already doing that for me."

"Trev, you acted as if this was normal for your other mortal friends."

"She's got a lot going on. This feels weird."

"The school board loves her. Rave reviews this far. They offered a permanent position."

"Stop," Trevin groaned and shoved the folder back toward his dad. "Shred it all. At least keep it locked up in the study at home."

"It will stay locked up," he said, shaking his head. Trevin rolled his eyes.

"What do you think is in her?" he asked. His dad looked at him.

"Nothing," he said, wrapping up his reports.

"You didn't sense anything in her last night?"

"Oh, I could feel something, but she isn't fae, at all. Family tree is there too. I wouldn't worry about it."

"She said when she was on our side of the boundary, colors were more vivid, her senses more aware. Then, when she went back to this side, she still had heightened senses. Is that normal?"

"Having a mortal cross through is not normal, Trev," he said. "Besides, I haven't heard of anything happening. They feel a little bit of pressure as we do, but nothing else has been reported. She could be making it up. Mortals can do that, say whatever sounds good with little thought."

Trevin sighed with a nod. He went to open his mouth, then shut it. Glancing at the trees outside, he thought about the surge in the air. He took an inhale to speak, but then let it go again.

"Out with it. What?" his dad asked, not looking at Trevin.

"Almost at the same time as that shift, I got a text from her crossing into Mendocino territory. It's weird, when the Old Giants call to her, the energy surge happens," Trevin said. His dad narrowed his eyes, then watched Trevin. He eventually let out a sigh.

"I'm sure it was a coincidence. Sometimes those with traces of fae blood have a hint of a sense, but she doesn't have any at all. I already checked her family tree back before California was a state, no forest sprite, no druid, nothing," he said.

"Dad!" he said. Lord Greenthistle shook his head and laughed. Trevin went back to reading the book she found.

"What is that you got there?"

"It's an odd old book on Falk. El found it at a used book store in Ferndale a few weeks back and let me borrow it," Trevin said, handing it over. Lord Greenthistle flipped through it, then looked at Trevin.

"The mortal girl found this? Then gave it to you? What does she know of our work there?" he asked sternly.

"She observes a lot. I thought I put my papers away, but I noticed a few nights later she had done some sketches of Falk. She said she looked it up. We talked about it later, and I told her we and State Parks want to preserve the artifacts there. I can see why she found the book so neat. For an artist it must be a ton of inspiration. She draws a lot and very well," he said.

Lord Greenthistle eyed him.

"Anything useful?" he asked.

"A few things. She mentioned on this page," he said, flipping to it. "It has the element for iron and then 'King' underneath. Mind you, this was before the iron cuff, so before she found out about us, she mentioned this page in particular," he said.

"Interesting. I'd assume King Range?" he asked.

"That was my guess. But iron? Where? We've done drills and assignments out there," Trevin said.

"Hmm. Well, keep searching. I will tell you that she is an odd occurrence. I am suspicious, but nothing in her background stands out any more than that boy Autumn is running around with."

"Charles? Yea, he and Elodie have moved around a lot, but she has stuck to the western states. He's moved a lot of places."

"As is the way with most transplants. I am sure they will both be on their way to something new soon. Though if the school offered her a permanent position, I'd assume she would stay longer. Who knows Marin might pull her back too, it's small here compared to there. We will have to figure out what to do with her when the time comes." A sigh escaped Lord Greenthistle.

Trevin frowned but remained quiet. *She was fleeting. Why her?*

"I will keep pawing through this book. I really hope the tome is in Falk," Trevin said.

"I do too. Go on and head home. Don't have that book out in public though, my study is probably the best," he said. Trevin nodded and packed up.

Chapter 22

The next day, she finished getting everything ready for dinner. She wore a green and black knee length sleeveless dress, with teal tights. Standing in front of the full-length mirror, Elodie snapped a quick selfie and debated on sending it to Trevin, he sent his good morning text but nothing else. She could not deny she felt something for him, but wasn't sure she was brave enough to cross that line with him. Trying to remain logical she shuffled through all the reasons it was not wise to even look at that line.

Elodie looked at the picture and hovered her thumb over the send button and let out a sigh. When the doorbell rang that impulse took over all the logical thinking she had done. She hit send then headed for the door.

She could feel the tension build as her extended family walked into the house.

"Oh, you are back?" her uncle asked, clearly not expecting to see her.

"I drove down for the break."

"So I guess it's working out up there?"

"It is actually. I've been really happy."

"I'm sure your dad would be happy with you here," he said, walking by.

Elodie let out a sigh, and noticed her aunt rolled her eyes.

"Nice to see you made the drive, though I don't know why you'd want to keep making it. Marin is lovely."

"It's a pretty drive," Elodie said.

"Oh Elodie has made such a nice sounding life up there. The school wants to keep her permanent, and she has a certain boy's eye," her dad chimed in.

"Oh, let's see where that goes," her aunt said with another eye roll. Elodie frowned then busied herself by setting the table. As her family sat and talked, she listened to the conversations.

"Ya know, I'm just glad that the state parks in the area enforce the curfew. People don't need to be on our beaches so late," her aunt said. Elodie glared.

Your beaches? she thought. *You do nothing for them. The high estates here probably do everything.* Her mind began to wander again. *What were they like? How old they were.* She came back to her thoughts when she heard her dad cough badly this time. Her mind went back to the previous night when she had come in and noticed his coughing.

Elodie watched him as he struggled to reach for his glass of water. It slipped out of his hand and hit the table, shattering when it hit the floor. She grabbed her water flask on the counter as her uncle helped him.

"Dad! Here." She rushed over to him and handed him the water bottle. He took it as he caught his breath.

"Ahh I'm fine. Thanks hun," he said, and he forced a weak smile.

"I will clean this up," she said. Her uncle sat back down and Elodie started to clean the glass up carefully. "Are you okay?"

"Yes, I'm fine. Don't worry yourself, Elodie."

Her aunt sighed causing her to flinch.

"Okay," she said. She walked to the kitchen and got a bag out to put the glass in and set it in the bag carefully, then gasped. She saw the blood and felt herself panic. She was getting overwhelmed. Clumsily she reached for a paper towel and applied pressure.

"Honestly, Elodie. Now you cut yourself?" her aunt sighed. "I guess I will tend to the glass. Just get cleaned up. Can't you get through one task before adding something else to your plate?" she hissed.

Elodie looked out of the window. Little trees and bushes, no ferns, not even young redwoods from her view. The ocean was too far. The Old Giants were too far.

Trevin, she called out in her mind, as if a mountain lion would come to her aid right now. With deep inhales, she saw her aunt nearly done with the glass.

She brought out the vacuum and got the small bits up and took the towel to the garage. Elodie sighed again.

"It's fine hun, are you? Do you need help? I'm usually the one to do this, I should be doing this," her dad said.

"I'm okay. I can do it." She checked on the food and watched her dad, his breathing labored. Elodie worried she had missed something, something he hadn't told her. While she was in Humboldt, falling into the world of the fae that she should have never found. She took a seat in the formal living room and sighed. The buzz of her phone refocused her attention. It was from Trevin.

You look lovely. Is your day going well?

All she could reply with was a yes. She turned to the window again, wanting to see the outline of the Old Giants. As though they were calling to her. Just as they always had. She wanted to be near them, to be tucked away in her little studio, and to feel the rain and mist of Eureka and Arcata. Her dad coughed again, snagging her attention. She got up and looked at him, worried. Her aunt shot her a glare. Her phone buzzed again, and she froze, one deep breath to return to the present moment. *What is happening to me?*

Want to video chat when you are free?

She frowned after reading Trevin's message and set her phone down, not responding.

I don't belong with him. I can't lean on him just because he has been nice. Am I going crazy? Tall old trees dragging me deeper into a forest full of fae. Why am I not more afraid?

The oven timer dinged. Instinctively, she got up to tend to the oven and checked the temperature. She pulled the turkey out then went to put things on the table, taking slow steady breaths. Her uncle got up.

"I will carve the turkey—it's gotta be done right. It needs to rest first," he said. Elodie nodded. She was too exhausted mentally to take it as anything but relief.

"What do you want to drink, Dad? I have water for you."

"Oh, just some tea is fine," he said, his voice and breathing still off. She nodded and went to get it. He was slower than she remembered. She frowned. One more reminder this was life for her. People she loved aged. Their bodies showed wear and tear. Trevin would not. His family and friends would not. His dad was four hundred years old. More than twice as old as California had been a state and yet he looked younger than her dad.

"Have a seat, hun. Is your hand okay?" her dad asked. She sat and nodded, looking at the bandage. The bleeding had slowed. "Your poor hands, do you remember when we were up in Arcata Community Forest, and you cut your hand?" he asked.

"Yeah, I remember. I did that trail recently." Elodie remembered when Trevin had been there. She smiled warmly now, imagining him sitting next to her, listening for any kind of danger. Her overseer. She should be upset with that, but she wasn't at all for some reason. Then she recalled the Old Giants telling her she was watched over that night. Trevin watched over her.

Knows a good thing right in front of him. Trevin, what am I going to do? Coincidence? Fate? Me going crazy?

"Ahh, I'm so happy you are back up there. You never stopped talking about the area," he said.

"I know, I miss you, though. Are you sure you are okay?"

"Yes. I promise. Are you? Everything is good up there? No dangers?"

She was silent for a moment, thinking of everything that had happened in the last month.

"I'm okay, Dad. Things are good up there. I have a great group of friends. My friend Cora runs a cute little café and we are close and my newest friend Anna, she's so kind and sweet. We get along like sisters almost and she's dating my friend Charles, who has traveled to more places than I have. They are cute together. My friend Justine has traveled and lived all over, too."

"That sounds wonderful. You know you can bring any of them for Christmas. Maybe that boy that told Ricky off?" he said with a laugh. "The politician's son? Tell me about him?" her dad asked. Her aunt and uncle walked back into the room with the last of the food.

"A politician's son, Elodie, I didn't think you had that in you. Is he from old money?" her aunt said.

"Now, now, you know she's never been interested in money. She has her own money," her dad said. "Tell me about him, not what his dad does."

"Um, he is my friend Anna's older brother. They have a younger brother but I don't think he likes me much, but Trev, Trevor, is nice. He has striking green eyes. They remind me of the ferns and redwoods themselves. He works for State Parks and interns with his dad. He hopes to be on the seat one day," she said, unsure what else she could say about the last month with Trevin.

The first thing he ever said to me was that I was odd. He held my chin and gazed into my eyes. He can see all my emotions. He's fae, immortal, and can change into a huge mountain lion whenever he wants. They roughhouse in the backyard and it's terrifying. I saved his life and his family's secret by cutting iron off him. And he is my overseer now.

"He sounds like a nice young man. I hope we get to meet him soon."

"I will see. I asked Anna if she wanted to come, but it was short notice for her."

"Well, ask when you get back. Has Trev traveled a lot?" he asked.

"Mostly stayed around Northern California."

"Has his family been there long?" her uncle asked.

"Yes. Generations," she said, not sure how many generations of Greenthistle there had been so far. She wondered how much his bloodline had seen the land change. They had seen the Old Giants as young saplings.

"Oh, I bet he gets to inherit a big old piece of land, no?" her aunt said.

"He does live in a large house, yes. It's nice," she said.

"If he doesn't get the county seat, you could always just move back down here and with that money, you could buy it easily," her aunt said.

Elodie rolled her eyes. *Never going to happen*, she thought.

"I don't think—" she started to say.

"Leave her be," her dad said.

"How have you guys been? How's Ollie? Still in Europe, I assume?" Elodie asked her aunt and uncle, just desperate to change the subject. She listened to them talk about more things they felt they were entitled to. They moved back to the living room and Elodie stayed to clean up.

Her phone buzzed once more.

Hope the night was good. The Humboldt dog and pony show was cold and drizzly. As it is the Humboldt way.

Trevin messaged her. He also sent a picture of him, Russ, and Q dressed up all and appearing mortal. She hadn't seen what Q or Russ looked like as fae, nor their feral forms. Then realized she had never responded to him. Letting out a sigh, she glanced at the time. Elodie debated on changing and going to the coast side but relented and retreated to the back patio. She sent him a response.

Hey sorry. It was a day. Glad yours was good.

Video?

She sighed in defeat then typed a yes.

A gasp escaped her when she answered. He was on his bed with no shirt on. She could see the line further where it went straight down and started to trace his ribs.

"Hey," he said, grinning.

"Hi," she said after a speechless moment.

"How's Marin?" he asked.

"Marin," she muttered. He frowned.

"Rough day I take it?"

"Sometimes I feel—" She stopped, her eyes scanning the trees and the city. She couldn't even make the trees out and she couldn't hear the water. "Never mind. It was a long day," she said.

"It sounds like it. I wanted to ask, have you been to the King Range area?" he asked. She was instantly relieved to be talking about something other than the day.

"I did the Lost Coast Trail solo two years ago. I took my time, spent four days out there because I liked the solitude of it," she said. "I know people do it in three-ish. Have you done Lost Coast?"

"Yes, sometimes we have to run it, at night, of course. My dad makes us. Sometimes we have to do it in mortal form. Done the King Crest trail?" he asked.

"No way. That one looks hard. But I don't know, the view from the ridge must be incredible. I think I could do it," she said with a small laugh. He smiled and rolled onto his stomach. "Other than the morning publicity thing, what did you do today?"

"We ran a drill, and then I looked through the book you gave me," he said. "How were the pies?" he asked.

"Good," she said. "It's my mom's recipe."

He smiled. Then she heard the door slide open.

"Elodie," her aunt said with some annoyance.

"Hi," Elodie said, trying to put a mask on. She glanced at Trevin, panicked and watched his mortal glamour slip on. She put the phone face down.

"You know he's sick, right? You should know this. He has COPD, it's why he has airflow and breathing problems. He's been in the hospital twice since you left," she said

Elodie gasped. "He didn't tell me! Why?" The hurt laced her voice.

"He doesn't want you to worry. You should really move back down here. Honestly, what is it you think you are doing up there? You can get trees here. You can take care of him."

"I can't leave mid-school year. It wouldn't be good for me to find a new position."

"Who cares? Just reapply here. I'm sure you will find something. How long were you going to stay up there, even if there are wealthy guys to marry? You need to take care of him."

"He doesn't let me! He told me to go. He's happy I am up there and I'm not looking for a wealthy guy to just take care of me, and there's no guy, anyway. I can't just get up and leave the life I've made up there right now. I will visit more," she pleaded.

"It's been less than five months—don't make this sound like it's been decades. Just move back home. I'm sure you can find someone else here, that boy likely is interested because you are a fresh face in a small town." she said. Elodie reared her head back now leaping from one emotion to the next.

"You know nothing about him and trust me I know how temporary I am in his life. I'm staying because I want to, because I like it up there. I like those redwoods." she said with such a certainty. "I will talk to Dad and see what he thinks. I do miss him, but I do not miss living here. I miss Dad a lot, but I miss the redwoods and Eureka too."

"Elodie, you know you can just go to Muir Woods, or Armstrong Redwoods, if you need a dose of them. You know your dad isn't going to tell you to move back here. You should have never given up that apartment, the rent has probably doubled. All I'm saying is consider it. He's sick. This is home," she said. "You know you are wasting time up there. It is so isolating, it's not good for your anxiety or whatever. You can't just keep running away from things." Elodie remained quiet. "Your uncle and I are heading out. I guess I will see you in December. Have a nice long drive," her aunt said and walked back inside.

Elodie paused and then wiped her eyes. She sniffed and looked out at the city again, before quietly asking, "Why do I feel them so strongly?" Anxiety had always swirled in her and she knew running away only buffered it.

"El," Trevin said softly, and she gasped and picked up the phone.

"I didn't put it on mute!" she said, mortified. She wiped her eyes again.

"What happened to your hand?" he asked, concern laced through his tone. She was near trembling. "Elodie, breathe," his voice soft. "Little mink, shhh."

"Sorry I'm such a mess. I apparently don't know what I need," she muttered. "I almost wish your dad would make me work for the estate, then I'd have to serve you all tea or something until all my fingers bled. That would be my only stressor."

"El, we don't do those things. Do you miss the redwoods? Humboldt's redwoods?" he asked softly.

"Yes. I feel like I look at—" she stopped again and sighed in defeat. She shouldn't be afraid to tell him. It was the truth after all.

"Look at me. You found my entire world all on your own. Odd things happen."

"Because I'm odd," she said, cutting her eyes away. Trevin sighed. "I look at the redwoods, I walk among them and run my fingers along their trunks and the ferns, and I find solace in them. Humboldt's are telling me to come back. I feel as though I need them, as though they want me? As if they are home? But Dad is sick. I don't know what to do," she said, the defeat and the exhaustion heavy in her voice.

"This calling, you said it was often? Before you crossed the boundary."

"Yes. Every time I have been up there, now every time I am on those trails." Elodie watched him glance off to the side in confusion and thought? "Nothing I do is right. I get told every little direction I should be going and when I pick one, it's wrong."

"Do you feel it in the redwoods there? Do they call you too, Muir Woods? Armstrong?" he asked.

"No. At first, I found solace in the young growths. Then I'd look around and realize how contained it all felt. I know state and national parks do what they need to, but the old growths of Humboldt feel different. Wild, primal, ancient." she said. "As though the roots are tethered to me somehow, and it's pulling me back. I've never told anyone that before. You might be the only one who might not think it's so crazy." She sighed and glanced down.

"I know we are new to this, whatever this is, and I never want to keep you from the things that are important to you, but I know when the lands like someone. The way the lands respond to you is unlike anything I've ever seen before. I guess what I'm saying is the lands would miss you if you left, and I would, too."

A small smile formed as she looked at him. "I always have missed Humboldt. I'd miss everyone up there too, maybe not Caleb or Russ, but I'd miss the awkward glances at the café from you too."

"You met Russ?" Trevin asked, his smirk fading to a frown. Her eyes widened for a second, remembering she never told him about the encounter at the bonfire. She nodded. "When?"

"At the bonfire, he introduced himself near the restrooms, but I wanted to get back to Cora and everyone else. I noticed Autumn with Charles and wanted to meet her finally," she said, hoping to change the subject, but she could see Trevin's mind working.

"That was right before I sat by you, wasn't it?" he asked, and she nodded. "What happened?"

Elodie swallowed. The interaction was uncomfortable. She figured if he couldn't lie, she shouldn't either.

"He kind of came out of nowhere, and started talking to me," she went on, and she could practically see Trevin's mind processing even more. "I'm sure he's just overly friendly and I have residual nerves left over from Ricky, but it felt weird. When I walked with you that night I was nervous but curious, safe. I didn't feel as though I was in danger. I got a gut feeling about walking off with him that I didn't get with you." She noted his narrowed eyes and inquisitive expression, then gasped. "I'm sorry! I know he's your good friend and an estate heir. I don't want to cause any unrest or disruption. It's fine."

"No, he needs to watch his boundaries. I don't want you to think we just touch and pull everyone however we want. He crossed a line, and I did too, which is why I knew I needed to apologize to you. Not just for Cora's sake, but yours too. We are never supposed to sway mortals to do anything. None of us should sway you to leave or stay in Humboldt before you want to. If you want to. It's always your choice. Remember that. It has to be your choice," he said, meeting her gaze. She nodded.

"Okay. I feel like I'm a point of contention in all your lives for some reason, and I don't know why. Was Justine or Cora ever? Charles or anyone that came before me?" she asked.

"We have our cautions with everyone. We have to. But you, little mink, are the first I've met who is so different. That energy in your veins, it's foreign and yet vaguely familiar. I want to make sure you are safe above everything else," he said. She smiled and nodded.

"Do the rules about swaying still apply to me? I mean, I found you all. You are my overseer. Doesn't that mean I can't leave?" she asked.

"El, this whole thing is uncharted territory. I'm never going to lock you up here. If the wind carries you somewhere else, it does. I'd renounce my role as your overseer. Greenthistle still would look after though, while in Humboldt. I'm not sure what my dad would require though," Trevin said, worried. Elodie frowned and nodded.

They continued to talk, sharing more about their childhood and how they each grew up. Elodie learned more about his mom and she shared memories of her mom. Eventually, she started nodding off from the long day.

Chapter 23

"How did we never know this was there before? State Parks reported nothing out of the ordinary on this section," Trevin asked, leaning over the desk in the study at Greenthistle Estate. Maps and guides of the land in the King Range were spread out.

"It's too close to the mortal trails for our drills. This appears to be an old trail. Unmarked and unmaintained. Mortals probably pass right by the turn off, not even realizing it," his dad responded.

"I wonder how much iron there is," Trevin followed up, thinking about how plausible it would be to access it.

"From what I can see from this book on Falk, the map is actually engraved into a piece of iron. So there is that. I'm not sure how in the world this was built."

"You think mortals made the map in the iron and buried it? In a box of iron too?" Trevin said, looking at the page again. He narrowed his eyes on a box with a lot of lines in it with only one opening, almost like a maze in a puzzle book. His eyes looked at the trail maps of the area unable to match anything up.

"Wait," Lord Greenthistle said. He got up and grabbed a map from a bundle of rolled up old papers. He unrolled a large map showing the southern part of the territory, indicating the boundaries. Greenthistle and Ashdale claims were clearly defined in blue, the mortal realm defined as well. A few small patches of the fae realm with no claim from any estate. Unconnected to the rest of the boundary lines. "It's in a patch of unclaimed land," his dad said, pointing to a small blue patch with a dotted pattern on the off-white paper of the map. It matched the exact location of the map Trevin had found at the Land Management archives.

"There is a patch of unclaimed land in the King Range on the mountain?" Trevin asked, stumped.

"Fae land patches are everywhere, not all connected. But this means that fae had to have brought mortals here if it was iron. That rules out the theory that mortals hid something from the fae. They both knew this was something that needed to be guarded even after they were gone. Your grandfather never said a word. I never recall the other high estates at the time saying anything either. And now with no mortals in our servitude, we are essentially stuck."

"Maybe not," Trevin said with some hesitancy. He wondered if Elodie would even be up for that hike. She had sounded like she thought she could do this trek. She had hiked a lot; he noticed a lot of the gear in her studio. His dad looked at him. "What if I asked Elodie?" he asked, a little worried his dad was going to get angry.

"The mortal girl?" he asked, confused. Trevin nodded.

"I mean, iron doesn't hurt her. She knows about us, so I don't need to hide or beat around the bush on anything. She can tell me where to step. We can both search and she can grab it, or get a rubbing or redraw the map. She hikes a ton, and she's camped and backpacked a lot of the western national parks from the sounds of it. She did The Lost Coast solo."

"I suppose if she gets injured or dies on the trail, you will have food and you are absolved of babysitting duty," Lord Greenthistle said in a half joking manner.

"Dad!" Trevin hissed.

His dad laughed, then frowned. "I don't know if she's exactly able to make the hike. The King Range is tough for most, and mortals are so fragile."

"She knows what she is doing. She has lots of gear, and she and Charles talk about backpacking stuff all the time. What else are we going to do? Disrupt everything in Falk?" Trevin asked. "I mean, I can try it. Maybe Cedar and I can go. One of us can get help if there's trouble with the iron?" he said.

Lord Greenthistle looked at the book with the symbols in it, then at the map.

"You know how hard it's going to be for her though, Trevin. I'm not trying to get her injured or need an air rescue for her. Then when she says she was with you on my account," his dad groaned. "The mess that would be."

"I will make sure she is okay, and she will make sure I'm okay. I think she was really worried about me. I'm sure if she saw me like that again, she'd help."

"When do you plan to go?" he asked.

"If I'm alone, tomorrow? Elodie is out of town till Saturday or Sunday, so next weekend with her. Cedar's got his stuff, so it depends."

"You and Cedar would need what, a night?"

"Probably, we could leave after our shifts, and be back by morning. As long as we can get around the iron," he said, looking at the map.

"How long with the girl?" his dad asked. Trevin thought about it for a moment.

"I think it has to be overnight. Two days. At that elevation plus the searching. Overnight for her."

"Okay. Inquire with the girl if she wants to go, do not force her, or trick her into going. Let her decide. I will take care of the permits."

Trevin nodded.

Down in Marin, Elodie made breakfast for her dad and herself, then went on a hike with a friend. She knew she was going to have to talk to her dad about things. If he asked her to, she would have to move back and somehow work something out with Lord Greenthistle to allow it. That would also mean giving up the last few months and the Old Giants, the trees that had told her to hurry back.

That evening as she made dinner with the leftovers, she thought about how the trees told her she was needed. She sighed and set the smaller table.

"Dad, can I talk to you?"

"Of course, hun, what is it?"

"How long have you had COPD?" she asked. He sighed.

"I should have known they'd tell you. To guilt you into moving back."

"Dad, please, I worry about you. Why wouldn't you tell me?"

"You wouldn't have gone up there," he said. Can I ask you something now?" She nodded. "Are you happy up there? Truly happy?"

"Yes. I am," she answered, without needing to think about it. She saw her dad smile.

"Then stay up there, El. Come visit, but don't move back. Whatever your aunt and uncle say, they are wrong. It's not your job to make sure everyone else is okay, it's your job to make sure you are."

"But it's my job to make sure you are okay too, to make sure you are taken care of."

"I am fine, Elodie. You are a few hours north, not the other side of the world. I want you up there as long as you want to stay up there. You have a good job that you enjoy from the sounds of it. Your mom is proud of you and she is happy you are up there building a life you love. I don't want to see the life drain out of you again," he said. She bit her lip.

"Do we want to look into in-home support?"

"Your aunt and uncle can help. Just be sure to visit. Bring that boy too. You know he would miss you if you moved back here."

She smiled bashfully and shook her head "Dad, there's no boy. He has a lot of admirers. We are just friends."

"If you insist, I still expect to meet him. Are you heading back tomorrow or Sunday?" he asked.

"I don't know."

"Let's get breakfast near the ocean and then you can head home. You should get one day off to decompress. Take Highway 1. Enjoy the drive."

"Are you sure?" she asked.

"Yes. I will see you for Christmas, right?" he asked, looking at her. She nodded again.

"Of course," Elodie said, then headed into the bedroom to change and crawl into bed. She called Trevin.

"How was your day today?" he asked.

"Better. Point Reyes is nice. It's not as busy this time of year. It was nice to see my friend too. It's been awhile. We did a hike, hit three trails in one on a loop—Dipsea, Mt. Tam, to Matt David trail. Are you familiar with it? I feel like everyone in Marin County knows it."

"I am familiar with Mt. Tamalpais and Dipsea," he said with a slight smile. "How many miles and elevation for today?"

"Well, my body says a lot, I'm pretty sore and tired. My app says eight miles, 1700 feet."

"Nice. How many of the California National Parks have you been to?"

"All of them. Even Channel Islands. Redwoods is my favorite though," she said. He smiled again.

"And now you live a short drive from them. I've only been to Redwoods, Lassen, and Yosemite," he said. She nodded. "What about in the country?"

"Counting the California ones, probably twenty. Olympic might be my second favorite."

"Been once, two years ago for a regional meeting. I got to go with my dad. Q and Russ went too."

"You guys get to see a lot of really neat places I'm sure we couldn't get to huh?" she asked.

"Yeah, I mean, you could get to them with some trailblazing and maybe some fines, and being on a lot of high estate radars. Though I suppose everything in Humboldt's land is open to you now," he said with a laugh.

"No thanks, I will stick to trails. I'm obviously already on your dad's radar and he is plenty intimidating. I couldn't imagine a bunch."

"Dad's fine, he certainly wants the residents of Humboldt to be safe, fae and mortal alike. Lord Ashdale and Lord Nightswift are the same. How's your hand?" he asked. She held it up, still bandaged. "It's fine. It was a little glass, and I was trying to get it all."

"I'm glad it's healing," he said. "You've had a busy few days from the sounds of it."

"Yeah, with the holiday and all. It was nice to be back on the Dipsea. It might be a favorite. Next to Angel Island."

"Sorry. I got distracted on work stuff, overseer stuff too," he said after a few moments of quiet. "There are a lot of projects we all have. I'm eventually going to run for Dad's seat, but I do a lot of work with State Parks of course. So I was thinking about the lands and what not."

"It's okay. You sound pretty busy. How do you keep track of everything, do you sleep normal mortal hours? Do you need less sleep?" she asked, and he laughed.

"Normal amount usually anywhere between five to eight hours. After field days are over, I could sleep for twenty hours but I don't. Usually if I am extra tired, I sleep in feral outside and it replenishes me," Trevin said and went on to answer a lot more of the questions she had. Hearing him talk about the forests and knowing the magic that she had found was real made Elodie even more eager to get back to Humboldt. It all made her want to be back on that soil. She had spent some time on her hike listening for any messages the lands may have had but she got none. Occasionally a small warm breeze would blow north. A small squeeze from a plant she ran her hand long, but nothing like the ferns and the redwoods. She would be back there tomorrow. She would take in the salty sea air in Mendocino and she would feel the lands welcome her back.

Back home.

CHAPTER 24

E lodie returned to Humboldt on Saturday evening. Life resumed, and she was back in the swing of things with work. She would text Trevin and Autumn with questions as they came to mind. On Tuesday Elodie went to the café, and was disappointed when Trevin did not show. Elodie tried not to read too much into it.

Trevin was fighting the urge to see her. He and Autumn had warded her place while she was away. While he did explain the ward, he knew he or Autumn would have to test it out. That would mean he would have to go to her place. Yet some part of him didn't want to just ask Autumn to test it out. He had thought about her a lot. He still was in denial that she was his vowed. Why now, at forty-five, would he meet her, a mortal? However, if he was going to get her help, he was going to have to face her.

When her thoughts about everything got too overwhelming, she found herself thinking about just him. Elodie pictured his face, his markings, his ears, his hands, his lips, and how soft his touch was. How green his eyes were. How the first kiss felt, and the second kiss. She wondered what the third might feel like, and what it might feel like to be engulfed in his arms and the way he smelled. A few times those thoughts would send her hand down her body, imagining him touching her. She would finish whispering his name.

Then she would take a deep breath and realize how stupid and weird all of her thoughts were. He had his pick of the fae. Ones that wouldn't age much or deteriorate with time. She could still dream and fantasize; that's what fairy tales were, after all, fantasy. She didn't move here to find a husband and have a bunch of kids. She came here to have a reset and breathe in the redwoods, and find that piece of her that she left behind. She wasn't sure if she could leave now, what would be required of her if she chose to.

Elodie thought back to Saturday, when her overseer seemed to know the moment she crossed the county line from Mendocino to Humboldt. Her phone lit up a few moments after she crossed the county line with his name. She pulled off at the One Log House in Cooks Valley to check his message. She had felt the redwoods welcome her home and Trevin's message asked if she was back in Humboldt. Elodie thought it was odd timing. Had he heard the redwoods speak to her, did they speak to him?

Welcome back.
She has returned.
Closer, closer she is to her awakening.

She wondered if she should ask him, but he hadn't mentioned seeing her. She almost asked Autumn if he was busy or okay, but thought better of it. *It will come off as desperate,* she told herself. Most likely, he enjoyed the break from babysitting duty. *He probably regrets being my overseer, resents me for it, even if he does answer all my questions.* She could only imagine if Caleb had to babysit her—he would always be angry with her. As it was, Caleb avoided her at all costs, and she was fine with that.

On Wednesday, she went to the café, again not seeing him. She shuffled through her emotions as she usually did. Jumping from disappointment to acceptance as she walked to the counter and ordered. Cora made her drink and smirked at her. Once she was seated and drawing in her sketchbook she noticed someone walk to her table. She knew who it was and let out a small sigh.

"Hello El." His voice caressed her ears. She lifted her head and met Trevin's eyes.

"Hello Trev," she said in a calm voice.

"Is this seat taken?" he asked with a smile. She bit her lip and then shook her head. She glanced at Cora who watched them briefly then turned around. Her eyes moved back to him.

He smiled at her then glanced down at her sketchbook. Her eyes roved his face and his ears. His human glamour, no markings and his ears were round.

"You draw really well. Your mountain lions are getting friendlier looking," he said. She glanced at her sketchbook. Her face burned as she saw the sketch of him and a mountain lion smiling. She closed it quickly, and he laughed.

"I'm sorry, I'm still weird about people seeing what I draw." Her insides shriveled up.

"No weirder than I've been," he said. She managed a small bashful grin as she eyed him.

"How was the drive back up here?" he asked, still smiling.

"It was good. I took Highway 1, stopped in Mendocino. I went to the bookstore, got coffee, and walked the headlands there before finishing the drive."

"Sounds like a grand time. The water is so blue there. It's been awhile since I have been to Mendo."

"Yeah, it's nice to be home though."

"Home," he said with a smile. "With the Old Giants in the north?"

She watched his expression with those eyes longing at her. She couldn't help but feel the butterflies. *It has to be your choice.* She remembered he said. *Such a dumb game, Elodie.*

"Yes." Her voice was small as she processed many thoughts. How she was looking forward to being back here and seeing everyone again. Seeing the Old Giants. She was happy to see Autumn and Trevin again. To know magic was real, and they were her friends. She wanted to see him again, not glamoured. She wanted to know that her mind had not made the image up.

"Do you have plans this upcoming weekend?" he asked, taking a sip of his coffee. She glanced at him.

"Um I don't think so," she answered with some unease.

"Would you like to go on an adventure with me?" he asked.

Elodie saw Cora's confused expression, clearly listening to their conversation, then looked at Trevin. Again her eyes moved to his ears then to his smile, genuine, not coy, then moved down his throat. No line. Then she met his eyes. A soft laugh slipped from his lips.

"What kind of adventure?"

"Just a little overnight backpacking trip. There's a place I want to go find and from the sounds of it, you are pretty good with that stuff. I came across it in that book you let me borrow."

"And you are asking me? What about your siblings or friends, Charles even?" Elodie asked, confused.

He nodded. "It's a place that I might not know how to navigate all that well but I think you might be great at it." He casually rubbed his wrist.

Her eyes shifted to his hands. She realized it had something to do with iron. *I'm the only mortal who knows this secret, who has this position of asset and liability.* Elodie swallowed hard, not sure how she felt about that position. She went to ask a question then stopped, knowing she couldn't say it out loud.

"Just us?" she finally asked.

"Yes, little mink, just us. Curious and observant, and a fresh set of eyes I might need for looking at things differently," he said with a confident smile.

"Can I think about it?" she asked.

"Of course. No pressure. Let me know? Yeah? I gotta run. Dad's wrapping up a big project and I need to be a good future candidate and learn," he said standing up with his drink. He smiled wider at her then left. She sighed and leaned back against the wall eyeing her sketchbook. Cora swiftly took Trevin's vacated seat.

"Okay what is going on? He's always here when you are now. Even if he can't stay for long, he stops by and you two text each other? Since when? He said you had a heart to heart."

"You said he was here a lot though. He came here often," Elodie said.

Cora laughed. "Elodie, he used to be here in the daytime. Then Halloween happens and now he's here when you are? Are you two dating?"

"What? No. He wasn't here last night," she said with a slow exhale. "What did he say about the heart to heart?"

"Just that you two talked, you opened up to him and he felt it only fair he opened up to you. Are you going backpacking with him?" she asked. Elodie started to glance around and Cora caught her attention. "Elodie, people are going to make assumptions, who cares? Are you going backpacking with him?"

"I probably shouldn't, huh? That's dangerous," she said. *Even more so now!* she thought but dared not voice aloud.

"Well, I and this entire café know who you will be with, a very public face here," Cora said. Elodie frowned.

"I need to talk to him more. I need more details."

"I need more details too," Cora laughed, getting back up to walk back to the counter.

After a few mindless doodles, Elodie said bye to Cora and headed home. Once she was settled, she sat on the couch and looked at her gear. She pulled her phone out and scrolled to his messages. There was a picture of a mountain lion next to his name.

What are the details of this adventure?

Are you home? I'm at my dad's office, but I'm on my way out. I can stop by and tell you all about it, I want you to know why we are going.

She tensed and took in the state of her studio. As soon as she replied telling him she was home and to come over, she jumped up cleaning the remaining clutter left out.

After twenty minutes she heard a knock and answered it. She pulled the door open to find him grinning. "Hi," she said, her voice oddly small.

"Hey," Trevin said, Elodie stepped aside and waited for him to enter. "So, about that," he said with hesitation. "Autumn and I warded your place while you were in Marin, so you have to ask me to come in, establish acceptance of me. If we did it correctly. We have practiced but never done it for real outside of the boundary."

"Oh. Okay, Trev. Please, come in," she said, feeling awkward.

He laughed. "My actual name needs to be used. Just my first name though."

Elodie's eyes widened for a moment and then she spoke. "Trevin, please come in."

"Of course, Lady Elodie." Trevin stepped forward, and once the door was closed he dropped his glamour, safe to be in fae form. She stared at him wide eyed.

"Sorry, I can put the glamour back on. I imagine its still unsettling to see me like this." He sighed.

She shook her head. "No, it's not that at all. It's breathtaking, amazing. I feel like it's a dream so when I see it, I know it's real," she said. "I want to see you. I like seeing you."

He gave her a bashful smile and when she motioned to the couch he followed her.

"So, there is a spot in King Range," he said.

"Let me guess, King Crest trail?"

"Yes."

"The fourteen mile one?" she asked. He nodded. "Wouldn't it be easier and quicker for you to just do it in your feral form? I'd imagine for a mountain lion, it's nothing," she said, confused.

He grinned at her. "It might, but I also think that it might be dangerous for me in a different way than it might be for you. If we worked together though, we would keep each other safe and we can get what we need," he said. She eyed him then took note of the elevation gain and loss of the trail.

"What we need? What do we need out of King Range, Mr. State Parks? Leave no trace."

Trevin laughed affectionately. Then pulled his phone out and sat closer.

"Well, I guess what Greenthistle needs, the fae need?" He got uneasy. She was clearly waiting on him to proceed. "So that book you found has a lot of information. Stuff State Parks does not have, and we discovered there is a map or layout of Falk there. The problem is it sounds as though it's in iron of some sort. Also there might be a lot of iron along the way." Trevin pointed to the map on his phone

Elodie looked at him confused and then at the map trying to figure out something.

"And it's in the middle of an unconnected, unclaimed patch of fae world, so there's a boundary line to cross." His unease grew with every new detail.

"So, you want me to hike 2600 ft. up a mountain to a random piece of a world I'm not supposed to know exists to help you get a map that might or might not be legible? It seems like a lot of effort to keep me quiet. Couldn't your dad just find me in the forest one night to scramble my brain or kill me," she asked and his heart skipped a beat. "Is this where the hold or whatever is?"

"El, no! That's not what this is, that's not what I want, neither does my dad. He was hesitant to consider you but my other option is going alone or with Caleb and he's not okay with either of those."

She sighed and then let out a small laugh. "What's one less mortal, right? I mean, I don't blame him, he loves his children. It makes sense he would be okay with me gone. I am a liability," she said and Trevin sighed.

"I promise you it's the last thing he wants. He doesn't want any harm to come to you or me, but he knows it is an asset to have you and me working together. Since you know everything, I don't have to be glamoured," he said, placing his hand on her knee. She looked at his hand.

Trust him.
El.
He will need you.

The voices just then, when she felt so unsure, caused her body to shiver for a moment.

"You will not hurt me? Your dad won't be waiting for us?" she asked, holding his gaze.

"No. We will not and do not want to hurt you. We just need to find something in Falk and this is the best lead we have so far."

"Will you or your dad ever hurt me?"

"No. Neither will Caleb nor Autumn. Greenthistle protects you. I made my dad swear to it."

"How many days? Saturday to Sunday?"

"Yes, that was my plan. Trek up, get the map then rest, and descend the next day."

"I can do seven and seven. The drive over there is two and half hours. So add that to a hike and the time to get back. We should rise early both days," she said, opening her sketch book and writing notes down—departure times, elevation gain, the supplies they'd need. "This weekend? King Range requires permits and they fill up."

"Yes, my dad said he will get the permits."

"I guess he has ways of pulling strings," she said with a nervous laugh.

"A few strings."

"What time do you want to leave? I'd say no later than 7:30? That way we can start the trail by ten," she said, writing that down too.

"You are really going to do this with me? Like go on this hike to help us get this map?" he asked, still stunned. She looked at him wide eyed.

"Is this a test? Agree and I keep my life here or refuse and become a servant to Greenthistle till I die?" she asked.

"What? No!" he gasped. He took her hand with both of his and held it. "I promise you, we don't want to hurt you, I don't want to hurt you or see you get hurt." He paused. Her eyes traveled down and she noticed his thumb rubbing the top of her hand. "You are extremely important to helping Humboldt. We essentially have to burn ourselves to get it with the iron. I have no idea how much iron there is but if the map we need is etched into iron, then we are screwed. We need a mortal and we have one who wants to help us. One who is kind."

"If I can help Humboldt and Greenthistle, I want to. I'll do it, for this place I call home," she said, looking at him and then down at her hand still cradled in his. Then back up to meet his dreamy gaze.

"I could kiss you right now, El."

"You could." It wasn't exactly a question. She wasn't exactly sure what was even happening, but she was going to go with it.

"May I?" he asked.

"You don't have to ask anymore, Trevin" she breathed.

With a smile and an inhale, he grinned then moved his fingertips to her chin. His lips met hers.

That feeling of a warm wave washed over them both again and she pressed into him. He pressed into her. His fingertips moved to cup her jaw and trace her ear. His other hand interlaced their fingers. She felt as though she would never tire of this; kissing him was such a euphoric sensation, and she never wanted it to end.

She wondered if this is what it felt like to kiss all fae, or if it was just Trevin because she felt so secure with him. She had never experienced this before. But maybe they all had this kind of power over mortals—to lure them in and catch them. She had never really been reckless, but alone in her studio, kissing Trevin, she wanted to be. She wanted him. Her fingers gripped him tighter and she ran her other hand through his hair, she curled her fingers and tugged as he let out a throaty moan.

He slid his tongue into her mouth and pressed into her, their tongues tangling together.

As soon as he laid her down on the couch, he straddled her. Elodie looked up at him and she moaned his name.

Trevin gasped and pushed himself up, still straddling her "I'm sorry! Fuck. I. El, I need to go," he said getting of her, his breathing heavy as he looked at her. She remained frozen, worry settling in as she held his gaze.

Elodie knew she had lost herself in the moment, so she swallowed hard and recollected herself. Her mind told her how stupid that was, to think he actually was interested in a mortal.

"Okay," she finally managed to say, taking a deep inhale. "Sorry. I got carried away." She stared at the floor, feeling a little insecure. "I know mortals are gross. And basic and stuff."

"It's not that. I need to go though. I'm needed at home," he said, standing up and grabbing his things frantically. She nodded and got up quickly. "Bye," he said before he rushed out the door.

Elodie sighed and leaned back on the couch savoring the fading scent of him. She figured that was as far as that would go and she probably wasn't backpacking with him. It would be awkward now. She frowned.

"What the hell happened? Does he like it when girls are mute? Jerk got me all hot and bothered. He wants to play fuckboy and then leave like that? He's just my overseer, not my friend. He doesn't want me," she muttered, frustrated. She certainly wasn't going to forget that sensation though. She undid her pants and closed her eyes imagining what could have happened as her hands wandered and moaned his name.

Chapter 25

Trevin's mind was racing as he ran home. He knew he was losing a battle he had never wanted to fight to begin with, he wanted Elodie but he couldn't have her.

He recalled all her emotions as clear as day on her face when he pulled away. The hurt, the embarrassment, and worry all made him just want to stay with her, to tell her he was being a complete moron about this because he did not know what was right. Yet even coddling her would start the battle all over again.

Mother above this is driving me insane. Why did I do that? Why did I get handsy with her? Then I just left her, panting, yearning, begging for more with her hand tangled in mine and her other hand tugging my hair. Fuck! I can't, I can't do this. I can't hurt her. I don't want to be hurt. He fought back the whimper, his thoughts spiraling.

When he crossed the boundary, he stopped. The edge that he was tottering on was too much. Heaving, his eyes stared straight ahead, then toward the tavern. Home or the tavern? He could have anyone and he could release this insane urge to run back over to Elodie and let loose on her. Round after round and she'd probably let him too.

"Fuck," he groaned and ran for the tavern, hating himself. A lot of eyes landed on him with interested gazes the second he walked inside. His eyes frantically searched for someone he felt was suitable. How could he be vowed to a mortal? He couldn't be vowed to anyone yet, at forty-five? Trevin ordered a drink and downed it instantly. The burn of the alcohol coated his throat, anything to shake this urge in him. He ordered another.

Elodie, he whispered, staring at the glass and the liquor in it. Imagining himself, downing this as liquid courage to run back there and take her. Shaking his head, he told himself to forget it, her, this desire building in him, between his legs. Never had he encountered this insane yearning before. With an inhale, he noticed how faint her scent was. Drowned out by distance, by the liquor, by the smoke of the hookahs, the floral scents that fae wore. He hated this place.

Fingertips ran across his back from one shoulder to the other.

"You look like you are on edge. I can help you down. You reek of mortal, couldn't bring yourself to get any closer to the trash?" A seductive voice caressed his ears. He saw the female with dazzling blue eyes, her skin a faint blue. Her cheeks had a scale pattern that also appeared on her chest. She was part river nymph. He downed the liquor and got up to follow her. As she smiled and pulled him along, Trevin noticed her hand didn't feel like Elodie's. He eyed the fingers, her nails done to points like little claws, and painted an opaque blue. It wasn't Elodie's hand and the river nymph was pulling him into a situation he did not want to be in.

Why are you thinking about her? The only reason you are here is to forget about what happened with her, Trevin thought.

She leaned against a wall and wrapped her arms around his waist, pulling him closer. He felt her against his hardness and tensed.

"You walked in here like that, naughty boy you are, Master Greenthistle. I didn't think you had it in you," she moaned and started to kiss him. "Nice to know you are well endowed, too."

Too. She's hooked up with Cedar.

His heart rate was pounding, Elodie's face flashed in his head. Her chest rising and falling, her hand tugging his hair. He thought about her and shook his head.

No, not her. Just get this out of your system. With a hard swallow, he pressed against the nymph and brought his hands to her hips. One hand ran up her body and he felt her breast and she moaned. *Not her moan.* The one that he would have gladly let chain him up for her to do as she pleased with.

Elodie. El, his mind moaned.

"How lucky I am to be with Master Greenthistle," she moaned and kissed him. She was rubbing herself on him. "Estate lady sounds fun."

Trevin, Elodie's voice said in his mind. He stopped for a moment and looked at the girl in front of him.

"What is your name?" he asked, breathing hard.

"Cassia," she said before kissing him and moaning again.

Cassia. Not Elodie. El. I want El, I can't. He felt her undo his pants and remembered the last time he randomly hooked up with someone. How many years ago? Seven? After the last mortal cheated on him. The empty and used feeling he would have after these types of nights. Elodie would be so disappointed in him, though he wasn't sure why it even mattered. He couldn't want Elodie, so what if she was his vowed. He could bring Cassia home, if she wanted it, if she wanted him, and not the title.

Would she have saved him from the iron cuff? Or left him there? Would she do the hike? *Fuck.* He still needed to figure that out, too. Elodie was their only shot. Would Cassia keep him safe? *What am I doing here?*

A hollowing chill suddenly shot down his spine and sat in the pit of his stomach the second she wrapped her hand around him and he felt himself deflate. He had lost all edge, but he certainly had not released anything. His body had shut down.

He met her eyes to see her disgusted at him.

"Daddy must be really proud of his heir, the Greenthistle disappointment. Caleb at least delivers," she said, pushing him off. "You act like you're above the hook ups and shit, but the hook ups are above you, aren't they? Better luck in the mortal world. Trash will do anything I suppose, even disappointments," she said, walking off. Her words sparked so much emotion in him. He could see her disappointment, her anger, her frustration. He adjusted himself and ran home, up to his room.

"Fuck!" he screamed into his pillow. "Elodie, you can't be, there's no way!" Rolling over on his back, he thought about her weird energy. He was vowed to it? To her? Then he wondered if he was kissing her against the wall of the tavern, and it was her hand. Would he have lost the heat? Kissing her on the couch certainly was the only reason he had it to begin with. What if she had undone his pants, and wrapped her hand around him, her fingers, pressing on him. He hadn't even realized he was wandering down that path again. Hadn't even caught himself opening the gate when he thought about their last kiss and her moan.

"Elodie," he moaned out, realizing his hand was now wrapped around himself and he was hard all over again. "Fuck," he whimpered. "Elodie," he moaned. He didn't stop to turn back, instead he kept down that path thinking about her, until that edge was released. He cleaned up and took a cold shower. He knew nothing else was going to tame this desire. Only she could. Trevin knew he had pushed open one of those gates he would never be able to close again and he didn't want to close it.

After Elodie had finished and processed the night again, her smile faded as the night replayed in her mind. "What am I doing?" With a frustrated sigh, she put on her hoodie and shoes and walked out toward the trail, knowing that being outside would help her process. Sadness crept in. As she walked toward the trees, she sighed. "What a mess you are, stupid little mink. That's what he would say." She walked to the first redwood she saw and pressed her hand to it. "Mom, I'm here, even if it is still all chaos in my head. I'm here in Humboldt again and it is just as magical as we always believed it was."

A warm breeze swirled around her as she pressed her head to the trunk.

Little One, do not weep. Awaken and you will see.
He needs you; they need you. We need you.

She backed up and stared up at the starry night sky.

"Trev," she said softly. "It's okay. We will both be okay, right?" she asked, and another warm breeze embraced her. She nodded and removed her hand. As she turned to head back for her studio, a raven cawed and took flight. She watched it, wondering if it was related to Nightswift, to Russ. She shook her head. "That's stupid, not every single animal is theirs."

Once she climbed into bed, slumber came quickly for her.

C̲H̲A̲P̲T̲E̲R̲ ̲2̲6̲

The next day Elodie awoke to a text message from Trevin. While excited to get it, she was also nervous about what it might say. She had a knack for not opening the emails, letters, or messages that could leave her upset. She also knew she would be uneasy all day, and that wasn't fair to the kids.

Her eyes moved towards the window at the tree line.

"Okay. If he's telling me we can't be friends or we can't talk anymore, then he is. If he's telling me he made a mistake and he needs time, then I have to respect that. He went too far, and he knows as well as I do, any feelings caught between us are stupid. His dad warned us." She nodded and read the message as her heart pounded.

El. I'm sorry for last night. I don't know what came over me. I don't know why I started that or why I ran away from that either. I imagine I sound like a dumbass, but I don't know what this is between us. This is all new and I'm not sure how fast or slow it should go. I also imagine the trip this weekend might be awkward. Don't worry about it. I do want to thank you for your willingness to help us and Humboldt. The lands thank you too.

What am I supposed to do with that? Is he telling me goodbye? To wait? To just brush it off? She sighed in defeat and finished getting ready. As she walked to her car, she remembered him lying there on the dirt, unresponsive. Remembered the gasp of air he took when she finally got the cuff off him. She wondered what would happen if he went alone or with his brother. Would they both end up like that with no help? She realized she was both Greenthistle's asset and liability, a unique position to be in. She looked at the trees and tilted her head.

Elodie wondered if they had brought her to them. This predicament she had stumbled into or had been dropped into.

They need you. He needs you.

As she drove to work, she started to think.

Trevin sighed in his dad's office, pulling a file from a drawer.

"I take it the girl doesn't want to go?" Lord Greenthistle asked.

"I don't know," Trevin groaned. *She was going to, she wanted to, and I messed it up.* Cassia's words stuck with him. He knew when he woke up he needed to apologize to Elodie. Even if she didn't know what he had intended to do at the tavern, where Cassia's hands had been. After typing and deleting his message four times, he finally typed something and clicked send. He had gotten no response.

"I assumed that's where you were last night, asking her? Or where you investigating the power surge?"

"What? Power surge?"

"You didn't feel it? Last night it didn't seem violent or anything, just calm, but it was there and it lingered. It was different than I felt before."

"What time was this?" he asked, considering how they felt before.

"Maybe nine or ten when I noticed it."

Trevin thought he was back from the chaos of the night. Had he missed because he was in the tavern? If this was related to Elodie, what was she doing to cause this? *Damn it, El, what are you?*

"I had a long night," he said, defeated.

"Well, obviously you did. Do I get permits, or no?"

"I asked her and she wanted to help, and was already writing details down. She plans a lot."

"Okay, she's a teacher. Does this surprise you? Teachers plan. She went to school to do this. Clearly she's good at it too," his dad said, puzzled.

"I know, but I messaged her this morning, and she didn't respond," he said, realizing he wasn't sure what he was expecting. It sounded more like a dismissal than anything she could respond to. He was frustrated, not with her, but with the universe. Why was his vowed, a mortal with a weird power? His best-case scenario was around seventy years with her, granted nothing happening to her sooner. He sighed again. He wanted her, though. Fighting it wasn't working, and he didn't want to ignore it anymore. Avoiding her was impossible now, she certainly wasn't out of his thoughts.

"Trevin," his dad said, looking at him concerned. Trevin met his dad's eyes. "Whatever is going through your head, take a deep breath. If you need a release, go find someone. Let the girl live the life she is trying to build."

Trevin sighed and slumped back in his chair. He deflated. "Okay."

"Don't go this week. Let's take a breather on locating the tome, and work out all this emotion. It's unnerving to see this in you. I will assign a sentry to oversee her."

"No, it's not her. I can still do my job," Trevin said, taking a breath of resolve. He looked at the clock and rolled his eyes. It was only 9:45 a.m. He opened the file he set down and the form book of civil codes and started reading when his phone buzzed.

"She wants to go! She will be ready Saturday morning by 7:30 a.m.," he said.

"Do not cross a line you will regret, Trev. It's for your own good," he said. Trevin nodded and went back to the message. Trevin's eyes read it again.

I am sorry, too. Whatever this is, was, between us is new. I can't say I hate it. If you are worried you are scaring me, you are not. About this weekend, I'd really feel better if I knew you'd be okay, if I was there to help when you need it. I will look out for you if you look out for me. I will keep my hands to myself too, if you do. Saturday at 7:30 a.m., my hatch will be open.

I will see you Saturday morning bright and early.

Trevin replied and put his phone down. He smiled to himself. *Little mink.*

Elodie skipped the café on Thursday and got the stuff she needed while talking to Cora.

"So, you are going with him? What are the details? One tent?"

"No way! He's bringing his own gear, and I'm bringing mine. I'm driving, it's in the King Range. We leave my place at 7:30."

"King Range? Lost Coast Trail? In two days?"

"No, King Crest trail."

"Oh, that's really tough. I did it years ago, like in my early twenties. Why the hell is he asking you to do that?"

"I don't know. He likes a challenge and I figure I can do it. I want the challenge too."

"Hell of a first date, I guess."

"It's not a date, Trust me. He doesn't like me. We are just friends. No sharing tents."

"You better text me in the morning and evenings when you have reception. Seriously! I trust him, but this is odd."

Elodie sighed and rolled her eyes.

I'm just the oddity of Humboldt, I guess, she thought to herself. "I will text you, I promise."

"Text me if you know, you two kiss again or something, too. You are going to be alone with him."

"Has he said he wants to kiss me again? I'm pretty sure he was put off from Halloween," she said in hopes of covering up any misconstrued assumptions.

"No, but I've never seen him give anyone those longing gazes before."

"I will be sure to give you a full report. Though I can tell you now, it will be boring come Sunday night," she said with a laugh before ending the call. She drove to the beach and backed her car in. Listening to the waves crash, she lay in the sleeper and watched the little breaks of white.

Elodie sighed and wondered what it was going to be like this weekend. So many unknowns, but what else could she do? Just worry about him until she saw him at the café or one of Cora's parties? She could ask him to text her when he was back? Even if he texted her if something went wrong, then what? Drive one hundred miles southwest, then run the seven miles to the boundary she couldn't cross?

This was to help Humboldt. Even if he didn't want her, she had to set that aside to help the fae keep the lands safe. If the tome would help them do it, she would help them. She didn't need to be the girl who went down in the fae tales as the one that caught the prince's eye. She could be the one who braved the iron for them. She focused her eyes on the trees.

The breeze blew past her and she reached her hand out, feeling the warm air even though it was the end of November. She smiled and then climbed out of the hatch and closed it. With one last glance at the dark ocean, she got in the car and drove home.

Friday came and went and she sorted through her gear. He had sent his good morning text to her, and she replied—her usual check in from her overseer, she assumed. As she packed her food, mostly snacks and beef jerky, she laughed and wondered if he was going to suffice on snacks like this? She sent him a text as she continued to put things in her bag.

Still on for tomorrow?

Of course.

Okay, good. Do I need the fire starter, or will you bring it?

I can start a fire, little mink, I do plan on cooking for you.

Thank you. That is good to know. I will have snacks.

Not sure what state she would be in on sunday night, she made sure to pack things to freshen up with. She would be far too self-conscious to ever look at him again, and that'd be that. She'd do this and he would just appear at gatherings and the café and they could act as though they were only acquaintances.

His dad wouldn't have to worry about a mortal girl fawning over his eldest and she would get on with her life. Then maybe she would reach an agreement with Lord Greenthistle and she could move on. She sighed in defeat and climbed into bed thinking of where she may go next and frowned at the thought of leaving Humboldt. Even if she went to Del Norte or Mendocino, what would be the point in leaving?

Chapter 27

The alarm rang, pulling Elodie from sleep. She shut it off, climbed out of bed, and walked into the bathroom to take a shower. "May as well start the weekend fresh. Who knows what state I will be in tomorrow." She put on her few layers and sandals, and grabbed her boots to change into when they got to the trail head. Once her hair was braided, she put her hat on and went over her list. Since it was overnight, she needed an extra change of clothes compared to what she'd take for just a day hike. Her sketchbook was easy to access, along with the charcoal and a few pens tucked away. She even brought the bigger sleeping bag since it was cozier and temperatures would be cold on top of the mountain. She lifted her pack and adjusted the straps to fit comfortably, then left.

With the door locked, she headed down the stairs to the parking lot, but as she got to the bottom, she saw him glamoured and walking toward her. He was in boots and cargo pants and a dark green hoodie. She smiled at him and figured this was the only version she'd see of him from now on. Her overseer, nothing more. She sighed, then reminded herself of the plan. *Just help get the map, that is all I need to do this weekend.* She opened the hatch and pulled her pack off then chucked it down.

"Hey. I got breakfast for us. Got you an iced coffee with cream too. What is all that?" he asked, confused.

"What do you mean? You said backpacking. We are overnighting it up there. Where's all your stuff?" she asked worriedly, noting he just had his usual backpack. He just looked at her.

"I know it's been a few days, I uh, I was busy, but did you forget already?" he pointed to his ears. They were round like hers. "What I am, in feral?"

"No, as much as I probably should at this rate, but like, okay."

"You are going to carry that for the entire fourteen miles?"

"Yes. That's what us mortals do, Trev. We need things like food, water, and shelter. It's kind of imperative for our survival," she said, obviously annoyed. "You don't actually backpack, do you?" She slumped on her hatch, realizing how stupid she was. Her whole body deflated with a sigh.

"Ummm, I have a backpack, yes. You really carried that whole thing on the Lost Coast Trail? On your other treks?"

"You've never gone backpacking with Cora? Or her brother? Charles? Do you even have a tent? A sleeping bag?" She looked at him, worried. "Oh. Oh no. I am an idiot."

"What?" he asked, confused. "El, no you aren't. I don't think you are dumb for having what you want to bring. It just seems like a lot of weight to carry. Cora? And Charles, they do this too? I go on overnights with Russ and Q, sometimes we have to, but we sleep in feral. I've gone with my family. What are we going to do with gear?"

"But what would you have done with the beach camping in Trinidad? Surely they would have freaked out with a fucking mountain lion at the campsite!" Elodie said, despite being at a loss for words.

"We usually don't camp with them, or we do. We just stay up till everyone else is asleep and then wake before everyone else. The hearing is top-notch. I just, I didn't realize you actually needed so much stuff as a mortal. It's okay. I'm not going to leave you behind. I will go slow but, you think you can do this in two days? I don't want you to miss work," he said.

She sighed and gave him a glare, hurt masked behind frustration. "Yes, I can do fourteen miles in two days. I'm not stupid, I'm not some beginner idiot trying to do this with a single bottle of water at noon either. Let's go, it's a long drive," she said. He nodded, and tossed his backpack in the hatch. She shut it and got in the car. She didn't talk much while she ate the breakfast he had brought.

Remember your plan. He is going to be baffled at how high maintenance we stupid mortals are. I will help Humboldt. They will be able to do whatever they need to do to keep it safe.

"El, I'm sorry about the other night. This is an odd situation to be in."

She gripped the steering wheel tighter.

The oddity of Humboldt, maybe that should be my nickname. Patron saint, my ass. The stupid little mink.

"Did you at least take care of whatever that was?" she snapped back.

"Yes." His voice was smaller than she had ever heard him use.

"Good. We can move on," she said. He nodded.

"Was the rest of your week good?" he asked.

"Eventually, yes," she said. "Yours?"

"It was okay. Winter break is coming up, right?" he said.

"Yes, it is."

"How long is it again? Two weeks?" he asked, desperately trying to make any conversation.

"About two and a half? Why, going to try to see if I can run another long trek into the wilderness with a mountain lion? Or does Q want to use me, too?"

"El! I'm sorry about Wednesday! I'm not using you, I swear. If you don't want to do this, you don't have to. It's okay, no hard feelings. You can pull over and drop me off," he said with a frown.

"No."

"Why?"

Elodie sighed. *Stop feeling things for him. He got it out of his system. He doesn't want to sleep with you. He wants a fae, not a mortal. You are nothing more than Greenthistle's asset and liability.*

"Because. I don't want something to happen to you. If there's any iron, it's a danger to you. I don't want to see you like that ever again. I'm sure whoever helped you on Wednesday night doesn't either, but they can't help you with this. I can at least do this one thing," she said with a gust of air through her nose, "The only thing I can do for you, handle iron."

"I didn't sleep with anyone, El! You want to know what I did? I ran to the tavern and downed two drinks to try to take the edge off. Then I thought I was going to get it out of my system with someone. Yet, the second she touched me I lost any and all desire. And then she called me the Greenthistle disappointment for it. So I sulked off and ended up in my room in bed and I took care of it myself if you must know. I felt like a stupid coward, because I instigated that then it overwhelmed me, and I don't know why," he said. "And stop thinking you are just a liability, you aren't. The lands like you, you are important to us."

"Okay," she said in a small voice. He sighed and watched the Old Giants pass on 101 South.

For a while they were both quiet. Elodie didn't want to fight with him. She didn't want to feel things for him either, and she hated that she did. She found herself hurt and confused with him.

Did he stop? Had that girl actually called him a disappointment? Even if he couldn't perform, he had so many other qualities she couldn't deny she liked. Elodie wondered how wounded his past relationship had left him. He was an estate heir and people really tossed him aside? No wonder he lacked confidence when people called him a disappointment. She questioned why she was rationalizing his crappy behavior. They had a job to do. This was the only thing she could do for him, the only thing that would ever require a fae and a mortal to work together. They were each other's only shot at keeping Humboldt safe.

The Old Giants told her they were all in danger. She had made a plan to do this one thing and move on. He needed to work himself out, she needed to find that thing she had left behind here. Getting distracted with each other was the dumbest thing they could do. Lord Greenthistle had told them both as much. She figured she would try to talk with him, they were friends, and friends talked. *Even if we are not friends the silence grows deafening,* she thought to herself.

"I think this might be the first time I've driven south on 101 knowing I'm not leaving Humboldt. It's the first time an immense sadness has not taken over," she said, not taking her eyes off the road.

"You feel sad on Avenue of the Giants?" he asked.

She nodded. "It usually meant my time in Humboldt was over, driving this direction at least. The only saving grace would be if I was taking Highway 1 and I could enjoy Fort Bragg and Mendo. Otherwise I'd take 101 and watch the trees change, watch the lands change. Say goodbye to the Old Giant's and hope it was a see you later, not a final farewell." She didn't want to meet his eyes.

"You don't hike here? Camp here? You sound like you do that a lot in Arcata, and Redwoods NP."

"No, normally I go north because it's the opposite way of Marin. This time though, I know I'm going back to my studio after this trip is over, I think." She glanced at him briefly and then went back to the road.

"You think?" he asked. She nodded.

"I mean, I don't know what could happen. But I'm willing to risk it." Her voice was riddled with fear now as they turned off 101. The lands were different, but she was still in Humboldt. The Old Giants hadn't spoken to her today.

"You still think we are going to hurt you? El, I don't know why you don't believe me. No one is going to be there from the estates other than me, and I'm not going to hurt you. You said it yourself, I look out for you, you look out for me," he said. "No one from the fae world will be there. If anyone is, they cannot attack me without the wrath of all three estates. Attacking a mortal under a high estate's direct protection is a death wish. You are safe."

She nodded. "But you are all so fast, I wouldn't see it coming. What if Caleb or anyone changes their mind?"

"Caleb would never do that. He doesn't want you to get hurt regardless of how he acts. He doesn't like when people are hurt, believe it or not, he gets a ton of compliments on the force."

"Okay, but this is an unclaimed patch of fae land, what if someone wants to claim it, how do you know it's unclaimed?"

"It's unclaimed. Fae can't just stroll up and call it theirs. Humboldt has three high estates who manage the lands. If someone did claim it, that'd be four and wouldn't work. You noticed I don't have a tent, that's because I sleep in feral, and in case anyone enters, I will know. I will defend you. Overseer duties."

"Okay," she said with a nod. She was driving slowly, and the unease was growing.

"What's wrong now? You still don't believe me?"

"The road is narrow and windy. I don't exactly have a high-profile vehicle," she said, now slightly agitated. He sighed again and looked off to the side.

"You are so nervous. Why are you actually doing this?" he asked.

"I told you why. I don't want you to get hurt."

"But you'd do so at the risk of you getting hurt?"

She slammed on the brakes, causing things in her car to slide forward, him included. The seatbelt locked across his chest.

"Shut the fuck up and let me drive. You are an idiot and you need to learn a whole lot more about us stupid needy mortals if you ever expect to run this place. I need to focus on what I'm doing. If this car goes off a cliff I don't have a magical cat form or nine infinite lives. I accept that I will die one day because I have to. But I do not want it to be this weekend. So either shut up and let me focus on this road, or you can get out of my car and meet me at the trailhead, okay? Why did you even ask me to do this then?" she nearly growled at him.

"I shouldn't have." Trevin crossed his arms. She felt her bottom lip quiver slightly and swallowed back any frustration she had.

Stop feeling things for him. He is so clueless. He's forty-five, yet he acts like a bratty twelve-year-old. She wondered if fae males took even longer to reach maturity. His dad didn't seem this dumb, his dad exuded every ounce of the cool, confident, and collected fae she ever read about. Yet Trevin was extra moody. *More reason to not want him.*

She slowed to make a sharp right and looked at the GPS and took a deep inhale. Elodie was breathing deeper, eyeing the tree line, waiting for anything but they were quiet. A relieved sigh came out when she finally saw the trailhead. She parked and stared at the trail for a moment. There were two other cars parked nearby. Both were SUVs. She swallowed hard and glanced at Trevin. Glamoured to appear mortal. Her frown made him roll his eyes.

"Seriously, El, you do not need to do this, I can see you are uncomfortable," he groaned.

She narrowed her eyes, fighting back the cry she knew she needed. Pushing an audible gust through her nose, she unlocked the doors then got out without another word. Trevin sighed and got out too. As she changed into her boots, Elodie swayed slightly off balance on one foot. She caught her balance on the edge of her car then noticed Trevin had reached his hands out to help her. Her eyes quickly went to the ground as she finished. He put his hands down to his side with a sigh. She didn't say anything as she made sure she had the trail maps downloaded.

"You have the trail map to the boundary line and after?"

"Yes I do."

"Can I take a picture of it, just in case?"

"Fine." He took his backpack off and opened it, pulling the book of Falk out and the map from his dad's office.

She sighed in distaste at him and took pictures of it. "Thank you," she muttered and put her phone in her pocket. He put his stuff back in his backpack and put it back on as she closed her hatch. A beep came from the car and then she put her keys in a small pocket with a clip on the inside near the top. She could feel his eyes on her as she hefted the pack on and clipped the straps. Without saying a word, she started walking.

Chapter 28

Elodie was still seething at him but she didn't want to be angry. She didn't want to let him go and she did not understand why she felt drawn to him. She eyed the trees and wondered why they were being silent. The redwoods did not grow here, firs and sugar pines did. This soil was still Humboldt's though. They had called to her from further away before so why not now? they were silent as she passed them on the drive here Worries crept into her head. Thoughts of what if they had stopped wanting to talk to her lead to a black hole.

What if I took too long to wake up? What if they don't like me being this aggravated or snapping at Greenthistle's heir? She swallowed through the painful thoughts. *What if they decided I wasn't worthy of this? Why do I even care? Trees talking to you makes you crazy.* As she approached a fir she let her palm slide across it only to be met with silence. She swallowed hard again. *Please, I need guidance.* She slide her palm across another tree, taking in the sensation of the trunk on her palm, they remained silent. Her other hand clenched into a fist and then she flexed her fingers out again. The air was still cool yet a pulse of heat through her body. She kept walking, feeling the mist on her face and the tears forming.

I'm going to have a breakdown in front of him and he's going to know I'm legitimately crazy. With a sigh, she kept walking, eventually taking a sip of water. She was grateful she always hiked with her camelback water bladder in her backpack. It had a hose that looped up through her shoulder strap to the bite valve so she could take easy sips and stay hydrated without having to stop for water breaks. Elodie's eyes fixed on another tree. They were thinning with the ascent. Steadying her breathing, she approached the tree. With a deep inhale, she reached out and pressed her palm to the fir.

She felt a warm breeze, but no words came. With a sigh, her shoulders slumped and she squeezed her eyes shut, swallowing back the cries. One slow exhale and she opened them, following the trunk up to the sky.

Trevin appeared in her peripheral. She flinched realizing how crazy she already appeared. She traced his face and ears, then met his eyes. *Trevin.* Just like she had in Marin, she pleaded silently for him.

"What's wrong?" Trevin asked her softly. They hadn't said anything to each other in the last forty minutes.

"Nothing." Elodie turned.

"Please talk to me, El. I see your emotions, what is wrong?"

She stopped but did not turn back to face him. "Nothing. Let's go." She started walking again hearing him sigh. After another twenty minutes of silence. Elodie took another sip of water and checked the trail on her phone then started walking again.

"I'm still not sure what you are trying to prove or to whom you think you need to?" he said, walking behind her again.

"I don't need to prove anything to you. I don't need to be told what I can and can't do," she hissed out.

"It was never my intent to assume you couldn't do this, I wouldn't have considered it, had you never spoken of your hikes and adventures. My intent is to keep you safe. I know this terrain. I've run nearly every square mile from the coast to Trinity's border. Del Norte and Mendo's too. Know I will always keep you safe. I see your despair though. I do not want them to weigh you down. Let me pull them off you."

"Do not dare." Her voice was stern. "These are not your emotions to bear."

"But it is my job to keep you safe, like you said you'd do for me. And at least knowing what is wrong is doing my job. I'm not going to tell you how you should feel, but if I can help make it better I will."

Elodie started walking again. "At least I know you can't read thoughts or get into my head."

"You're right, I can't read minds. All I can do is see waves of emotions crashing down on you. You're struggling to keep your head above water. I don't know what the point of this gift is because I cannot figure out what is causing it all."

"Count it as a blessing," Elodie said, annoyed.

El. Wake up.
He will need you.
Danger awaits him.

She stopped dead in her tracks. He stopped close behind her.

"What is it? What's wrong?" he asked in a quiet tone. "I felt that shift in the air and you clearly did too," he said quietly.

"What's around us?" she asked worriedly.

"Nothing. I can sense a few mortals but they are far away. They do not stand a chance. If any assholes think they can one up me and attack you they are in for a rude awakening. If they try, I need you to run back toward your car at least for a bit. I will run off trail and change and they will have a mountain lion encounter, then I will find you again, understood?" he said, placing his hand on her shoulder and giving it a small squeeze. She nodded.

"Okay. I run and play scared and then the mountain lion handles it, you will find me, right? You will come for me, right?"

"Always," he said. "Even when you hate me."

"What if?" She paused. "What if a fae is in the unmarked area? Then what?" she asked.

"Then I fight them. Caleb, Q, Russ, and I don't thrash each other around for shits and giggles, most of the time. Our dads require us to for reasons like that. Attacks on us are stupid but they can happen, do happen obviously. Be on alert and know I have your back."

She nodded and swallowed hard again. "What if they hurt you or render you unconscious again, and I'm stuck in that patch of land?"

"If it's with iron, Dad, Autumn, and Caleb will know I went rogue again and they all know I am here, with you. They will come," he said. She nodded. "Can I ask you to do something in the event I am rendered unconscious? It might be scary, but it might be your last solid defense," he said.

"Okay," she said in a small voice. He nodded and reached into his pocket. He held up a thin vial of a pink shimmering oil.

"This is floss flower oil. It has no effect on you. It's just a floral smelling oil, like lavender or something, but it is poisonous to us."

"Trev! Why do you have this?"

"We can't be too careful," he said, lifting his hoodie up revealing the hilt of a knife. It was a bronze color and had green stones inlaid into it. Her eyes widened. "If a fae somehow gets me incapacitated, I want you to grab my dagger and line it with the floss flower then stab them with it."

She swallowed hard and nodded.

"Can you do that?"

"I think so, in the city I usually kept my keys between my fingers when I was walking alone. I do it here sometimes too. But floss flower was how your—" She stopped and cut her eyes down.

"I know. We all keep a vial on us. I want you to keep this, even when we get back. I am the defense, but you are the offense. I don't want you to fight, I want you to run and not worry about me. The ravens will see, Greenthistle will know, every mountain lion will know. They will know the dagger, they will scent me on you. Understood? You run, and you stay safe."

"You will fight, right? Even if I run, you will get out of a bad situation? You will tell me you got out of a situation I left you in? Abandoned you to?" she asked, feeling her eyes tear up.

He had remained quiet making her look up at him. Her eyes met his. Something like confusion shown in his face.

"Trev," she said, worried. "You'd tell me you were safe, that you made it home?" she asked. He smiled slightly.

"Yes. I will fight with everything in me to get you home and to be able to tell you I am home too," he said.

"I will keep the floss flower safe. And I will only use it if I have to."

"Good. Let's go, we have a few more miles till we head off trail."

The long break of them talking about plans helped with the trek up the incline. They took a few breaks, and closer to the top, they stopped so she could eat a snack. She held it out, offering him some.

"Thanks," he said, and she nodded. "I noticed you run your hand along the trees, I see you do that a lot on walks. Why?"

Elodie looked at him and frowned.

"I don't think it's nothing, El. I think, something is on your mind and you're right, I can't read minds, but I don't want you to feel like this on this trek. I'm sorry I suck at backpacking and I'm sorry, I made assumptions about you. I'm sorry about everything. I don't think that I've fucked up this much around anyone before."

She sighed and looked down. "It's okay. I was—I am emotional, but I don't want to talk about it." She put the food away and loaded up the pack, taking a sip of water before she started walking again, knowing she had to stay hydrated.

"I respect that," he said. She nodded. "But will you tell me about the trees? Why do you do that?" She kept walking, remaining quiet. "El."

"I just like trees and ferns," she answered with a defeated sigh.

"Lying is pretty pointless when I can see all your emotions, ya know."

"You think I'm lying and I'm not. You think I'm lying about liking trees and ferns."

"Fuck," he groaned out. "You know what I mean. You are trying to bottle everything up, and I can see you are hurt. You're scared, you're worried, and you feel dejected. You watch your steps enough and you know you are fine with the hike. You are looking forward to summiting the mountain, you're embarrassed and you are angry. I can see all that dragging you under and the weight of your pack is pushing you down. I hear your breaths deepen and your heart beating faster. Yet what I cannot figure out and I do not understand, is why you feel all those things inside. I get the heart rate, and the breathing, that's obvious. Let me take the pack so you at least have one less thing."

"No," she said, he sighed again.

"Why not?"

"Because I know what I can carry. I've been doing it all my life. I know that doesn't mean much to you, but it's a long chunk of time for me."

"I know you have and maybe you can let someone help you now."

"I know I can do this."

"I do not doubt that you can. I wouldn't have asked you to come if I didn't think you could have. But you don't have to do it alone. You don't have to prove it to me. Are you trying to prove it to yourself?" he asked. She narrowed her eyes.

"No."

"When you rub your hand along the trees and the ferns, does it give you comfort? Or relieve your stress? El, you say you feel them calling you, pulling you here, they have been. You found me, you cut the noose from my neck and saved me. You know what I am, what my whole family is and can turn into. You know about Ashdale and Nightswift. You know magic exists, you know it's real. You proved to yourself that the Old Giants are magic, they fuel these lands, even if they are not present in King Range, they are still the entities of this land." He sighed. "Have I told you what happens when you walk these lands?"

"No," she said shortly. He sighed quietly.

"I see the Old Giants shift toward you, I see the ferns sway toward you, they appear brighter. When you went to Marin last week, I was in my dad's office and I felt a shift in the air. As though the redwoods let out a collective sigh and then the air returned to normal. Then my phone lit up and when I opened it, it was your picture of the Mendo County line. And it wasn't just me who felt it. My dad did, Lord Ashdale, Lord Nightswift, Q, Russ, we were all in that conference room totally zoning out on how some ordinance affects something in Arcata's building codes. But that moment they all looked out the window, and we all felt it. Scouts out and they found nothing off. You know it was the damnedest thing that the trees would react that way, to anything really. Collectively watching something go, someone cross that line. You."

"You think I did that? I made the redwoods sigh?" she asked, confused. *They had said come back, but he felt them sigh? They all felt it? How? Why?*

"It sure was an odd coincidence."

"Odd," she said.

"And when you returned, everything felt more content. I wondered if it was you returning, so I asked. You were back in Humboldt's territory." He smiled wide.

"Oh," she said, confusion growing.

"So these lands like you, want you here, wanted you here for some time from the sounds of it. I am curious why you reach out for them as much as they seem to reach out for you," he said. She deflated.

"If I tell anyone, I'm going to lose my job. I need my job, and I love teaching. It is the only thing that allows me to live this vagabond life where I don't have to rely or depend on anyone else. Something like being labeled mentally unstable means I'm done as a teacher."

"Mortals might label you as that. The only reason fae would say it is because they would not believe it. I see it though, El. I know there is a connection, we all see it. I believe it even if I don't understand it. Your connection to these Old Giants is different from ours."

Elodie let out a long exhale. "Okay. I hear them. They tell me things, and have every time I've been here. When I left for Marin, they told me to come back, to not be gone too long. When I came back, they said they were happy the little one had returned." Her face burned with embarrassment.

"The Old Giants speak to you? With words? It's not a sensation or intuition?" Trevin asked dumbfounded. "They actually talk to you?"

"Yes. In my headspace, similar to you in feral. Whispers. I hear them calling to me, wanting me to walk with them. You don't hear them?" she asked.

"They don't talk to us, El. We feel their energy, they are the entities of our territory, all counties have something that is the essence of their county. The rivers in Sacramento, the Bristlecone Pines of Inyo, older than the Old Giants. San Diego has Torrey Pines. There can be more than one entity too. El Capitan and Half Dome in Yosemite for Mariposa County. We honor them, we protect them for they are all tied to the earth as we are, they make our bloodlines up. Over the years bloodlines mix, my mom was from Everoak, dad from Humboldt. When you described my eyes, that I was made of the redwoods and ferns themselves. I couldn't just say it was mere coincidence or an odd occurrence. No one has ever described my eyes as anything other than a striking green at most. To describe them as the essence in my blood. Then you spoke of bears, mountain lions, and ravens as the protectors of the redwoods. I desperately want to know what it is in you. How they talk to you."

"Because I'm some oddity. A circus attraction for the fae to gawk at? Slowly going insane," she said, wiping her eyes,

"Elodie, I don't know how to make this situation any better. I want to, but I don't know how to. I've never seen this before. Never heard about a mortal, no one with a sixteenth fae blood, not a halfling, nor a high fae who could talk to the Old Giants. I don't want your brain to be scrambled, or you to be our servant, it does no good. To anyone one. In fact if Dad did that, it'd probably just piss off the Old Giants. They've called you here. I also don't want it to fall into the wrong hands or territory, I don't want you falling into the wrong hands or territory."

"Fitting I suppose that I have an overseer. The asset and the liability," she muttered, feeling her eyes water. She hated herself when she got in these stubborn cycles of trying to push everything away. Absolutely hated how alone it left her feeling. He could and would leave at a moment's notice, anyway. It was better to prepare for another occurrence like Wednesday night. The fae prince didn't want her. He never would. He wanted her power? Blood? Whatever it was that was in her that made her so *odd*.

"I never said that," he snapped back.

Trevin hadn't wanted it to go this way. She was so insistent on proving she could do everything herself. They had miles of steep terrain between them and the car. He had forgotten things had to be done correctly for humans on the trail.

He wondered how she would feel knowing she was his vowed, but he realized how bad an idea it was to tell her now. *When was a good place to tell her? Not now. At her place? At the* café*? The estate? Ask Autumn to do it?* He thought about all those places and then sighed. There were a million reasons why he should never tell her.

Focused on her once again, he slowed his steps as he listened to her breaths and stood next to her. She was sweating and tired, but she kept going. Not one complaint about her feet hurting, her back hurting, or being tired though, she just kept going. He realized she would push herself into the earth if she had to. Why did she do that? She was everything he wanted. Strong, kind, loyal, trustworthy, she was beautiful. Had the Old Giants really brought her here, and vowed them together? She still was so hesitant and recoiled from him because he was fae. He sighed again.

He watched even more despair and sadness pour off her. Not being able to comfort her was driving him mad. *Vowed.* His dad would never accept her, even with this strange power in her. He was so worried something would hurt her, take her away. The level of trust he had in her was one he didn't think he'd find again. She had never once slipped and used his real name or Autumn's, and she had saved him and his family, she continued to.

"Elodie, let me take the pack."

"No."

He walked in front of her and faced her, stopping them both. "Stop trying to carry everything. I didn't bring you to be a pack mule. I brought you because I wanted your help," he said. She walked around and past him, unable to meet his eyes.

"You brought me because iron is involved, just let me do what I need to," she muttered. Her throat tightened and she kept trying to listen for the Old Giants but they were still quiet. She took a deep inhale. *Please talk to me.*

Elodie wasn't sure what she was doing anymore. The Old Giants hadn't spoken to her. They did not grow here at the higher altitudes but she had heard them on the beach and in Eureka where they were near, just as they were now. She hadn't realized how jarring their absence would be. Trevin was the one person who didn't deem her crazy or think she was joking because he could sense it. He could sense everything she felt and she could tell how desperately he wanted to soothe her. She also knew what her heart wanted and that it was such a dangerous line to cross. The consequences it could bring. *Some force out there brought us together. Regardless of all the things he was and could be to her, they were here, in each other's lives. Bound to remain so.* She took a sip of water before speaking.

"Why did you start going to the café at night after Halloween?"

"What?" he asked, clearly confused.

"Cora said you went in the daytime before we met."

"I think you have your answer right there. I wasn't trying to eavesdrop on you, I just heard Cora introduce you to Justine and when you said what you did for work, I figured you'd be there at night."

"But you hardly talked to me the next week. You just watched."

He smiled. "I didn't really understand why I was doing it either. I just had such a curiosity about you. At first I told myself it was out of alarm, the way you spoke of high fae, the Old Giants, and the earth. Then when I would hear you talk I just was mesmerized. The way your words flow—it's beautiful. You intrigue me. That energy in you had me baffled but you, my little mink, are amazing. The chance to see you and hear you speak—talk about things I take for granted. Hearing you talk to Charles about the Old Giants, hearing you talk to your students about the magic here. There is something different about you in so many facets. And I'm pretty sure you could have gotten any guy you wanted that night. Caleb certainly would have tried to kiss you had I not glared at him. Honestly I was about to leave after you pushed me away, but then Caleb made that game and I didn't want him or Q getting to you first."

She smiled for a moment, feeling relieved. Then she frowned remembering that first encounter. "You said I was odd."

"I am sorry for using that word. I saw that energy in you and I wanted to know what it was. I wanted to see if I could identify it. So I gazed into your eyes, coy smiles, pretty words and all. I realized how creepy I was being. It's something new, but it feels ancient? It's foreign but familiar."

"The patron saint of Humboldt, no?"

"Never to become a martyr. Not on Greenthistle's watch," he said with a smile. "You are very strong by the way. I didn't expect you to be able to push me back that much." He laughed.

"I wasn't sure where that came from. I was rather shocked." She formed a quick smile then dropped it into a frown. "They have been quiet," she said softly.

He heard her drink out of the hose on her pack. "Who?"

"The Old Giants, they haven't spoken to me much today. Usually they do every time I'm in the forest. I—" She paused and frowned. "I'm worried that they are mad at me for being such an irrational bitch to you, to Greenthistle's heir."

A soft laugh escaped him. "You have not been irrational or a bitch. I am a fool and have to ask myself if I learned anything about mortals."

"I was irrational and bitchy today and I'm sorry. Trust is a funny thing. I don't trust people to help me because so many offer and fall short. I have friends and acquaintances everywhere I've lived, but I have always been the lone wolf. I tend to feel like I need to hide who I am because of this thing I feel toward the trees and ferns. I wonder if at times I am actually going crazy. Now that they are quiet, I'm worried they are not talking to me. As if I'm not listening to them and they are done trying with me, like, people do."

"You are not going crazy, El. Being defensive helps. Being the lone wolf makes it easier, right? I guess it's similar to why we estate kids just go after the transplants, it's easier. They leave and we don't have to worry. None of us ever went for Cora even before she was with her partner because the café is a staple in Eureka. She will always stay."

"That makes sense. What about situations like Q and Justine? She left and came back?" Elodie asked.

"That's a good question. It's never happened honestly. She's the first to come back. How long do you think she will stay? Charles seems hell bent on leaving in the summer, much to Autumn's dismay."

"I don't know about Justine. She said she's scared to call it official, to let herself act like they are a thing so she denied it at first. Scared she will end up stuck here. I didn't think it'd be a bad thing. She and Q are cute together. But I guess, she probably should—if Q is going to have to leave her, I wish Charles would stay too. Autumn really likes him, huh? She clings to him a lot."

"She does. She loves the adventure van type, but she usually isn't this clingy with them. If they are together, their arms are around each other. Q definitely bragged last time Justine was here, but now he is tight-lipped about it. It's a different side of him too."

"And I guess that leaves me of Cora's transplants."

"Cora really wants you to stay. She makes friends with the vagabond type here and there. I was hurt she'd uninvite me to things on your account," he said with a laugh. "So where does that leave you, little mink?"

"I don't know. I guess one day you will leave me when you go into hiding or however the fae are supposed to do that."

"But we don't have to hide from you. I think the harder thing will be when you leave. I dread that day when you decide to pack up and go, I'm not sure what the lands will feel like, you think they will pull you back? I know I will miss you. Autumn will too."

She was quiet for a moment. "You'd actually miss me and my oddness if I left?"

"I would, you are not odd, I never should have used that word. It led you here. Elodie, I will never forget what you have done for us, what you did for me. That is a promise," he said, looking at her. She smiled.

He slowed their pace about a half a mile from the summit, they were adjacent to King Crest. She glanced at him then stared ahead with unease

"Boundary line. Take my hand. The dread is a ward to keep mortals from getting too close to our boundaries," he said. She nodded and took his outstretched hand, watching him hold his dagger with the other. "If anyone is there, take this and I will change." She nodded and bit her lip with unease. They stepped through and Trevin dropped his glamour. He was fae again and scanned the surroundings. Elodie let out an exhale and felt her senses more attuned. She could hear the faint wind and the sun was bright. She looked at him and took in his features.

He held onto his dagger and walked in front of her, dropping their hands so they could keep walking. As they reached the summit, they saw a mound of rocks with a cave entrance, but it was as though it was carved. Right angles making up the entrance instead of the irregularities of weathered rocks. There were large rocks all around them.

"This isn't visible from the other side of the boundary. It's the top of a mountain and yet there's structure? This entrance. A cave? Built by fae?" Elodie was confused as Trevin eyed the entrance and then looked at the map.

"It's a literal maze," he said. "That's why it is enclosed in the book. Oh," he said walking to the entrance. Then he noticed slats above open and they shined with the sunlight. "Oh."

She followed his gaze and squinted her eyes then they widened. "Are those slats iron?" she asked, confused still. She turned her attention to the rocks along the entrance and ran her fingers over them. "This is stone, I think."

Trevin placed his hand on the rock and nodded then his eyes shifted to the wall and he tilted his head. He slowly reached to the dirt above the rock and flung his hand back. "Oh fuck!" he said, shaking his hand out. Elodie seeing his reaction brushed the dirt off. He felt his sinuses burn with the dust and stepped back. "Fuck." He pushed air through his nose and rubbed it. His eyes teared up. Elodie's eyes shot wide. She put her hand to her mouth.

"I'm sorry!" she whined, wiping her hands on her leggings.

"It's fine, you didn't know. This entire thing is iron. It's eroded and in the dirt. This is insane. I just, we are going to have to disrupt so many plots in Falk. This isn't feasible to do." He groaned then sighed in defeat. He ran his fingers through his hair. Elodie took a deep inhale and took the pack off, needing a break from wearing it and knowing they needed to figure out a new plan.

"I guess it's on me then," she said with a shaky exhale. As she opened it Trevin placed his hand on her shoulder.

"Not alone, you are not going in there, El," he said. "I can't let you do that."

"That tiny bit of dust made your eyes red and bothered your nose. The ceiling and the walls are made out of it! No, Trev. You have to wait here."

"Can you even see more than six feet in there? I'm not trying to insult you or your senses but this is just dangerous. I'm not about to watch you walk into those shadows alone and never see you again."

She felt her mouth fall open slightly and then looked down at her pack. "I have a headlamp," she said, pulling it out of her pack and turning it on. "I will leave the pack here, there is food in it and stuff. Let me use your backpack to take my charcoal and sketchbook in and I will follow the map. I can't drag you into your death, Trevin. I can't do that," she said, "I will not."

"The ground is still earth. I will stand behind you, we walk in the middle and do not touch the walls. We stay together. If you get injured in there, I'm going to run in there anyway and then we are both screwed. So we may as well go together. The first sign that it is too much for either of us, we turn around. No discussion, no 'just five more steps.' We turn and come back here."

She glanced at him then down at the ground, and eventually to the entrance. She nodded. Then reached into her pack again. She pulled out a teal, black and white chevron print fabric and handed it to him. "Put this over your nose and mouth, it's like a bandana but better. It isn't going to keep everything out, but it will keep larger particles out. I used one when I thought I could trail run. I don't have anything for your eyes, unfortunately. Snow isn't exactly my favorite thing," she said.

He took the fabric, and slipped it over his head and around his neck. He pulled it up over his nose and nodded.

"I cleaned it, I clean it after every use." She put her headlamp on, shifting things around between the two packs so they could stash her bigger pack in between some rocks.

She looked nervously at the entrance, and then he walked up beside her and took her hand. "We do this together, El. I keep you safe, you keep me safe, right?"

She looked at their hands and nodded with a faint blush. "Guess neither of us is keeping our hands to ourselves," she said, and he laughed a little.

"Life is a whole lot better when we are friends, El," he said.

She gave him a nervous smile, and they walked into the dark void encased in iron.

Chapter 29

With each step, she could feel more tension, neither knowing what to expect. They could only see what her head lamp shined on, and use the flashlight on his phone for the map.

"Are these old railroad spikes? With rust?" she asked, not needing an answer. "What the hell?"

"I guess they didn't want anyone wandering in here, mortal or fae. Your tetanus shot isn't near due, right?"

"No, I got it a year ago, and they're good for a decade."

"That's a relief."

"Does tetanus affect you?"

"No, viruses and bacteria don't affect us. That's why we tend to track those animals that turn up with things like rabies. We can usually talk it down to capture it. We have a certain number we have to let go for population control, but generally Dad tries to heal them. Usually," he said.

"Oh. I guess that is a perk. Did you encounter rabies recently?" she asked. "If you are talking about it."

"That busted lip I had, mountain lion with something. We thought it was rabies, but something worse got it and we hope that the tome will have a record of something about it. It attacked Russ really badly, clawed up Q's chest and when I tried to pull it off Russ, it clawed my face. Lord Ashdale pulled it off me, but my dad lost it and snapped its neck. It was the first time I've ever seen my dad lose control like that. We were all pretty messed up that night. It was when you went to Trinidad. Autumn offered to check on you all, but I didn't want her or Caleb outside. I just asked her to text Charles, who said you were in your tent. I'm not sure my dad slept that night. We didn't do drills on Monday. Russ was still recovering."

"I'm sorry. I had no idea, and then I yelled at you at the café and you still looked out for me?" she asked, stunned.

"The thought of that mountain lion locking its eyes with you filled me with absolute dread. I was nervous I'd face something like it alone. Russ was high up in the tree keeping an eye out. He had just taken flight again that night. I thought it was too soon, but honestly, he recovered really fast. I'd probably have just carried you back to your car if something like had shown up. No other traces of whatever it is have come up, only the odd growth in Falk. We are worried the tome will be lost forever if we don't get it soon."

She smiled and gave his hand a small squeeze. "Thanks again for watching over me, Trev. Even if your dad hates me." With every ounce of warmth and longing, she also felt dread that he was forbidden. He felt like home, as though he was a part of what she was searching for. The ferns and the redwoods, and the magic in them, she felt it. Then she realized that he was. Trevin was the magic that had been calling to her and she could never have it. It was dangling in front of her. She couldn't hear the trees, but she remembered the danger that he was in, now and ongoing. She needed to wake up to help him, help them all.

"He is just cautious of you, and with everything changing so fast, he's nervous. We've never had a mortal discover us. I've never heard of a mortal coming to our side honestly. My dad has only ever experienced one mortal knowing about us, and he was younger than I am when it happened. Ever since then, he said he can't get over their void eyes. Mortals are so expressive and he hated it. He swore he'd take every precaution to not have to be in that position again."

"And I messed it all up. Your dad does love you, a lot. He is terrified of losing you. He is protective of you. He went papa bear over you—papa lion, I guess. Lord Ashdale is the papa bear," she said with a laugh.

"He was genuinely concerned with you doing this and not because you know, but because he doesn't want to see you hurt either."

"That's nice of him. I hope I can help you all," Elodie said. They continued to follow the path, not letting their guard down.

"You have helped us. You *are* helping us. He knows that and appreciates you—I appreciate you,"

They turned a corner and Elodie's foot hit something, causing her to stumble and fall forward. The light showed a spike shooting up from the floor just as Trevin wrapped an arm around her and pulled her back to him.

"I got you. I got you," he said, letting out a slow, shaky exhale. "I got you."

She felt the embrace from behind and took note of how strong he was, how quickly he reacted and how much that startled him.

"Thank you." She turned the headlight to face down at a 45-degree angle.

"Always, little mink," he said, noticing he was getting warm, as though the walls were closing in. "Not much further."

A few minutes later, they stopped. There were three dark openings facing them.

"What now? I don't remember seeing anything on the map like this."

"Because it's not. Nothing was in the book either that I had read through. It'd take too long to keep reading it here. There's so much in that book that it's overwhelming to try to decipher it all," he said.

"I thought the same thing when I picked it up. It's weird that it was made a year after the founding of the town. I could spend hours looking at that book."

"After this, you will have plenty of time to read it. I will make sure of it."

She glanced up, no slats. "Do we pick a random one? Splitting up isn't an option."

"No. it is not an option," he said, tightening his grip on her palm despite the sweat. He was starting to overheat, and he didn't know why.

"Okay." Her eyes searched for any foliage or ferns. As she turned around, she could see the walls that had roots sticking out of them. She wondered if she would get any signs or guidance in here. The trees had been quiet this trip. "I'm going to try something. It's probably going to be dumb but just, let me try. I don't know what else to do."

"What is it?" he asked. She turned, then reached for the wall. Trevin stepped toward her, giving her some more slack but not letting her hand go.

He watched her press her palm to the wall and her fingers intertwine with the roots. He could have sworn they wrapped around her fingers, but it must have been the light and shadows.

"Middle," Elodie said and gave the roots a small squeeze and then removed her hand. He cringed, seeing the iron shine from the dirt that fell. Clinging to her side, holding his breath, they entered the middle hall, trusting her instinct. A wall of spikes faced them. They turned to the left and could see the sun beaming down on a pillar.

"There," he said. Elodie looked at him for a moment, then walked to the pillar.

It read 'City of Falk, sub terrain.' Not a map, but a layout of the city buildings and listing for things underneath. She rubbed the dirt and dust away.

"It's just got some dirt on it, no rust even. It's amazing that it's in this good of condition," she beamed.

Trevin nodded. He didn't speak. He couldn't anymore. His eyes watched her, then scanned the entire chamber they were in. They were in a tomb and one's only option was to rot into dust and bones and become one with the earth all over again. He tried to slow his breathing. He couldn't leave her, but he had to get out of here. The burning in his lungs and eyes was becoming too much, and panic was setting in.

Elodie took a picture first and then got the rubbing. The image was surprisingly clear, she noted. Turning to him, she noticed his shoulders heaved up and down with each labored breath. He was starting to sway.

"Trevin."

"El. Go! Get out of here." he heaved out, then stumbled back against the wall and cried out. She could see him struggling to breathe as he fell forward on his hands and knees, gasping for breath.

Elodie knelt down next to him. "Trevin!" she whimpered. She put her hand on his head and pulled it away instantly. She looked at the ground and rubbed it away. "No. No! What is this place?" Elodie saw the iron on the ground, the walls, the ceiling. It was draining him! She gasped again, realizing if the iron cuff could kill him in a week, this much could be killing him right this second. "No! Hang on please. Please Trevin."

Familiar whispers graced Elodie's mind. The message clear. Save him.

Elodie tucked the map into her sketchbook, then shoved it in the backpack and her phone back into her pocket. She could retrace their steps. She had to get him out. They were going to keep each other safe. She would keep him safe.

Elodie knelt down in the dirt and slipped the backpack on him, then debated on how to best hoist him on her back. Her legs would hate her tomorrow and well into the week. All she had to do was get him out of here. She had dealt with sore legs before and a sore back, sore everything before, she could do it again, she would endure it again.

Pushing herself up, pressing her palms into the layer of dirt, she gasped again. A charge shot up her hands and into her body. She froze for a moment, feeling the energy surge, the power. Exhaling with no further comprehension of what or how, she grabbed his arm with both hands and rolled him onto her back. He was heavier than she realized, but she had this strength. Had the earth given this to her or was it adrenaline?

"Hold on Trev, stay with me. Greenthistle needs you." *Just get him out of here and don't trip.* She followed their steps in the dirt, retracing them and avoiding the spikes in the ground.

"Stay with me, Kitty Cat. Hold on. We're getting out of here," she said.

"You know, when we get out of this, you can laugh all you want at me. After Halloween, I did want to kiss you again. I did think about it, do think about it. I like kissing you and I know I shouldn't. I don't know what we are, Trevin, but I like you, a lot. I hope you do laugh in my face for this, so I know you are still with me," she said with labored breath.

"I hate the thought of you with any of them, because I know how pretty they are. They are literally out of a fairy tale and I'm not. I am hurt that you ran off Wednesday night to hook up with someone, but part of me is glad you ended up in your room, alone. There's my big confession about why I was being such a moody bitch all day. It hurts to know it will never be me. I find myself thinking about you a lot and I know I shouldn't." Elodie was not sure why she just confessed that to him, but talking kept her distracted as she retraced their steps out of the cave. She had to make it, she had to help him. These lands needed him far more than they'd need her.

She kept walking and saw bright light. *Okay. Closer. Closer.* Her knees were shaky and the deep breaths strained her lungs. Elodie knew how gross she was. He would be disgusted by the sweat coming off her. *At least he'd be alive to be disgusted.*

Finally, she took a deep inhale and that fresh air hit her with relief. Late afternoon low sun upon them. Her feet dragged with each step, causing her to stumble forward, dropping to her knees. A rock sliced her leg deep as she fell forward and cried out in pain.

Trevin started coughing, life slowly returning as he tried to take gulps of fresh air. The fire all over his body fizzled out, then her cries pulled him back to the present and his surroundings. He realized he was lying on top of her then quickly got up, taking the backpack off and kneeling beside her.

"Elodie!" he exclaimed, rolling her over. She was breathing hard, clearly exhausted. Tears ran down her cheeks and there were scuffs on her face. "El!" he said, hugging her tight. "Thank you!"

She had saved him again and strained herself to do so this time, too. Weakly, she hugged him back and sobbed, trying to wipe her eyes.

"That was worse than the iron cuff," she said, catching her breath. He laughed, glad he was finally able to.

"Thank you. Thank you," he repeated. He pressed his forehead to hers and noticed she was still crying. Her energy and emotions overflowed. "Shhh, what's wrong?" he asked. A whiff of iron and of blood hit his nose and examined her. "Let me tend to that, okay?" She nodded and took a deep inhale. "Rest. You deserve it, little mink."

His palms cupped her jaw, his thumb traced her cheek, wiping the tears away.

"Thank you, Elodie, I am forever grateful for you," he said. She looked at him. "Shhh, I'm here. Breathe, breathe. You are feeling a lot right now. I see all it crashing down on you. Do you want me to calm you or take the burden off? I can, I don't mind," he asked softly, still rubbing her cheeks.

"I'm fine," she whimpered.

He frowned. "El, you saved my life again. Let me help, please?"

"Just don't leave me here. Please! I don't want to be alone right now. The person from Wednesday is probably way hotter, and clean. Just don't go yet. Please?" she said, whimpering again. "I don't want to be alone up here."

Trevin felt his own heart hurt without even taking her emotions on. How badly he wanted to hold her and take all her pain away. He pressed a light, calming sensation into her.

"Never. I would never leave you up here. I'll never leave you, Elodie. I give you my word. Don't compare yourself to her. The tavern was a mistake. I was a disappointment that night, to her and to you. I don't care what she thinks of me, but I'm not going to be one to you anymore. You are so strong and I'm lucky as hell to be in your company," Trevin said, leaning over to kiss her forehead. "I'm going to take care of your injury, okay? It won't take long," he said softly. She nodded and sniffed. He laid her back down gently and got up heading towards her pack.

Once her found the first aid kit he sat down next to her. "You really did think of everything to bring. And we got the map because of you and your tenacity. This might sting, but we don't need to bring an infection back," he said, carefully wiping the blood away.

"You're okay. All done. Now the relief can come." His voice was calm as he wrapped his hand around her calf muscle and cupped his hand over the shin.

As he held her leg, he noticed the muscle tone. He thought about her body now. Then his eyes traced the contours of her leg to her hips that flared. How they had felt in his hands and under him. He thought about how small and petite Cassia was in his hands and how he had wanted to feel Elodie instead. How stamina and strength were apparent in Elodie, how lovely she was. He knew the strength river nymphs and fae had—Cassia was a deception. She looked tiny but could drag anyone, mortal and fae alike, to a watery grave. Elodie didn't need glamours, though. She was a mortal made of pure earth. Her body showed the weight her bones would carry. She was the girl who watched and processed her observations fairly. A decision she would carry out with strength and valor every time. Elodie was the perfect living organism in Humboldt. Already was the very essence of Nightswift, Ashdale, and Greenthistle and the lands knew this, could see it in her. She had no use for glamours. And through all her strength and determination, she had found him. Found all of them and the Old Giants loved her, had led them to be here now, and had graced her to him. He really was vowed to her? This beautiful, strong and brave person. He smiled at her with such endearment.

Trevin noticed she had fallen asleep. Smiling softly now, he assessed her leg, fully healed. He moved carefully and knelt by her.

"I'm not going to fight this anymore, Elodie. I can't. I want you," he said, softly kissing her forehead again. He sorted through her backpack, pulling out her tent and sleeping bag—not surprised they were a mix of her favorite colors. He had set up tents a few times for appearance's sake, but it had been awhile so he struggled at first to put together her teal and white tent. When he was finished, he put her goldenrod colored sleeping bag inside. He wondered what she'd look like at a Spring Equinox ball. A gown in these rich colors would be beautiful against her tan skin. She would stand out against everyone's soft greens, pinks and lilacs. She'd outshine everyone even if she did wear the dusty hues. He thought about her in a sapphire blue and white gown for the Winter Solstice at Greenthistle Estate. If she went as his lady, she'd get to wear a diadem and be radiant. Hints of bronze to reflect the bit of sunlight the shortest day of the year would bring, then carry them into the longest night. He smiled at the thought, knowing he'd end up with this fantasy in his dreams.

"Oh Elodie. How did we find ourselves wrapped up in this trope of forbidden lovers?" His eyes rested on her. He felt a small tug on some strand deep inside him and though he had never felt this before, Trevin knew what that was.

Chapter 30

As Elodie slept, she could hear someone call her name. She turned to see Trevin smiling at her as he took her hand. "My little mink," he said softly, "I will never leave you," he said. A warm happy feeling came over her. She realized they were in her car overlooking the ocean, laying on the sleeper in her hatch. "I'm going to get dinner going for us."

"Okay, but I just bought snacks."

He laughed softly and rubbed her head. "I told you I planned on cooking for us."

"You don't have to, though."

Trevin laughed again and climbed out of the hatch. Elodie glanced at her sketchbook. "I must have fallen asleep," she said, feeling groggy. She opened to the last thing drawn and saw a loose paper with a rubbing of a map of the town of Falk. Confused, she got out of the car and froze. She met the green eyes of a mountain lion—a dead rabbit in its mouth, another dead one at its paws. It dropped it and she saw the blood on the mountain lion's teeth. Her eyes went wide as the mountain lion chuffed and nudged the rabbits toward her. She took a step back and tripped over something, falling backward.

Her body jerked with a gasp as she opened her eyes, and it took a few moments to realize it was a dream. It was nearly dusk and there was a fire going. Something was being chopped and her eyes darted around. Her head was on a bundled-up hoodie on the ground where she lay. She pushed herself up, still groggy and sore, and a groan escaped her.

"Take it easy," Trevin said as he wiped blood from his dagger. She trembled and scooted back. "El. You are okay. You are safe."

She looked at him and then at the food, then cringed. "Is that rabbit?"

"Yes, you know your small game."

"That you caught with your teeth?" she asked nervously. He laughed gently.

"Not these teeth. They were slightly longer and sharper. You're not vegetarian, are you?" he asked, confused.

"No. I just, getting a rabbit dropped at my feet by a mountain lion isn't a common occurrence in my life. Wasn't a common occurrence."

Another soft laugh escaped him. "I'm not exactly dropping it at your feet. It will be cooked." He wrapped something in foil and then tossed it into the fire. He placed flatter rocks on top. She nodded, then noticed her tent with a light on in it, her LED lantern sitting next to it.

"You set the tent up?"

"It took me a minute, but I do know how to camp a little, mostly about how to cook on a campfire. Dad has a rather fancy palette, so he taught us all how to catch small game and cook it. I brought spices and dinner stuff. I do apologize for not realizing how useful all that stuff is. You're amazing."

She blushed. She started to get up, and he set his knife down.

"Easy. Don't overdo it. Your leg is healed, but let me know if it hurts. I'm not exactly an expert at that yet."

"Thank you, Trevin. I'm sorry for being emotional earlier. I don't know what came over me."

"Me acting like a dumbass," he said with a grin, and she nodded bashfully. "We are going to be alright, El."

"I'm thirsty, and I need to freshen up. I feel gross," she said with a small exhale.

He nodded. "You aren't, but your pack is just outside the tent. I think there's some good human bathroom spots around those rocks," he said.

She cringed. "Do you just go in feral form?"

He smirked. "Cats are going to cat. I did freshen up some too, including cleaning the blood off my muzzle and fur and rinsing my mouth out in human form."

"Riiight," she said, somewhat uneasily. "Things I never thought about."

Elodie took her boots and socks off, and put her sandals on, then walked behind the rocks. After she took care of relieving herself and freshening up, she stood up and peered out at the land, and noticed how still everything appeared. The fog was coming in over the ocean and soon it would surround the peak they camped on. When she crawled into the tent, she changed into spandex shorts under her sweats and a T-shirt under and hoodie. As she packed the dirty clothes away, she noticed her phone charging on the power brick with no signal and thought about how much had happened today. How much Cora was going to want to know, and could never know. Elodie grabbed her pencil pouch and water bottle, then returned to the fire.

Trevin smiled at her. "You look more awake. Dinner should be ready just after sunset," he said with a smile, cleaning off his knife. She noticed all the food scraps were disposed of, too.

He sat down next to her as they both watched the golden hour sun over the ocean. Elodie noticed he was sitting close.

"I cannot thank you enough. El. Iron really sucks. I think I've encountered enough for a lifetime."

She frowned and brought her knees to her chest. "I hate seeing you like that. I don't know what happened, but the Old Giant's told me to save you. They told me I had the strength and somehow, I found it. I put my palms on the ground to push back up and a surge of energy came over me, then I just pulled you on my back."

He leaned against her. "You are lovely. I think the Old Giants chose you to be here because you already are the essence of all three estates."

"I should have listened. They said you were in danger earlier and you were. I feel bad I didn't tell you because talking to trees and trees talking to me makes me sound crazy. I sounded crazy all day. I got overwhelmed with all those emotions you told me not to bottle up, and I felt gross and I just didn't want to be alone," she said, rubbing her eyes.

He wrapped his arm around her. "You are beautiful, Elodie. Your body is made of earth itself, strong and sturdy. You don't need glamours like they do on the other side of the boundary. Deceptions or disguises are meaningless to you because you know your strength and wear it proudly, like a goddess," he said, giving her a hug.

She wiped her eyes and sighed. "You don't have to say those things, Trev."

"They are all true. I figure I should confess something to you since you made some confessions to me back there." Her shoulders slumped. "I think about you a lot too, and not just because of your energy. Your kisses spark something in me and I can't explain them. I hate pulling away from them, hated pulling away Wednesday night. I don't know why I did. I got overwhelmed too, that it would get out of hand and I don't want to scare you. The feeling is new to me."

She could feel her cheeks heat. "You heard all that? And you think of me often? You wanted it to go further?"

"Yes. I do think about you often, in a few different ways." He grinned at her.

She took in his features then looked down, blushing. "Oh," she said nervously.

He chuckled and gave her a small kiss on her cheek. She smiled, placing her hand on his leg.

"My body was locked up in there. I think the deeper we got, the more dust got through the cloth. Then it got in my lungs and once I backed up it burned, and then the floor was covered in iron. I've never been so scared. I couldn't move, couldn't do anything but burn and scream in my head. I wanted you to run. To go, to stick to our plan. Then I felt weightless and I could hear you talking. I wanted to laugh, cry, hug, and kiss you but I couldn't. I hated every second."

"Seeing you unresponsive is terrifying. All that went through my head was to help you. You make Humboldt feel like home as much as these Old Giants do. Something new sparks in me when we kiss."

"What a wild day it's been, little mink," he said. She smiled. "I'm glad it was you who found me. I'm so glad the trees called you back here. When was the last time you visited up here?"

"Probably two years ago. Some friends and I drove up. We left way too late on Thursday and got to our campsite late. But it was a fun trip, Avenue hikes, and stuff along the Eel River. That absolute dread came on Sunday when we drove South on Avenue of the Giants because I was leaving."

"You came back though. You are building a life for yourself here."

She was content as they watched the sun make its final descent.

"We are in a bubble up here and the air is hauntingly still up here. The world is turning out there but in here, it feels as though time forgot about this place. That iron maze is proof of that. When my dad and I were looking at this map, he realized it was in a patch of fae realm and it wasn't Greenthistle's or Ashdale's. Some territories have a lot of splotches like this. Marin being one of them. Humboldt only has a few patches and I think my dad had forgotten about this one. I'd never run to it. It's odd how much of the fae history we are missing surrounding Falk and all its relics. Dad isn't sure why."

"And yet, these stones and trees may be the only things that know. Maybe the trees are silent because they can't speak of the history. I wonder if I went to Falk if they would be quiet?" she asked, watching the deep red of the sun.

"I wonder if Falk is going to have a lot of iron too," Trevin said, glancing at the water.

"I can go with you if you need my hands."

He smiled at her. "I think I will be okay, it's not exactly a well-preserved ghost town. There are remains of buildings and a water tower, but we don't want to disrupt anything there. It wasn't even a high priority until the earthquake hit in October. Another building gave way and my dad said we had to move it up before the overgrowth reclaimed everything. Nightswift ravens reported the surge in the overgrowth."

"Were fae always hidden from mortals? Is it like that everywhere?"

"I've heard talk of some territories where they both live in harmony but it's all far away. Not anywhere in the western region. There is an annual council meeting, where all the Northern California territories meet. The high estates gather and address concerns. We just had it at the end of September. Our dads go, as well as the heirs. It's usually over in Sutter or Yuba County, central but with fewer people than Sacramento. Sacramento always has a ton of stuff to report because it's the state capital. Marin, and San Francisco too, just more people. Mendo, Del Norte, and us are usually pretty quiet. None of the counties co mingle with mortals though. They report on their mortal discoveries as we call them and they state what they did with them. Even the neighboring territories with Oregon keep the boundaries hidden. Dad said it's been separate for as long as he can remember too."

"I take it Humboldt has something to report now?"

"Admittedly I have not wanted to really think about it. When you got that cuff off me and I realized the weight of the situation I knew I had to be very careful with my words so as not to sway you, to keep it as much your choice as possible. I wanted to get inside before a scout saw us. I knew how scared you were and felt like if I told you I was your overseer it would make it worse. So I made that bargain with you as a means to explain what was needed in order to let you remain safe.

If anyone seizes you or puts you in the hold they interfere with our bargain and they break it, not you. It gives you an extra play. Since it is our bargain, I have to remain by your side as your overseer. Once you agreed it remained a Greenthistle issue and not one that needed to be escalated. I declared myself as your overseer to my family when I got home. Anything regarding you, now has to go through me. It has to be reported to them though. Your overseer will ensure the bargain is upheld."

"That was a lot to process after being tranquilized."

Trevin smirked. "I never want to see you ripped from this place, or your life here. Another reason I was quick to bind myself as your overseer. I wanted to be the one to keep an eye on you. I know you are good, I trust you. I know you will not out any of us, so that wasn't my concern. What worries me is this power in you. It's clearly tied to our Old Giants. I'm worried if I saw it, if we can all feel it, others will too and they might try to pull you away. I don't want that to happen. If you wanted to leave, I'm not sure what would happen either, and I don't think my dad knows either."

"So, I guess I have to stay in Humboldt then?" she asked curiously. She met Trevin's pensive eyes.

"El, I'm not supposed to sway you in any direction. We are never supposed to. I can't stop you—I won't stop you from doing what you want. I will never chain you up and lock you here, but with everything that's happened, I'm worried what might be yet to come. I'm worried even if you do want to stay here with the Old Giant's others might sense you and try to steal you for their own."

"Like ripping a redwood out of the earth?"

Elodie tensed when those voices hit her. Again they told her she was home.

"You okay?" he asked. She nodded. "I think it might be exactly like that. They clearly wanted you for something, and I want so desperately to know why. It's as though someone dumped a puzzle out over Humboldt. I can't put it together quickly enough to figure out what's going on. It's far more than just getting an artifact or a tome out of the ground. It is much bigger than that, it's our home. One of our own residents seems to be trapped in the puzzle too." He wrapped his arm around her tighter.

"They tell me there's something here too, they tell me to wake up. Let him see, he will see, they all will, they will need you," she said, meeting his eyes.

"Me? They tell you about me? That I will see you?"

"They do, they have," she said, keeping the rest of what they said to herself, about the bond that cannot be undone. Elodie worried he might think she was lying about everything.

Trevin smirked and kissed her head. "I did see you—I do see you. I just hate that I don't know what else I see aside from a beautiful, brilliant, strong, and kind person with a big heart. Who wants to protect my home too because I think, or maybe I hope it's her home now too."

She smiled and wrapped her arms around him. "I think I might be home—I think I want this to be home," she said, laughing. "Justine would think I'm stupid."

Trevin laughed too. "The heart wants what it wants," he said. He felt her nod against his chest and they watched the sun vanish behind the horizon. "I'm going to get dinner. I hope you don't mind if I grabbed your dish ware in your pack. Seriously, you brought everything."

Chapter 31

As they ate, Elodie was amazed at how good it all tasted. She could picture his dad eating this with a glass of wine, while camping. Somehow looking so high and mighty, and not dirty. Then again Trevin didn't look all that dirty either. They talked about their lives growing up and she drew him, the tent, a mountain lion, the Old Giants, the ferns and redrew the map of Falk. Eventually they cleaned up, and she crawled in the tent, grateful she had brought her bigger sleeping bag. After she took off her sweats, and hoodie she got cozy in the sleeping bag and tried to make herself small.

Despite freshening up as best as she could, she still felt the dire need for a shower. Oakmoss and amber still flooded her senses much to her surprise. It seemed to be the only thing she ever smelled on him, but she had never noticed it on his friends or siblings. His hair was only slightly messier, and his clothes were hardly dirty all things considered. Trevin certainly didn't look as though he trekked 2600 feet up a mountain.

"I hope you sleep well, little mink," he said, sitting back on his haunches in front of the tent.

"Trev, do you think it's safe here tonight? No fae will come?"

"I strongly doubt it. We are so close to that iron death trap it'd be foolish. You are safe, I will keep you safe."

"Thank you," she said softly and glanced down; she couldn't believe she was about to ask this. That she wanted to do this, especially given the state she was in.

"Any time, El." Trevin smiled, turning to leave her.

"Trev, can you, will you sleep in the tent with me? I don't want to be alone. I don't want you alone out there," she blurted out, feeling her cheeks heat.

He gave her a knowing look. "Of course, El. Let me put some stuff away and smother the fire."

She nodded, letting out a deep exhale. A few minutes later, Trevin crawled inside and removed his boots. He took his hoodie and his pants off, and bunched the hoodie up for a pillow, then crawled in next to her.

She took a steady inhale and tensed when she felt him press his body into her back. He slid an arm under her and the other over her waist. She let out a steady exhale.

"Is this too much? I can keep some distance between us," he said softly. His voice swirled in her ears. His scent enveloped her.

"It's okay."

"You can tell me if it's not. I said I wasn't going to hurt you, nor would I force myself on you. I will never do that."

"I suppose your words hold more truth than a fuckboy's?" she said with a playful tone. He nuzzled into her and laughed. A warmth swelled in her.

"I'd suppose so too."

"Guess I don't have to keep my hands to myself, since you didn't?" she said, pushing back into him and putting her arm over his to keep him where he was. He smiled then kissed her neck and rubbed her stomach. Her breathing hitched.

"I didn't want to keep my hands to myself. I was hoping you wouldn't either," he said, giving her ear a light tug with his teeth. She shifted and arched her back, feeling him as he let out a throaty moan.

"No running away this time, right?" she said. He let out a slow exhale and slid his hand under her shirt. His other hand was near her navel.

"No. No running away. I moaned your name out on Wednesday in my room. You were who I knew I wanted all night."

"I moaned yours too." Another hitched breath from her as his hand slid up her shirt, feeling her chest.

"Elodie," he moaned heavily in her ear. He slid his fingers just under the band of her spandex shorts. "I've said your name every time for a while now." She moaned as his fingers inched down further.

"Trevin," she moaned, pushing back against him, rubbing herself against him.

"I've imagined you moaning my name just like that, Elodie."

His fingers found her apex, and he moaned deeper. Another moan filled the tent as she writhed, pressing into him more. He licked her ear, and she trembled. "I moan it often because I can't get you out of my head. I don't want you out of my head. Or out of my grip."

"Trevin," she moaned again.

"I like hearing you say my name, hearing you moan it."

She rubbed against him, arching her back. "Trevin."

"I will not take you here. I will do it in a proper bed, where I can have my way with you. Spread wide for me." His sultry voice was heavy in her ear. "The things I want to do to you, Elodie."

She let out a whimper and trembled. Her panting filled the tent and he gave her ear a gentle tug again.

"Trevin," she panted out then turned around to see his eyes filled with lust. Moments later, her lips were pressing against his neck. "Then will you let me return the favor?" she asked softly, kissing up to his lips.

He smiled. "Is that an order?" he said, kissing her and nibbling on her bottom lip.

"Yes, Trevin." Her moaning turned into a laugh.

"Of course, Lady Elodie," he said.

Her hand reached down and gripped him, and she started to stroke and kiss him. Her other hand braced his head and she ran her fingers along his ear.

Trevin kissed her neck. "Elodie," he moaned as she stroked him.

She felt her eyes go heavy when he kissed her neck. The size of him, the firmness. Even just being wrapped in his arms felt as though she was falling deeper and deeper for him. She had found him breathtaking from the first moment they locked eyes.

"Elodie," he moaned out. "This feels so good," he said, moving back to kissing her hard. She breathed heavily and stroked him faster. Her fingers ran through his hair and tugged, feeling him tense before his release spilled against her hand and between them. He held her gaze, breathing hard. "Fuck," he said, panting and then kissed her. "It's been awhile, and that felt amazing," he said. She pulled her hand out.

"There's tissue in the front of the pack," she said heavily. "Sorry it got a little messy, we didn't keep our hands to ourselves."

"No, we didn't and I'm not at all upset about it," he said, grabbing the tissue out and cleaning them up.

"You really haven't been with anyone in a while?" she asked.

"No. Didn't want to, didn't care too. After the last mortal cheated on me and the last fae said I wasn't worth it, I tried a mindless hook up, like Caleb and Russ do. I just didn't like it. Not that I needed a huge commitment, but the same conversations every time, just to get some seemed dumb. As more and more fae would try to flirt, my title always got thrown in there and I knew they cared more for it than me. Mortals could never know the title but I didn't want to get cheated on again so, I gave up on both. Five years ago," he said.

"It has been a bit for me too. I stopped doing anything with Ricky a few months before I moved up here. I didn't trust him, I don't trust him obviously, getting cheated on sucks. I really wasn't looking when I moved up here, but when I saw you, I was speechless. For a split-second I wondered if you were going to kiss me in front of the fireplace. I thought I'd be in a fantasy romance. Then I realized those situations don't happen in real life. But I did meet a fae prince that night."

He laughed and nuzzled into her. "You have been on my mind so much since that party. When I woke up after that iron cuff was off me and saw you, I thought I was dreaming again. Everything came back to me and I realized you brought me back. You found me. I was in a fantasy romance too." He laughed.

They lay there talking softly about things until sleep quickly engulfed them both, the exhaustion of the whole day finally settling in.

Trevin awoke first to the scent of ocean breeze and lavender. He nuzzled into her and she roused. She gripped his hand and gave it a squeeze. "Morning, little mink."

"I'm not dreaming, right?"

"No. We are here, on top of the world, hidden away from everything."

"Away from reality. Above the clouds."

"Above that fog at least," he said.

"What time is it? Going down is usually quicker than going up," she asked. He rolled over and checked. "It's 7:30. We both passed out pretty early last night."

"I was exhausted."

"You carried everything on your back yesterday, including me. I'm carrying the pack down to the car. I will get a small fire started and grab us some breakfast, rabbit okay again or shall I try to find a raccoon? Deer might be too much food? I could eat it though."

"Rabbit will do. The least environmental impact."

"So conscious of the lands you are." He laughed still holding onto her.

"I know it's the natural order, mountain lions need to eat too but I do feel bad." Elodie turned and he saw the dreamy look in her eyes as she took in his features. He was seeing the desire, attraction and so much happiness in her expression. A relief from yesterday. She was happy and so was he.

Trevin laughed. "And you are beautiful, El," he said, kissing her. He rolled her on her back and straddled her. "My little mink," he murmured, kissing her. *Not here.* He smiled at her and then got off her. She let out a sigh of defeat. "I'm going to get a fire going."

Elodie nodded as he slipped out of the sleeping bag and tuck her back in. Awkwardly he slipped on his pants and grabbed his boots. He gazed at her longingly, then opened the tent, where Elodie saw the sun under the fog. Once she had her hoodie on, she crawled to the edge of the tent and took it in the view. She could hear the waves below and smell the sea salt in the air, it was mixed with oakmoss and amber.

Home. This is home. How could I ever leave this place, leave him? she thought.

Embrace this.
Never let it go.
You are home.

A warm embrace of the air hit her and she smiled.

"Did they speak to you again?" he asked as their eyes met. She nodded and repeated their words. "I'm glad you chose Humboldt, El." She watched him stand up. "I'm going to change, okay." She nodded still fixed on him. He turned and in the blink of an eye he was a mountain lion. Her smile grew wide.

"Trevin," she said. He let out a chuff and took off down the mountain.

Elodie changed quickly and freshened up before preparing instant coffee. When she was nearly finished packing the tent up the sound of soft footsteps made her freeze. She spun around locked eyes with a mountain lion. Striking green eyes met hers, a rabbit lifeless in its mouth. It let out another chuff and she smiled. He padded over to the cutting mat and set the rabbit down gently.

"I'm going to clean my muzzle, it's not pretty when I'm back in fae form. I look a bit wild," he said and she could hear him in her head. She nodded.

"I made you some coffee. Nothing like Cora's but it works for camping. There's creamer. I have English muffins and butter too." He chuffed again.

"So prepared. I will research how to backpack, and hopefully I can go next time Cora arranges something."

"I'd like that, Trev. Would we share a tent again?" she asked, watching him lick his paws and rub his muzzle.

"If you ordered me to, I guess I'd have to oblige," he said with a smirk. She laughed.

"I will never abuse that power, I promise you, Trevin," she said.

"I trust you, El. I wouldn't mind if you ordered me to share a tent with you though, because I'd very much like to share one with you again."

She felt her cheeks flush, and laughed. After his muzzle was clean, he changed back to fae form, and grabbed some things out of his backpack including a small vial. He added a few drops to his coffee before taking a sip.

"What's that?" she asked as he put the vile back into his backpack and pulled out some eggs.

"Stress relief tonic. I take it every morning to make it efficient."

"Oh. You get that stressed out?" she asked, confused. "I'm sorry I certainly didn't help yesterday, did I?"

"This is to prevent a certain type of stress from forming, Autumn has her own blend and Caleb has the same as me. He definitely needs to take it. Dad makes us," he said with a coy smile as he took another sip then got to prepping the food.

Elodie thought for a moment, processing the information he had volunteered. Then wondered about its actual intended use as she finished packing everything back up. She sketched the cave entrance and the campfire while he cooked. After they ate, cleaned, and packed the last of the stuff up, Trevin threw the pack on and nodded at her. She put his backpack on and they descended through the boundary line and down the mountain.

The hike back down went so much quicker. They made it back to the car, and after the slow drive on the dirt road, Elodie let out a sigh of relief once they hit 101 North.

As they told more stories from their lives, Elodie had a nagging fear that this fairy tale would end. That he would vanish now that he didn't need her help. Her self-doubt was creeping in even after everything he had said.

Is crossing this line worth it? she asked herself. The Old Giants were once again silent. *Embrace it. Home,* she reminded herself.

Chapter 32

Elodie pulled the car into the covered parking area and grabbed her gear out. He helped her unload and walked in with her, eyeing her often.

I want her so bad. I shouldn't do this but I don't want to fight this anymore.

"I think that's the last of it. I closed the hatch and the doors," he said and beeped her car. Her eyes traveled up his body now that he had dropped the glamour.

They both looked up when they heard it start to rain.

"If you are not sick of me, you can stay," she said. "I just need a shower. I'm disgusting," she added.

He nodded, not taking his eyes off her. "You are not disgusting El, but I probably could use one too, after you of course," he said. She nodded. "I will order something, my treat. Go on and take a shower, get comfy," he said.

"Do you have a change of clothes?"

"I do. I might have left some in your car, just in case something came up," he said. She blushed.

Trevin ordered food, and then sat down at the table and started to unpack and clean off some of the gear. When he pulled out her sketchbook, he flipped to the drawings of the rubbings she had done. She had redrawn it in her sketch book and it was nearly identical to the rubbing. He snapped a picture of them both just in case one got damaged. His eyes roved to the next page she had drawn, and he smirked at the drawing of him in his fae form. Just generic to look like anyone but the markings were undeniably his. Then he flipped back to the front of the book. Drawings before they met, of her car, a small town with the sign for the town of Mendocino, and a café window. He continued to browse, seeing more sketches of places in Eureka, Arcata, the café, the bagel shop. She had drawn Cora, Charles, and Justine. Then he saw a drawing of what could have been him with round ears. He smiled.

Sketches of a mountain lion looking mean, and the words 'one good thing,' on the next page. Lots of sketches of the Old Giants. She had written it—she had written the word 'home?'. She had little notes and things too. She wrote 'El' in frilly little letters 'Maybe it's time you let someone call you that again?' written next to it.

He had never asked her why she held that name in such high regard and he wasn't sure he should ask her in case it upset her. As he flipped through more pages, he noticed a lot of raven sketches. She usually drew what she saw, but there hadn't been many around when he was. Usually he was always aware of any Nightswift ravens present. His eyes went to the little mink she drew with the flower crown. He closed it and set it on the coffee table. He sighed.

"Elodie. My vowed?" he said to himself softly. "I would give you everything I could, if I knew you'd stay." Glancing at the window in the living room he could hardly make out the outline of the trees. "I hope she really is home here."

He heard the water stop, and he took an inhale, not sure what she would be wearing when she walked out. A few minutes later, she stepped out of the bathroom in thin pants and a fitted camisole. It was clear she was not wearing a bra. He took a long slow inhale and tried to not stare too hard.

She held a towel out for him. He stood up from the couch and walked to meet her, taking the towel.

"Here, you can just leave it in there when you are done. Feel free to use anything you need," she said, feeling her heart rate increase.

He smiled and glanced down then back up. She too took a deep inhale. "Thanks, food is on its way. Feel free to start when it gets here."

She nodded and her eyes followed him into the bathroom. The door shut and she let out an exhale.

With another deep breath, she sat on the couch and saw her sketchbook, then started to draw. As she sketched, she thought about him, how he felt. She had felt him, his abs, chest, and other parts, but she had not seen him in the darkness of the tent

Elodie sighed again, thinking about his body and had to cool down. The food arrived, and she welcomed the rush of cold air and rain.

"Calm down. He will probably leave after he eats," she said quietly. A few minutes later, the bathroom door opened, and he walked out in a black T-shirt and athletic shorts, much like she had seen him wearing at the estate. The shorts had the Greenthistle crest on them. Her eyes traveled back up to his. "Do you all have a family crest on your clothes?"

"On some things. Personal tailors and all." He smirked. They ate on her couch and watched TV, but her mind was wandering.

Elodie was getting nervous and the food was getting harder to eat. She set hers down and took a deep inhale. She went to adjust and groaned. The aftermath of the trek, and while she had stretched when they got back to the car, she hadn't when they got home.

"What's wrong?" he asked with concern.

"Soreness is setting in. I suppose fae don't deal with that? I did stretch, just not enough apparently," she said, and he nodded slowly.

"We get sore, but it takes more. Honestly, sometimes on Monday nights I'm exhausted and I soak for a long time in the spa. If Lord Nightswift is doing drills, we change between feral and human so many times and it wears us down. It's conditioning though," he said, setting his food down.

After some awkwardness, she cleaned up and then headed to the bathroom and brushed her teeth then glanced in the mirror.

Are you going to do this, with him, a fae, and estate heir? Greenthistle's heir? she asked herself. *Maybe he doesn't want to, maybe he will head home now. It'd really be best if he did.* She walked out of the bathroom and he stood up.

"If you'd like, I can help relieve the soreness," he said, looking at her. Her eyes widened.

"Like a massage?" she asked, feeling her cheeks heat.

"I can do that or I can use some healing magic again. Though I'm still learning it all, I haven't been practicing as long as my dad. Or I can do a combination. A healing touch massage if you will," he laughed.

Elodie nervously inhaled, realizing his hands would be on her body again, only they wouldn't be in a tent this time, they would be on a bed. "Okay, how should I lay or sit?" she asked.

"Depends on which one you want. If you want quick healing, then I'd need to brace your head like this," he said, reaching his hands to the back of her head. She met his eyes and noticed how vulnerable a position this had her in. While she knew she could trust him, it still didn't feel comfortable for her.

"Umm, not this, maybe a healing massage?" she asked. He smiled and nodded.

"On your stomach then. I assume your legs are sore?" he asked. She nodded.

"And my abs, and back," she laughed.

"I had better get to work and make you feel better, since I dragged you on that trek. Then you dragged me out of it," he said with a smile. "It is the least I can do."

She nodded and laid down. Trevin pressed his thumbs into the soles of her feet and massaged. Her tenseness faded with the soothing touch of his magic as he applied just the right amount of pressure. She could feel that thing in her humming. Her eyelids were heavy. He moved to her calf muscles and Elodie's breathing was getting heavier and slower.

"If I'm pressing too hard, let me know," he said softly. She nodded.

"It's perfect. Thank you." Her voice was evident of how good it felt. "You do drills on Mondays? Like boot camp type stuff?" she asked.

"Every Monday one of the high estate lords will lead Russ, Q, and I through a bunch of physical exercises. Six Rivers, Lost Coast, Redwoods NP, Humboldt redwoods, all over the county. We do mental problem solving and come up with a strategy before we can run a course. We always have to work together and rely on each other. I'm usually pretty tired Monday nights, they run us hard, so I just want to eat and sleep." Trevin explained his weekly schedule, which was a combination of State Parks work and being in the office with his dad. He moved to massage her thighs. "Is this okay?" he asked. She nodded.

"The mountain lion, the bear and the raven all have to rely on each other?" she asked.

"Yea. Nightswift watches and observes, Ashdale is loyal and fair, and Greenthistle is strength and valor. We always practice them though," he said. She tensed when he straddled her legs and started working on her lower back. "This okay? Not too much?" he asked.

"No, it's fine, just wasn't expecting it. You can keep going, if you'd like," she said in a relaxed voice.

"I would like to, El," he said. "That energy in you seems to like the magic of a fae."

"I think maybe I like the magic of a fae too." The words slipped out before she could think about what she was about to say. She gasped and heard him chuckle. As he leaned forward, she felt him press against her as he massaged her shoulders.

"I am happy to help you, you helped me, you helped Greenthistle, and Humboldt. Thank you."

"I wasn't going to leave you in there. I hate seeing you like that."

"Nice to know someone's watching out for me."

"It's only fair I suppose."

"Yeah," he agreed, climbing off her. "On your back," he said. She nodded and rolled onto her back, realizing she wasn't at all sore.

"I don't feel sore at all, thank you, Trev," she said, smiling.

"Anytime." His eyes trailing down her body then back up to met her eyes. He laid next to her and they stared at each other for a moment. He took a deep breath. "If you say stop, I will."

She looked at his lips for a moment then met his eyes. "I don't want you to stop. I never did."

"I knew that and knew how stupid I was. I didn't want to stop either. So I won't, ever again." He leaned in and kissed her. She pressed back into him and he ran his fingers through her hair. He climbed on top of her and a gasp slipped out of her as he kissed her neck and up to her ears.

"Trevin," she moaned.

"Elodie," he whimpered, rocking into her. He pulled her tank top off and eyed her topless. Only a few thin layers of fabric remained between them now. "Fuck," he whispered, then began to grope and lick her chest, her moans followed soon after.

He was so good with his touch. Every time he touched her it sent a current through her. She ran her finger along his ear to the point. He shivered and moaned.

One hand slid down to her rear, and he squeezed. Then he moved both hands to untie her pants. She inhaled nervously and he stopped. "Too much?" he asked.

"No, I just, I'm too soft. I don't look like the girls you could have."

"I don't want to think about any of them right now. Only you, you are perfect. You are a goddess, El. Your curves, the softness and the perfect transition of tone. Stamina, perseverance, strength, written into your skin," he said, kissing her on the lips passionately. He pressed himself against her and she could feel him. She moaned, and he rocked against her again.

"I have an IUD. What? How does it work for fae?"

"That stress relief tonic you asked me about this morning, it's fae birth control for males. Autumn's got her own mix designed for females. Pretty sure Dad would kill me if I made an heir right now, half or high fae."

"Oh," she said. Her eyes roved over him taking in his fae form with the markings. She ran her finger lightly along his cheekbone and he let out a soft moan.

"No one has ever done that before. That felt good," he whispered. She did it once more, and he moaned again. He sat back and took his shirt, off revealing the markings across his chest and outlining his ribcage. Her eyes widened. Then her hands were touching his body, tracing the markings. His eyelids were heavy, and he moaned. "Elodie."

Her eyes traveled down his body, the smooth skin over the muscle and tendons that made him what he was. He was fae, and he was on top of her, he wanted her. She wouldn't just ride the fairy tale out, she would seize it. He didn't care much for mortals but he cared for her and she did not doubt that. Her eyes traveled down to the top of his shorts and she pulled him out and started to stroke.

She fixed on his face that was engulfed in pleasure. "Yes," he moaned.

"Trevin, I want you," she said.

Trevin leaned over her and kissed her hard. "And I want you, Elodie, more than anything," he murmured.

At that moment something in Elodie went taut. She felt him kiss down her breast, soft and sensual. His tongue traced her stomach and his hands hastily tugged down her pants.

What is this feeling? Elodie asked herself. She had been in this exact position before, and a few guys even told her similar things. Yet never had she experienced this tug, this tether form before. Something told her she would never be out of his sight. He would always watch over her even if his dad told him not to. Had she bound him to her, actually bound him? What if he didn't want it after the heat of the moment?

When she realized he had slid down between her legs, she lifted her head as he eyed her apex, his coy smile formed.

"El?" he asked. She nodded with a nervous inhale. She flung her head back and writhed as he started to lick her.

"Trevin," she moaned. She ran her fingers through his hair and along his ears. He moaned as her hips writhed under him. "Trevin," Elodie moaned again, feeling him, his strong grip on her hips, his tongue pleasuring her. She tugged his hair, causing him to moan.

"Trevin. I'm close," she panted out.

He stopped for a moment and listened to her breathing. Then he went back to licking her, feeling her fingers in his hair. She trembled then moaned louder, and he kept going, not letting her go. His strong grip held her down as she orgasmed.

"Trevin," she moaned again, panting hard. "Trevin. Please. St-stop," she panted out, trying to catch her breath, her pelvis convulsing. He stopped and gave her one last lick causing her to tremble then pulled away. "Trev," she moaned again, meeting his lust filled eyes.

He shifted up to his knees and he met his eyes.

"Are you ready?" he asked. She let out an exhale and nodded.

"Yes, I'm ready."

A smile graced his lips as he brought his knees to her thighs and spread her wider. He leaned forward and put his hands on either side of her.

"You are beautiful, El." His eyes locked with hers and he eased into her. He pulled back and pushed back in, and she felt everything. "Elodie," he moaned and thrusted again, and started kissing her neck. His arms wrapped around her, pressing her into him.

When she gazed into his eyes and felt him, Elodie saw so much emotion in him. The way he embraced her now as if he needed her, could not let her go. And something in her, deep in her core felt the same. It was the forest, this place she had been missing. This connection to him was what she needed. It could not be wrong. She wrapped her arms around him just as tight. With his lips on her neck, she laughed a dazed intoxicated laugh.

"What have you found so amusing, little mink?" he asked.

"The first night we spoke, you said you could see that I wanted to kiss down your neck."

He laughed and ran his tongue along her jaw and up to her ear. She moaned again. "How does it feel to have a breathtaking fae kiss down your neck, on top of you?" he asked in a seductive tone.

She wrapped her legs around him and ran her fingers through his hair. "More amazing than I ever dreamed," she answered before kissing his neck.

Trevin let out a soft moan. She rolled him over and pushed herself up, and started to ride him. He watched her face as he touched her chest.

"Elodie. He sat up and hugged her tightly, and she raked her fingers through his hair.

"Trevin." A moan as she sank down on top of him again. She traced his ear with her fingers and knew he'd stay in her mind and heart forever. As though everything had led them to this moment, Elodie thought about how lucky she was to have felt the pull of the Old Giants. To have been able to help him and have this bond with him. She knew magic existed because of him. This place had become her home. He felt like home. The ferns and redwoods, and the soil that she felt flowed through her. She would savor every second she had, because for as right as this felt, time would never be on their side. Time would always be that finite resource she could never have a surplus of. She knew he could be robbed of it one day and she had been brought here to help him and the high estates from ever being robbed of that surplus they had.

In the center of her heart, she knew this was love that would never be replicated. A love for him as much as she loved the earth, the stars, and the oceans. Though she wouldn't dare say it to him right now, she knew it was true. She would love him until she became one with the earth, despite all the harsh realities of knowing he may have to disappear from her life. He may meet someone on the other side of the boundary who his dad would approve of, his brother wouldn't despise, and who could give him heirs and offspring and be there forever for them, for Greenthistle. She did love him.

Elodie realized no sadness came to her, only the deepness of their bond. The certainty that this was right. Was this that thing that couldn't be undone, she wondered. As though she and he were binding themselves to each other and she could see that tether of their very essence at this moment. She felt more aligned in the universe.

Trevin, how far I've fallen for you, my brave beautiful mountain lion. I will always protect you from the coldness the world throws out at you. Her thoughts flowed in her mind; she pushed them toward him. Words could be spoken later, right now intent meant far more than words.

His grip tightened even more on her and he let out a groan as he slowed his thrusting and she felt him release. He laid her back down on top of him and then rolled her on her back. They gazed at each other. Her finger traced his cheekbone, his face markings.

"Trevin," she moaned with love and affection flowing from her voice into him.

"That felt amazing. You're amazing," she said, kissing him.

"You are too, Elodie. It's never felt like this before. You are very passionate. Absolutely amazing in every way, and I need more of it, of you," he moaned. "Do you need a break or are you ready for round two or three, or however you are keeping track?" he said, kissing her jaw again.

"You're ready that fast, for round two or three, or whatever number?" she asked, noticing he was thrusting gently and how hard he was.

"Yes," a heavy moan slipped out from him.

"I take it you were just getting started." She met his eyes with a coy smile. He smiled back and pushed himself up to his knees, still holding her in place. He gripped her hips, lifting her and started to thrust.

"You have no idea how wild you drive me. If you say stop I will, always, but until then, you are all mine."

"I'm not going to say it because I don't want you to stop," she moaned. He inhaled deep and smiled lustfully at her. After he released, he wasted little time between the next round mounting her from behind and kissing her shoulders and back.

After he finished he pulled out and sat back with a long pleased exhale. "Elodie, I can't get enough of you," he said, running his fingers along her back and rear. She remained on her stomach, her breaths slowing. Her lustful eyes met his. They had done three rounds, and he told her he wasn't done, it was just a breather.

She looked up at him as he rested against the headboard of her bed then reached her hand up to stroke him. Trevin moaned as she pushed herself up and straddled him. Cupping his jaw with her other hand she kissed him.

She kissed along his jaw, turning his head to the side. Light kisses up to his ear, running her tongue along to the point. He moaned again.

"Fae have a lot of stamina, don't they?" she asked in a coy tone.

"Yes," he moaned, playing with her breasts. "We do. Especially with someone amazing."

She kissed back down his jaw and kissed him again, then ran her tongue down his chin and down his throat. Down his chest along the line her tongue traveled, and she moved back still stroking him.

"I have to build up to that, but I can pleasure you in the meantime," she said, and he moaned again as she licked a path along his ribs and back to the center where the line stopped and ended with a dot. Running her tongue closer to the object her hand was stroking, he sucked in a breath.

She then watched him as she licked up the length to the tip. His hands gripped the sheets as his head tapped back against the wall and moans escaped his lips.

She licked and ran her tongue up and down then took him in her mouth. He moaned louder and moved his hand to her head, fingers threading through her hair.

"This feels incredible. Fuck," he moaned out.

"I can tell you are trying to hold back, don't. I'm not made of glass," she said between licks and then took him back in her mouth.

Trevin sucked in a gasp of air. "Elodie." Her name was sheathed by his moan.

She moved in sync with his thrust, her hand following her mouth. His body writhed with the vibrations of her moans on him.

A grunt escaped him as Elodie felt him tense, then he released down her throat. It was oddly floral tasting which she did not expect. She pulled back, and he caught his breath.

"El!" he moaned. He sat up and embraced her. Then he eased back into her and thrusted again. "That was so incredibly hot. No one has ever licked down my markings and they are sensitive. Tell me to stop if you need a break. Please, I just can't get enough of you," he said, kissing her neck and sucking lightly as he thrusted deep into her again.

"Trevin," she moaned. "There's nowhere else I'd rather be than right here with you," she told him. He kissed her hard, cupping her jaw.

"I love hearing my name on your lips," he moaned.

"Trevin, you feel so good." He gently tugged on her bottom lip with his teeth and then moved to her ear. She gasped.

After the fourth round, they laid together, her under him. He kissed her neck and jaw lightly and she hugged him tight.

"El," he said. She was running her nails lightly along his back and enjoying the warm feeling in her.

"Yeah?" she said softly.

"I want you, all of you. As mine," he said.

"As in your girlfriend? No longer just an overseer?" she asked, moving her hand up to his head, running her fingers through his hair.

"Yes. I want to be more than just your overseer and friend. Know that you mean so much to me and please never question it, do not doubt that."

She hugged him then pulled back to take him in. She took in his eyes, his face markings, his ears.

"I'd never imagined meeting someone like you, meeting you, feeling this. I promise to keep your secrets safe, to look out for you, Trev, you are mine." As she said the words, Elodie felt that thing in her tug and tensed. "I want you to be forever," she said, pressing into him and it tugged again. When she assessed the feeling in her, it was as though she was tethered to something. Her mind followed the direction of that tether outward toward him. She looked at him as her eyes widened.

"What is it? Tell me if you aren't sure please. Don't feel pressured to be with me if you don't want to be," he said.

"No, Trev, that's not it, I meant it, I want you in every way too, but this feels like I tethered you to me when I told you that. Did my words do something?" she asked worriedly.

Trevin laughed and kissed her neck. His finger traced her ear.

"El, you are who I want, I never expected someone like you to walk into my life. I was suspicious at first, but you are unlike anyone I've encountered and you want me. You saved my life, you helped keep my family safe. You are my everything, I mean it, my everything."

"What is your dad going to say? I want to stay here with you but I don't want to make your life hard though. I know this whole thing is forbidden, I guess in fantasy books it usually is." She hugged him tighter, as though she was going to lose him instead of the other way around.

"And in your fantasy books, they get their happily ever after. We will figure this out, we will fight to get our happy ending too. We can make it as public or as private as you like. My dad, nor Caleb will do anything to you. Q likes you—he is amused when you snap back at us all. You already know Autumn loves you," he said, looking at her. "My dad hasn't done anything to Charles, Lord Ashdale hasn't done anything to Justine. However you want us to appear in public is up to you. I will gladly make out with you and call you mine the next time you cross that boundary. Everyone will know you're mine." She laughed bashfully and pulled him closer, kissing him. Running her fingers up his spine and wrapping her leg around him, she pressed against him. Trevin kissed her again and they went into the next round.

Eventually sleep took hold of her and he followed shortly after.

Chapter 33

The next morning came and they needed to get back to their usual Monday routine. Elodie got ready for work and Trevin would leave when she did for his drills.

"Got everything?" she asked. He nodded and put on his backpack, casually leaving a shirt behind for her. She walked over to him and he kissed her passionately, before cupping her cheek and kissing along her jaw. "Trev, easy," she said, with a laugh.

"I know, I know. I'm sorry. I wish we had another day off. A month off," he said, smiling.

"Your scent is intoxicating," she said. He looked at her with a slight grin.

"What scent might that be?" he asked.

"Oakmoss and amber. I've smelled it on you since Halloween. Don't stop wearing whatever it is you use, okay?"

He grinned wider. *We are doomed. I'm her vowed, no doubt, but how do I have a scent for her?* "I'm surprised you picked that up."

She rolled her eyes and grinned at him. "Come on, I can smell things too." She laughed and kissed him lightly.

Of course you can. My vowed. What are you, El?

"We are going to keep this under wraps for a bit, yeah? I just, your dad and you are very high-profile. Small towns, I'm nervous, but you are worth every ounce of nerves."

"We can make it public whenever you'd like. Though, there is no easing this into the fae world, everyone will scent you all over me," he said, kissing her again. A small laugh escaped him when she cringed. "It's not a bad scent, mortals have a scent, fae can tell. It's how I knew Autumn and Charles hooked up on Halloween and knew about Q and Justine. I know when Russ and Caleb get lucky too."

"I am happy you are mine, happy to be yours." He felt that tug again, and it looked like she had too. He grinned. *There is no way she can be feeling this.*

"My little mink. You will be mine forever."

"I hope so," she said with a pensive smile. She ran her fingers through his hair.

"You will be. We never lie, we can't," he said, kissing her again. She laughed and kissed him back, then grabbed her keys.

"If you want a ride to the trailhead, we gotta go now, otherwise you walk home from here," she said, and they walked towards the door.

After running home, Trevin ran inside and went right to his room to shower where he took care of himself again. He still had a lot of drive pent-up. Once he finished scrubbing himself down twice and finished rinsing off, he ran off to drills. After a day of drills and another shower, Trevin hoped her scent would be off him enough to give his dad the map. He did not want to have this argument with his dad. Part of him didn't even want to sit at the table for dinner tonight either. He just wanted to go back to her place. They had made plans to meet at the café tomorrow night.

When he got to Ashdale Estate he saw Quinn and Cyrus. Lord Ashdale was not there yet. They gave him a grin.

"Finally went feral on the mortal girl?" Cyrus grinned wide. Trevin tensed.

"Her scent is still all over you. Good job, that must have been some release," Quinn said with a laugh.

"There, I got laid. Now you guys can stop with the jokes," Trevin scoffed.

"Awww, Trevy finally got some. Five-year dry spell, over," Quinn said, patting him on the back.

"Maybe now you will come out more," Cyrus said. "Dry spells over, you wouldn't want to let it go dry again."

"Not going to happen. We are a thing, but we are keeping it quiet for now."

"What happens over here—" Cyrus started.

"Absolutely not. I will not do that to her," Trevin said, cutting him off.

"Dang, you finally took your claim and now you latched on hard," Quinn said.

"You are one to talk, Ashdale, you never go out either," Cyrus said with a grin.

"What can I say, I like mine a lot too."

"Figures you both would simp over some dumb mortal girls," Cyrus said, rolling his eyes.

Quinn's dad, Lord Ashdale, walked out; he glanced at Trevin and shook his head in annoyance.

Trevin ran drills with a newly found fire and Lord Ashdale was impressed. Usually when Quinn or Cyrus came to drills after a rowdy night, they were reckless and mouthy, but Trevin had razor sharp focus and didn't miss a step.

When the day was over Trevin ran home and then to his room and took another shower. A very long one and scrubbed himself twice again. Once he got out, he got dressed and grabbed the map. With his hand on his door he took a deep inhale then went into the study. His dad eyed him with narrowed eyes. Trevin lifted the cover and Lord Greenthistle's eyes examined the diagram.

"Look at that," Lord Greenthistle said. "It's actually a layout of the town."

"She thought of everything. She's a resourceful little mink. Headlamp, bandana material, first aid kit, spray finish for charcoal stuff," Trevin said, watching his dad look at the layout of Falk's former buildings.

"It lines up perfectly." Lord Greenthistle compared notes using the old book Elodie had found open nearby. Trevin flipped to the page with the map of King Range. "So, I assume the girl returned to work today? There were no missing person's reports or absence from the school staff?"

"Yes, we got back okay, but I wouldn't be standing here with this if it were not for her. This map was in an enclosed maze of iron. It is unreal. There are open slats on the top and then they get smaller and smaller. Erosion has caused bits of iron to get into the soil. Elodie was uneasy with just how deep and enclosed it was getting, there were old rail spikes shooting out. Tetanus and all as a deterrent for mortals, fortunately she is currently up to date with her shots," Trevin said with a sigh of relief they had both made it out of that. They had both made it back to her studio. A small smile crept over his lips.

"Did you send her in alone?" his dad asked him, stunned.

"No! She was about to but I couldn't let her go in there by herself. It was way too dark. She had the headlamp but I just couldn't let her. There are two other areas, cells almost. Elodie tapped into some kind of earth magic and figured out which cell Falk was in, it was weird. She got the rubbing no problem despite the tiny rays of light but I think the iron was in the air, too. I tried not to talk, tried to keep my nose and mouth covered but I inhaled it and it was bad," he said, looking down. "The ground, the walls, all iron. My entire body burned—my lungs burned. I couldn't move."

"What happened? How did you get out?" his dad asked, concerned. "I noticed you went rogue again for about an hour, dipping in and out to where I could sense you for moments, then gone. I was about to send sentries over there but you reappeared."

"El," he said with a slight smile. "Elodie saw me fall, and figured out the ground was iron. She was already upset with my lack of backpacking knowledge, and she was so prepared for everything. Somehow she dug deep, pulled me onto her back then carried me the mile out of the maze. She kept talking to me, but I couldn't move." Trevin went on to explain her fall and how he healed the deep gash on her leg. He noticed a small relieved smile grace his dad's face.

"Tell me, is she angry with you, us, for that expedition?"

"No. She's not at all. It did take her some convincing that this wasn't a trap to kill her at first." He laughed. "But she does want to help us when she can. She thinks she is insignificant but I mean that's twice now she's saved me."

Lord Greenthistle looked at his son. "And as a reward, you bedded her?" he asked. Trevin inhaled deep and then rolled his eyes.

"Yes! Do you ask Cedar about all his conquests? Autumn about Charles? Do you want all the details? Want to know how many times? Six, six rounds, Dad," Trevin spat out.

His dad smiled at him with a wry grin. "You mostly washed it off you, but I can see it in you. Lord Ashdale said you had a lot of drive today. A focus and determination he's never seen out of you. Just do not do something you will regret. She could have been seriously hurt—you know how fragile she is."

"I know. I know," he said. *I will not regret any of this with her. My vowed.*

"You said there are other rooms, areas with maps?" his dad asked, glancing back at the map. Trevin pulled his phone out and showed him a picture of the map she drew.

"Yeah, but we didn't go into them. It was alarmingly quiet inside the boundary. Not a single other fae was there. Hardly any sounds. It was almost haunting."

"Hmm I suppose it's not unheard of. It is pretty remote, especially if there is a big iron structure there. That is a good drawing, she did this, up there?"

"Yea, she draws a lot of what she sees. There are a lot of ravens in her sketchbook, but I don't notice any when I'm around her," Trevin said.

"They are birds. They get to hang out closer to the mortals than we and Ashdale do."

"Yeah, I guess so."

"Well let's pinpoint which plot the tome is in and if you like you can get it or I can send Cedar or Autumn."

"I will go. I can do it," Trevin said. His dad smiled.

"You are a good brother, looking out for them, you don't want to risk them getting hurt." Trevin nodded. "Will you take the mortal girl?" he asked.

"No. I don't think I need to nor want to. She should relax and enjoy her day. The life she built for herself here, or something," he said. Lord Greenthistle gave him the same wry grin.

"Of course she should, son."

"Elodie asked why the maze would be there, how it got made."

"Things we hope to find out. She does ask some odd questions."

"She's got a unique way of taking her world in. I guess ours now too," Trevin said.

"Don't get too hung up on her though and do not sway her from her life she has established here, understood?" he said. "She brings a fire out in you but you have to remember she is temporary. If you must, go ahead and use her for whatever play you see fit, but do not trap her here, okay? Do not get attached to her, or I will have to remove you as her overseer and appoint someone else."

Trevin rolled his eyes but nodded anyway, then went up to his room. He glanced at the drawing she made him and he smiled. "My little mink, you saved my life again. And I am going to try to find a way to give you a choice," he said before flopping back on his bed and thought about something in him pulling taut. When he fixed on her eyes, knowing how wrong it was to keep going he didn't care. She was his vowed, and that tug was her tether pulling him in. He knew they would both be hurt somehow but he couldn't fight it anymore. The want in his heart was something he no longer would fight. Trevin wondered how she would react to knowing she was his vowed. How would he handle losing her one day? It was selfish to keep going but if he ignored her he'd go mad. He wanted her, she wanted him. His vowed was here in his hands, he could not waste this precious time with her a second more.

When his eyes traveled up to her face again, the roundness of her ear and the realization of how fleeting his vowed was hit him. If he could find a way to offer her forever, he would. There had to be a way. He knew in his core this was something he could never put into words. And he now realized what vowed meant. Elodie had saved him, she had shown him the beauty these lands had. Showed him how to be brave and strong. Had done so with all the grace and beauty of the Old Giants. He wanted nothing more than to be that for her, to be that for Greenthistle, for their home.

He grabbed his phone and started to read about vowed bonds and if mortals could feel it or not. These were things he'd never mention to his dad yet. Eventually he would but not yet.

Chapter 34

As Friday night rolled around, Trevin and Autumn ran toward Eureka for the party at Cora's.

"You've been with Elodie a lot this week. Like *been* with her," she commented, "You went so long between partners too. Poor girl." Autumn laughed.

"Yeah, poor girl. Trust me, I take care of her plenty. Her dreamy eyes tell me I do, and she never tells me to stop. She's perfect in every way."

"You really like her, don't you?" Autumn smiled.

"Yes. I mean, after what she's done for us, for me. How can I not?"

"She is something else. That's for sure. You know it's going to hurt though the more attached you get, but then again, she does know about us. How long would you stay with her if she didn't leave?"

"Forever. And she's not leaving. Is she?" he asked worriedly.

"I guess you could technically stay with her for her entire life now, but there will be a day, you know?"

"Stop! Why do I have to think about it? I have her here and now. I know Dad glares at me every day I come home reeking of mortal. It doesn't matter that you do or Cedar does because you aren't the heirs. Autumn, I almost took her on her couch a few days before the King Range trek. I stopped because I knew it was wrong. Just left her there panting and yearning for more and ran like a damn coward. Then I ran to the tavern to try to get this outta my system and the second Cassia grabbed me I deflated, lost the edge. Cassia called me the Greenthistle disappointment. As if my body only wants Elodie, and you know what, I am done trying to fight it. I do like her. A lot. I don't know what I'm going to do, but ignoring it doesn't work. I tried."

"I'm sorry, Trev. I had no idea it was this strong. She is good for you and I can see how much the lands like her. I'm glad she's here. She's part of Greenthistle, no matter what Dad says. I hear her, Charles, and Justine talk about where to go next. Maybe So Cal with Charles, he mentioned she talked about Hawaii or even Denver. She does mention how drawn to the Old Giants she is too, though. She might not leave."

"I obviously can't keep her chained down here, but I hope she at least sticks out the next school year. If she stayed beyond that even better, but she can make her own choice, for her. If I felt like I was holding her back, I'd let her go though."

"Vagabonds are said to be easier to deal with and yet, it doesn't seem that way," she said with a sigh.

"He's certain he's moving?" Trevin asked.

"He talked about job searches in San Diego."

"It sounds as though you like him more than the last few."

"He's great. Laid back yet so attentive, but what can I do? You are lucky, you know? She cares for you deeply and we both know how far she would go for you. Honestly, I might be more upset that she's mortal than Charles leaving." She laughed.

"I dunno why the lands led her to me. I don't know why any of this is happening, but you know what? I wouldn't change it. Just have to ride it out," he said.

When they approached the town they changed and put their glamours on then headed into Cora's. Quinn was already there. Cora eyed Trevin with a grin. He smiled innocently back. He knew Elodie wasn't here yet, he couldn't scent her. As he walked over to Quinn, he watched as Charles walked in. Autumn smiled widely.

"Let's grab a drink," Charles said to Autumn. She nodded and held his hand.

"She is so starry-eyed with him. He's nice. Super chill dude," Quinn said.

"He is." Trevin agreed.

"Your girl coming tonight?" Quinn asked, taking a sip out of the bottle in his hand.

"Yes. Is yours?"

Quinn smirked at him. "Of course. Feels weird being domesticated and stuff. Even weirder than you are."

"Elodie is something special," Trevin said.

"Was that what you were waiting on, someone to find us? You could have been waiting forever."

"No, I wasn't waiting. I tried to ignore her, but the power in her is incredible, and now, she's mine," he said, feeling the tug. "I'm going to grab a drink," he said. Quinn followed him.

"Is she going to give you the starry eyes, too?" Quinn asked, glancing at Autumn. Charles laughed with a nod as Trevin laughed.

"Wait and find out," he said, grabbing a beer. "She wanted it kept quiet for a bit, but it's hard to keep my hands to myself," Trevin laughed with a genuine smile.

Trevin, Charles, and Autumn all walked outside to the back patio. He took the bench, leaving enough room for Elodie when she showed up. Cora walked out a short while later.

Justine and Elodie arrived around the same time.

"Hey Justine. Good timing."

"Right! Let's get a drink," Justine said. Elodie smiled and they headed to the kitchen. "Cora mentioned you and Trev went on a backpacking trip last weekend?" Justine said. Elodie smiled and nodded bashfully. "Wow. You two have the weirdest dynamic." She laughed. "I love it."

"It has been odd. How's Q?" she asked.

"He's great. I don't know though. I want to travel and he never wants to go anywhere. Says work is too busy for him to just take off. He's amazing though. It would be nice to travel with him. Why he wants to stay I will never understand."

"Yeah, I imagine it's hard for them. Trev and Anna both said it was hard for them to travel much. Sometimes it's hard for people to want to leave home."

"You guys are really close now. From yelling at him and Caleb in the café to being around each other a lot. Have you been to his place? What is Mr. Greenthistle like off hours? I've never actually met Mr. Ashdale."

"No. His dad is super intimidating. I met him once at the office. Trev introduced me. Very proper, respectful. I am not sure he likes me much. Caleb certainly doesn't," Elodie said, glad she could lie. She was trying to learn from Autumn on how to be quicker with what she said. Often, she listened to Trevin and Autumn interact with mortals. How no one had any idea except for her. Two of her mortal friends were sleeping with fae and had no idea.

"Caleb seems like he gives Trev a hard time a lot. Usually the older brother usually picks on the younger, but you wouldn't know it was the other way around with those two."

Elodie laughed, some nerves seeping in.

"This might be TMI, but does Q ever want to do multiple rounds?" Elodie asked. She was genuinely curious about how that went. She felt herself blush at the thought of him.

"You guys moved super fast! Q and I usually have two or three rounds. Trev probably has so much pent-up frustration too. I don't know if I've seen him with anyone. You are definitely something special, Elodie. How many rounds? I have to know!"

"Six. I hope he finds something special with me. I—I'm kind of enamored with him," she laughed bashfully.

"That's so cute. I'm happy he didn't end up a creep, because he could have been with how he acted. Cora says he's nice, but I haven't interacted with him much. Q and him are good friends," Justine laughed. "I take it you've finally met Russ?" Justine asked. Elodie nodded.

The way Russ watched her made her uncomfortable. It had made Trevin extra alert. "He has gotten much creepier. I don't know what happened. It used to be little gazes and grins and then he'd lose interest when they were not returned, but now he's like a vulture just watching."

"Observing and assessing," Elodie said. Nightswift's traits, the raven ever present. She wondered what he saw in her, what he had intended to do at the beach now that she knew what he was. She wondered what he and Q thought about her knowing.

"Yes! Like Seriously, eww. He is good looking, if the blond hair and blue eyes is your type. He doesn't need to be creepy to flirt."

"Yeah, I don't think he means any harm," she said, also lying. Her intuition had never been wrong. It seemed even stronger since moving to Humboldt.

"Let's go out to the fire pit. Cora's out there, so are Charles and Anna," Justine said. Elodie nodded.

They walked outside and Trevin met her eyes with a smile. They arranged to arrive separately, then go home together. He would drive her car regardless if she was tipsy or not.

He scooted over on the bench, making room for her as Elodie took the seat. Cora glanced at them curiously. Thus far, Cora only knew they had kissed a few times. Elodie hadn't said much else despite her asking a lot.

Elodie wasn't sure what it would look like being with a 'politician's son' or what the other fae would think. She was pretty sure Autumn and Caleb knew, though. His dad had to have known, but she hadn't had her memory wiped clean or been forced to work for them yet. Then again she knew fae upheld their bargains, it was usually the mortal who messed up. She was determined to not jeopardize any of them with an accidental slip of a name or their estates.

After taking a sip of her drink, Elodie smiled at Trevin. She glanced over at Cora and then at the ground, nervous.

Trevin scooted closer, and he put his arm around Elodie pressing a kiss to her temple. "I want everyone to know you're mine," he said softly. She felt her cheeks heat and her smile grew.

"I'm glad you're mine too, Trev," she said back quietly.

"I knew it! I have been trying to get details from the backpacking trip all week!" Cora laughed. "How long?"

Elodie met her friend's eyes and hesitantly put a hand on Trevin's leg.

"Since Halloween? Just kidding. A few weeks ago, it was shortly before Thanksgiving. I was stressing she might have stayed in Marin," Trevin said.

"That long? What happened? And you didn't tell me? I thought we were friends, Elodie," Cora joked.

Elodie laughed nervously and saw Q and Autumn's grin, probably wondering how she was going to lie this time.

"I was in Sequoia Community Park and he was out for a jog and we literally bumped into each other. His clothes got dirty and I was mortified. We just decided after how weird everything had been we could have dinner and talk. We did and yeah."

Trevin smirked.

"I knew I had been completely out of line with her and wanted to make it right. After dinner I realized I did like her," Trevin followed up.

"Glad the kissing game paid off that night," Q said, giving him a head shake.

"There ya go Cora, all us transplants with the estate kids," Justine joked.

Elodie and Trevin laughed.

"Maybe if I'm lucky, she won't be a transplant," Trevin said

"Maybe," Elodie said. The fear in her mind lingered though, that he would leave her one day that this was temporary.

Elodie's eyes glanced at the tree line.

Home. With him.
It cannot be undone.
Soon, awaken.
Bound.

"I hope Elodie stays for a long time, and that I'm invited to the wedding," Cora laughed.

"Not to insinuate, but I hope all three of us are in Elodie's bridal party," Autumn gushed and looked at Elodie and her brother with the biggest grin.

"Oh, I hope so too," Cora said. "Let me bake your cake. I promise it will be good."

"Stop, you will scare him off," Elodie said, and glanced at him. Marriage was not something that would ever come for them. She fought a frown knowing that this thing with him was fleeting.

"Never, I said you were mine, and I am yours, little mink," he said, hugging her again.

"I wondered who would catch your eye, Elodie," Charles said, pulling Autumn into him.

Trevin was nervous to tell her that she was his vowed, that he would always love her as long as he lived. Part of him too feared she would leave him, be it from time or someone else. He didn't think she would ever cheat on him, but if she didn't

realize what being vowed meant, someone else might sway her. He did not know how vowed bonds worked for mortals.

As the night went on, Trev and Q stepped out front to talk.

"What was that shift? I've felt it a few times, and she always reacts to it. What is she?" Quinn asked him. Trev leaned against her car.

"I still don't know. I can't figure it out. You should see the lands when she is on them. The ferns and the Old Giants shift toward her. The Old Giants talk to her."

"She hangs out with Charles too much. I'd keep an eye on the camping trips we are not invited to," Quinn laughed.

"No, she's being serious. I just don't know what it is about her. I've seen her pull power from the soil. She hefted me on her back and carried me a mile out of that iron death trap."

"Well, whatever it is, Cyrus is aware of it, too. He gave her a super creepy grin when that shift happened."

"Bastard. He better leave her alone. He was trying to challenge me at the bonfire too," Trevin said, clenching his fist.

"You've been near territorial over her since Halloween. This girl got her claws in you good, why? This mortal with the weird thing in her?"

"Q," he groaned. "I hope she knows I am hers. Only hers. I can't tell anyone either." Trevin deflated with a long sigh.

"Do you think you lo—?"

"Stop! Don't say it please," Trevin interrupted, knowing he'd have to answer, and have this snap into place here. Quinn looked at him, confused.

"Okay. I mean, it's obvious you do. I say it to Justine. It's fine. You can say it to her."

Trevin sighed. He always had trusted Quinn, much more now than he did Cyrus and Cedar. "What scent do you get off her?"

"Other than you?" Quinn laughed. Trevin rolled his eyes, unamused. "I dunno. A sweet floral scent? Whatever products she uses? I've smelled it on lots of people. Mortal scent."

"What scent do you get from this car?" Trevin asked with a sigh. This just confirmed what he already knew to be true.

"What? Why are you asking? It smells like dirt, rain, exhaust. I can pick up that sweet cherry blossom or whatever that smells like. Justine has a similar scent. I've looked at the body spray she uses. It's pink and says cherry blossom."

"My senses have been enveloped by the same scent on her since Halloween. I scented it on the trails late at night before then too. The scent of ocean breeze and lavender. I smell it on her car. I could find her place on scent alone if I went blind. I smell it now from the house," Trevin said. "I crave it. Cannot get enough of it. Hate leaving it," he said, shaking his head.

Quinn looked at him confused, then shock crawled over his face. "Oh."

"Please don't tell anyone. I don't know if Autumn even realizes it and I can't tell my dad. That's why I am territorial. I love you guys, but I will fight you all if any of you try anything with her."

"Elodie is your vowed?" Quinn said. "And she knows about us because she saved you from the iron cuff? Your vowed saved you," he said, putting his hand on his head. Trevin hung his head low. "There is a weird connection between you two. Autumn and I both noticed it, she gave me a confused glance. Mortals can feel the vowed bond?"

"I don't know!" Trevin groaned. "I have been so careful not to tell her those words. I've seen it nearly snap in her too though. She looks at me with some deep-rooted knowledge we need each other and I will never deny her. I just can't figure out how the bond works with her, too. I looked it up and everything said mortals don't feel the tug that we do, but it appears she does."

"Damn. You found your vowed, now?" Quinn said, stopping himself. Trevin knew what he meant. Trevin found his vowed at forty-five. Forty-five years of an immortal life, when she was in her mid thirties, well past a quarter of her life, if she was lucky.

"Keep an eye on her please?" Trevin asked.

"Sure thing. You know it's only going to hurt though, right?"

"I know."

"But anything other than her is living a lie," Quinn responded.

"There's too much happening all at once. She has some kind of power in her. She's my vowed. She knows about us. I can't help but feel like it's no coincidence."

"Yeah, I'd say it's not, but what does it all mean?" Quinn asked. Trevin sighed again.

"I wish I knew. I hope she isn't in any danger. If I can sense something in her, I'm worried others might too and try to hurt her," Trevin said.

"You got the map to Falk, yea?" Quinn said. Trevin nodded.

"I hope it will have some insight on anything."

"I hope so too. It certainly is making my dad nervous."

"Mine too," Trevin sighed.

"Did you bed her on the backpacking trip?" Quinn asked. Trevin leaned back against her car.

"No. We kissed and got handsy in the tent. But it was after we got back to her place that Sunday."

"How was it? You must have gone wild," Quinn laughed.

"Six times and then when I got home, I was still anxious," he said. Quinn laughed.

"Good for you. Enjoy it?" he said.

"I never imagined anyone could be that passionate. She's an absolute goddess. Do you know our markings are super sensitive? I've never had a partner like her. The way she eyes me. She is beautiful."

"She's your vowed. I wish Justine could see my markings. I wish I could show her any part of me without glamour. Hell, she can't even know my real name."

"You are starting to really like her, aren't you?" Trevin asked.

"She's lovely, the way she dreams and talks about the world. She's laid back, but blunt as can be. I missed her. I will miss her when she leaves. All I can do is enjoy what I have of her, though. I see her eye other guys on occasion," Quinn said with a frown.

"I dread the day when Elodie decides this place has run her course. The Old Giants will dull ever so slightly."

"You'd let her just leave, let whatever is in her go? You wouldn't even ask her to stay? Tell her what she means to you?" Quinn asked, confused.

"I can't, it's forbidden," he said. "I can't trap her here with the vowed bond either."

"It's forbidden for any of them to know about us, yet she does. She's been to the other side of the boundary. You are her overseer. You can't just let her go. You have to tell her she's your vowed, Trev. It's for the better of both of you."

"Why? Tell her something she should have but can't? My dad's not going to let her be an estate lady. If she even wants all that. A half-breed heir? Dad would scramble her brain and drop her somewhere secret."

"But you can't keep this from her. You can't just let her walk away, either. What about her choice? Plus others will know, they will sense her power and they might hurt her. It's going to hurt you to lose her, yeah, but you don't want to see anyone hurt her. Have to hear about it months later at the regional meeting."

"I want to give her the choice, to become like us."

"Trev, I don't know if that's possible. I'm sorry, I can't imagine how rough this is for you," he said.

Trevin sighed. He took a deep inhale and exhaled, and fought back all the fears and uncertainty. "I know. Let's get back inside. I don't want to lose a single moment with her."

"I get it, bro. We may have forever, but they don't."

Trevin glanced at the trees.

Please. Please, I want her to have the choice, he pleaded before heading back inside.

Chapter 35

The following week Trevin sat with his family during dinner at Greenthistle Estate.

"Daddy?" Autumn asked in a slightly higher tone than she normally spoke. Cedar rolled his eyes. Trevin didn't pay any attention.

"Yes, hun?" Lord Greenthistle responded. "What would you like me to say yes to but you have a good feeling I am going to say no initially?" he asked with a sigh and set his fork down.

"Well, the Winter Solstice ball is coming up," she said. This caused Trevin to glance up and see his dad was already not amused or interested.

"It is. Let me guess, you'd really love to bring that boy and just have him dealt with afterward? You know I cannot do that," Lord Greenthistle sighed.

Autumn shook her head. "I don't want Charles to forget me. I don't even think he'd be interested in that as much fun as it would be," she said, and Trevin's jaw dropped when Autumn glanced at him. His dad glanced at him, too. "I was hoping with everything in my little heart that Elodie would be allowed since she knows about us," Autumn said with her sweetest smile and biggest eyes.

Trevin looked at his dad in complete shock. Cedar tossed his fork down.

"That's stupid and you know it. She can't be allowed," Cedar huffed out.

"Why not? Dad said he'd allow her at the house," Autumn retorted. "And she doesn't even come over."

"Everyone will know she's a mortal. They will paw at her, Master Greenthistle will lose his shit, and the house will be in shambles. You really want to risk ruining a seasonal ball?" Cedar quipped back.

Trevin thought about what it would take for no one to be able to touch her. He looked at his dad, whose attention was no longer on his daughter, but on him with a contemplating gaze, followed by a sigh.

"Did you tell her to ask me?"

"No sir. I didn't even know what she was going to ask."

"Do you want her to attend?"

Cedar groaned as Trevin was about to open his mouth.

"Obviously he wants her here all dolled up with a pretty bow. It's a horrible idea," Cedar huffed out.

"I did not ask you, I asked Trevin," Lord Greenthistle said.

"In order for no one to touch her, I would have to announce her as my lady, wouldn't I? And as the master of the hosting estate, I have to do the opening dance? With all eyes on us," he said. He wondered what asking her to be his lady would do with being vowed. He knew he wanted her there and to see her dressed up. Autumn would make Elodie's fairytale dreams come true.

"Yes, you would," his dad said with a pensive smile.

"I would do it in a heartbeat, if you'd ever allow it. I know that's not going to happen, though." Trevin looked back down and heard his dad sigh.

"Then you will escort her into the ball. School will be closed anyway and she will stay the night before you go to Marin with her," he said. All three of his kids looked at him, shocked.

"You mean it. She can be my lady at the solstice ball?" Trevin asked, confused.

"I can allow this for you. Just do not do something stupid. You are walking a very fine line, Trevin, and I do fear for you. What she might do to you."

"Yes, sir. Thank you, Dad. She will not cause a problem—I will not cause a problem. I'll give you my word," he said. Cedar let out an even bigger sigh.

"Thank you, Daddy!" Autumn squealed.

"Great," Cedar sighed.

"Cedar, you will look out for her along with Autumn. She will be an honorary guest of Greenthistle Estate," Lord Greenthistle said. Cedar sighed and rolled his eyes. "This is to remain in this room though, lest anyone get any ideas in advance. Understood?"

"Fine," Cedar groaned.

"Thank you!" Trevin said.

The next day Elodie heard tapping on glass. Trevin glanced over with a smirk.

"You are going to want to open that."

Elodie opened the window where a squirrel set down an envelope.

"Your presence is most anticipated at Greenthistle Estate with Lord Greenthistle's blessing," the squirrel said, then ran off.

She stared dumbfounded then looked at the envelope again. It read 'Lady Elodie Santiago of Humboldt' in a shimmering blue ink and fancy script. She carefully opened it and slid out a soft woven paper with black and blue shimmer ink.

You are cordially invited to attend the Winter Solstice Ball at Greenthistle Estate on Dec 21st, as an honorary guest of the Estate.

Elodie stared at it for a moment stunned, then glanced over at Trevin who was smiling.

"I was wondering when that was going to show up." He stood up and walked over to her.

"Winter Solstice?"

"I must admit it wasn't my idea, but I certainly did have to answer for it. Autumn asked in her most precious voice. She always does this when she wants something that Dad would say no to if it was Caleb or me," he said with a laugh. "No doubt about it, she is Dad's favorite."

Elodie laughed. "When she told me about the Autumn Equinox ball it sounded magical, and with winter I can't even imagine."

"If she has her way, you will probably get an invitation to the Spring Equinox too. Ashdale Estate is hosting it," he said, and her eyes lit up.

"I will order a dress online. I don't want to look poor."

"So, I wanted to talk to you about that. Autumn is more than excited to do your hair and makeup. If you are free tomorrow, she would like to send your gown selection and requests off to our tailors. Also help you pick out your jewelry and your, uh diadem." Her eyes went wide, processing.

"I get a diadem? A real one? Greenthistle's personal tailor is going to make my gown, specifically for me?" she asked.

He nodded. "Yes, Autumn asked but then Dad asked what I wanted and as you know, we have rules for everything, even our revelries. There hasn't been a mortal guest in decades, centuries. Not even in any surrounding territory either. So, if you are okay with all this, you will be attending as my lady, hence the diadem."

"Your lady?" she asked, hands still covering her mouth.

"I don't know that Greenthistle has ever had a mortal guest. If you went just as a guest, any fae could approach you just as they could a fae attendee. Something bad could happen. I'd not let it of course but to ensure there would be dire consequences if anyone tried, you will be announced as the master's lady. It will certainly yield some whispers and murmurs, and some snide looks, all eyes will be on us," he said, uneasy.

"Mostly me though?" she asked. He nodded and cleared his throat.

"There is also the tradition of the young master of the hosting estate and his lady to open the revelry with a dance," he said. Elodie exhaled loudly.

"Oh," she said.

"I leave this entirely up to you, I know this is a lot. I know you are more comfortable in hiking gear in the forests or at the café with your sketchbook. So I understand entirely if you would rather not go. It is always your choice. I do have to attend though," he said, deflated.

"Do you have another lady you'd rather go with? One better suited for the formalities? Maybe less clueless about everything?" She lowered her eyes.

"I don't have to have a lady by my side for this regardless of who hosts. The opening dance would then be a rotation or partners," he said. She nodded. "If you are worried that I'd rather go with someone else, you shouldn't be. I can only imagine what Autumn has in store for you. There is no one I'd want by my side more than you as my lady, El. I've gone to the last fifteen revelries alone, even the ones we hosted."

"You want me as your lady? You want me by your side for your solstice ball?" she asked, shocked.

"I want nothing more than to walk arms linked with you, El. Never doubt what you mean to me," he said with a hopeful gaze.

She smiled too and threw her arms around him. "I would love to be your lady, Master Greenthistle."

He hugged her tightly. "I cannot wait to take you formally as my lady in front of everyone. Dad also is requesting you stay the night before until we go to Marin."

"What?" she asked, confused.

"Well it will take time to get ready and stuff. Also, we want to gauge your reaction to fae wine. It can lock mortals in a trance and make really sick. So we want to test it in a safe environment first. Some half fae have trouble with it too. So you'd have to sleep it off and be monitored. By your overseer of course."

She smiled wide. "I have to practice dancing, huh? I've never done any kind of ballroom dancing, the most I've done is belly dancing."

He raised an eyebrow. "It is not a difficult dance. I will show you," he said, standing up. As he set music to play on her speaker from his phone, he walked up and took her hand and wrapped the other around her waist.

She met his eyes and felt her mouth part slightly in awe.

"My dearest Lady Elodie. I am honored you have accepted my invite," he said softly, showing her the steps and spins. Delighted to see how quickly she learned.

Chapter 36

After a night of observing Elodie's reaction to fae wine, the Winter Solstice had arrived. Sitting at breakfast, they were all impressed that Elodie seemed normal, more awake even. As if she had rested well.

"I look forward to seeing you both get anxious tonight," Cedar said, taking a bite of bacon. "Also, you might want to freshen up for sure, I can scent you all over each other. Not that it's a secret Trev's dating a mortal. Bedding one." He laughed out loud. Trevin sighed and gripped her hand tighter.

"Caleb, please," Trevin said, mindful of using his real name around Elodie.

"Your kissing game ends at that? And you guys make a big deal about a kiss from a mortal?" Elodie asked with some snark.

"Yeah, what about Alena? Who is she attending with, you or Russ?" Autumn asked.

"Mortals require less effort to bed. Easier to impress them, right Trev? And Alena will be here, as my date," he snickered.

"So you like being lazy then?" Autumn quipped up. "Trev isn't. It took some work to get her. Elodie is special. You just wish you'd be lucky enough to find someone like her," Autumn said, pouring another mimosa for Elodie—it would be her third.

"I thought I had seen her first if we are being honest." Cedar grinned as Trevin narrowed his eyes. Cedar laughed and shook his head.

"Please don't get her drunk before the ball even starts," Trevin groaned noticing Elodie take the full glass Autumn had set on front of her. "Eat more, please, you are going to be drinking a lot tonight, I think."

"She's fine," Autumn laughed.

"I don't want her to be sick or black out and forget the entire thing," Trevin said with a groan. "In fact, El don't take any beverage offered to you, Autumn and I will hand you drinks." Elodie nodded and eventually they finished their plates, and then Autumn took Elodie's arm.

"She is all mine for the day, Trevy. I will take good care of her. Here, take this one with you," she said, pushing another mimosa toward Elodie. She grabbed herself one too, and they headed upstairs.

"Five bucks says you punch someone in the face in the first hour. You know how many eyes are going to be on her?" Cedar asked.

"Stop. You are making me regret inviting her." Trevin groaned again and finished the last half of his mimosa in one gulp. Cedar laughed and patted him hard on the back.

"She will look stunning when Autumn is done with her," he said.

"You better watch out for her, Cedar."

"I will, I will, I don't have a choice, it shouldn't have taken her to make you into a Greenthistle heir," he said. Trevin sighed and got up, heading to the fitting room in the study.

"She has an oddly high tolerance to the fae wine," Lord Greenthistle said. "I'd still require you both to keep a close eye on her. I have no doubt my daughter will."

"You doubt Trev will?" Cedar said. Both Trevin and Cedar were confused.

"No. I doubt you will be as attentive as they will. It's not her I'm worried about tonight, it's everyone else. She knows exactly what she wants," he said, looking at his eldest son who was smiling wide.

Trevin recalled the night prior, she did certainly get drunk off the fae wine. His dad had baited both her and him to see what might happen. Despite her want for the wine glass Lord Greenthistle held just out of reach, Elodie's true desire was clear as day when Trev got mentioned. The increased heart rate they all heard, the bashful smile, that look of absolute need in her eyes. Trevin was so grateful she hadn't said she loved him at that moment. Then the realization she might say it tonight, at the opening dance in front of everyone.

In Autumn's room, Elodie was led to the bathroom. "Go on and put on the robe. There's some fun lingerie too," Autumn said nonchalantly.

Elodie blushed and then looked at the robe and the small bundle wrapped in a sage green tissue. "You had a robe made for me?" Elodie asked.

"Please, it's got an E embroidered on it. This is nothing. This way I can get your hair and makeup done and help you into your dress. Also, your diadem has been made too. It's arriving shortly," Autumn asked.

"Do you wear one?" Elodie asked.

"No. Only the hosting house's firstborn and partner get to wear one. I wore one when I went as Russ's lady and they hosted," she said, Elodie blushed and frowned. She put her hands on her cheeks. "You clearly need more to drink." She laughed, requesting some sparkling wine.

"I can't believe I'm doing this, that I'm here, with him." She took a deep inhale and then another large gulp of her drink. Autumn laughed again.

"You are good for him. I've never seen him act this way around anyone. Elodie, I do love Charles, but I know it's temporary, and it works for us. I will be sad to see him leave but it is for the best. Just ride the fairy tale out," she said, and Elodie nodded. "I don't know how or when it will end, but one day it has to. Remember that, okay? We never know what a future holds for our mortals."

"I know, that's what I tell myself when I look at him. One day I will not be here. I hope he will remember me though. I will always remember this as long as I am still breathing." Elodie laughed and swallowed back her pain. Autumn smiled but not as big as before.

"I don't think he will ever forget you, Elodie," she said.

Elodie smiled but felt a twinge in her heart. *'Never doubt what you mean to me.'* His words repeated in her mind. She knew she had never felt this way before, this love. How fast things had happened. He would meet her dad tomorrow, would meet her family and see where she was from. She hoped he wouldn't get too bored, that her extended family wouldn't scare him off. She wondered about when she was her dad's age, where would he be? *Just ride out the fairy tale. Right now is all you have.* Focused back on the mirror, she watched Autumn brushing out her hair and pinning a few strands to the front. She held up a few small sparkly clips and held the comb in her mouth.

"It had been a while for Trev, before me?" she asked.

"At least five years," she said, Elodie's eyes widened.

"Why? He's pursued people right? Fae?"

"No one I know of. So the fact he has a lady at a ball we are hosting, one he is loyal too, is a big deal. Especially one who pulled him out of harm's way and helped us out. Definitely turning some heads."

"Why though? Me? I never felt very special or even very confident. I feel so clueless with all the rules and customs. As though I'm going to embarrass Greenthistle," Elodie said. "Sure, I hike and know how to backpack but as if that is even a desirable skill for you all. Mountain lions don't need tents and sleeping bags. But this, a seasonal ball alongside the master of a high estate?"

Autumn shook her head laughing, continuing to braid Elodie's hair while making sure it was a perfect French Braid.

"You are special, Elodie. Trev sees it, we all do. You bring out so much in him and I think even Dad is warming up to you."

"That is wishful thinking. I'm ready to grovel at his feet for everything he has allotted me."

"Stop worrying. He knows you are good. Caleb does too. You are not embarrassing any of us either. Just be yourself, you needn't worry about what they think. You have the protection of Greenthistle." She smiled. "And Trev does really like you. I've never seen him this protective. Relax and enjoy it okay," Autumn said, putting a hand on her shoulder. Then she took another jeweled clip and continued to work. Staff helped Autumn with her own hair and took final measurements on Elodie. Some small fruit tarts and finger sandwiches were brought in with more champagne.

"What are Trev and Caleb doing, surely it doesn't take them this long to get into their attire?" Elodie asked.

"No, they are probably drinking, maybe even having a scrap in the yard. They have to be with Dad to make sure everything is going where it should downstairs, and in the yard too. Making sure the diadem is to Trev's liking, finalizing things. Probably taking a nap too."

Eventually Autumn moved onto makeup, and kept Elodie's pretty light but did put the wire ear cuffs on her.

The ball was getting nearer and Elodie's nerves were growing.

"Relax, Elodie, you will be okay."

"I have to walk out in front of everyone. I'm going to dance in front of everyone. All fae," she said, letting out a deep exhale.

"Girls dream of doing this. Just like one of your fantasy books, right?"

"Those don't actually happen, yet here I am," she said, watching Autumn put her makeup on. Elodie was enamored when she was done. Autumn looked at her. "You're beautiful, Autumn. I shouldn't be the one to look at," she said, Autumn laughed.

"Please, everyone has seen me countless times. They all know I'm the second-born and young Lady Greenthistle, though, it does sound weird. Mom should be here. She should be here to see you, and see you dance with him. She would be happy to see him like this. I think Mom would have liked you a lot," she said then paused. "You've been to Everoak?"

Elodie nodded. "Eastern Sierra and stuff. It's small. Not very populated. Like only three thousand people. It's pretty. We were road tripping on the eastern side of the state, Lassen, Lake Tahoe, Yosemite, Death Valley."

"You've really been all over the state huh?" Autumn asked. Elodie nodded

"You could say that," she laughed. "I've been up through Oregon and Washington. Traveled to the southwest and Chicago and New York, Hawaii, and then abroad some. Mom and Dad instilled it in me early. We traveled a lot as a family, before, and then we stopped," she said, getting quiet.

"I know it's hard sometimes. I miss my mom a lot. Trev took it really hard though, you know with his empathic gifts. Whether it was intentional or not, he sucked the grief out of us; but that meant he took it on himself. I think maybe he still hangs onto it. Seeing him with you though is like getting a new Trev back. Like the old one but different. You are pretty special, El. He will never forget you," Autumn said. Elodie smiled.

When she went behind the screen and saw her dress she gasped. She had seen a sketch of it but she couldn't believe this was what she would wear. Carefully she stepped into it and then stepped out for the staff to help tie and zip. They helped her into her boots as someone knocked on the door. One of the attending staff walked to the door then nodded and went to Autumn.

"Lady Santiago's diadem has arrived."

"Perfect timing. Let's get it on her," Autumn said, walking out from the other screen in her dress. Elodie gasped when she saw herself in the mirror. Autumn glanced over and smiled.

A man walked in with a box and set it down. Elodie noticed his ears were not as pointed, he appeared more human and wondered if he was half fae. He smiled in delight at the sight of the girls. Carefully, he removed the lid and lifted the diadem gently with gloved hands. Elodie was speechless. She looked at him and then down at the diadem again.

"I just delivered Master Greenthistle's. He was eager to see the lady's, but I did not show him," he said.

"This is beautiful, I don't know if I can do this justice." She looked up at the man and then at Autumn. They both smiled at her.

"You look stunning, my lady," he said. "Let me know if any adjustments need to be made. The ferns are a frosted silver and the crystals are raw fluorite with the perfect frosted green. His is similar and likely will be the only hints of green out there tonight," he said.

Autumn placed it on her head and adjusted some loose strands of hair. "Does it feel okay? Not tight or pinching anywhere? I'm going to pin in it. Just in case," she said.

"Yes it feels perfect," Elodie said with glee.

"Good because it will be Trev's job to remove it, if he can follow the tradition," Autumn said with a laugh. The man blushed and hurried out of the room.

"What tradition?"

"After our vow ceremony, it's customary for the pair to retreat back to their quarters at the end of the evening. Where the lord or lady of the estate is to undress their partner fully. Then she has to undress him, the diadems come off last before he can bed her. Otherwise it's said to be bad luck."

"Vowed? Wait, this is a solstice ball, right? This is beginning to sound like a wedding." Elodie panicked and blushed more. Her ears even heated red and Autumn laughed.

"No, it's not your wedding you are walking into, don't worry. Dad would flip. Sometimes it's fun to play make-believe, Russ and I did that after a few revelries and no way am I ever going to marry him." She laughed again, shaking her head. "Q has done it a few times too, I heard. But I don't know if Trev has. So given that I assume you are staying with him again, I'm pretty sure he is going to want to play along," she said, Elodie nodded nervously.

"Vowed is like a soulmate? Spouse?" Elodie asked. Autumn nodded.

"Something like that. Don't worry though, you are not going to be married off to Trevin tonight," she said. Elodie nodded and sighed. Her thoughts raced through everything he said. They couldn't lie, but they could omit. He had never mentioned the vowed thing before. She knew she wasn't his though. Would never fully be his but she was enjoying the experience. What would she do if his vowed showed up before her time? Her thoughts were interrupted by another knock. Both her and Autumn watched one of the staff hurry to the door and open it a crack. She nodded and took a box. It was wrapped in brown paper and had a green satin ribbon.

"A gift for Lady Santiago from Master Greenthistle," she said and set the box down. Elodie stared at it and then turned to Autumn.

"What's this?" Elodie asked. It was long and flat.

"I don't know. Go on, open it. It is solstice, so he got you a gift," she said, and Elodie nodded. She pulled the ribbon and opened it. Her eyes widened again.

"He had a dagger made for you, and a hip belt?" Autumn said, looking at it then at Elodie. "I suppose it makes sense. Usually if someone is dating the master of the hosting estate, they can wear an honorary weapon. But this looks similar to his own dagger. He's never given anyone one to wear before despite having gone with partners before."

"It's amazing, this must've cost a fortune," she said, holding it up. The blade was sharp and shined bright. The hilt was bronze and had an inlay of raw peridot and emerald nestled in a fern pattern. The hip belt was dark leather with a place for the blade and a few small pouches. There was a small scroll sealed with a green wax seal and the Greenthistle emblem with a T over it. She opened it carefully without breaking the seal. Then her eyes read the fine penmanship.

El, I cannot wait to formally ask you to be my lady tonight in front of everyone. No matter who says what, I want you here, by my side, always. I had a gift made for you in hopes you feel safer, even when I cannot be there. Wear this tonight please. Remember you mean so much to me. I'm not sure I know how to explain it but I am desperately searching for the words and maybe the courage too. My little mink, you are so very special. See you soon. – Ever yours, Trev

She swallowed and put her hand to her chest. She ran her fingers over the hilt. "Are you sure fae can't lie?" she asked, looking at Autumn who read the note and then stared at Elodie shocked.

"You are something special to him, Elodie," Autumn said and heard the chimes. "It's time, let's get this on you and get you down to the hall. Don't worry, you will be in good hands and I will be in the crowd. Trevin will be on the other side of the doors waiting for you," she said with a smile. She picked up the hip belt and helped Elodie put it on.

Elodie took a deep breath and slid the dagger into the sheath.

Autumn handed her the lip gloss. "Come on, just a little bit. Trev loves it. He's told me it's his weakness." Autumn laughed as Elodie put the gloss on.

They took a few selfies and then made for the door.

Elodie felt her heart pound with nerves but also with eager curiosity to see Trevin, for him to see her as fae as she was ever going to be.

"Okay. Just down that hall. He will be waiting for you." Autumn gave her a hug then ran off as she heard an announcement made.

A staff person ushered her to the door where two other staff people stood ready to open them.

CHAPTER 37

"Announcing the arrival of Master Greenthistle," a voice said as everyone quieted. Trevin walked the top of the steps off the sunken ball area. Attendees gathered around the edge. If this were any other ball he would walk forward and choose his first dance partner. He saw Autumn beaming with excitement and his father's pensive gaze. Cyrus and Quinn stood near their parents and Cedar, along with Delia, Coral, and Poppy. All dressed in their finery. Only those in the Greenthistle Estate knew that Elodie was here. Her scent was masked by everyone else in attendance. He saw the eager faces hoping for a chance to dance with him too.

A smug smile was plastered on his lips as he awaited the next announcement. This was the moment where challenges would arise, talk of the mortal and speak of the girl becoming estate lady. He would fight for her and he would fight for Greenthistle. He almost dared anyone to challenge him or threaten her. Yet he was nervous that he would break rules by telling her she was his vowed. That if she said she loved him tonight in front of everyone, they would see it, his dad would see it and take her from him. He had to slow his breathing, the mountain lion was restless.

"What is he waiting for?" Trevin heard Lord Ashdale ask with the room so quiet.

"You will see, Autumn asked, and I felt that given what she has done for us, I could grant him this," Lord Greenthistle's response stirred a lot of emotions in Trevin.

"Announcing Lady Elodie of Humboldt, a guest of Greenthistle Estate," the announcer said. Some murmurs occurred, and the doors opened to reveal Elodie. Trevin had not seen her since breakfast. As he turned to face her, she stepped into the light, and more murmurs and gasps occurred. Trevin tuned everything out when the doors opened and he was utterly awestruck by the sight of her. The pure hum of energy pouring out of her. How radiant she was.

Her hair pulled back and braided to the side with jewelry clipped in. Wire ear cuffs formed a point lined with jewels and small strands of silver. Her tan skin shimmered across her chest. Small hints of highlight on her cheeks and a shiny gloss on her lips kept her makeup light and natural. The scent of sea breeze and lavender enveloped him. A gown came off the shoulder with long sleeves and a blue bodice with silver embroidery. Around her hips was the belt and dagger he gifted her. The gown cascaded into a white flowy dress with a shimmering blue gossamer overlay. He eyed the diadem and smiled. It was perfect for her. The light hit her in all the right ways. *She could be a goddess of the earth,* he thought.

He watched as Elodie took in the sight of him dressed in his revelry attire. Autumn had only given him details but he tailored it to fit those details. Trevin donned a long-sleeved dark gray button-up shirt, the first two buttons undone. A corset vest in a light shimmering blue matched her bodice with the silver embroidery. The Greenthistle emblem embroidered the chest pocket. Gray fitted pants and black boots completed the outfit. Around his belt he had a saber and his dagger with the hilt that matched hers.

Elodie eyed everyone in the audience, only able to make a few faces out near her. Trevin took her hand.

"Lady Elodie, will you bestow the honor of the first dance as my lady?" he asked with a bow. She felt her heart yearn for him.

"Master Greenthistle, the honor would be mine," she said, doing a curtsy as she was taught today.

He smiled wide and led her to the dance floor and pulled her close. They did the steps as she had practiced and they hardly broke eye contact.

"El, you are stunning. And the energy pouring off you is unlike anything I've ever seen," he said softly in her ear.

"I'm in a fairy tale," she said, smiling.

"I am happy you are my lady," he said, pulling her close. "Never doubt how much you mean to me, Elodie," he said in a quiet tone.

"I am glad we met. I'm not sure I've ever felt this way before. I can't imagine feeling it with anyone else, Trev, I lo—"

"Be very careful with that word, my dear little mink. I see it in your eyes, and feel it in your touch. I know what you mean. I hope you know how much you mean to me," he said, interrupting her softly. "Not yet, El. Those words mean more for you and I. Soon, I promise. Never question what you are to me though. Please?"

"Okay. I trust you. I am happy we have this here and now." Her voice was small and fighting the faltering that loomed.

"I am glad," he said. "Oh Elodie, how beautiful you are. I can see the heads turning and the eyes admiring you, they all know you are mine, and I am yours. I will be yours for much longer than you realize too."

Elodie felt that tugging and confusion brewed inside of her.

"And you will be mine. My mountain lion, so brave and beautiful," she said, meeting his gaze. "For a long time I hope." He smiled and with the final crescendo of the music and spun her around and then wrapped her in his arms. Everyone clapped as the music faded and the dance floor became much more crowded. They continued to dance once more, and then he led her to his dad and the other lords.

"This is the one, the mortal who runs with the fae, with the odd energy in her. I can feel it," Lord Nightswift said. Elodie curtseyed to the high estate lords and ladies. Putting forth her best formalities she had practiced over and over.

"It is a pleasure to meet you, Lord and Lady Nightswift, Lord and Lady Ashdale," Elodie said with a smile, taking them in as fae. They nodded, watching her closely. She turned to Lord Greenthistle and curtseyed again. "Lord Greenthistle, I thank you from the bottom of my heart for allowing me to be here. Thank you for your hospitality. I do hope to remain quiet and not be a burden," she said. He nodded and smiled.

"For you what you did for my son, and for Greenthistle, I thank you. This was a small request to fulfill." He smiled. "Heed my warnings though." Both Trevin and Elodie frowned and nodded.

She was introduced to people who worked with the estate lords, and those who taught the estate children. Countless introductions were made by people she had seen around town and not realized were fae. Small plates and desserts were enjoyed, and she only took drinks from Autumn and Trevin. There was more dancing with Trevin and a few with Autumn. Even a dance with Q who dared not touch her, and Trevin watched the entire time. A few glares, looks of disgust, and gazes of awe and wonder all came in Elodie's direction. There were also smiles and even compliments that sounded genuine for her too. She avoided Russ and Caleb. They seemed busy with a girl that Elodie could only assume was Alena.

"That's the one he got so worked up over?" She heard a girl say. She fought the urge to turn her head.

"If that's what gets him off I guess, he went all soft on me. Just the Greenthistle disappointment, right?" The girls laughed. Elodie sighed and frowned.

Autumn took Elodie's hand. "Come on, ignore them," she said, leading her away toward a bench. She stole a glance back and was stunned at the girl who spoke last.

"Is she high fae? She looks different. Beautiful."

"River nymph and fae. A different sort of half-breed. And don't worry, I know he didn't do anything with her. That was before King Range."

Elodie frowned. "I remember the night."

"It was also the night he decided he wasn't going to ignore his feelings for you anymore."

"I was a complete bitch to him the entire way up that mountain. I got worried with each step that the Old Giants gave up on me. They were so quiet. Trev never did though. He kept trying to help me."

Autumn smiled. "It's odd you have that connection to them."

"Always odd, I suppose." She frowned.

"El, it's neat that you do. I can definitely see something in you, but I can't pinpoint what. Fascinating, is a better way to put it."

Q walked over to them. Her eyes cut to the ground. Q laughed as he sat down next to her. It was her first night seeing everyone as fae.

"I'm glad you could be here, he looks so happy, and you look as though you belong here, El," Q said to her.

She smiled and her cheeks flushed with heat. With a hard swallow her eyes met his. He had called her El. She felt it was a form of acceptance. "Thank you, Q. I know I don't belong here with him, but getting to experience this is a dream come true. Trevin is a dream come true. I know this is stupid and forbidden but I feel like I know I lo—like him so much. I never imagined meeting someone like him and to know that this is real, that magic does exist. To know that in some tiny way I can help you all and these lands. The Old Giants." She smiled.

Q smiled too.

"He won't let you say that word, will he?" he asked. She nodded. "He's a damned fool. I see it in his longing gazes, I've never known him to be like this. He does, Elodie, know that he does."

"I'm glad. Because I do too," she said. "When he tells me how much I mean to him I almost feel a tap on a strand deep inside me. I know that sounds stupid. I've never felt this way before, but then again, I've never been to fae revelry before, never had fae wine." An awkward laugh escaped her.

As the night went on, Elodie decided to be brave enough to get some water on her own. She took a large gulp, then felt someone walk up behind her.

"Lady Santiago, with the odd power in you, how it boils and simmers. How it caresses and coddles Master Greenthistle. As if you were a siren luring him in," Russ said.

Instantly, Elodie's body tensed and she saw his sly grin and the evil in his eyes.

"Hello, Master Nightswift," she said with a curtsey. He placed a hand on her elbow. It was tense as if he was struggling.

"Please, call me Cyrus," he said, forcing his hand to her waist. She gasped.

Is this his real name? Russ. Cyrus?

"You are blessed with good graces I see. Autumn has done a fine job of making you an estate lady." He pulled her toward him, her body locked. The earth was still and she could feel it as though it locked up with her.

"I'm not Lady Greenthistle. It is only his lady tonight, so no one touches me." Her heart pounded. It only seemed to make him smile more. His grip on her arm trembled. He took a deep inhale.

"Perhaps I could show you otherwise, estate lady of Nightswift? Maybe Trevin doesn't want a mortal as his lady. I can see the pure energy in you too you know.

I can show you what it is." His voice was so close to her ear as he pressed his body against hers.

"Stop! How do you know what it is? And you gave me your name? Why?"

"I think you are trustworthy. You wouldn't dare abuse it. Not with Trevin, or dear sweet Autumn. Not me, right? And besides you know I cannot lie." His lips were so close to her skin. Short, labored breaths escaped her as she swallowed back a cry. He grabbed a glass of wine with a shimmer in it. Fae wine.

"I should get back to Trev," she said.

"Aww why? I can follow you into the forest just as easily as Trev does. I can take to the skies. We can get to know each other, maybe I should kiss you?" He held up a flute of the shimmery gold liquid she drank last night.

"Cyrus, stop," she said, he let out an evil little laugh and gripped her arm tighter. *He's not listening to my command? How?*

"I'm not going to hurt you, little mink," he said to her. She froze and felt a pit in her stomach. She did not like hearing him call her that. That was Trevin's name for her.

"Cyrus," she said, trying to pull away. His breath graced her neck. She whimpered and swallowed hard in fear, she was about to scream.

"Master Trevin is occupied. Wouldn't want to cause a scene would you? Let me show you your power, we just need a short walk. You could see your true potential on the winter solstice, the longest night of the year," he said. Elodie watched, worried to see Trevin with Caleb and Alena. The girl laughed and put her hand on Trevin's chest. Elodie watched as he narrowed his eyes and backed up away from her.

Trevin! Elodie pleaded in her head.

"Cyrus, Stop, please," she whimpered. Just then Cyrus let her go and walked away as she locked eyes with Trevin. He instantly hurried to her side.

"Elodie, what's wrong? Who got you shaken up? I got interrupted on my way to find you," he said, holding her hands gently. She glanced over and couldn't see Cyrus anymore.

"No one." She shook her head

"El, I announced you as my lady, if anyone even gives you bedroom eyes there will be dire consequences."

Why would Cyrus do this? He knows the rules. He's an heir. Even Q kept his distance.

"Was that Alena?" she asked, trying to change the subject. He sighed and pulled her in for a hug. She gripped him tightly.

"Yes, she is kind of seeing Russ and Caleb."

Elodie nodded uneasy. "Oh, is that normal? To be with both?" she asked clearly, still shaken.

"It is for some, yes. What happened?"

"Nothing. It's fine, I don't want to be the one to cause a scene. Not here, not now."

"Something did happen, didn't it? Who?" he asked, his rage building.

"No, I wanted to get water and bumped into someone by accident and they glared at me. I am okay. They just rolled their eyes and walked away, I'm not even sure I could point them out to be honest. There weren't even words, just a glare, not worth getting upset over," she said, and Trevin sighed.

"El, please tell me the second anyone else ever makes you uncomfortable. Keep your dagger on you and the floss flower oil. Okay?" he asked, holding her hand.

"I will, Trev." She hugged him tightly.

"I dunno about you, but I'm about done bumping into people and getting pulled in every direction. I'm sorry I left you. I just didn't want to smother, plus I know Autumn and Caleb are looking out. What do you say we retire for the evening?" he said, leaning in to kiss her softly, save for the nibble on her bottom lip.

"Do you need to make a grand announcement or something?"

"No. We simply go to my room, there's an extra ward on it tonight." He smiled at her. She nodded.

"Okay," she said nervously. He held up his arm, and she took it as they left the ball getting some snide looks.

Chapter 38

As soon as they were out of the grand hall Elodie let out a sigh of relief. Trevin led her upstairs to his grand suite, where candles were lit in and the lights were dimmed. He started to kiss her, tasting the cherry lip gloss.

"It drives me absolutely wild to see your glossy lips. Kissing you is euphoric." A groan slipped out of him. Her hands ran down his chest and over the corset vest to his waist. She noticed he was undoing her hip belt and set it to the side.

"Thank you for the gift. I need to get you something. I just don't know where to begin."

Kissing her neck, he walked her back to the bench in front of his bed.

"It is something I had been wanting to give you since the King Range trek. I want you to have it. I want everyone to know what you are to me. How special you are. I will teach you how to use it. I noticed you and Q talking," he said as he sat her down and knelt in front of her, untying her boots then removing them.

"He is nice. Justine does like him, even if she acts like it's not serious." She frowned and met his eyes, as he removed her other boot.

"He likes her a lot. Russ and Caleb give him shit for it, but he doesn't care," Trevin stood up to kiss her and took her hand. Smiling at her, he began to kiss her neck. Then he moved behind her and pressed himself into her, his breath hitched in her ear. He was already getting hard, as he moved his hands down her chest and wrapped them around her. "El," he said in a near moan, pressing himself against her.

"Are we going to follow tradition?" she asked. A soft laugh caressed her ear as his hand untied her bodice and felt it loosen. Her posture slumped, and he smirked.

Tell her, you idiot, he told himself. "Autumn told you about the vowed ceremony tradition, I take it?" he asked, removing the corset slowly. *Tell her that she is your everything. That you love her.*

"She did."

"And how would you feel if we did stick to tradition?" He kissed her neck and nape, and watched her shiver.

"I think I would like that. It would be fun to play along." A nervous exhale slipped out as he pushed the corset down slowly.

If only this were real, you are my vowed. I am yours, El. "Yet you are nervous. Why?" he asked.

"I'm not sure. It's silly at this point since we've slept together. It's been magic every time," she said. He smiled and rubbed his hands up and down her body. She still had undergarments and the diadem on. Her breathing picked up as his fingertips skimmed back and chest. He embraced her for a moment.

"El, you are..." he whispered and kissed her neck. "Beautiful," he said softly and walked around to face her, kissing her again. "You look as though you are entranced." He grinned. *Say it, chain her down. Sway her. She needs to know.* His thoughts battled themselves. He didn't know what was right.

"Your touch is intoxicating. It always is," she said, unaware of the battle raging in Trevin.

He kissed her and worked his way down to his knees licking and sucking on her chest. She had to take a deep inhale. He was just above the underwear line and he glanced up at her. His hands rested on the small of her back, fingers just above the elastic.

"You mean so much to me, Elodie and I want you in every possible way. Remember that always," he said. His fingers slid down her underwear squeezing her rear. Then he pulled the garment down and started to kiss what was in front of him, using his tongue ever so slightly. He heard her moan and her body swayed, his arms supported her as he pressed into her.

He felt a wave wash over him and pulled her closer, knowing how much he loved her.

"Trevin," she moaned. "The diadem." Her breath was so full of lust and want. He laughed and kissed back up to her neck.

"I know what traditions say, and I can be patient. Despite how much I want to just rip these clothes off and take you on the bed right now," he said. Next, he slowly removed her hair clips and the hair tie letting her hair unravel. "Your turn," he whispered and led her out of the mess of her clothes on the floor she was standing in.

His words flowed through her head. *I want you in every way possible. Does he want me as his lady, his vowed?* She couldn't imagine feeling this way again with someone else. She knew she wouldn't have this kind of love with anyone else. This was the storybook love with her prince, her vowed? He would leave one day, she wouldn't be attractive to him, she would age. Even if he wanted to stay, she would be fifty and he would look like this. What about when she was too frail to do the hike to the estate? This was not forever, it was temporary and yet she would vow herself to him if he asked. In a way she felt as though she already had. *Just ride the fairy tale out,* she thought.

She took an uneasy inhale and undid his saber belt. Carefully setting it down next to hers, her eyes traveled up to him. Elodie took in his face, his eyes, his markings, the ears, the diadem. She looked at him in awe. Her fingertip ran along his ear and she watched his eyes go heavy, his lips pulling to a smile. Then she ran the back of her finger along his cheek bone and his breath hitched as he closed his eyes.

"You are breathtaking. I can't believe I am here right now. As your lady."

"You always will be, El."

The tap pulsed through her again as she stared at him for a moment. Then her eyes traveled down his shirt. Her fingertip traced down from his lip to the point where his vest began.

"Your touch is intoxicating too."

A small smile graced her lips as she lightly tugged his collar of this shirt, pulling him down to a kiss. Her hands moved to un-fastening the corset vest, and she kissed his neck.

"You look regal enough to be a king," she said quietly. He laughed.

"That would make you my queen."

"A title of true honor."

She placed her hand on his hip and lightly brushed across him walking behind him to remove the corset vest. She could feel how hard he was.

"I've never seen a corset vest before, you look very regal in it."

"I wanted to match yours, Autumn would only tell me colors and basic design. We will look into getting the Greenthistle sigil on your Spring Equinox gown," he said.

"You want me at the Spring Equinox?" she asked, unbuttoning his shirt. He cupped her jaw and looked at her.

"I want you in every possible way, El," he repeated. "As my lady at every seasonal revelry and every night," he said, kissing her. She gently pushed him and walked him back to the bench. He smiled going with her lead. She knelt in front of him and removed his shoes.

"Even to remove your shoes on my knees, naked save for a diadem to match yours?"

He laughed. She slid his socks off. "Did you not enjoy it when I removed yours?"

She stood up, stepping between his legs and started to rub her hands up and down his chest. Kissing him, she slid her tongue in his mouth and he moaned reaching up for her chest. She undid his pants and kissed down his chest. Her tongue traced his lines as she tugged his pants down. He moaned again and tipped his head back. Her mouth hovered over his hardness and she wrapped a hand around him then licked down and up his length.

He moaned again loudly.

"I like the sensation of you undressing me. I like undressing you, knowing what is waiting for me underneath. Knowing what's mine," she said with a hint of possessiveness she seldom used.

"Elodie," he whimpered.

She stood up seeing him naked, save for his diadem then took his hand and pulled him to stand.

Trevin took a step back and spun her around. "Radiant as a queen should be."

"As breathtaking as a king should be," she replied, taking him in. He stepped forward and assessed her again.

"Once these diadems are off, I am going to take you on my bed and have my way with you, little mink," he said quietly, as her hands roved over his body.

He let out a small shaky sigh as he undid the pins around the back of her diadem.

Elodie felt his change in demeanor was odd, then she remembered Autumn said he had never done this before.

"You've never done this before?" she asked.

"You are the first, El," he said with a smile. With the pins out, he lifted it off her head carefully so as not to pull her hair. He set it down on the dresser and looked at her. "I've never felt this strongly about anyone. Your kind heart, your curious nature, your brave soul, you are beautiful. And how far you have gone for me, my family, these lands. I will never chain you down. If you chose to go, you would be free to, but I do hope you know, Humboldt loves you, you are home here, Elodie. These lands are as much a part of you as they are me. Whatever great forces out there led you here, I am grateful for you. You are my—Elodie, you are everything to me. You mean so much to me," he said and a small exhale escaped him.

Elodie watched him, his words had her entranced. For a moment she wondered if he was going to tell her she was his vowed. Yet he didn't. She was his everything, granted more than she ever should have been by being here. She would ride this fairy tale until they no longer could. Surely, he would have said it if they were vowed. The idea likely was just as bittersweet to him as it was her.

They had tonight, and whatever tomorrow brought. She knew he cared for her, and maybe, it was the same way Autumn cared for Charles, and Q cared for Justine. One day it would end. *Am I allowed to really leave? The bargain though. I don't want to leave this place or him. Ride it out till you can't. You would ruin this bloodline and this estate. A half-breed born to lose their mother. As he had lost his, as I lost Mom. I am not sure I even want to be a parent, how would I raise a half-breed?* Again all her thoughts cascaded down but this time she stopped herself. With an inhale, she smiled in soft sad acceptance, she wouldn't continue that cycle, wouldn't break Greenthistle of being high fae. He was hers here and now. She'd give him everything until she couldn't, she was temporary after all.

Stepping forward, she looked at him. She felt she could cry, but not out of sadness or that inevitable loss that would one day come. Elodie wasn't exactly sure how to put this emotion into words.

"Trevin, my mountain lion, my king, my dashing fae prince who keeps me safe. Who I have been blessed with."

A sudden surge and swell jolted through her. He watched her concerned.

Wake up. Wake up. You are his. He is yours.
They need you. Wake up, you are home.

The voices said and instead of feeling tense, she felt warm. Any lingering sadness that this was not real, that he and she were temporary was gone. Her eyes widened, and she looked at him. She was his, and he was hers, she loved him. No matter what their future together held, his lands were her home. She smiled wide, she wouldn't leave this place, even if he left her. He had shown her home, she had found it. Trevin was not her overseer, and he had told her as much. He was much more than that, he was home.

"You feel like home to me. Whatever our future brings, you have shown me home," she said, lifting her arms and removing his diadem.

Trevin processed the range of emotions then the surge in her, the shock in her face and the smile, then her words. Suddenly he felt that regardless of being careful, of not saying the words specifically, if somehow this was real. This was not make-believe and fun as his friends had all done before. As though their intent was strong enough that they had become vowed.

This was them both, stripped to their barest form. She had found home in him. He had to let her decide if it would remain her home forever. Until then, she was here. They had the longest night of the year and he would not waste a second more fearing what the sunrise might bring.

He scooped her up in his arms effortlessly and laid her on the bed. Their hands began to wander as they kissed each other, pouring every ounce of passion over each other.

CHAPTER 39

After an early departure and long drive down Highway 1, Elodie pulled her car into the driveway of a house in Novato. Trevin was somewhat uneasy meeting Elodie's dad. He wanted to make a good impression but was nervous she would decide she needed to be back here with him. He knew he wouldn't stop her; he hoped maybe she would come back after a while and they would pick up where they left off if she moved back.

"Hello, sir. It is an honor to meet you, Mr. Santiago," Trevin said, bowing.

"You are not what I expected from a politician's son. You are almost like royalty, Trevor."

"My father holds us to a high expectation, especially me, as his eldest. I set an example," he said with a smile. Elodie grinned with some unease.

"Well, I certainly would say you are a worthy suitor of my little princess," he said.

Elodie felt her cheeks heat. "Dad!" she said, "Stop, please." Trevin laughed.

"And I do hope to remain worthy of Lady Elodie's affections," he said with confidence.

"Stop. Both of you," Elodie said nervously.

"El, you are so very lovely," he said. Her dad raised his eyebrows.

"She must really like you—she never lets anyone call her El. Even scolds me for it," her dad said. Elodie frowned as Trevin glanced at her curiously. "Her mom used to call her that. I miss her a lot. She loved the redwoods and Humboldt, and loved taking Elodie up there. The way Elodie's eyes would light up looking at the ferns and redwoods, and up to the tops of the old trees. I swear she could see magic in them. It is a memory I hold dear. I know her mother did too," he said with a smile, glancing over at the family picture on the bookshelf.

Trevin's eyes followed, seeing where Elodie got her features. Her mother was Native American and Irish. Her dad was Mexican and Spanish.

"There is a lot of magic in the Old Giants, Elodie helps me see more of it every day despite growing up there," Trevin said with a warm smile in her direction, and Elodie smiled back, knowing this was their secret.

"I miss her, but I am so happy she took the step to make a life there. I think she has needed a place like that for a long time," her dad said.

Trevin smiled. "I think the Old Giants needed her for some time, too. I think maybe I do too."

"You are the oldest?" her dad asked him.

"Yes sir. A younger sister and a younger brother. Though my brother is taller and stockier than me," Trevin laughed.

"Tell me about them?" her dad asked as they sat down in the living room and talked. Eventually Elodie got up to start making pies and getting things prepped. Trevin watched her, amazed at everything she was doing as he conversed with her dad.

At some point, her dad coughed hard. Elodie saw his glass empty. She instantly rushed over and replaced it with a new glass of water.

"I'm sorry. I should have made sure you had a glass. Are you okay?" she said.

Trevin watched this dynamic closely. He could see her fear pounding, and her energy simmered again. Her face was plastered with worry. As he observed her dad, Trevin noticed his irregular heartbeat, watching small hints of shame form in him. He didn't understand at first. Her dad was omitting something, the heartbeat that he could feel, but Elodie couldn't. This was not the omission he and his family did every day; it was not to protect himself. Then his eyes went wide, and he looked at Elodie. He thought back to what she had said over Thanksgiving about the cough that had started. He was omitting things to protect her.

"Oh I'm fine, hun. Don't worry," he said, catching his breath. Trevin heard the lie and frowned, realizing he was facing a moral dilemma.

The people in the café, who had their own reasons for lying or omitting, Trevin simply watched. He was no more involved in their lives than they were in his. Just people in the same space at the same time. He recalled when Cora's grandfather passed away a few years ago. He was there for her. He absorbed her sorrow and he processed it. It hadn't bothered him. It didn't take him back to the place he had been when his own mother was lost. He just helped as needed and moved on.

Yet this was his vowed potentially being kept in the dark about something that would break her. Something that might pull her away from him and the Old Giants. He wanted to give her the choice, not force her into forever, and wanted her to choose it. If she didn't choose Humboldt, what choice did he have? He wondered what he would do if this were his dad? Death was now a real thing in his life. He had always been ignorantly unaware until he had lost his mom. Elodie had lost her mom, and the day would come when he would lose her too if he didn't find a way to give her that choice.

"I'm fine hun. I'm sorry, Trevor. The old lungs ain't what they used to be anymore. Don't ever get old, okay?" he said with a laugh. Elodie glanced tight-lipped at Trevin. He gave a half smile and nodded.

"Of course," Trevin said, composing his nerves. "Let me know if I can be of help. My dad has some medical knowledge, and I have picked some up from him, not much admittedly," he said.

"Ahh, so well rounded your family sounds. I'm happy to hear," he said. He began to tell the story of when Elodie cut her hand open in Arcata Community Forest. Trevin spoke of the trails up there with familiarity.

Elodie cooked for them all and cleaned up after while they watched TV. Trevin had offered to help, but she insisted she was okay. He frowned and nodded. When they went to her room, he saw a glimpse of her life here. Pictures with friends and far-off places he wasn't sure he'd ever see. Old sketchbooks, patches, and rocks lined the shelves. She walked out of her bathroom. He smiled, seeing her and when she climbed into bed, he held her close to him.

"Is this what life is like down here? Tending to everyone's needs? No one tends to yours?" he asked, and she sighed.

"It's what we do. Wait until you meet the extended family. They will give you the impression I'm selfish and putting myself before anyone else. All I need is the forest and the ocean. Those are the needs that replenish me. And maybe my mountain lion," she said, rubbing his cheek. He smiled and brought her hand to his mouth and kissed it.

"You jumped up, ready to dig deep for some magic healing power every time your dad looked strained. You did all that prep work, you're going to cook the entire meal tomorrow too?" he asked. She remained quiet. He rubbed her head.

"It wasn't always like this. They were nice until I started to travel again on weekends or on breaks. I was running away, they'd say. I went away to college and came back and I was silly for moving that far, yet Dad always told me I should go. To honor my mom, who loved to go explore. So I did. Then I got a job here. I had my own little apartment, too. I found a higher paying job in the city and took that. Got burned out on commuting and the work environment, so I came back to Marin County. The entire time I was away, I was told I could be doing something better, closer, less time consuming, for more pay, you name it. There was always something better, right here in Marin."

"The Old Giants got louder. It felt as though they were reaching for me, the roots were reaching out trying to grab me. I started browsing jobs, just to see, then apartments, things I remembered, new things I didn't know about. Then on a whim I applied, and then another and another, then video interviews. I remember the night I walked in on Ricky in bed with someone else. I stayed a night in Jenner. I got the job offer the next day and that night I sat in my hatch at Stinson Beach. I listened to those waves and thought real hard about what I already knew in my heart I was going to do. It scared me that night. More than almost anything else in my life had. Yet I knew I could stay here, shriveling up more and more or I could go, give in to that pull of the Old Giants. Let them pull me out of that hole I crawled into. Start over, find out magic is real, and that my fae prince was there, waiting for me to cut the iron off him."

"I am forever grateful you made that choice. That you took that chance," he said, trailing off. "Death is a very scary thing for me. It shouldn't be. We are immortal. We can heal quickly. I have strength and heightened senses. I can become a beast most people are terrified of, but death is not something we think about. But I lost my mom, who was always supposed to be there for me. I hear you and your acceptance of the matter and it hurts to think about. I hadn't realized part of being human was that life is finite. Your drive to do extraordinary things is precious, it is amazing. I see what you do in the cities and towns. I hate that people make their contributions and then fade away," he said, kissing her and hugging her tightly. "Don't wear yourself so thin that you become dust and soil, please."

"Trev, we know this is a reality. We ride this out until we can't. What else can we do? My forever and your forever are very different. I want you forever, whatever that looks like." He felt another tap, more violent than before.

"You have it, El. Never doubt that, forever," he said, kissing her and crawling on top of her. She ran her fingers through his hair.

"Trevin," she said. He tugged on her lip with his teeth. "We have to go easy. Quiet."

"I know, we will. Lay back, Let me take care of you," he said, running his hand up her shirt and playing with her chest. Three rounds and she was spent. He kissed her softly, listening to her deepening breaths, eventually following her into slumber.

Chapter 40

Trevin awoke the next morning and jumped up uneasily. His eyes scanned the room as the familiar scent of sea breeze and lavender hit him. *In Novato.* A sigh, then he got up, got dressed, and walked to the kitchen where the smell of food overtook his senses. He was shocked to see everything she had done and prepared. He knew there was no kitchen staff here, no servers, no one but her doing this.

"El," he said softly. She looked at him and smiled.

"Have a seat. Help yourself," she said, putting a slice of French toast on a plate, then set a bowl of fruit down on the table.

"How long have you been at this?"

She glanced at the clock. "Maybe an hour? I had to get the turkey and stuff."

"By yourself?"

"No kitchen staff in Lord Santiago's Estate." She laughed nervously. He walked up and hugged her, giving her a kiss.

"Never feel like you have to do this for me, okay? Ever."

"It's nothing really. I just don't because there's no room at my place in Humboldt."

"Even if you get a bigger place, don't feel like I expect this, okay? I appreciate it though. I've never had a partner make me breakfast before." He kissed her head.

"Really?" she asked. He shook his head. "Go on, sit down. Help yourself," she said. "I'm going to wake Dad. Unless you want it to just be us."

"It'd only be polite to eat with Lord Santiago while he hosts me." He laughed.

They ate and Trevin helped when he could. They all got cleaned up and presentable, and then her extended family showed up.

Trevin was in the kitchen, still trying to help while Elodie ran and got the door. He cursed himself for being clueless about cooking—something he now knew he needed to learn. He didn't want to rely on the staff to feed him anymore and certainly wasn't about to rely on Elodie to feed him all the time. His ears took in the conversation happening at the door.

"You're here. Good job," Elodie's aunt greeted, unenthused.

"Yes," Elodie responded with a sigh.

"Are you moving back yet? End of the semester, surely you can just move closer now?" a man asked. Trevin glanced at the doorway, not yet seeing them.

"You know I can't do that. Mid-year is the same as any other time, and they offered me a permanent job," she said. "Oh, hi Ollie. It's been awhile," he heard Elodie say.

"Yeah, I figured I could pop back here. I am jetting back to Spain on the 26th, for New Year's and all. It's pretty amazing. It doesn't make me miss the Bay at all."

"No, I'd imagine not. I have been busy too, and haven't even given New Year's much thought. Probably a get together or bonfire or something."

"I'd imagine it's super boring up north. Where'd you go again? Sonoma or something?"

"Humboldt and actually it's great, thanks. I just attended a big solstice celebration," she said as Trevin listened and stirred gravy.

He heard a timer ding and went to tend to it but heard Elodie say, "Oh shoot. Let me grab the rolls." And quicker than he thought possible for a mortal she was in front of him taking the dish out of the oven. He saw the three walk in and lock eyes on him.

"And this is?" her aunt asked. Trevin read her assessing gaze.

"This is Trevor. My boyfriend," she said confidently. He felt that light tapping, and exchanged a quick glance and small smile with Elodie.

"Hello, it is a pleasure to meet you all," he said with a slight bow.

"Where'd you find this guy?" Ollie said, laughing.

"Humboldt, duh."

"Oh, you must be the politician's son, those eyes of yours. I see why she might have given you the time of day," her aunt said with some sass.

"Stop!" Elodie hissed. "Trevor is so important to me and to Humboldt," she said as Trevin smiled.

"I must admit, I am very lucky she gave me a second glance. She has become an important person to me too," Trevin said. Her aunt rolled her eyes and her uncle walked to the couch, unimpressed.

"Let's see if you say that in a year. She gets restless," her aunt said and walked off.

"Your dad is a politician in Humboldt?" Ollie eyed him up and down.

"Yes, he is."

"Let me guess. You all just sit around and smoke all day?"

Trevin smirked. He could sense Elodie's nerves building and surging.

"Oh you know it, then you know what we do? We go out hiking in the trees and wander through the redwoods. Like a bunch of hippies. Winter Solstice was a grand party. El and I had the time of our lives that night," he said in his wry voice. Ollie and her aunt snapped their heads back at him.

"Okay." Elodie laughed nervously. "I think dinner's about ready," she said. Her aunt shook her head and Trevin smiled warmly at Elodie.

"Sorry I'm not as much help with cooking. I will get better. This is amazing," he said, closing the oven door after she set the turkey down.

"Really it's fine. I'm not sure I'd know how to do any of this if I had kitchen staff either," she said with a smile.

"You hire people to cook for you? You must be old money. Elodie says your family has been in the area for some time," her aunt said.

"We have. My grandfather went into politics and then my dad followed. I hope to do the same as the area is home and important to me. My dad has a more expensive pallet, and he's pretty busy so he hires a cooking staff for us. That's not to say I can't hunt and camp for a few days if need be. My dad taught my siblings and I. Plus I work with BLM and State Parks. I do some overnight trips," he said, stretching the truth, of course.

"Real outdoorsy type. That explains why she likes you," her uncle said. "Let me guess, you have an adventure van."

"Actually, I drive a truck. I camp out in the forest more than I stay at campgrounds. El and I had a rather wild adventure in King Range recently. She's very good at backpacking. I certainly learned a good bit from her," he said. She smiled widely.

"Oh, she has been to so many places with her little car. She loves it. I bet you had a lot of fun up there. That is a steep climb," her dad said.

"It was steep. I was exhausted. Then we both had to work the next day."

"Yes, it should have been three days but poor planning on my part. She was so brave, too. So prepared where I was not." Trevin gave her hand a gentle squeeze.

"You got yourself in a whole situation and a half up there and you want to stay?" her aunt said "Even if there is old money involved."

"Stop, it's not like that. At all. He has helped me a lot, too. He's very good with the wildlife up there."

"And he told that ex of hers off," her dad chimed up and stood. "Let her be. Trevor here is a perfect match for her. Her mother would be thrilled."

"Seriously, you should just go back abroad. It's much more fun. You were in Asia, ever think about going back there or Europe? Plenty of teaching jobs in both," Ollie said.

Elodie's shoulders slumped and Trevin noticed just how tired she was. He could see it not only in her eyes, but also mentally. This was draining her. Part of him couldn't help but wonder if it was because she was too far from the Old Giants. If the lands did give her some kind of life.

"I miss it, but I knew it was time. It ran its course. I honestly missed the redwoods even over there. There was a magic I found over there. If I had the opportunity to go back for a visit, I would, but I also like the magic I found up north. The magic I found before and after Trev and I even met."

Happiness washed over Trevin. "She shows me the magic up there all the time, and we got off to a rocky start. I messed up pretty bad the first time we met."

Her aunt stood up now and gave Elodie a smug look. "Sounds really healthy. I'm sure that turkey has rested enough."

"Always gotta be carved right," her uncle said. Elodie was once again grateful for the topic change. She made sure her dad had what he needed, and that Trevin did too, and then finally sat down. She remained quiet, even though the conversation was grating to her.

Trevin watched her and observed her family. He drew conclusions and realized this place drained her. Even if Humboldt was not where she settled, this was a strange place for her.

After they left, Elodie started doing the dishes after she made sure her dad was set. Trevin walked over to the sink. "El, sit. Let me do them."

"It's fine, it's just dishes."

"And you are both mentally and physically exhausted. Let me help you. It's the least I can do for being so pathetic in the kitchen." He ran his fingers along her spine, sending a relaxing energy through her. "Go sit, please," he said.

Her eyes got heavy, and she nodded.

The doorbell startled them both.

"I'll get it," Elodie sighed, heading off to the door.

"She works so hard, she always has. Please look after her, Trevor," her dad said. Trevin met his eyes and nodded.

"I always will. I give you my word, sir. She has burrowed into my heart and I never want to lose her," Trevin said, as he felt another strong tap. Then he heard Elodie gasp.

"I had a feeling you'd be here. Let's talk," he heard a vaguely familiar male voice say. Trevin narrowed his eyes, trying to place it.

"You need to leave. You need to stop bothering my dad, too. Leave now, Ricky," she said, backing up. Trevin was by her in an instant, glaring at Ricky.

"You heard her, leave."

"You're that asshole from before," Ricky said.

They assessed each other. Ricky had more bulk, but Trevin knew he was of little worry. It would hardly be an effort for Trevin. He'd thank Cedar later for all the practice. Cedar was bigger than this guy. Quinn would have towered over him.

"Leave," Trevin growled.

"Elodie, come on, you can't really think whatever he offers is good for you," Ricky said. Trevin felt her energy surging, and he took her hand, trying to calm it down. Elodie looked at their fingers laced together, a soft soothing sensation flowed into her. Ricky turned his attention to Trevin. "What are you, rich or something? She and I have a history, bro."

"She and I have a future. Learn to listen and be more respectful. Stop acting as if you own her. No one does," Trevin said.

"Just leave Ricky, seriously," she said, with an assertion, gripping Trevin's hand back.

Ricky narrowed his eyes then looked at Elodie.

"I know I messed up. I'm sorry, I apologized before. Can I at least know where you moved to? I know we had something, something real, two years' worth. You've had six months with this guy at most? You know he's probably out fucking around on you too," Ricky said. Trevin snapped. He was so tired of people assuming things about him like this. He pinned Ricky against the wall and Ricky tried to fight back, but Trevin effortlessly pinned his wrists.

"You make very wrong assumptions about me. I have never fucked around on anyone, and I never will when it comes to her. I told you before that I know a good thing when it's right in front of me, and meeting her was the best thing to ever cross my path."

"Oh, you went and found yourself a charming prince, didn't you?" Ricky said, scowling at her.

"Just leave. I'm telling you this for your own good. We are done," she said. Trevin hadn't taken his eyes off Ricky once.

"Just going to run away, like you do best. Good job landing this overbearing asshole."

"Ricky!" she hissed.

Trevin glared at him.

"One more word, or text, to her and you regret everything you've ever done to her. I see it in your eyes. You think you are entitled to her, you fully intend to hurt her again too," Trevin said with a near growl. "You fucked up, you lost her. Learn to listen," he said, shoving Ricky away from the door, then turned to walk back inside.

"Yeah, whatever, fucking prick," Ricky said.

Trevin heard Ricky's heavy steps, heard Elodie gasp, felt Ricky grab his shoulder and yank him back. Trevin swung his fist around and punched Ricky in the face, nearly knocking him over. Trevin didn't say anything; he just stood there and loomed over Ricky.

"Please Ricky, just leave. I didn't want to see you get hurt, but this is over," Elodie sighed out. Ricky glared at Trevin, who narrowed his eyes, daring him for one more comment. Ricky remained silent then shook his head and walked to his car. Trevin walked back in and closed the door, pulling her into a hug.

"El, are you ok?" he asked softly, rubbing her head.

Elodie nodded. "Thank you. I'm sorry."

"You have nothing to apologize for. I've been wanting to punch him since Halloween," he laughed.

Elodie sniffed and laughed too. "Is your hand okay? That was a hard punch."

Trevin cupped her jaw and gazed into her eyes. "I'm fine. Let's go sit back down. You are so tired I can see it in you."

She nodded and walked back into the living room. Her dad glanced at her. "I'm okay Dad. I think he might have gotten the message," she said. "I hope he did."

"Thank you, Trevor. I don't normally condone violence, but the way you rushed to her side, I'm glad to know my little girl is looked after."

"She is very special and I don't want to see her upset or stressed."

"Does Ricky know where you moved?" her dad asked.

"I doubt it, I certainly never told him."

"Well good. No matter who says what to you here, I want you to stay where you are happy. You were miserable here. You are building a life up there. As long as it keeps you happy, I want you to stay. Don't worry about me. I am fine," he said. Elodie looked at him and smiled. "If he does find out where you moved, or he shows up there, look into a restraining order."

Elodie nodded and sighed. Trevin watched him, hearing his breathing sound off again. He could see the shame in her dad's eyes, knowing he was going to crush his little girl with whatever health issues he was hiding.

"You're going to look out for her for a long time up there right, Trevor?" he asked him. Trevin looked at him, slightly stunned. He heard the pleading in his voice. He was trying to push her away, hoping she'd somehow be okay.

"Always, sir. I give you my word. I will look after her until I am no longer breathing." Trevin felt the tap and noticed Elodie's body flinch, as if someone pulled a tether on her too. He wasn't sure how to feel about this. Would he shield her from this pain, too? Could he watch her lose her dad? He realized he was going to have to. Her dad was begging him to help her and he couldn't leave her. He'd carry her through it; however, she needed him to. She had saved him twice; he would do this for her. Trevin wanted to do this for her.

Her dad sighed and took a sip of water. "Did you two really have a big Winter Solstice party?" her dad asked.

Elodie and Trevin looked at each other.

"Yes, we did, but it wasn't a big pot infused hippie festival, it was more like a gala or a ball. I got to wear a pretty dress and his sister did my hair and makeup and it was so magical." She beamed.

"Sounds like something out of a fairy tale. I bet you looked stunning," he said.

"She did. It was a true honor to be by her side that night."

Elodie got up and showed her dad the picture of her and Autumn. Autumn and Trevin had taken some glamoured with her. "That's Trev's sister, Anna and I."

Her dad looked at it, then at Trevin. He smiled. "You sister is beautiful, and Elodie, my little princess, that dress and you even have a crown on. You always did love your ear cuff things. Stunning." She laughed. Trevin smiled remembering her. Remembering holding his vowed and dancing with her.

"The guest of honor and the host family got to wear diadems, and it was my family's turn to host," Trevin said.

"Absolutely stunning. You two look like a Lord and Lady of Humboldt with the redwoods and the ferns there. She has found her fairy tale."

Trevin met Elodie's eyes, and she smiled wide.

"She is always going to be my lady," he said.

"I am so happy you found each other," Elodie's dad said. He yawned, and he turned in for the night.

He looked at her and she sighed. She was tired and drained. Her energy was spent.

"Are you sure your hand is okay?" she asked him. Trev laughed.

"Please, that was nothing, you've seen light days with my brother, and believe it or not I can pin Q about half the time. Caleb will be proud I punched him out," he said.

As they got ready for bed he rubbed her back, soothing her and seeing the energy come back.

"Are you going to see the Marin Estate Lords tomorrow?"

"Yeah. Their neutral meeting spot is Marin Headlands. I'm not sure what all I will do with them but I will be back in the afternoon at the latest."

"What would they do if they knew about me? Aren't they going to ask?"

"I am allowed to date mortals, it's fine."

"What if they ask if I know about you? Them?"

"I'll tell them the truth. You helped Greenthistle with projects involving iron. In turn Dad made a bargain and you agreed. You are under Greenthistle's eye and know the consequences of speaking. I can't lie and neither can they. The most they can do is ask my dad and he will say the same thing." She nodded and kissed him.

Chapter 41

They returned to Humboldt establishing a routine of half the week together and half the week apart. Slowly they became more open with what they were. Cora commented on how they had cut back on their days at the café only really going Wednesdays and Thursdays. Fridays usually consisted of them out at the beach or gatherings.

Elodie was enjoying work more each day. The school board was so impressed with her lesson plans, parents were always quick to say hello to her. There was talk of the elementary school teacher and the budding politician circulated. Her cheeks heated every time. She wondered why it was never the budding politician Ashdale and the accountant Justine, or the music teacher, Charles and the PR rep, Autumn. Elodie and Autumn often hung out around town and went on hikes together, much to Trevin's relief. Autumn said Elodie always had her dagger and would laugh at the odd looks passersby would give her.

Trevin too continued to excel at all his drills and work tasks, giving more public facing announcements and reports on TV. Quinn and Cyrus were also put more in the public role. Trevin and Quinn couldn't help but notice Cyrus often seemed more and more exhausted as the days went on. Trevin hardly went to the tavern with Cyrus or Cedar. The few times he did, Cyrus would continue to make sly remarks about Elodie. He noticed he never said anything about Justine, leaving that to Alena.

Cedar usually rolled his eyes but did nothing to stop the talk, though he did not participate in it. Cyrus never said anything bad about Autumn, but would make the occasional comment about counting down the days until Charles left. This made Trevin and Cedar uneasy.

Cedar had a week away in Siskiyou County and would have another one in Trinity. Trevin had told Elodie in the fall he would be on assignment with the police academy in Mendocino. Quinn too had assignments away with CALFire. Trevin's job usually did not send him far but he did have some weekends he had to work.

Cora hosted parties and arranged bonfires and Elodie always stayed close to Trevin, especially if Cyrus was there.

Quinn liked Elodie, he had told Trevin a few times he needed to tell Elodie what she meant to him. He was unaware what had all occurred the night of the solstice. Trevin was still hesitant, saddened he couldn't give her his forever and he so desperately wanted to. With the spring equinox approaching Trevin agreed to Quinn's bargain; if they could find a way for her to go, Trevin had to tell her. Though he was still unsure what rules applied. Part of him couldn't help but feel selfish.

Trevin had decided to go to Falk. With the winter months ending, the more likely people would be hiking nearby. He had been studying and working with his dad on the exact location and now they felt they finally had it. Though the retrieval mission left Trevin shaken and Lord Greenthistle was concerned. For once actually encouraging him to spend a weekend with Elodie to relax and take the edge off. Trevin was downright spooked with what he had found and only told his dad weeks later, nervous the entire time.

They looked at the tome which had an iron lock and covers made of iron. Trevin had to wrap his hoodie in it and tie some rope around it to get it back. It sat on a podium in the study at Greenthistle Estate. A sigh of defeat escaped them every time they looked at it. They debated having Elodie help briefly with it but they were not sure if wards were on it. They were also not sure if the lock broke what might happen to Elodie. It was mentioned once, then not again. Trevin didn't want her to stress anymore over this and his dad did not want to harm her.

One Friday morning Elodie and Trevin were getting ready for work when her phone rang. It was her aunt, saying her dad was in the hospital with a ruptured lung. She went still as death and Trevin instantly felt her emotions and watched her as though she were going to break. He had a feeling he knew what this was about and cursed himself for letting it slip his mind.

"Elodie, do you want me to go with you?" he asked softly. She looked at him then down for a moment.

"I have to go, soon, like today. Now."

"I don't mind requesting, we just usually give more notice. Emergencies happen though," he said, watching her. "I will meet you later if I need to."

"Five in Marin, right?"

"Yes. I send word and it reaches them all."

"Isn't your dad going to be pissed?" she asked. She was looking off at nothing, as if she was going numb.

"He may not find it the best idea, but he will understand. He mourns friends and family too. He passes to other counties to mourn them. Fae and mortal alike. I am your overseer, it's my duty to Greenthistle if he has a problem. I do not want you alone for this."

She remained silent.

"Okay," she said in a small voice.

"I will run home and send word to Marin and then run back here. Fourty minutes tops," he said, rubbing her arm.

She nodded but didn't move. He watched her looking to see what the energy in her would do. He hated seeing her in distress but that was when it seemed to get clearer. It was never clear enough though, as though the mist of Humboldt kept it just out of his vision.

"El," he said softly. She wiped her eyes and nodded.

"Okay," she said, with an inhale. He embraced her in a hug and kissed her head.

"I will come back here in a bit, okay?"

She nodded and he let her go. "Trevin," she said, wiping her eyes again. "Thank you for being here," she whimpered.

He smiled and rubbed her tears away with his thumbs. "I will always be here, little mink," he said. She gave him a split-second of a smile and nodded. "See you soon," he said, heading out of the door, then changed into his mountain lion and ran.

He ran inside and went to the study. He thumbed through the parchments and found the herbs for Marin's High Estate. He wrote the message and double checked it.

Master Greenthistle of Humboldt requesting entry into Marin.
For reasons of aiding a former resident with a family emergency.
Appointed Overseer.
Length of stay not to exceed seven days.

He put the drop of blood on the parchment and sent it off by tossing into the bowl of flames. Once upstairs, he packed his backpack with clothes, a charger, and tablet, then ran back to the study. A sealed parchment appeared with all five high estates' approval and well wishes. A small bit of relief passed through him, knowing they were not fond of such short notice and turned around, then gasped.

His dad stood there with his arms crossed and leaned on the door jamb.

"Marin? Are you planning on running all night?" Lord Greenthistle asked.

"No. We are taking her car," Trevin said. His dad gave him a condescending smirk.

"You are going back to the mortal girl's home, so soon?" Trevin narrowed his eyes on his dad.

"She lives here. She's visiting her sick father," he said. "What are you trying to imply?"

"This is two trips to Marin County in the last few months. You are my first born and heir to this estate and you will remain. For someone who wanted little to do with mortals you are rushing out of here to go over two hundred miles south with one?"

"I don't want her alone for this, not on that road. I am her overseer and her friend. This is what friends do for each other. Everyone was here for us when we lost Mom," Trevin said. He took a step forward now. "She calls Humboldt home, we look out for our residents, fae and mortal alike. If she wants to stay there, do you have requests? Wish that I drag her back crying and screaming?" Trevin said with seriousness. His words echoed defiance he had never taken with his father before. His dad did not move.

"No, the request is if she wishes to stay, you hand her over to Marin and you return without her. Do not do anything to piss off the Marin Lords. Understood? Report to them and me."

"Yes sir," Trevin said with irritation walking toward the door.

He was stopped by his father's hand on his chest.

"Trevin, the other request is that you be very careful if she returns with you too. A mortal will not be lady of this estate. It will only ruin you," Lord Greenthistle said.

Trevin looked his dad in the eyes with shock and disdain.

"I'm not trying to make her lady of the estate. You made it loud and clear she can't be." Trevin did not back down.

"I'd highly recommend you remind yourself of that, I worry for you, son. She is kind, but she's fleeting," he said, stepping out of the way. Trevin sighed. "Tell her I send my condolences."

He stood there for a second and before he said anything stupid, he ran off.

Chapter 42

E lodie walked out and locked the door in a daze. She wiped her eyes again and took a deep inhale. Trevin walked over to her and offered to take her bag, but she paid him no mind and stood at her car. She had her hand on the door handle and she stopped and stared at the trees.

Come back, little one.
Make your peace, embrace your gifts.
We will be drained.

"El," Trevin said, standing next to her. She snapped back and looked at him.

Those eyes. He will be drained; his family will fall. Her lip started to quiver again.

"Let me drive. It will be okay. He will be so happy to see you. I've been granted seven days. Dad sends his regards," Trevin said.

His family will be drained if I leave?

"I can drive, I'm fine," she said, hesitantly putting her hand on his arm and giving a small squeeze. "Thank you again, Trev. I'm okay to drive."

Trevin nodded and opened her door then set a cup of iced coffee in the cup holder for her. He closed it when she was in and walked to the passenger side. He had also gotten them breakfast. She smiled and her eyes nearly welled up at the thought. The coffee was just the way she liked it. *He is so thoughtful.*

They drove in silence for the first few miles taking 101 south and bypassing Avenue of the Giants. With each mile passing, her heart rate increased.

I need to see Dad. I need to see him. I'm going to Marin, she told herself. *I'm from Marin. Humboldt has been calling me back here. Why? I left Dad behind.* Her eyes watered, and she sniffed. The pull of these trees got stronger as they reached Humboldt's territory line. Every time she did this drive south it was becoming a struggle. Avenue of the Giants had become a sad place, a place that meant she was leaving. Ripping the roots out of her heart.

"El. Pull the car over," Trevin said softly.

"I'm fine," she said, voice breaking.

"I know how to drive. Just pull over and let me drive, let me help you. I know you're overwhelmed and scared. I'm here. I always will be." Trevin's words tugged on her. She kept driving and then saw the Grandfather Tree and pulled the car over.

"I've driven this way dozens of times, and I drove it in November, and I drove it in December, with you." Elodie fixed on the redwoods ahead of her, watching them as though they were worried.

"I know you can do it, but I'm telling you that you don't have to," Trevin said, placing his hand on her shoulder. "You don't have to this time. Little mink."

She looked at him finally. Now fixed on his eyes and thought about what the trees said and then she caught a glimpse of the trees in Mendocino. The trees never spoke to her anywhere else, only Humboldt's redwoods did.

She sighed, and a nervous feeling crept into her core. Elodie nodded.

"Okay," she said with slow deep breaths, "Okay," she repeated then put the car in park. Once out of the car, she stood staring at the redwoods around the parking lot.

Do not wander off for long. Evil lurks.
He will be drained, his family bound.

A chill shot through her despite the voices being a faint whisper. She got in the car and looked at him again. He glanced at her then checked the mirrors and slid the seat back.

What am I supposed to do? she thought. She noticed her coffee moved to the center console now and took a sip of the iced coffee with the cream. She could taste the caramel in it.

"Thank you," she said. She felt like she had barely spoken to him other than to tell him no. "I appreciate it, a lot."

"Anytime, El," he said, putting his hand on her knee.

"How was the trip to Falk, the map was correct, right? You seemed distracted afterward."

"It was correct. The trail is getting overrun, as are a lot of things in the town but I found it. There is a trail that leads there from the Headwaters Forest Reserve. Most people think only one building still stands, but there's more, they are not very stable though. I'm not sure Q could do it in feral, Russ would have trouble flying in too. Luckily there wasn't a lot of iron around. I found the ancient tome in an underground storage section of a collapsed house. Unfortunately, we can't open the tome. It's locked with iron, and has iron plates on the front and back. So we are all stumped, but we have it."

"More iron? Were you okay?" she asked, glancing at his hands. He nodded and explained how he got it, with the supplies he brought.

"So the Old Giants are taking back the site they fell in?"

"Yes, but the overgrowth is alarming to a lot of fae. The three estate lords are uneasy." Trevin sighed.

"What is it?" she asked. "What makes them so uneasy?"

"It's nothing we won't figure out. I think it has to be a fae thing to handle. I don't want to add another stressor to your plate," he said then sighed with defeat. She frowned and looked down.

"Is it that you can't speak of it? Or you think I'm going to get scared?" she asked.

"It's not either of those things. It's that, I don't want—I don't want to upset you. I have been processing what I saw at Falk. It was disturbing. Only my dad knows and I didn't tell him until weeks later."

She turned to him.

"Oh. If three high fae estate lords can't handle it, what is a mortal going to do? Is that what you were trying to avoid saying?" she asked. Her tone was level, not angry but not in agreement.

"Yes, but no. Do you remember the very first thing I said to you? At Cora's Halloween party?"

"How could I forget, 'You are an odd one,'" she scoffed.

"Yes. I didn't lie. I could have picked a better word than odd, but it was true. The way you speak of the Old Giants is similar to how we view them. The way you stop to look at them and the energy I feel when they speak to you. It is not that I think you are less than us, please do not take it that way. I cannot figure out what it is in you. Dad sees it though, and he doesn't know either. I'm just worried that somehow, you and it are connected and I don't want you in danger. There are dips and dried up old streams and sharp jagged rocks. It'd be a challenge for anyone, us included. Eleven miles round trip plus the trailblazing."

"Which estate does Falk and preserve fall under? Greenthistle or Ashdale?"

"Neither. It's part of the federal lands. It is part of the territory, not anyone's estate. A lot of ancient or important artifacts get placed on federal lands so as not to give automatic claim to any one estate granting them more power. It would take a fae's eyes or a clever little mink to find these things. Since most mortals don't really know what they are looking for, it's safest on federal lands," Trevin explained with a small smirk.

She smiled too and then frowned. "The overgrowth is more than just some ferns sprouting up, I take it? An invasive species?" she asked.

He sighed then went to speak, but paused. "I saw a stone pillar or tall monument marker of some kind, broken. It looked old. I'm sure it was a result of the earthquake last fall. There were animal bones scattered around it. After I crawled out of the structure and had the tome though, was when I saw what spooked me. Around the broken stone looked like dark soil. When I looked closer, I noticed the soil was dried blood. Then I saw bones, and the fur stood up on my back and a chill passed through me. It wasn't just rabbits or squirrels. It was the bones of ravens, bears, and mountain lions. A few of each and their skulls all lined up facing me." Elodie stared at him wide eyed.

"Trev," she said uneasily.

"I bolted as fast as I could. I didn't detect any fae around nor in the bones, they were animals. Our estate animals specifically," he said.

"Oh."

"So, that's why I am glad you didn't go. I do not want any human bones or blood there, certainly not yours. I do not want whatever was there to sense you there, with this power in you," he said. She nodded. "These puzzle pieces keep falling, and I don't think you can avoid getting buried by them now."

"I see," she said, breathing deep. "Does power ever shift between estates? You said yours is the oldest, the strongest?" she asked, thinking back to the iron cuff.

"The power balance should always be close to equal. Greenthistle is the oldest, Nightswift, then Ashdale is the newest. The lineage determines what abilities the earth grants the high estates. Dad has the power to sedate and heal, rendering anything unconscious should he need to. Also the ability to scramble minds, I guess in some ways, Greenthistle has a lot of power.

"Nightswift can see through their aligned animal, we can't and having line of sight in the skies is a huge advantage. It's one reason I think Lord Nightswift wants to remain second. He has said Russ will succeed after me but before Q. Ashdale can pull strength from nearby aligned animals at no expense to the animal. An advantage for a bear. They can also calm, kind of like a living weighted blanket. Q looks intimidating, but he's rather gentle. I can calm others too, but that's only because I'm an empathic seeker and receiver. I know how to shift emotions. Q just calms them but can't pull or shift emotions.

"The power shifts reflect in our feral forms most. We will be bigger or smaller depending on which estate has more or less influence on the land. Depending on the generation that causes the power shift it affects them most. So if Dad broke rules, we all feel the loss, but he and the other lords would feel the loss or gain the most. Power can be earned back or shifted. Breaking rules, hurting mortals, hurting those the lands favor, hurting other fae or high estates, all those things can lead to a power shift."

"Oh. Has power been pretty equal in your lifetime?" she asked, wondering about his example.

"It has."

"I assume there wasn't any power shift from the iron cuff? So that ruled out Ashdale and Nightswift?"

"Ya know, it was odd. Quinn had mentioned he felt a small push of power. I was unconscious and then it was crazy with you finding me. I think I gained. Russ didn't mention anything, but he did have that accident prior and seemed to recover faster than we all expected. So, we assumed we gained, somehow which also has us all baffled. Q is the only one who felt it clearly."

"Another estate trying to get power?" she asked.

"We searched. No estates were involved, they were horrified and worried."

Elodie was trying to think. *It couldn't have been Cyrus if he was able to recover, he had strength. It wouldn't be Nightswift or Ashdale with those succession gifts either.*

"I must make everyone extra nervous then. Plus I have something weird in me around the time some rogue assassin puts iron on you? I'm surprised they didn't just put me in the hold or whatever it is," she laughed nervously. Trevin sighed.

"No one wants to harm you. That bargain just made it so no one could. You have been a huge help to us. One I think even Dad realizes we have needed."

"Does your dad think I am linked to everything happening?"

"He tries to write a lot of this off to coincidence but I think he's starting to see it's too much coincidence. He feels the surges that are linked to you too."

She nodded. "Do you think this thing in me is bad? Or a danger to you all?" she asked with a worried frown.

Trevin instantly shook his head. "No, not at all. The Old Giants talk to you, they act as though they need you. That tells me you are not evil or malicious."

"They don't need me. I'm worried I might be unknowingly putting you all in danger and now, you are driving far away from your lands to help me. I hope they don't smite me for pulling their heir away for seven days." She frowned, and he squeezed her knee.

"Little mink, this must be so overwhelming for you and I'm sorry. I never expected this to happen, to meet someone like you. Never expected someone to have the effect on me that you do. To be the very embodiment of all three estates," he said.

She looked at him as though he was crazy. "Ummm, what? I don't have any neat animal forms. I'm limited to two feet and slow ass healing when I trip and fall like an idiot on trails."

He laughed and shook his head. "Elodie, you are so observant and cunning like Nightswift. Loyal and kind like Ashdale. Strong and brave just like Greenthistle. When Caleb started talking about kisses from mortals, I knew I didn't want either of those assholes to kiss you. I saw something in you that night and I wonder if it was all the estates that made you. When I heard how Ricky spoke to you, as if he owned you, like you were a toy he'd pick up when he pleased, I was pissed. Then you wanted, needed help, and I had to get a kiss, and you were the only one who caught my eye. The only one who catches my eye," he said. She blushed and smiled.

Elodie shook her head. Then she wondered if Cyrus actually knew what was in her or just wanted to do something to her. She went to speak and then stopped. She looked at him then back down.

"Come on, El. You have nothing to be afraid of. Let me help. What is on your mind?"

With a nod and a hard swallow, she asked the question.

"Is Russ's real name Cyrus?" she asked. Trevin narrowed his eyes.

"It is. Clever mink, what was your thought process on that?"

"I can't take credit for being clever. He told me to call him Cyrus." She watched Trevin look at her shocked then back ahead at the road.

"When? Why?" he asked, shocked. "You didn't ask him for it?"

Elodie shook her head. "Um, at solstice. I saw you and Caleb talking with Alena, I think was her name. And he came up behind me and said I'd cause a scene if I cried out. He said he wanted to take a walk with me, to show me what was inside of me. But I've read and watched enough horror stories to know that wandering off leads to trouble." She noticed his grip on the steering wheel tighten.

"That bastard. That's what had you shaken up? Why didn't you tell me? He knows how stupid that was."

"I didn't want to cause a scene. I know I was allotted an immense privilege being able to attend. I didn't want more eyes on me, thinking I was trouble or to be cast out. Didn't want your dad to have more reasons to dislike me."

"Cyrus tried to lure you away from me, he knows you are under my specific watch and Greenthistle's. He tried to challenge me for you at the bonfire last November, before you found out about us too. When I was still fighting what I felt for you."

"It filled me with dread and the trees warned me not to. I didn't feel that dread walking alone with you so that's why I stayed by you or with Cora the rest of the night of the bonfire."

"Elodie," Trevin said, heaving slightly, trying to control his anger and protectiveness. She looked over at him. "Will you promise me if he touches you or tries to get you alone ever again you will tell me immediately?"

"I don't want it to be my word against his. His dad and yours just staring me down." She started to panic.

"He cannot lie. It would never come to that. Q and Autumn have noticed the looks he gives you too. Please, Elodie, promise me. I bound myself to be your overseer because I needed to make sure you were safe. Brothers don't go after each other's partners. We made a pact years ago. I'd never in a million years go for Justine or Alena or anyone they have been with. This is the second time he has broken that pact. Promise me, please," he pleaded.

"Okay, I promise you, Trevin. I will tell you." She watched him sigh in relief and nod.

"Thank you. I do not want you in any danger or to feel uncomfortable." Elodie nodded and looked at him. A shaky sigh slipped out. "What is it?" he groaned.

"Um at solstice, he pressed his body against mine from behind. He told me if I wanted, he would make me Estate Lady of Nightswift. I panicked, I saw you tense and step away from Alena but you didn't look up. He faded back into the crowd and you were there."

"He was trying to lure you in. He is trying to fill your head with inconsistencies. Unless. Unless you want to be Nightswift's lady."

"No! Greenthistle, you. I don't want him or Q. I want you, Trevin."

"Would you want to be an estate lady? Mine?" he asked nervously. She swallowed.

"I am not sure what that entails. I want you Trev. In whatever way you will offer me," she said, "I don't want you to hurt though because we both know one day, it will." She frowned.

"If I could, I would make you an estate lady in a heartbeat. I want to offer you everything," he said. She sighed and smiled at him.

It cannot be undone, as though he is actually vowed to me but he doesn't know it yet? One thing at a time. Dad first.

"I'd like that, Trevin. Our happily ever after. One thing at a time though. Dad first," she said.

Trevin nodded with a hopeful smile and a plea that they would find it.

Chapter 43

As soon as Trevin parked the car, Elodie ran inside. He kept his eyes on her, scanning for anyone watching her. Trevin was nervous with her emotional state being so wild that Marin would seize her. He'd be damned if anyone took her.

When they entered the room, they found her dad hooked up to multiple machines, but he smiled at Elodie.

"Dad!" she cried out.

"Oh, my little girl. You rushed down here so fast. I hope you weren't speeding," he said, gripping her hand weakly and smiling. Trevin could see he was not doing well. He stayed by the door, giving them space.

"No, I wasn't. The school gave me time off. But let me know what you need. I will take more time off or quit if I need to," she said.

Trevin's heart hurt, and he felt sad knowing he could not sway her any more than he already had.

"Elodie, I am okay, it will be okay. I am just glad you are here now," he said. He gripped her hand with some more strength and she smiled, hopeful. He glanced over and smiled wider at the sight of Trevin leaning against the door. "Trevor. It's nice to see you. Thank you for being with her."

"Always, sir," he said with a bow. He walked closer and smiled.

"I'm glad to see you two. I hope I'm not pulling you from your work, Trev. I don't want to pull her from hers."

"Not at all, Mr. Santiago. Dad sends his thoughts," Trevin said and her dad smiled. Just then a knock occurred and someone walked in. Trevin stepped aside.

"Hello, I'm Dr. Latham. You must be Elodie?" he asked.

"Yes. This is my partner, Trevor," Elodie said hastily. The doctor and Trevin nodded at each other.

After a few moments, Trevin stepped out giving them some privacy though he could still hear the entire conversation. Her dad was not doing well, which confirmed what he already knew. He kept his eyes peeled as he felt her energy simmering, worried someone would see it. With a deep inhale and texted his dad.

Can Marin take her from us? They can't, right? She's one of ours.

They can hold her until I confirm the bargain, but they cannot do anything to her. Just because you are her overseer doesn't give you the right to override the local estate orders. Is there an issue?

No. Her dad isn't doing well, and he kept it from her. Her energy is simmering and I'm worried they will sense it.

Remember you cannot sway her, Trevin.

I'm not trying to! They shouldn't force her into their hold though. She trusts me and I don't want her to be separated from me by estates she doesn't know, especially not right now.

I know, son, we cannot chain her up here, just as they cannot keep her from us. She needs to decide and if they scent you all over her, it may be seen as influenced. This was one reason I warned you about getting too close with her. I will speak to them should there be a problem.

Trevin sighed, putting his phone away, and then saw her aunt and uncle walk up. They stared at him, stunned.

"You are here? Why?" her uncle asked.

"I was with her when you called. I offered to come for support. It's what partners do."

"Well great," her aunt snapped and went to walk in the room. Trevin stood up and blocked her and she looked at him appalled.

"She's talking with the doctor now and she is under a lot of stress."

"We are too. He's my brother! I don't know why he left her to decide everything when she's not even here. She's off gallivanting in the trees high as a kite with you!"

"She's not. She works really hard. Please all I am asking is for you to show her some sympathy too, this is her dad," Trevin said, stepping aside and taking a deep breath.

"Whatever," she said.

"You know she doesn't need someone speaking on her behalf," her uncle said.

"I'm not. I am out here giving her some space. She doesn't need people deciding things for her either," Trevin said, sitting down. Her uncle walked in and then a few moments later he heard her aunt speak.

"Nice of you to show up."

Trevin felt Elodie's energy plummet and jumped up to see her heaving. He could see how overwhelmed she was, how scared she was. She was recoiling inward. The doctor was assessing her, likely for a panic attack. Trevin didn't waste another second debating. This was his vowed, and she was in distress. He rushed to her side and took her hand.

"El, you are okay. We are here. You do not have to do this alone, little mink," he said softly. As though the words coddled her, she took a deep breath and her breathing slowed. He was careful to not shield her from any emotions, letting her process things.

She gripped his hand and glanced at him with a nod. The doctor assessed Trevin and then her aunt and uncle, noting their narrowed eyes at him. He called her aunt and uncle out of the room, and Elodie hugged Trevin.

The rest of the night went much smoother, and her aunt and uncle apologized to her and offered her support. Trevin apologized for offending them and being combative, and after a few hours they left.

"I'm so happy to see you rushing to help, Trevor. You are a good man," her dad said.

"I hope I always will be. For her up in Humboldt," he said. Elodie smiled. "Uphold your promise to look out for her, okay?"

Trevin tensed suddenly hearing the irregularities in his heart. "I will, always."

Elodie smiled and Trevin took her hand and placed it in her dad's. He stood by her side and placed his hand on her back. He was getting uneasy with this surge. Her dad had said goodbye to her aunt and uncle before they left, and had told him to look out for his daughter. Now it was Elodie's turn.

"Elodie, I'm so proud of you. You have built the life you always wanted, your mother always wanted, and she is proud of you too. I love you. Never lose sight of the magic, always reach for it okay. You found it up there in those redwoods," he said.

"I will, Dad. I love you. That magic Mom talked about up there is real. I did find it, in the trees," she said with a smile. "It's in those Old Giants and the ferns, I feel it," she said, smiling so wide.

"Ahh the earth has blessed you? How wonderful. I love you hun," he said. Elodie smiled too.

Trevin narrowed his eyes at the words. *Blessed by the earth? Her?* He had heard something like that somewhere a long time ago. When he was little but he couldn't remember it, a memory that was blurred. Something his mom may have told his sister, but what was the context? He was yanked hard out of his thoughts when the machines started beeping and Elodie whimpered. Her energy was boiling.

Elodie watched her dad close his eyes. For a moment she thought he was nodding off to sleep. Then she heard the wheezing escape him, the machines went off and his hand went weak. The nurses rushed in seconds later. Elodie cried out as Trevin pulled her back. She fought him, trying to get out of his grip.

"Let them work, El. I'm here."

"Let me go! I don't want you to see this," she screamed. "Dad!" she screamed again, her hands heated. One of the nurses eyed him and he nodded, pulling her out. "Stop. Trev—" she said, biting her tongue. She panicked for a moment, debating if she was actually going to order him, use his real name. Then the Old

Giants and the ferns flashed in her head, the very thing she felt safe with, him. Home. She stopped fighting and her energy plummeted again causing her to go weak. He sat her down and held her tight.

"I'm sorry," she sniffed out.

"You have nothing to be sorry for. I know what it's like. And I know it hurts. I don't want you alone for this. I'm here, and I will be here. You are not alone. Breathe, little mink," he said. She nodded, and he rubbed her back.

A short while later the doctor walked out with a solemn expression. "Ms. Santiago. I'm so sorry. We tried everything, did everything we could, but your dad didn't make it."

Elodie felt her lip quiver and then the wave of grief cascaded over her. "El," Trevin said softly in her ear. She gripped him and he held her tight, she clung to him so tight as if she were going to fall. "Let's step outside for a moment, then you can see him," he said softly.

"I wasn't here! I lost the last eight months! I'm a horrible person," she cried. He led her outside. "Ricky was right, I just ran away," she said. Trevin cupped her chin and locked eyes with her.

"No, you are not. You visited him. You left the Old Giant's that called to you and came here, back home," he said.

"I don't know where home is. I ran away from this one to try to hide in the forests," she cried out.

"And you helped me. You made friends and taught children to see the magic in their home. You show me new ways of seeing the home that made me. He's proud of you Elodie," he said softly. She flung her arms around him crying into his chest. He rubbed her back and held her close. "Want something to soothe the pain, or would you rather feel it and process it?"

"Please. Not a lot though. Don't pull anything onto yourself either," she pleaded, tugging on his shirt but not looking at him.

"Of course." He placed his palm on the back of her neck and pushed some calming magic into her.

Eventually they both said their goodbyes and headed back to the house.

Chapter 44

The next morning, she cried as he rubbed her back, letting her process the emotions. He told her about when Cora's grandfather passed, how he was at the hospital in Eureka with her and her partner.

Elodie asked if he had sensed it was coming. She noted how he made her hold her dad's hand one more time. Trevin fessed up, and said he was worried she would be mad at him. She was grateful he had been able to prepare her.

When Elodie eventually got up, she went to cook but Trevin stopped her, insisting they order something. She relented and agreed, sitting still was never something she had been good at. She started to sort through things and he helped until he had to go. It was shortly after sunset and he realized she hadn't eaten since they got up. He had been snacking since his metabolism was higher.

"We will get dinner when I get back, okay? Don't cook though, please. I will be as quick as I can," he said. She nodded and hugged him tightly. He kissed her head. "My little mink."

"Thank you, Trev. For everything," she said, letting him go and watching him leave.

Elodie went back to sorting through things and trying to busy her mind. The house began to close in on her. The quietness and the stillness she had felt when her mom passed. Only now she was much more aware of everything, now that she was older. She was trying to maintain normal breaths. Occasionally she would stand in the backyard trying to feel the earth, the call of the redwoods. Yet all she felt was how far they were. She saw the stars become clearer and longed to walk the trail by her studio, the trail to Greenthistle, the trail in Arcata. She glanced back at the house and for a moment Elodie debated on driving to the coast somewhere. Point Reyes was closed, and Stinson Beach felt lonely. Sighing, she went to her car and sat in the driver's seat. She eyed the ignition, holding the keys in her hand.

Trevin would be livid. No, he'd be worried. He is so kind. To be here with me and he wants to give me forever. She looked up to the tree line, some were young redwoods nestled with various other types of trees. *I do love him, but I can't tell him, can I? I won't tell him, but I hope he knows. He has to know.*

Elodie sighed and dragged herself back inside the house. Once she was in the door, the severity of the situation weighed back down on her. *Just keep your hands busy. Keep getting things ready to close this chapter. Marin isn't home. Humboldt is home. Forever. Remember that, El,* she said to herself.

Trevin tried to control his nerves, anxious about leaving her alone, but he had a responsibility to be at Marin Headlands.

One mountain lion, a coyote, a large stag, a crow, and a hawk landed in front of him, then changed. They watched him bow his head and kneel down.

"On behalf of Greenthistle Estate, I thank you all for the approved passage on short notice. My father, Lord Greenthistle, sends his regards."

"Rise, Young Master Greenthistle," the mountain lion said. He stood. "Your friend, a mortal? Otherwise, I'd assume you'd say which fae estate."

"Yes ma'am," he said. "She relocated to our territory late last summer."

"Hmmm interesting, your father approved this," the crow asked.

"Yes, sir, eventually."

The estate leaders exchanged glances.

"Will the mortal be regularly returning with you escorting her? Should we be aware of her name and history?" the hawk asked.

"No, ma'am, that's not necessary. She is not in servitude to Greenthistle, Nightswift, or Ashdale. She is a friend to the three estates and ally of Greenthistle Estate." He saw them all murmur and whisper.

"A friend and ally? Humboldt has not had any mortal discoveries in centuries. Your father was a mere cub the last time one was in their hold," the coyote said.

"She has proven trustworthy and is no danger to us, nor you. She understands to speak of us means she will have the option of servitude or her memory wiped. She has agreed to our bargain to help us with iron on artifacts and where iron and floss flower may be involved. She will remain quiet. I have been appointed as her overseer," Trevin said.

"And your plaything?" the stag asked and smirked. Trevin remained steadfast.

"No. We have developed a fondness for each other. It is mutual."

"Very well then. What is her profession and reason for choosing Humboldt?" The stag followed up.

"She is a primary school teacher, sir. She likes the redwoods—the National Park is her favorite. She is a vagabond and has lived all over the state and West Coast. The Humboldt High Estates will report any and all details of her status to the council in September."

The hawk nodded. "Understood. One more question, there was an odd power surge last night. Did you feel it?"

"Yes, ma'am." He remained calm, aware of their eyes on him.

"Had you felt it before, in Humboldt perhaps?"

"I have. The estate lords of Humboldt and heirs are looking into it. We are diligently researching it."

"Humboldt encounters it?"

"Yes," he said, unable to lie.

"Interesting. It felt like a very ancient power, an old power that has not been seen in some time," the stag said.

"Do you know much about it?" Trevin asked.

"It is a power of the earth, that of something very old but in a new form. Yet it is a foreign energy on these lands. We would like to learn more of your research on it in the event we encounter it again."

"Understood. We do not have much, but I will relay the information to my father upon return to Humboldt."

"Thank you, Master Greenthistle. We do wonder if it has something to do with your Old Giants. The old growth in Muir Woods seemed to respond to it most, but it is feels more ancient than they are."

Trevin nodded. "We are looking into that, too. Our Old Giants and ferns react to it."

"Interesting. Should we encounter it again, we will be in touch with your father and the other Humboldt estates. Be well, Master Greenthistle," one of the mountain lions said. Trevin nodded and knelt down again.

"Be well, Lords and Ladies of Marin. I thank you immensely for the passage to your lands," he said and watched them all run off. He remained frozen, listening for any movement before he sighed in relief, then changed into a mountain lion and sprinted for Novato. Once it was clear, he changed into his glamour, then ran down the street to her house. The kitchen light was on, but the living room was dark. He opened the screen and went to knock, noticing the door was slightly ajar. His heart tensed for a moment. Had he not closed it, had she? Had someone else entered? His heart pounded.

Trevin walked inside and saw a light in the back room, her dad's room. He heard her sniff and that energy quietly trickled out. Sensing she was upset, despair pouring out from her, he closed the door and ran back to the room. Elodie was on her knees, hunched over with her arms around herself. He knelt in front of her and placed his hands on her shoulders, supporting her, calming her. She looked up at him and threw her arms around him, and cried into him. Instantly he wrapped his arms around her.

"Elodie," he said softly.

"They're both gone. Both of my parents," she cried. He looked around and saw the photos of her as a kid with her mom and dad. He saw the photos of them in Yosemite, and Joshua Tree. Photos of her older with her dad in Seattle and Sedona. The medical supplies and prescriptions near the bed. A picture of Elodie in a cap and gown in front of an older mission style building and palm trees on the wall. Then he saw a bigger picture of her mom, with the same warm smile Elodie had. "They aren't here and I don't know what to do," she cried out. He rubbed her back, and he felt his heart break for her.

Trevin knew everything she was feeling, and he had no idea what she was feeling all at once. He wasn't sure what would happen if he ever lost his dad. He looked up to his dad for guidance, even if his own foundations were fracturing. One day, that legacy would fall on him.

"Shhh. I'm here for you. I always will be. Always. I promise you," he said. Knowing he would keep that promise. He'd always watch over her regardless if he was or wasn't a presence in her life. The *tap, tap* preparing to tug, hit them both.

"I know. It's just that they are gone. They aren't here. This house is like a ghostly shell of memories that will never be spoken again. It's so hollowing here." She trembled. "I don't know why I walked in here. The house feels hollow but when I walked in here, it hit me, crashed down on me like a net and I couldn't get out," she cried into him.

"Let's go to the living room, or your room maybe?"

"I don't think I can stay here tonight."

"We can get a hotel. Near the water. We still have five days left. I will do what you need me to here if you can't look at it. I will talk to your extended family too. Let's get something over in Tiburon or somewhere," he said. She nodded and held his hand as he grabbed their bags and turned the lights off. "Do you have the keys?" he asked. With a nod, she locked the door, trembling the entire time. He took them and led her to the passenger side door. Then pulled out his phone and sat back, booking a room.

Elodie pulled out her wallet and handed him her card. He looked at it, then her and shook his head. Her shoulder slumped.

"Don't worry about it. I got two nights and we will see where we are, okay?" he said, starting her car and driving south. She nodded. "Let's grab food and get checked in."

"Thank you," she said in a small voice.

"Anytime, little mink. I'm always going to be here for you. I promise." *Tap, tap.*

"I'm not sure I'd be able to do this alone," she said. He felt a chill, imagining her there with no one to pull her out, her not asking for anyone's help.

"I'm happy to help. You've done so much for me and my family that this is the least I can do for you and yours. You are important to me, El. If you want me to take some of the load off, let me know."

"I can't put this on you. Not when I know how much it hurts. You know how much it hurts."

"It does, but I will be okay. This is what people with my gifts do."

"Do you know a lot of other people with your power?"

"I know a few. One of the judges in Humboldt's court system, actually."

"We have a fae judge?"

"We do. When we get settled, I will pull up a picture of our judges, see if you recognize them from solstice."

He pulled the car into a spot and turned to her. "Would you like to stay here or come in?"

"I can go in," she said. He nodded, and they walked hand in hand.

"Checking in Master Greenthistle?" a female's voice said.

"Tanya?" Trevin said, shocked.

"I thought for sure it was Caleb when I saw Greenthistle." She glanced at Elodie.

Elodie looked at her and then cut her eyes down, realizing this was a fae, likely a high estate one. Her eyes were a deep blue, much darker than Cyrus's. She wondered if there was purple in her unglamoured eyes. If her name had something to do with tanzanite.

She found it odd that Trevin's was so unique when it came to fae names, with little name history, or to do with nature.

"Is everything okay? With her?" Tanya asked. Elodie's heart pounded

"This is my girlfriend, Elodie. Elodie, meet Tanya Lillyleaf. The visit here is an unexpected and unfortunate one," he said giving Elodie's hand a small squeeze. She looked at the girl behind the counter and gave a small nod.

"Oh. My apologies. Our best room is on the third floor," she said, sliding the keys across the counter. "Let me know if you need anything." He nodded.

"Thanks. It's not cause for attention. She's an ally of Greenthistle. I told your mom a little while ago when I met with the estates," he said. Tanya nodded.

"You know I'm good for it, Trev," Tanya said.

Trevin led Elodie out of the lobby and up to the room. She could see both bridges and the water. Angel Island was visible too and Elodie wondered if she would camp or even hike there ever again. Her thoughts distracted her from the weight in her heart, what she was going to have to do until she heard Trevin sigh. She turned around to face him.

"I didn't realize she worked in hospitality, but it makes sense. Front facing public job. She's an heir and usually heirs have government jobs. Lillyleaf's animal is a hawk. Wisdom and protection. She can read a situation quickly and report on it. Lillyleaf makes a lot of split-second decisions when the stakes are tense. So that was why she asked if you were okay. She and I had um had a few nights when I had a state parks assignment down here."

"Oh. She is very pretty."

"She is fierce and kind of scares me at times. Hiding things is pointless from her. It was a tryst years ago. It was fun that week, but I was empty after I came back," he said, taking her hand. "Not like you though. I want to hold on to you forever, El," he said. "I didn't tell you about Tanya to upset you. I just want to be honest and open with you."

"I'm not upset. We both had partners before we met, and I trust you when you say that. You wouldn't be here if you didn't care for me. I care a lot about you, too. I want to hang on to you forever, too. I'm grateful you are here. I don't know how I'm going to get through this week. I miss him," she said, wiping her eyes.

"I know. Let me know what you need and I will do it," he said, and she nodded and reached up to kiss him. "I will be here with you every step of the way." He hugged her and rubbed her back for a little while, before they got settled for the night, ate dinner, and prepared for the next day.

Throughout the week, Elodie made difficult decisions and told her extended family this was what his wishes were. They had gone back to the house after the two nights in Tiburon. Elodie even spent a few hours talking to Tanya and seeing her unglamoured. They packed up things and prepared for a small ceremony to see her dad off. She had found an updated will in his documents and read over it.

Trevin heard her gasp and looked over at her, seeing her emotions flicker over her very quickly. He saw gratitude to despair, to sadness, to fear, to unease, to excitement, and then nothing. Her body went blank of emotions. She brought her hand to her mouth and took a deep inhale. She looked around at the house.

"El," he said softly. "That was a lot of emotion and now it's nothing."

She swallowed hard before she spoke. "He left the house to me, everything to me. The truck, his estate, nothing to them," she said, her wide eyes met him. A pit formed in his stomach. She sat in a chair nearby. "I mean, I knew he would leave me something, of course, but not everything." She paused and checked the date and then looked at Trevin. "He updated this after the holiday, after Christmas and solstice. He knew, and he wanted me to be okay," she said, tearing up. Trevin knelt beside her. "He didn't want me to move back. This was his way of making sure I wouldn't have to."

"I could sense he wasn't telling you everything at Christmas. His breathing and heart rate sounded off and I knew I was facing a moral dilemma. I didn't know what was going on, what or why he was not telling you how bad it was. When Ricky showed up and you went to answer the door, he asked me to always look out for you. I promised him I would. I will."

"Thank you, Trevin. I don't want you to bear my burden. I don't want you to pull any emotions off me, ever. Especially not one like this. These are things you never should have experienced. Even with everything I feel now, I worry that you are reliving things you never should have had to experience."

He looked at her as though he were falling in love with her all over again. *How big her heart is, to hold all of this? She wants to protect me. Humboldt wanted her with me? I hope she doesn't leave.* "Elodie. You are so kind. I am glad I could be here. I meant it, whatever and however you need me."

"I'm glad, Trev. You show me so much care and kindness."

He was certain she would say she loved him. She hadn't yet, and he knew it was coming. Then he would tell her how much he did.

"Let's get done what we can this week. I will probably have to come back to finalize things to sell the house and close out my life here. I think that this was the last thread I was holding onto," Elodie said with an exhale.

His eyes roved over her. He couldn't believe she was this certain that she would leave this lifeline to fall back on. That maybe the possibility of her staying in Humboldt was real. She had told him she wanted him forever. He told her she had it already, and he fully meant it. Yet worry, fears, and doubts crept in that it was wrong to tether her down. Even if those Old Giants seemed to be doing so already. Fae had rules, and he would damn them both if he broke them.

"You want to go back to Humboldt, right? You are not going because you feel as though you need to take me back?"

"You can't be away for that long. I shouldn't be away. I can take care of the house sale in a weekend, a day probably," she said with a frown.

"I can run back. I've run further," he said. "If you need to stay, if you want to stay," he said as he swallowed hard. "I understand. This was your life."

"You're telling me if I want to move back here, you're okay with it?"

"I'm not, but it's selfish of me to want to keep you up there. So selfish. I want you up there not just because I want it, but because you want it. This is a place you could easily return to. Elodie, we are not supposed to sway mortals to do anything. To stay or go. I'm worried I have crossed a line, though."

She placed her hand on his cheeks and rubbed her thumbs along his cheekbone. "Trevin, this is not home. Humboldt is. It has felt like home for some time. It always called me. Maybe it did because it was calling me home. My dad told me numerous times to stay up there. I hate being away from the Old Giants, from you and Cora and Autumn and everyone. Even if I stayed, I would feel haunted living in this house by myself. I built a life I want up there. I was building it the day I drove north on Avenue. I made a choice to be up there. I was happy up there before Halloween. I am happy up there now."

He smiled and cupped her hands. "I am so glad, little mink. We will get through this week and we will say goodbye, then go home, together?" he said with a hint of a question. She laced her fingers in his hand.

"Yes. Back home to the Old Giants." A knowing smile graced her lips. He stood up and kissed her.

A small service was held with her extended family and some of her dad's friends. It was what he wanted, nothing big. A small gathering in Point Reyes. Trevin and Elodie were heading home the next morning.

Trevin took a few moments to say a blessing for him from the earth. To tell him she was going to be okay. He would ensure she found home and a sense of family somewhere. If not with him and Greenthistle, then at least with Cora and Humboldt. He told him the Old Giants would always watch over her while she was on the lands, too. When he walked out, he felt her emotions well up but stopped short of the corner overhearing the conversation with her aunt and uncle.

"You are just going to sell the house? I guess why wouldn't you at this rate, though. You have him and his rich family now."

"I don't rely on any of his money or his dad's. I make my own money. I still work and hold my job. The school district has been kind to give me the bereavement leave too. Marin wouldn't have yielded this much. I get opportunities up there I never would have had with the county and the city too. They want me there. Dad wants me there too."

"You are lucky he left it all to you know. Now you can just go and roam the planet, running from everything."

Trevin listened and felt sad for a moment that she was closing this chapter out like this. His eyes shifted down to the ground. Then he heard her speak with confidence.

"Do you still want me to visit? If I make an effort, will you maintain this relationship too? Dad wanted that for us. I know he told you because he would tell me. So if you still want me in your lives, if you can look at me and know I am his and Mom's, I will make the effort. Otherwise, stop telling me what I should do when you make little effort to be part of my life. The life I found in Humboldt is more than I ever imagined I'd find. Trips and travel may happen, but I honestly don't know if I see anywhere else as home now."

The happiness that hit Trevin at this moment was monumental. Still fixed on the grass under his boots, he pleaded with the Great Mother. *Please let me find a way to give her forever.*

"Good luck, Elodie. I suppose this is goodbye," her uncle said.

"Take care of yourselves. Respect these lands too. Remember, they do not belong to you," Elodie said.

Trevin heard her aunt sigh and walk off. He heard Elodie sniff, then walked around the corner and securely took her hand. She gripped it tight.

"I know you don't want me to pull anything off you, but if you ever do, tell me. Any time, for anything."

"Thank you, Trev. You are so important. The Old Giants wanted you to see me, but I needed to see you too."

They spent the final night in Marin watching the sunset at the beach. After pushing through a lot in the house, they were headed home early. Elodie would handle the house sale remotely. They took the day and drove Highway 1 and then after the road took them back inland to 101, they did take Avenue of the Giants, north. Elodie felt the Old Giants rejoice that she was back. Home.

Chapter 45

Once they returned to her studio in Humboldt, Trevin helped bring the boxes of stuff she was keeping up the stairs. She sighed.

"I'm home." Her eyes roved over the apartment. Trevin stood next to her.

"I'm glad Humboldt is your home," he said. "Are you sure you are okay? I can stay tonight if you want and just head home tomorrow. I don't mind."

"I am okay. I think I need to get back to the routine. Sitting still is not good. I think I'm going to let work know I'm back and will finish the week out. I will meet you at the trailhead tomorrow afternoon," she said, giving him a kiss.

"Of course, little mink. Don't push yourself, though. If you need time, then take it. I will see you tomorrow."

"I don't want to pull you away from work and stuff any longer or make your dad more pissed at me. I hope he doesn't ban me from seeing you."

"He can't. Autumn and Charles spend so much time together and he hasn't said anything about them," he said. Elodie nodded, hugging him tightly as they shared a deep kiss. "You are home, El."

Trevin sighed and dragged himself back into the house. He saw his dad sitting there waiting for him. Another sigh.

"Study please," Lord Greenthistle said, standing up. Trevin knew he would not repeat himself and reluctantly followed. "Close the door. Sit." Trevin did as he was told.

"You are back early?"

"Yes, we, well she took care of a lot this week."

Lord Greenthistle nodded. "Well, she has my sympathies. I imagine she is scared. She seemed close to her father."

"She was. He loved her a lot. She does thank you for the words and for letting me go. She is grateful that she didn't have to do all that alone. The thought scares me, seeing how sad she was alone in that dark house. The Marin Estates felt the power surge and asked me about it though," he recounted the meeting. Lord Greenthistle narrowed his eyes and nodded.

His dad slid a small blue book with gold detailing on the cover across the table. Trevin looked at it and then at his dad. "Open it," he said.

Trevin did and flipped through the pages. Photos of his dad, glamoured, looking younger. His heart began to pound with each page. Photos of his dad with a woman who was certainly mortal and most definitely not Trevin's mother. Small notes taped in, the names Earl and Shirley. Trevin's eyes widened as he flipped through more pages of memories. Them at gatherings with friends, them in at the beach, bowling, on the bridge at Redwoods. His dad smiling and so happy, the woman looked much the same. Trevin saw her age and his dad did not and on the last page was a letter.

"Read it," His dad said. Trevin opened it. The penmanship was excellent.

Earl,

I hope you are happy with your actions. I hope it stays with you for the rest of your miserable life. I cannot say you wasted thirteen years of mine, because I loved you. Some small part of me thinks you loved me too, but you are a lying cheating drunk. I will not be that woman, I will leave. So you do not need to worry about sneaking over late, no need to choose between your booze or a ring. Enjoy life as a slob and shame your father's legacy. Good riddance! By the time you sober up, I will be gone—far, far away from you. I feel sorry for her, she is too pretty for you to break her heart too.
- Shirley.

Trevin's eyes were wide, and he stared at his dad. "Who was she?" Trevin asked. "What happened to her?"

"She left, moved to San Diego, met a nice man, and they had three kids too. She died at the age of seventy-nine," his dad said as though he were fighting pain back as he spoke.

"Mom?" Trevin asked, worried everything he had seen was a lie. Worried he might not be high fae. A half-breed?

"I loved your mother, and she was there when I was so down about letting Shirley go. I cursed everything when Selene was taken from us. Swore I would do anything to protect you kids, and I fought hard to give you the best chance you had. After the accident with Cyrus I was worried I failed, and after the iron cuff I feared again I failed. I might have and I'm so sorry. I'm not sure why the Old Giants or the earth deemed this a fun game. Trevin, I will not see this estate tied to a mortal, not with me, not with you."

"Dad," Trevin whimpered. "Wait, am I? Was Mom actually my mom or?"

"You are Lady Selene Greenthistle's son, and she loved you so much. So much, Trevin. Never doubt that her blood courses through you. Sometimes I think it overrides Greenthistle's, you are the firstborn of mine, a high fae and brilliant and strong one at that."

"You loved a mortal? Enough to build over a decade with her?" Trevin's heart was pounding. "She never knew about you? The estate?"

Lord Greenthistle shook his head. "Shirley was to me what Elodie is to you. Vowed," his dad said. Trevin's eyes shot wide.

"You, you know? How? Dad! A mortal? You were vowed to a mortal? Not Mom?"

"I knew it the day your mortal walked in here. You puffed your chest out to me, you stood between her and I. I know a lovestruck fool when I see it because of that tether. What a cruel sick card the universe played. It was her that found you and saved you from the iron cuff. It was her that helped you get the map of Falk and the tome. Of course it would be her. You cannot think this will end well, you will watch her die, Trevin and it will hurt you."

"Stop!" Trevin heaved out.

"Does it upset you to think about it? Her taking her last breath, an animal attack, a gunshot, a car accident. Some mortal ailment. Hell, what if she's late on her tetanus shot and steps on a rusty nail?"

"Stop it!" Trevin shouted. "Did you ever tell her what she was to you? Did she ever know?" he asked, his eyes wide.

"No. It's forbidden to tell anyone. It's forbidden to know about us. The vowed bond makes no sense to mortals, they cannot even define love it seems."

"Did you ever take her through the boundary? How do we know what happens to mortals here, on this side? Elodie seemed so alert even after a night full of fae wine!" Trevin asked.

"It's forbidden! I made exceptions for the girl because of what she did. I can allow you and Autumn to be friends with her, but I will not let you make her the lady of the estate. I will not watch you suffer. You have to understand that. You will have to distance yourself from her."

"Yet you seemed to know everything about Shirley! You still watched, didn't you?" Trevin said, getting angry. "You watched her. You put up a complete facade that you were a drunken fool. Let her run away, fall in love, have kids, a family and you still watched her die! While you raised us? Did you spare yourself any grief? Or you just missed out on a life with her!" Trevin spat out.

"All those things I watched, but I also watched her fall in love. I saw wedding photos, I saw her thrive and live her best damn life. Blissfully unaware of what would have happened. I see her legacy carry on through her kids. That's what vowed do, we want them to become the best versions of themselves and we want to become it too, even if they are not here to see it."

"El isn't blissfully unaware of shit! I acted like a creep to her. I avoided talking to her. I did all those things I was supposed to do! She still figured everything out, and she still saved my life! Twice! This isn't the same. She's at home here. We just have to go on and pretend we don't like each other? We have to go on being miserable now? You were vowed to a mortal, and you kept me from them. You'd keep me from my vowed? She just lost her dad. The rest of her family treats her horribly, and her ex is a royal piece of shit and now, you want me to just act like it's nothing?" Trevin heaved out. "And that power in her. Dad! I do want to see her become the best version of herself. That power is so strong. Marin said it was ancient but in a new form. I can't. I won't let this go."

"I'm telling you, that I am not going to watch you break. I was worried you'd forfeit your title for her if she stayed there, but now I see the real problem. Her presence." His dad sighed. "Every breath of hers is sand slipping through your fingers, Trevin. You know it and you know how much it hurts you to think about."

"This is the thanks we're going to show her for risking her life for me? To get that iron cuff off me, to do that backpacking trip and carry me on her back. And what happens if Cyrus does try for her or anyone else? Just not me, right? I'm the only one who can't have the one I'm vowed to? I'm her overseer. You will not take that from me!"

Lord Greenthistle leveled his gaze at his son. "This is for the future of Greenthistle. I loved her. But I loved your mother too, I was blessed with three brilliant and brave kids that will make the estate proud. I see you grow more and more every day, and I see this newly found drive to excel at being heir. Don't throw it away now. She is coming between you and Cyrus."

"Because Cyrus is acting like an asshole! He touched her, he tried to lure her away to get her alone. He is swaying her to leave—" Trevin paused and looked at his dad. "You are fine with him swaying her to leave aren't you?"

"Fix your relationship with Cyrus. The girl is not important. You both are teetering on breaking rules."

"You'd let whatever is in Elodie go?" He couldn't let her go. He wouldn't.

"So she has something we can't figure out, nothing adds up, it's having an adverse reaction on all of you. The lands like her. Great. She's a kind person who loves the Old Giants. I will give you that. But it doesn't mean she is something to break yourself for, we see dozens of kind mortals who love trees pass through. It's not that you would give her up, son, it's that she may leave you one day. For another, for new lands, what then? She's been running from life in Marin. She lived abroad and ran from that, what happens when she leaves for the next place?"

"The Old Giants tell her she's home—they tell her to embrace this, they tell her things often. I think she can feel this bond too. Dad, I can't just let any of this go. I'm trying not to trap her here. If she said she was leaving for Maine or Florida or India tomorrow, I'd let her go, but she says this is her home. Ignoring her doesn't work. I tried to ignore her, I tried to hook up with someone like Caleb does and I couldn't go through with it. Cassia called me the Greenthistle disappointment. I don't give a shit what Cassia thinks about me but that's all I am, to all of you. All I ever will be to Elodie too. No matter what, I am the disappointment."

"You are not a disappointment, Trev, but she is a mortal. Even if she had some great power, she does not have this vowed bond. She will leave you either from her choice, old age, better opportunity, someone else. She is not forever, vowed are not forever."

"I've never told her what I feel for her, I've never told her I loved her and she hasn't said it to me, but I see it tug on her. When she says she wants me, when she says she's mine, every time she says I'm her mountain lion. She feels it and she is drawn to this place, because the Old Giants want her here. I have a scent to her, oakmoss and amber. How? How does a mortal scent her vowed?" Trevin heaved out. Lord Greenthistle narrowed his eyes in confusion. "I just watched her close the chapter in Marin. She says she is home here—they tell her she's home. It can't be undone. They tell her we are in danger and that I need to see her."

"And you and I see this power in her, that doesn't make any sense. Trevin," he said with a sigh. "I gave you solstice because I see how much you smile with her and I haven't seen this side of you in so long. I just know what she is going to do to you though. I wanted to give you a solstice with her but I fear it might have been a mistake. It planted seeds in your head and now it's near impossible to rip them out."

"You are wrong! About everything. She is special to these lands. They have warned her about danger for all of us. And she won't leave me. She doesn't want to. Are you going to tell Autumn to leave Charles too?"

"Autumn knows better. He isn't her vowed. You have a fire lit in you because of her. You lacked confidence before. A mortal girl makes you want to fight for your birthright? You should have had it all along. Will you lose your confidence when you lose her?" Lord Greenthistle said as if even having to speak the words was absurd.

Trevin glared. He wanted to scream and shout and tell his dad he was wrong all over again. Instead he stood up and went upstairs to his room with out a word. His eyes fixed the drawing, the mink and the mountain lion. She was his, he was hers, and they were both at home with these Old Giants. Hastily he repacked his backpack and left as quickly as he could.

<u>Chapter 46</u>

Cora walked up to Trevin and set his drink down. "Everything okay? I heard you guys were back early. How is she? I haven't talked to her yet."

"She's okay. Still sad. It was odd seeing her pull through that. She had so many emotions and was so sad. Then, as though someone flipped a switch, she closed out her life in Marin. Her dad left her everything, and she's selling the house there. Not sure what she's doing with his truck yet. Suppose we—she will figure it out when the house sells."

"That seems sudden, but I mean, she would get sad whenever she talked about leaving here, leaving these trees. She never seemed like she wanted to be in Marin when she talked about it," Cora said.

"I feel like she is home, she feels like this is home and it's only been a few months. She's not even from here, but—" He paused and looked at Cora. His friend for years. His mortal friend who had known him without the titles and the responsibilities of being an estate heir. "She feels like home to me. I feel selfish for wanting her to stay, for being happy she chose this."

Cora smiled at him. "It's called love, Trevor. Home doesn't have to just be a place, it's a feeling and sometimes people bring up those feelings. Are you upset you love her?" Cora asked. Trevin looked at her stunned.

"No. Not at all. I'm scared that I'm chaining her down. I'm keeping her from her best self. I want to be better around her, I want to be better in general, but what if there's more for her out there than me or this? She can go anywhere," he groaned.

"Trev, what in the world has gotten into you? She loves you and you love her. She had a major loss, and she feels at peace here. With you and these trees. Embrace it. I've never seen you so lost before. Like you don't know which way to go. What happened last week?"

"Fight with my dad. He's a dick sometimes."

"He doesn't dislike her, does he? Why on earth would he? He better not expect you to be single forever."

"No he doesn't dislike her." Trevin took a deep breath. He hoped she was okay with a house guest for a few days. He needed to rationalize things. "I'm glad we are back. Thanks Cora. Sometimes I don't realize how much emotion I carry." Cora shook her head.

"She's good for you Trev. I hope she stays for a long time. I love her too," she said and walked off. Trevin took a sip of his drink then chewed on the straw. He took out his phone and sighed. It was around 4 p.m. and he wondered if she wanted to be alone. He supposed he could camp, or rent a room somewhere in Eureka, maybe he'd go hang at Ashdale for a few days. It was their day for drills anyway on Monday. He sighed and relented, grabbing his stuff then headed to her place. Once on the property, he saw her car and the lights on. Emotions appeared to be calm and the energy she had was still. The scent engulfed him the closer he got.

Trevin stopped and looked at the tree line. The entities that made his home, the spirits that called her here so he could be lost in this scent. *Let me find a way, please. I can't let her go. I'm going to dump this on her after everything she just went through. How horrible am I?*

With one deep inhale he walked up the stairs, toward the door and then knocked. He exhaled slowly and tensed as the locks turned. Her eyes widened and then she smiled.

Trevin saw affection and excitement as her eyes fixed on him. He then watched the concern creep over her face.

"Trev, Come in. Please." He nodded and dropped his bag once he was inside. Elodie closed the door locking it and watched him drop the glamour as he faced her. He watched her eyes take him in, and she smiled. *She does this every time. My vowed. I should have let you say it at solstice. Hers, I'm hers, I want to be hers.*

"I hate to ask this, especially after the week you've had, but can I stay here for a few days. I don't want to see Greenthistle Estate." He noticed her tense.

"Your dad is mad you went with me, huh?"

"It's not that. I had an argument with him and he's being an asshole. Fae have skeletons in the closet too and I'm not sure what I'm supposed to do with this one. I will help cook, I promise, and I will clean and pay for food. I just need a few days to figure out what I'm supposed to do with Greenthistle," he said.

Elodie nodded and walked up to him, talking his hand.

"We are going to find our happily ever after right? You and me?" she asked. He brought his fingers under her chin and kissed her.

"We will find it, El. I am yours," he said.

Tap, Tap.

Chapter 47

Trevin stayed with Elodie for five days, only dealing with his dad at the city office. Elodie taught him how to cook a few of her favorite dishes. When they grocery shopped, she no longer worried about the curious glances they got. Trevin noticed she was working harder, not talking much about things. She was dealing with the house sale in Marin, certifying and mailing documents. Over her spring break she would be going to Marin to finalize everything and drive her dad's truck back up. Trevin had already requested the visit much to his dad's disdain. He was still trying to find a way to bring her to the Spring Equinox. Autumn had even started designing her dress.

Once Trevin had gone back to Greenthistle, he stayed in and they talked most nights. He stayed with her on Wednesday night where they met at the café and left together. Elodie hadn't been back to Greenthistle Estate since the Winter Solstice. She was too nervous to ask or take up Autumn's offers. Trevin hadn't offered, and she figured it had something to do with his dad.

Another Friday afternoon was upon them and he would spend the weekend with her.

She parked her car knowing she was early. He was still finishing up work stuff that probably would take another hour. Something had pulled her as she looked at the stairs to the trail in her side-view mirror. Something that she couldn't place but she wanted to seek out.

Elodie.
Come to us.

Elodie checked the time again and then glanced at the sky. It was likely going to rain but her phone said it wouldn't start until after sundown.

"Three miles is probably ok. Maybe I can surprise him at the boundary?" She hadn't eaten today, she hadn't slept well either. The stress of dealing with everything from her dad still weighed on her.

She got out, tucking her keys in her pocket and started walking. An older couple passed with a smile and nod, and a mile later one more person crossed her path. Everyone headed the opposite direction as her, toward Sunny Brae. Elodie figured it must be the hour, she wouldn't go that far. Three miles was nothing for her.

Some force she couldn't identify kept her walking. Deep inside her something swelled, pulling her deeper and deeper into the forest. She was on a part of the trail she had not been on and she wondered how close to the boundary line she was. It was as though she could almost see it but her eyes must be playing tricks on her. With every fern and redwood she passed she let her hand slide across taking in the sensations on her skin. A soft gentle squeeze of her hand was returned, and a smile slowly graced her lips.

"This is home," she said softly.

A light gentle rain started and the sounds of a waterfall graced her ears. The ferns popping bright against the black soil. Her eyes traveled up seeing trees and mist.

Elodie, rest your soul.
You are home, dear child.

The voices said. She climbed the rocks near the small waterfall and flinched when she sliced her palm on a sharp rock. The same hand that she had gotten stitches on when she was little.

"Ouch!" she yelped, examining the wound. It wasn't too deep, but it still stung. She pulled her sleeve over her hand as a small buffer. Hunger and exhaustion were forming a haze over her mind. Her appetite had been nonexistent lately with her dad gone. Trevin had been mindful of her needs and made her food often. She always smiled at the thought of him.

Carefully she continued up the rocks.

He needs you.
Greenthistle needs you.
The lands need you. Come now, child.
You must wake up.

The voices said all around her and she gazed at the massive trunk of the redwood that seemed to talk to her. She pressed her palm to the bark and her body swayed as something coursed through her. This was not just the pull of the redwoods, this was life, old and ancient, wild and wise. Her fingers gripped the tree trying to stabilize herself but she had to slide down on her haunches. The scrape on her hand made her stare at the tree then she saw the blood. Her eyes traveled up the redwood again.

"Oh." The rain got heavier. Her head slumped forward on the tree and the sound of the rain falling filled her ears. One deep inhale filled her lungs.

Elodie, return to us.
Let him see, let them all see it.
You belong here, home.
Home.

The voices were louder now as though someone was behind her. Bracing herself on the tree, she turned her gaze and saw no one. An energy swirled inside her she had never felt before.

"Home," she said with a smile, focusing on the trees and ferns. His smiling face appeared in her mind. "Trevin."

A sudden shiver shot through her and she realized it was getting dark. She needed to get back to her car, she was soaked and freezing. This was supposed to be an after-work hike, he would be on his way to her car soon. She pressed her hands against the redwood to push herself up.

Greenthistle needs you,
Nightswift needs you.
Ashdale needs you.
Evil is waiting for them.

Whispers caressed her ears and her head dipped forward again. Another pulse shot through her. She jerked her head up and the dizzy hunger hit. With a deep inhale she stood up slowly. Exhaling, she eyed the rocks, now dark with a wet shine. They would be slick but she had climbed up and down wet rocks before. Taking another deep breath, she pulled her sleeve over her hand and began her climb down. It wasn't more than three feet worth but the rocks were slippery and the small stream had grown. A sound nearby caused her to freeze. A hum from a large animal filled the air. This was no familiar chuffing or purring sound, it wasn't even a mountain lion but a bear. One quick breath and she assessed her next step with a pounding heart.

Please be Q, please be Q, be an Ashdale, she pleaded to herself. A slow breath in and out this time as she went to step down.

As soon as she let go, a weightlessness took hold of her body and a gasp escaped her. She fell on the rocks and cried out in pain. She closed her mouth as the bear went silent. Trying to push herself up to run, a pain shot through her arm and she collapsed in the stream. It was getting dark and her ability to see clearly was fading. She dragged herself out of the stream on the opposite side and looked at her leg. The leggings were torn and bloody from a deep gash. Her arm cramped up and she couldn't move it without a lot of effort. She feared a broken bone. A whimper escaped her despite fighting to hold it back, then she heard and felt the bear behind her.

She looked up at the brown bear.

"Q!" she cried out. "Friend of Ashdale!"

It roared at her and then went back on its hind legs. Too terrified to cry, Elodie thought about her mom and her dad. Her eyes locked on the trees.

"Help me, please," she pleaded to the giants.

A low growl followed by a loud roar caught her attention. A blur passed by and a mountain lion ripped the bear down to the ground. Oakmoss and amber filled her nose. She gasped in pain and saw the bear and mountain lion facing each other.

The mountain lion arched its back, fur standing up and ears flat. He was nearly the size of a bear. Something in her peripheral caught her attention. Her eyes focused on the glow in the water, the soil, mud caked on her wounds. Despite the numbness, she could feel a pulsing power flow into her.

Her head was heavy as though the power was pulling her down into a deep sleep.

Another growl pulled her out of slumber.

"Trevin," she said weakly. His tail twitched.

"Stay with me, I need to get the bear away from you. I'm here," he communicated silently. She nodded and pressed her palm into the dirt to push herself up and noticed the ground illuminated teal. The pulse shifted to a surge and then a swell, completely engulfing her. Her head felt heavy, a warm embrace was surrounding her. Ferns reached for her.

"What's happening?" she asked, slurring and struggling to keep herself up. "Trevin," she whimpered and fell back.

"El!" she heard him say, his hands cradled her head. She saw his emerald green eyes, the markings on his face, his ears. The worry on his face. "Elodie, stay with me," he said, rubbing her cheek.

Trevin held her close. "I have you, you're safe now. Just stay with me, El," he said softly, pulling her into him. She was so tired.

Soon.

You are home.

Protect him, they need you.

She saw the trees, then focused on Trevin. He was carrying her in his arms, holding her tight.

"Trevin," she said, gripping onto his shirt nudging into him closer.

"I have you, little mink. You will be okay. I'm going to take you to my dad. He will heal you. Just stay with me," he said.

Listen little one.
Let the boy's estate bring you home.
Let him heal you. Bind you.
They need you.

"Trevin." Her eyes watered. "Trevin," she cried out.

"Shhh you are okay. I have you, El. I always will." A tug pulled inside her.

"Trevin," she whimpered again, pulling on his shirt. "Something happened. The earth," she said, "I felt—"

"Stay with me, what did you feel?" he asked. She was trying so hard to stay awake.

"I feel it." Her words were sluggish.

"Elodie, you feel it? How?"

Home.
He will take you home to bind you.
Listen to him.

Her eyes closed and her grip weakened.

"Home," she said, her voice faltering as the exhaustion wiped her out. "Home." Her words slurred as her body fell limp.

Chapter 48

Trevin felt her go limp. She let go of his shirt and he noticed the blood on it.

"Fuck! How much blood have you lost?" He was on the estate property and the doors opened.

"Dad!" he cried out. "Help her!" Autumn ran down the stairs and gasped.

"No! What happened?" she cried out. Cedar ran into the room and froze at the sight of Elodie.

Trevin looked at his dad who had rushed out from the study, there was remorse all over his dad's face.

"Please, I don't know what to do! Help her, something happened, on our lands, she's one of ours," he whimpered. "Please!"

"Take her to bed," Lord Greenthistle said calmly. Trevin carried her to his room and laid her on the bed. Cedar let out a sigh and Autumn glared at him.

Trevin wiped her face down.

"El, you are safe," Trevin said softly, removing her boots. He stood up when his dad walked in, Autumn followed, as estate staff came in with supplies.

When Lord Greenthistle put his hands on Elodie's head, ensuring she was fully sedated. He sighed before he spoke.

"Her body is exhausted. She's already in such a deep slumber. Her energy well is spent," he said, assessing her injuries. He healed her broken arm then moved to her leg. Then noticed her palm, caked with blood and dirt. With a frown he took her hand and cleaned it gently, then cradled it in his. In this moment Lord Greenthistle could feel his heart hurt for what he had lost, for Shirley, and Selene. He looked at this girl, who he knew his son was vowed to and sorrow formed, for them. He rubbed his thumbs over the wrist and healed the wound. Tears formed in his eyes mourning for Shirley, for Selene, for this girl who had pushed herself so hard for his estate. He mourned for what this would do to his son.

Thank you, little cub. You are so kind, he said to himself and he realized he cared for Elodie too. He set her hand down gently and stood back with a shaky sigh then turned to his son.

"This is what it's like, Trevin. They are so fragile." His voice solemn.

"She said she felt something, earth, before she passed out. I tried to keep her talking, but she was exhausted," Trevin said.

"Are you hurt? What happened?"

"I'm fine. I was heading to her place and saw her car at the trailhead, but she wasn't in it. It was raining too hard, so I followed her scent." He paused. "She smells of ocean breeze and lavender to me," he said. "She must have been five miles in, I heard her cry out and I heard the bear. She pleaded with it to be Quinn or an Ashdale. I got the bear to leave and ran to her, she was talking deliriously. I know you feel it, there's something in her blood. Tell me what it is. I've been trying to figure it out since the first night," Trevin pleaded. "The lands are calling her, why?"

"I do not know what she has in her. She is important but you have to let her be important, you have to let her find out what that means. We cannot push these things."

"She hasn't been eating much. She's sad a lot, misses her dad, and is still grieving. She feels like she should have been there, in Marin last year, but she said being anywhere but here is haunting," Trevin said, looking at her. "She says leaving here hurts her too. To be away from the Old Giants."

Everyone was silent for a moment.

"Can she help with the tome, to get it open?" Autumn asked. "Obviously, iron doesn't hurt her. She's here. I mean once she's recovered of course."

Lord Greenthistle and Trevin stared at each other, assessing each other's reaction.

"I don't think it is my decision when it comes to her. Her overseer will need to determine what he feels is best. Greenthistle is my decision though," he said sternly, looking at Trevin. "Autumn, let's give them some privacy."

When Elodie came to, she could see light through her closed eyes and she registered that someone was in bed with her, holding her. She opened her eyes for a moment and realized she wasn't at home, that the bed and room were both bigger. It was his room, at the estate. She curled up and nuzzled into Trevin. She had stayed at the estate she realized trying to remember last night as her heart pounded.

"El. Relax," Trevin said softly, holding her. She let go and pushed herself up, taking in the large lavish room and looked at him, then at her hands. "Relax. You are safe," he said, sitting up, rubbing her back and leaning his chin on her shoulder.

"What happened?"

"You must have gone out for a hike?"

"I went up the rocks and cut my hand." She rubbed her palm, no sign of a wound or infection. She remembered it caked with dirt and when she rubbed it, the teal glow came to mind. She met his eyes. "The Old Giants were calling to me, saying my name. I hate that I sound so crazy." With a sigh she dropped her head into her hand. "You fought a bear, for me? I'm sorry."

"El, look at me," he said, meeting her eyes. "I'm a fae that turns into a mountain lion. I told a bear to always leave you alone. Trees talking to you isn't weird to me. I got to your car at the trailhead and followed your scent, then I heard you cry out."

She blushed and let out a sigh. "Am I that rancid? I'm in your bed? House?" She panicked, eyeing the bathroom.

He laughed softly. "No, you are not. When I first spoke to you, your scent struck me. You smelled of ocean breeze and lavender. It intoxicated me. When I saw your car and you were nowhere near, I changed and followed it. Five miles, El, on an unmarked and unmanaged trail. It paralleled the boundary line." She looked at him shocked then her hand. She felt her leg, no gash. "I brought you here and my dad healed you. I knew I couldn't take you into town and I was too worried to take you home and try to heal you myself."

"I guess we are even now? The iron cuff for my stupid hike and the bear?"

"Maybe, but I'm still your overseer and I'm still yours." He laughed and rubbed her back. She smiled at him meekly. "And I'm not at all upset by it."

"Thank you, for last night. Is your dad pissed?"

"I think he was genuinely worried for you," he said. "I took your clothes off and sent them to be mended and cleaned, I hope I wasn't too invasive. I will call for breakfast. Dad said you were dehydrated too. When did you last eat?" he asked.

Elodie noticed she was just in her underwear and one of his shirts. Her cheeks heated then she met his eyes.

"The appetite still hasn't returned. Stress sort of kills the allure of food."

"Well hopefully this weekend can relieve some of the stress. Go on and get cleaned up and I will grab breakfast. Autumn left some clothes for you too."

"That's really sweet of you both. Are you sure I'm not inconveniencing anyone? Or making anyone uncomfortable? Caleb?"

"Caleb can deal, and it is really no inconvenience to us. I promise. After we eat, my dad needs to talk to you, he wants to monitor you until tomorrow, to make sure you are okay."

"What?" she gasped. "I'm staying here this weekend?"

"He and I want you to rest. And there is something you might be able to help us with, it involves more iron. But it can wait. Please try to eat first."

"Okay," she said, she looked at him and rubbed her thumb along his cheek, before she kissed him. "Thank you. Thank you for caring about me as much as you do. I am grateful for you," she said, kissing him again. He hugged her tightly.

"Little mink. You know I will always be there," he said. *Tap and Tug.*

She nodded then got up. Her eyes took in the large green and white bathroom with lots of plants and brass fixtures. Amber tinted glass bottles with brass pumps lined a shelf. The wood was dark, and the window let a lot of light in. The shower head dropped down from the ceiling. She turned the knob and took a deep inhale. She felt so embarrassed for even ending up in this position. She really did know better.

She flinched when she felt his hand on her stomach pulling her into him. He pressed his lips to her head.

"Use anything in here. Your robe from solstice is on the back of the door, and the hairbrush Autumn used is on the counter. I set the clothes on the bed for you. Maybe it's time you have a drawer at my place too," he said. She blushed. "You are not intruding, I'm happy you are here," he said. She nodded.

"Thank you." Her words were soft as she felt him kiss her head.

He pulled the bathroom door to almost a full close, revealing the dark green robe with the 'E' embodied into it. She sighed and removed the few clothes she had on.

The shower reminded her of the tropical ones she had been in while on Okinawa or Hawaii. She rinsed her hair and used a body wash that smelled of sea breezes. She smiled and then wondered if anything smelled of lavender. She wondered why he picked up a lavender scent from her, she still had yet to wear anything with that scent. Once finished, she brushed her hair out and remembered how she looked at the solstice ball. She thought about spring equinox ball? How many more of those would she have? Would he want her at?

"This is far more than any fairy tale. Just let this run its course," she told herself, wrapping her robe around her. Bashfully she walked back into the room finding a neatly folded stack of clothes. A small package with green tissue and a twine string. She opened it and saw undergarments made of green lace but enough coverage. She blushed and put them on. The bra was a harness style, and she loved how it made her feel. She slid the green long sleeve tunic dress on with the jagged edge and v-neck. The dress came down just below her rear and she was grateful for the black leggings. She put the goldenrod socks on and her boots, and smiled at herself in the mirror. She loved it. She was finishing braiding her hair to the side when the door opened.

Trevin walked in with a large tray of food. A groan escaped her stomach. He eyed her up and down with a grin, then set the tray down at the small table near the window and offered her the seat.

"You look really cute. I'm glad Autumn's stuff fits you. She has so many clothes. She said she pulled all from her new to be sorted pile. A lot of designers give her things to try so it's all new," he said, sitting down across from her. "We all get things from designers being the high estates. Even dad gets stuff."

"The colors were a good choice, I was a bit worried when you said they were from Autumn, they might fit too snug but I like these." she said, "I will thank her and get them washed, I promise."

"Autumn said they are yours, she said she'd have a new set for you tomorrow," he said, feigning a smile.

"Trevin, I want to stay. I'm just embarrassed by the scene I must have caused yesterday. I don't want to make the estate staff uncomfortable either. It's somewhat of a shock that your dad said to stay. It was so nice he offered me what he did for solstice," she said and Trevin smiled.

"I'm glad. I'm happy you are here. Dad and Caleb don't hate you. They just are cautious, new territory for us all."

"Like my namesake?" she asked. He smiled and nodded.

"My little mink," he said with a smile. "Eat please and drink water. Dad said you were dehydrated. You know better. Ms. Candytuft said no wine until dinner," he said with a slight laugh. Elodie blushed and laughed too.

She nodded and drank the glass of water. "So after I eat, I have to talk to your dad?" she asked, picking up her fork.

"Eventually but don't rush," he said then paused, grabbing a piece of toast. He inhaled as if to speak then stopped. She looked at him and froze. He smiled and took another inhale. "We, the Greenthistle Estate would like your help with something. If you are up to it but you are under no obligation to help if you don't want to. Do not feel pressured."

"What exactly would I have to do?" Elodie asked, uneasy. She reached for her fork again.

"The tome I got out of Falk is still unable to be opened by us. Since iron doesn't hurt you, we were wondering if you would be willing to try. Autumn suggested it but if you are too tired or don't want to, it's okay. We understand," he said. She looked at her palm again and then at him with a nod.

"Isn't this part of my bargain, to help you with iron stuff?"

"It was never expected, just a hope. I never made that part of the bargain. We are not going to force you to do this. Dad will not, given recent events. We didn't want to ask you in the event there were wards on it. I didn't want anything to happen to you. It has been examined though and no wards are detected."

"I will try but if it's some combination or something I don't know what use l will really be. I'm no code cracker."

"Thank you. You have a fresh set of eyes and you can at least touch it. Dad just gritted his teeth and burned his fingers to get it on its stand."

She nodded and was quiet for a moment. "Trev?" she said after she finished the plate of cooked food. She had grabbed a muffin now and savored the taste of berries and cinnamon in it.

"Yes, little mink?"

"You say you are bound to me, but I still don't understand what exactly I did to you. I don't want to accidentally lock you into something you might not have been ready for."

He laughed softly. "No, it's nothing like that. You didn't lock me in anything, and I want you, want to be with you. Everything I have done I assure you, I have been happy to do, glad to be able to do for you." He sighed. "El, it's hard to explain, but like I said before, never question or doubt how much you mean to me. How much I want to be with you. When you tell me you want me, something goes taut in me and I know that this is right. You are worth fighting for our happily ever after. We will find it," he said.

She smiled and blushed. "I feel it too, when you tell me that, when I tell you those things. I've never experienced this before. I've never felt more certain that I need to keep you safe, keep this world safe," she said. He tilted his head curiously.

"You feel something in you, a tug on a strand or thread?" he asked, tracing her features, her ears, and her eyes as she nodded.

"Exactly like that, I just, I didn't know how to describe it, that I could describe it, this tether." she said.

He took her hand and met her gaze. "Elodie, please understand and believe me that you mean more to me than I think you realize, then I think I can tell you right now. Fae have a lot of rules that mortals don't. I don't want to rob you of your life, especially if I can't deliver. I want you to always have a choice."

She frowned. "You want me to have a choice but what about yours? If I chose something, what if it doesn't line up with yours?" She looked at their hands, fingers intertwined.

"I know what I want. I'm holding her hand. I am trying to figure out what it means for us, but I'm asking you to believe me. I know that regardless of what happens in the future this cannot be replicated again, what I feel for you."

Elodie met his eyes. The sincerity behind them.

"I don't want you to hurt when—you know, my time comes." Her eyes broke away from him, glossing over.

"El, it's hard to explain, or I guess I'm scared to explain it. What could happen if I do. My dad knows, so does Q. I think Autumn suspects it. I will find a way though. I will give you the choice when I do and respect your choice. Because I cannot rob you of your life out there. And while every choice is yours, it still is a choice, and takes one option away."

She looked at him, confused. "Are you talking about the mortality thing? A way to make me fae?"

"That's part of it. Don't answer—please think really hard about what it might mean, and I don't even know if there is a way. It's been so long since we've had a mortal over here. I'm researching what these things do to mortals," he pleaded.

"You'd really want me, enough to even consider it, I'd have to learn so much. I'd be so behind."

"You are the patron saint of Humboldt, Elodie. I will not let you become a martyr, ever. You crossed my path and you spark this new life inside me. I want it so badly. But you deserve a choice. This fairy tale could turn into a nightmare very quickly if there is a way. This life you built for yourself will have to end one day and you will have to vanish, letting everyone go. We will have to do that one day and we all know it. Dad's done it, so have Lord and Lady Ashdale, Lord and Lady Nightswift too. It is a part of our lives as high estates that have to integrate for the benefit of the lands. The severity of it, what that really means is not something I'd force on you."

She nodded thinking about what it would mean to be immortal. "I do want you, Trevin. Know that whatever my mortal heart is worth, I do feel it for you," she said, looking at him.

"Little mink, how lucky I am. How blessed I am," he said.

Elodie suddenly felt something different. Not a tug or a pull but a bounding embrace. Stronger this time.

Blessed. Blessed.
Wake up.
Little one.
Let them see what newness walks the lands.

She let out a deep exhale as the whispers passed.

"Blessed," she said, he tilted his head and raised his eyebrows.

"What?"

"A whisper of a thought passed through me. The Old Giants said blessed, you said it, Let them see what newness walks these lands." she repeated while embarrassed.

"You are blessed. The lands like you, they want you, you are new, Elodie. Your dad said you were blessed by the earth," he said smiling.

"Home," Elodie saw him smile wide at the word.

"Ready to tackle the tome?" he asked. She took a deep breath.

"I am ready. Nervous but ready," she said, standing up. He took her hand and they headed towards the door.

Chapter 49

Elodie took a deep inhale as Trevin led her to the study.

"You will be okay. Dad isn't going to banish you. He just needs to ensure you are alright and if you can help with the tome," he said with his hand on the doorknob. She nodded, and they walked in. She saw Lord Greenthistle at the desk, Caleb stood off to the side, and Autumn sat in the window.

Elodie held her head low and frowned. She fought the lump in her throat. During the solstice she was nervous, and had flinched at the comments, but Trevin made it all better. She felt like royalty in that outfit next to him, as though none of the comments mattered. He wanted her and she was his lady that night. At this moment though, she was scared. They stood in front of the desk and Elodie bowed her head.

"Thank you, sir. I'm sorry for the disruption I caused—I am happy to try to help where I can." Her voice faltered as she gripped Trevin's hand tightly.

Lord Greenthistle let out a deep exhale.

"Lady Santiago," he said with a calmness that made her flinch. "You need not fear having your memory erased or being locked up into servitude here. You are trustworthy and have proven as much. I will admit it is always scary to see one of our residents in that condition. Mortals are easier to heal than fae, so it was no strain on me. I'm sure it was more of a strain on my son to see you like that. For his sake, I must ask that you please use caution when hiking."

She finally met his eyes and nodded. "Yes, sir. I will not cause another disruption again."

"Good. I'm also not here to talk about bonds and such matters," he said.

Elodie noticed Trevin's grip on her hand tighten and she frowned. She cursed her mortality and her rounded ears. She thought about the rift she would cause in this family. A family that had been around long before her and should be around long after her.

"Yes, sir." Her voice was so small and fragile.

"That said, I can grant you some privileges as I am asking for your help in dealing with this tome. You have been a great asset in finding this. Greenthistle, Nightswift, and Ashdale are appreciative," he said. She nodded.

"I want to help, sir," she said in a small voice.

"I thank you, Lady Santiago," Lord Greenthistle said. He stood up and walked to the tome resting atop a podium, avoiding touching it. "We have no progress on opening it, if it even can be opened. Since you can handle it without burning yourself, we would appreciate any assistance. There are no wards we can detect on it, either. The iron seems to be the deterrent," he said.

Elodie examined the old book with its fancy iron capped corners and inlay plate on the front. It was in excellent condition for how old it must be and being stored underground. Characters she couldn't read along with a redwood etched on the cover. The lock appeared to be a circular dial of sorts, also made of old iron. She glanced at Trevin and he nodded. She let out a small exhale, stepping closer to it. The etching of the redwood reminded her of the book she found last fall. She had forgotten about it. There were symbols on the dial and she couldn't read those either. She ran her fingers over the etching, feeling dirt in the lines.

Soon.
Awaken.

She pulled her hand away quickly and looked at the Greenthistle family. They all watched with curiosity. Elodie turned her gaze past them toward the large bay window.

"Does it hurt you?" Trevin asked, walking toward her. Elodie shook her head, then glanced at her hand. She rubbed where the cut was and felt nothing. "Can you do it again? Hold your hand there, unless it hurts you, then stop."

She nodded and fixed her eyes back at the book, then put her palm flat on the etching. Her eyes locked on her hand, seeing ferns in her mind, watching them travel up the trunk of a redwood.

El. Let them see.
You are bound.
You are home.

Something Elodie could not see caressed her hand and her palm got warm. She was almost locked in a trance. As though she could see past her hand, past the etching. As though she was really seeing the ferns wrap around the redwoods.

"El," Trevin said, but she didn't respond. "Elodie."

How do I wake up? What do I need to show them? What do I need to open this? Show me. Please, I want to help them. I love him. She said in her mind, trying to communicate with the book. She had heard these things since she moved here, even more since meeting Trevin.

"Elodie," Trevin said louder.

Open the tome. Show them.
You know how.
Awaken. Return home.
You are ours. We belong to you.
He is yours. Let them see. It cannot be undone.
El. The boy is trapped.

Suddenly Elodie saw the ferns and redwoods fizzle into smoke. When it cleared, Trevin was screaming on his knees. His hands gripping his head, crying out in pain as hundreds of blackbirds swarmed. No, these were shadows. Blackbirds on on the ground lifeless.

Instinct took over her body, forcing her to rip her hand away and backed up, stumbling into Trevin. She was heaving.

"What happened? What is it?" Trevin pleaded. She stared at the book, her heart pounding. "Elodie, breathe," he said softly. She finally ripped her eyes away and looked at Trevin. Her eyes scanned his face, his body. Then she met Lord Greenthistle's concerned gaze.

Lord Greenthistle's eyes widened.

"What is in that book? Why do you want to open it?" she asked, trying to catch her breath. Shock appeared on his face at her question.

"It's an ancient fae tomb we had yet to find. You helped Trev find the exact location of it and the book you gave him had information on Falk we didn't know about. We think there might be useful information in it. There's something in the lands that's—"

"There's evil in the lands. It's a danger to you all, and if you fall, mortals have no chance," she said. Lord Greenthistle gasped at her words. "You think this book has the answers in it? The solution or cure?" she asked, taking another deep breath.

"We have reason to believe it might help."

"How?" she asked, her heart was pounding. Her thoughts trying to figure out the message.

"Our hope is that something in there will tell us about the evil. How to fight it. Trev told you about his findings in Falk? If you know of the evil?" he said. She nodded.

"And about Cyrus and the mountain lion," she said sadly. Lord Greenthistle sighed in defeat.

"We need to get this under control. We need to figure out how to open this book," he said.

She sighed in defeat too now and eyed the book again and walked closer to it. Her hand hovered just above it anticipation.

"Please be careful. I don't want you to slip into that trance again," Trevin said.

"I want to help. I'll be okay," she said, then picked up the book and turned it over. She saw another iron plaque set on the back and rubbed her fingers over it slowly.

Wake up El.
Open it. You know how.
He will be the first to fall. One by one, they will follow.
Open it. It knows you are here; time is running out.

She trembled and bit her lip, fighting back a whimper. She pulled her hand back again. Another hard swallow before she spoke.

"I don't recognize these characters, is it a fae language?" she asked. Trevin and his dad leaned closer.

"It's hard to see it. It is a very old language, not commonly used anymore. I'd have to take some time to translate it. Maybe Lord Ashdale or Lord Nightswift know it better. My father never taught it to me. Claiming he was too busy—it was not needed," Lord Greenthistle said. Elodie looked at them, confused.

"If this is a fae tome, why is there so much iron on it? Why was the map to its exact location through a maze of iron that seriously hurts fae? Mortals had to have helped, known? That map was in a tomb of iron and tetanus for fae and mortal. What if this wasn't meant to be found? They put it in a hard to find place, to keep you and I out?" she asked. Trevin looked at his dad.

"Or they were told to it away while in servitude. We never figured out who put the iron cuff on Trev?" Caleb asked.

"But what was supposed to be hidden, then? So the fae made a bunch of mortals make this book and then led them to a patch surrounded by boundary lines to keep themselves out?" she asked.

Trevin looked at her. "All the more reason to open it?" he asked.

"I need some kind of clearer image of the back of the book if you want me to translate it," Lord Greenthistle said. Elodie tilted her head and ran her fingers over it.

Yes, little one. Keep going.

"What if I got a rubbing of it so you could see it better? Paper and charcoal or a crayon, even dirt," she said. Trevin looked at her, remembering the other book.

"You mentioned it with the book you loaned me. It's here, you said you wanted a rubbing of a page or image in it?" he asked. She nodded.

"May as well," Autumn said. "I will grab stuff," she said, walking off. Caleb crossed his arms. Trevin went to the shelf and grabbed her book on Falk.

"If you can't figure it out, just say so," Caleb snapped. She frowned, thinking about what she heard. She had to be crazy. She wanted to be.

"Caleb, we are getting further than we were," Trevin said.

"You don't find this odd as soon as she shows up. This plight on the land shows up?" he said, looking right at his dad.

"Let her work. She's trying," Lord Greenthistle sighed.

"Literally the week they start talking, Cyrus almost dies, and Trev gets his face ripped open. What if the mortals locked this information away on how to solve this plight, because it's them?"

Elodie felt her lip tremble. She glanced at Lord Greenthistle who was watching her. Elodie shrank back into herself.

"Shut up! How dare you say that about her!" Trevin growled. "She wants to help! You think she put that cuff on me? Even knew what it was? Somehow got over the boundary line and nailed me with a tranquilizer? You're being stupid!" he snapped.

"When was the last time a mortal was allowed to leave here? Even knew about us? Since when did you even start liking them? Trev, you hated them more than you hate fae. Now you're bedding one!" he shouted.

Elodie went rigid. She could feel the tears in her eyes. Lord Greenthistle and she hadn't broken eye contact. The mountain lion watching the mink. Trevin shot his dad a glare.

"Enough. If you do not care to help, leave, Caleb," Lord Greenthistle said.

Trevin put his arm around her waist and handed her the book. She shook her head pulling away from him. He held her tighter.

"Don't," he said softly to her. "Please never doubt what you mean to me, El."

Elodie lifted her eyes to Lord Greenthistle, terrified of his reaction. *He knows I love Trevin, and he's going to cut this bond.* She cut her eyes down to the ground.

"Whatever. She can't do it and she knows it. We're just wasting time."

Trevin spun around toward him and glared. "Get out!" he growled.

"Enough! Behave or you both leave. Autumn will help us," Lord Greenthistle said sternly.

Elodie shook her head. She was too scared to reveal what it told her, but she knew she had too. All their lives could depend on it, most of all, Trevin's. She also feared she was driving a wedge between them. She looked to Lord Greenthistle and, for a moment, wanted to beg him to wipe her memory of everything. Of Humboldt. But if this plight that may be linked to her was going to hurt them, it would start with her. How safe would they be if that hold couldn't contain it? She sank to her knees and pressed her palms into her eyes.

"They keep telling me to wake up. To return. That I'm home, I'm theirs, bound, can't be undone. Wake up. Awaken, but I don't know how to, he will see it, they all will let him see it. I don't know what I'm supposed to do!" she cried out.

"Shh El, just breathe," Trevin said in her ear. "I have you." She shook her head.

"It will come for him first. One by one, they will all fall. I don't know what to do, how to stop it. They say wake up. Show them, let them see, it knows I'm here," she repeated the words. She met Lord Greenthistle's eyes again. "What is in me? What do you see? I want to help you. I have to help him."

"I do not know. It's not something I've ever seen before. I can't place it," he said with a sigh. She dropped her head. "It's grown stronger, Elodie. I do see it, but I do not know what it is or where else to turn for answers. I have searched though. I want to know too."

"When I last met with the Marin Estates, they felt her surge. They said it was something old, ancient in a new form. It was foreign. They also said it could have something to do with the Old Giants, but they didn't understand it either," Trevin said.

"New, foreign, odd," Elodie said, pressing her palms into her eyes. "Just odd."

Trevin sighed. "I will never be able to take back those first words I said to you. I wish I could do it all over, Elodie," he said softly.

Autumn set paper and the charcoal down on the desk and stood back silently trying to give Elodie space.

"If you want to take a break, it's okay," Trevin said.

She exhaled sharply. She couldn't waste any more time. Not with him. The luxury of time was never on her side and now it may not be on theirs either.

Standing up, she wiped her eyes. Trevin stood back, letting her do what she needed. Grabbing the paper and the charcoal, she got the rubbing on the back of the book then blew the dust off and set it on the desk. They examined it, much clearer now and in the old language that Greenthistle had never learned.

Elodie examined the tome again and flipped it back to the front. "Wake up, I have the code. I know how, right in front of me." she repeated to herself, racking her brain. She turned to the window again, the trees silent. She sighed. "Wake up."

"Who or what tells you this? Are these thoughts? Voices?" Lord Greenthistle asked. She shifted her eyes to him.

"The Old Giants I assume. I look at them and I hear them, feel them. They tell me things and have told me all this since I moved here. Even before I met Trev," she said, "I swear I do. I'm not crazy. I don't do drugs. I will take a drug test. I hear them though and now they are silent," she said, feeling as though she was failing. "I don't know how to wake up. I don't think I'm dreaming. If I am, why can't I wake up? Is this a dream?"

She trembled suddenly, fearing she truly was insane. What if this was a fever dream, and she was at home in Marin with her dad? Or next to Ricky? She suddenly felt sick.

"This is all very real. I fear that maybe this is what this side of the boundary does to mortals. Slowly alters your mind," Lord Greenthistle said with a remorseful sigh.

"Then how would she have felt called to this place before she ever moved here? How would I see this power in her at that party when she was completely oblivious to this, to us? Marin has five estates and you know she's crossed paths with at least one or their heirs. Hell, she's been to Everoak! Thank the Great Mother they never saw her there with whatever this is in her," Trevin said, fixing his gaze on her. "You are not going insane. You are here. We are real, I'm here, El. Right in front of you," he said softer as he held her hand.

Right in front of you. His words echoed in her head.

She looked at his face. She had grown to love him in the last few months, how much he cared for her, had been by her side, and he wanted to fight for their own happily ever after despite everything pulling them apart. *Right in front of you.*

Her eyes cut to the window again, seeing the trees. The Old Giants, redwoods right in front of her.

She spun around to the tome, flipping it over. She saw the tree, then went to the desk and flipped through the other book to that sigil. Grabbing the paper and charcoal again, she lightly rubbed it and four symbols emerged. The rubbing wasn't very clear with the softness of the paper but the symbols could be matched up well enough, so Elodie wasted no time going back to the tome.

Turning the dial to the corresponding symbol, each click was followed by a release sound. When the last symbol lined up, she felt the click, pressed her palm down and the latch released.

You are home.
Home. Forever.
Ours. His.

The voices shouted in her head, causing her to gasp. Her body seized up and Elodie suddenly fell unconscious.

Trevin grabbed her before she hit the ground, not even concerned with the book.

"El, wake up!" he said, worried.

"What is that symbol? It didn't even match the book cover," Autumn said.

"Damn it! The whole tome is in that language. It will take forever to decode," Lord Greenthistle sighed in defeat.

"Dad! What's wrong with her? Her pulse is weaker!" Trevin pleaded.

Lord Greenthistle walked around and looked at her, unconscious, in Trevin arms. He knelt down and assessed her vitals.

"It's coming back, Let's monitor her to make sure she is okay. I think she's just exhausted. She opened it, though. She figured it out. How did she know that symbol had the key? What is it?" he asked.

"I don't know. She told me there were neat illustrations. One that'd make a cool tattoo."

"Get her back into bed. Stay with her. I will need to talk to her again when she wakes up."

"You felt that immense surge. I know you all did. The redwoods and the ferns nearly pulsed with energy in unison. You know the Old Giants talk to her. They told her she was home."

"Humboldt told her she was home. Not Greenthistle. Be with her for now," Lord Greenthistle said softly. Trevin glared but nodded, gently lifting her in his arms.

"She's something odd if she did that. Not normal, Trevin. Dangerous," his brother said with a glare.

"If you are not going to help. Leave!" Trevin hissed and took her to his room.

Trevin took her boots off and laid her down in bed.

"El, you have to know what I feel for you. I know you feel it for me too, we are vowed. If you say it first, I will confess everything, but I cannot sway you," he said softly, rubbing her head. He kissed her temple. He looked at the tree line. "Please let her hear this. Please tell her," he begged.

Chapter 50

Still in the study Autumn, Cedar, and Lord Greenthistle flipped through the tome, just taking the scale of it. The amount of information that must be sitting in here all in a language they could not read.

"This is just insane. This has been stowed away there this entire time?" Lord Greenthistle was nearly dumbfounded.

"We have it now, can that mortal be put in the hold finally?" Cedar hissed.

"Absolutely not!" Lord Greenthistle snapped. "We do not break bargains, she hasn't."

"How does any of this make sense? How are you ok with this? Something is happening and she is the cause of it all. What if that is why Trevin is acting like the heir should be, it's his instinct to shield us from the danger, from her."

"You're an absolute idiot if you think that's what it is. She is not dangerous, she's not evil or mean," Autumn quipped back.

"The girl is not your fight, Cedar." Lord Greenthistle's voice was stern. "Stop provoking him."

"It is this entire estate's fight! Dad, a mortal allowed to go free?"

"Stop stressing her out! She wants to help and she's overwhelmed!" Autumn said, getting annoyed.

"Either you help me decode this or you can leave. I have too much to figure out. Let Trevin handle her," Lord Greenthistle said.

Autumn and Cedar both took a seat and got to work. Cedar tried to translate the tome, with finding the symbols that repeated a lot. Autumn eyed the symbol in the book on the desk. She scanned the page.

"Why do you think she flipped to this in particular? What stood out about this one thing so much to her? There are odd illustrations of trees and mountains, maps and diagrams with things pressed into these margins all over. This in particular called to her, though. Yet it's the one thing in here without a reference number?" Autumn said, flipping pages.

"Questions you will have to ask her, I suppose, if we don't end up draining the poor girl," Lord Greenthistle said.

"She thought it'd make a cool tattoo. Of course she would say that." Cedar rolled his eyes. "So stupid."

"You just cannot stand that she did something you couldn't. That a mortal girl was able and willing to help us and not once has she slipped in her world with my name nor Trev's. Not once has she given anyone, not even Cora, a hint as to what we are. Is it that? She's given you zero reasons to hate her? Or is it that Trevin will fight you for her? You are used to the apathetic Trevin who never stood up to you?" Autumn spat back at her brother.

"Trevin doesn't trust anyone aside from us—he only went to Cora's parties to watch them on Dad's behalf. Now it's like Trevin and Quinn are all buddy-buddy and Quinn acts like Justine is all he needs. Quinn loved flirting and messing with them. Trevin just simps over Elodie, the little mink," he said in a sarcastic tone.

"So what? Maybe Quinn wants to slow down. Let them enjoy things. Let Trevin learn from her. They are good for each other. She has a finite amount of time, Cedar. He finally puts trust in someone new and you want to ward him away from that? You know he feels things so deeply and losing mom really hurt him. Elodie is exactly what he needs. They both know she doesn't have forever," Autumn said with a hint of sadness.

Lord Greenthistle sighed in remorse. He knew Autumn was right. To push the girl away now would only hurt Trevin. Might make him hesitant to trust like this again. Might hurt his trust in Greenthistle. He sat back defeated, realizing he had made a grave mistake.

"What did she do for you that was so great? That you want her around this much? You begged for her to be at solstice, but not Charles? Why?" Cedar reared his head back.

"She saved his life, for starters. She's nice and an overall great person. She's curious and wise, and she has a big heart. Even for you. She wants to help us because she knows how important we are to Trevin. Plus she loves it here, she loves the Old Giants and the coast. They bring her peace."

"She can lie, though. She will fuck him over, just like the last mortal did. He hurt over that, too. Remember? Elodie just sunk her claws into him and he just took the bait after a few weeks? She is not normal."

"What about the last fae he dated? The one who flat out told him he was not worth the hassle? Or Cassia, who called him a disappointment because he wouldn't put out? You're right, Elodie can lie. She has been lying to her friends for us this entire time. And she does have a power in her. I see it now too. It has gotten bigger, stronger. What if Everoak had seen it in her? I don't even want to think about what horrible things she would be facing there. I will bind her to me if Trev won't do it. I don't want to lose her!"

Lord Greenthistle paused for a moment, imagining her power being this loud in Everoak. What any territory might do to the poor girl. A chill shot through him at the thought. He wondered what Marin would do if they had kept her. He didn't want to lose whatever it was. The possibility of what it might grow into now, and the knowledge that iron would no longer bar them from accessing things. Whatever it was in her was something rare and new. Yet he knew he was setting Trevin up for a devastating blow.

When Elodie had locked eyes with Lord Greenthistle, he could see her pleading with him to let her help. She was willing to slice her hand open for a blood oath. He could see the honesty in her. That she was loyal to them. She would be loyal to Trevin and she would bleed herself dry doing so. Lord Greenthistle knew how much Elodie loved Trevin. Would love him for as long as she was breathing. How unfair this was to not only Trevin but to her too. A sigh escaped him at how unprepared he was for this. He had let his own vowed go, but he had not once considered his son would be vowed to one so rare. He looked over at the window and asked why she couldn't have just been fae.

Because if she was fae, she'd never have found Trevin. She'd never have been able to get that cuff off him. Or handle the maze of iron or open this damned book. Lord Greenthistle was so defeated. He hated the bitter reality his son and Elodie were facing. He sat back and rubbed his face.

"The omens are too close to home now. She might have claimed she wanted to save him, but she will drag him down." Cedar scoffed.

Lord Greenthistle thought of the omen and sat back. *When one estate is bound, the forests shall be born anew.* He stared at the ceiling trying to sort all his emotions. Never would he let his kids know he was feeling. It was always better to be a hardass than an emotional wreck. Lord Greenthistle knew Trevin had to wear his heart on his sleeve. Knew it the moment he was born what he was.

He thought about something very old, ancient in a new form, it was foreign. *The Old Giants.* He sat back thinking about Elodie. *Did she harvest their power? How? They spoke to her before she had ever laid eyes on Trevin. She wasn't born here, she wasn't of Humboldt blood. Her parents weren't. She was foreign. New.*

He sighed as he stood up and left the study without a word, walked upstairs to Trevin's room, and knocked.

The door opened and he saw his son clearly stressed and uneasy now with his arrival.

"May I see how she's doing?" Lord Greenthistle asked calmly.

"She's still sleeping."

"May I see how she is doing?" He repeated his question.

Trevin stepped aside and Lord Greenthistle walked in and saw her curled up on her side. He pressed his fingers to her neck, her heart rate was calm and steady. His eyes traced her features, her ears. He saw her power, louder than he had ever seen it. A calm but steady stream forging on. *How can this be?*

"Trevin, I will not tell you to stay away from her anymore. I will not be the one to break this trust in you, son. I truly hope she doesn't break it either. I don't want Humboldt to lose this power in her. But remember you cannot force her into things she cannot comprehend. We cannot break those rules. She has to want this, to understand that we can't tell her what might happen because we don't know."

He heard Trevin let out a slow exhale. "Thank you, Dad. I will accept any and all responsibility that falls on me with her. I give you my word. I understand if she speaks of us, she will go into the hold."

"Good. Please inform me when she wakes," he said.

"Yes, sir," Trevin said with a smile.

Lord Greenthistle nodded and walked out, closing the door behind him. He walked out of the house, changed and then bolted deep in the redwoods.

He noticed a couple of ravens nearby and remembered Trevin mentioning she had seen a lot. As he ran, he thought about Trevin, Elodie, Shirley, and Lady Greenthistle. He thought about everything in all their lives that had brought him to this crossroad. How he now did not know where any one path led. Could not see around any of the bends and that terrified him. To know the laws and rules never accounted for something like this. How a mortal with a strange power could emerge, could be vowed to his son, to Trevin of all people.

Chapter 51

Some hours later in Trevin's room, Elodie gasped awake. The light pounded into her head causing her to whimper.

"I'm here. You are safe. You are okay," he said, rubbing her back.

She took deeper breaths then pressed herself up to sitting. The air in the room was different on her skin and her eyes needed to adjust, but to what she didn't know. She held up her hand and rubbed it.

"Is your hand bothering you? Dad cleaned the dirt out of it before he healed it last night. He usually always checks for early signs of infection."

She rubbed her thumb over her palm again. Remembering how she pressed it on the redwood trunk.

"El? Are you hurt somewhere?" Concern sat in Trevin's words. She swallowed hard.

"No. I just feel weird. Dizzy but not, disoriented but I'm not. Tired but I don't think my body wants to sleep anymore, I'm wide awake. Hazy but not. Something is different."

"Hungry? You should probably hydrate." He motioned to the glass of water on the table next to her.

"I don't feel hungry," she said, reaching for the water. Once she drank it, the hazy feeling faded and her senses were sharper.

"Eat something anyway, dinner will be soon. We can eat up here." He set down a bowl of blackberries.

"I told Cora I'd be there tonight, I don't know if I can do that walk though. My car has been there overnight?" She started to panic. Her usual self was getting overwhelmed.

"A sentry took it home, your keys are on my desk. Dad thinks you should stay here too."

"Does he think I am the plight? Do you? Maybe I should be put in the hold," she asked worriedly.

"No, you are not the plight. You are good. The lands like you, Dad likes you, he's concerned for you. I don't want you to leave, ever. Dad said he wasn't going to tell us to stay away from each other anymore. He appreciates everything you've done. He doesn't want to lose you, doesn't want Humboldt to lose you."

Elodie wanted to be happy about that, she was happy about it. She could love Trevin and not feel the disappointment in his dad's eyes. She would see fear and unease in them, for she might be something that would damn Greenthistle into a grave. One they never should see. She might be damning these Old Giants too. She took his hand and gripped it.

"Are you relieved by that? You are mine. I am yours, and no one will take that from us, El. No one."

Tap, tap.

"I don't want to go. If I go, all of this will just be in my head. Your dad wouldn't need to scramble my memory because everyone would already know I really am crazy."

"Then don't go. You are not crazy. You are brave, little mink."

"I don't want to leave you." Elodie saw him smile wide.

Shortly before dinner, his dad checked on her and told her she was safe and watched over. She was welcomed at Greenthistle and he wanted her here. Elodie could only nod, trying to sort through her senses. How heightened they seemed.

Autumn too had visited Elodie before meeting up with Charles for Cora's party. Elodie felt bad she couldn't go but Autumn assured her she would cover for them. Trevin naturally stayed by her side. He suggested they go for a swim in the pool. Autumn of course left her a new swimsuit to wear mentioning how it was fine to go in sans suit too. Elodie blushed and nodded.

Before Cedar left for Cora's, he found his dad back in the study.

"Dad, you have to do something about her! She knows way too much! She's here, just put her in the hold!"

Lord Greenthistle sighed. He couldn't admit to his youngest that his own vowed was a mortal. Nor that he had grown a fondness for Elodie. A pride at the man his eldest was becoming as of late because of her. Nor the hurt and anger he knew Autumn would direct at them both. Pride and excitement formed at what his eldest and the girl had accomplished together. Their ability to work together, to listen to each other. Most of all trust each other despite centuries of tales and myths telling them not to.

"This is not your fight, Cedar. Leave Trev to sort through it."

"You see that look in his eyes when it comes to her. He would take a bullet for her, stand in hell's wake for her, for a mortal!"

Lord Greenthistle leveled his gaze at his youngest. The boisterous ball of energy that would protect his home and his other siblings without fail. Yet his fears were guiding him in the wrong direction. Elodie was not the danger.

"Why do you think that is, Cedar?"

"I don't know, because he's stupid?" Cedar spat out and crossed his arms.

Lord Greenthistle sighed and shook his head. "The school board loves her, it would be a disservice to not only her lineage but to Humboldt too if I erase her memory. She would be done as a teacher. Same if I lock her up. And honestly what do you think Trevin is going to do if I did either thing to the girl? Tell me, Cedar, what do you think your older brother is going to do as a result of either action? He would find her no matter where I dropped her and he would start over with her if he had to. You know it and that's why it bothers you so much."

Cedar remained quiet.

"She's trustworthy. I am not sure what the lands will do if I scramble her mind either, honestly," Lord Greenthistle said with a sigh. "So she is and will remain under Greenthistle's direct protection," he said sternly. Cedar sighed and rolled his eyes.

"What if she brought this evil though? I don't think she did it on purpose, I will give you that. She's kind, obviously, but what if it's tied to her power? She's going to drag him down and we will follow, one by one," Cedar huffed out.

"That's not exactly how it went, Cedar. And what if this evil awoke something in her? Something dormant, she has been a major asset to us, you cannot deny that. We never would have been able to get that tome and Trevin could have been taken from us."

"So lock her into servitude and keep her in the hold."

"She has not broken the bargain. I cannot and will not go against these rules. It would cost Greenthistle power. We have to trust her, Trevin does. "

"Fine, when your first born damns the estate."

"Cedar, you are dismissed. We are a family, support your brother," he said, turning his attention to the papers on the desk. Cedar narrowed his eyes and walked out of the office and off estate property to head to Cora's. Lord Greenthistle sighed and went back to the books on his desk. He flipped back to the page with the sigil and began to rack his brain for its meaning.

Chapter 52

Over the next few days, Elodie knew they were trying to decipher the tome along with the book she had left behind. Trevin and Autumn tried figuring the sigil out.

Trevin stayed at her house for two nights during the week and updated her on everything. Restlessness had grabbed hold of her. She was jumpy and looking over her shoulder a lot, staring out of the window a fair amount. Most sounds made her flinch even if they seemed far away.

"Are you okay? What's wrong?" Trevin asked worriedly. He held her hands, but she pulled them away.

"I'm fine," she said. "I feel fine."

"Please stop lying. What's wrong?" he asked.

"I just feel anxious, I'm okay. I will tell you if something happens," she said, but she was worried something was happening to her. Something to do with the boundary line, but not being able to go see him was the last thing she wanted.

He leaned in and kissed her. "I never get enough of you, little mink. Tell me when to stop."

Nodding, she pressed into his kiss while feeling his body. She ran her fingers under his shirt and down the line on his chest causing him moan heavily and kiss her again as he walked her back to the bed. Trevin noticed she had gotten even more passionate as of late and after four rounds she slept soundly in his arms.

The next morning they headed off to work, and Elodie dropped him off at his dad's office. He would see her the next day at the café and stay with her again. His usual every one or two days. He was busy most nights this week with the book.

That night he and Cedar met up with Cyrus and Quinn at the tavern.

Alena looked at him and shook her head in disgust.

"Reeks of mortals at this table," she scoffed, sitting on Cyrus's lap. He laughed.

"One is extra annoying, the other is pretty naïve," Cyrus said.

"Don't start," Trevin snapped.

"He smells of her most nights, now that he's glued to her hip. At least Q takes a break," Cedar added.

"I guess we can cut him some slack, it's been awhile. As if she has anything he can't get over here," Alena cooed. Trevin rolled his eyes.

"Leave it be. So you dislike mortals now. We don't," Quinn said.

"He used to dislike them, a lot." Cedar scowled.

"I came out to clear my head from work. I didn't think you were just going to talk shit all night," Trevin said, annoyed. He tried to block out their conversation and thought about Elodie more. He was getting worried about her mental state. Once he finished his drink and stood up, he noticed Cyrus's wry grin, and rolled his eyes. It grated him as of late.

"Taking off?" Quinn asked. Trevin nodded.

"I want to get some more stuff translated before work tomorrow."

"Later," Cedar said. Quinn nodded.

Trevin left, heading back home and into the study where he stared at the tome.

He thought about her questions and he too wondered. How and why was this tome made? Had mortals been to this side of the boundary? Were they mentally altered after? He sighed in frustration. His dad had done too good of a job at keeping mortals out, so there were not enough records. Del Norte and Mendocino hadn't had an issue in so long either. He wasn't comfortable asking the other territories. Then he sat back and sighed, staring up at the ceiling.

Elodie loved the life she built. He couldn't trap her on this side of the boundary. She needed to be in Eureka, Cora needed her. It was selfish to tell her about the vowed bond.

He sent her a good night text, and got a 'sleep well' response from her. "Please let me find a way to give her forever," he said, looking at the trees. Exhaustion from work took over him. He wanted to curl up next to her and part of him was tempted to ask if he could but he didn't want to smother her.

The next morning Trevin woke up to a gentle caress down his face. It was a temple to chin motion, not Elodie's usual along his cheek. He felt someone kiss him and half dazed he pressed into it, glad he had gone to Elodie's last night after all.

Then he realized the absence of her scent in the air. This scent reminded him of the tavern. He heard a laugh that was certainly not Elodie and opened his eyes, meeting Alena's smug grin. Trevin pushed himself back stunned. He saw Alena smiling at him lustfully.

"Morning, Master Greenthistle."

"Get the fuck out of my room, now!" he growled. He realized she was topless and his face paled. "Nothing fucking happened, why are you in my room?"

Alena laughed again.

"Trevy, I always wanted to see what you were like, Cedar is so much fun, I bet you are amazing. Tell me, is the little mortal trash a good enough release?" she said, reaching out for him.

He jumped out of his bed. "Do not touch me and do not speak of her. Go crawl back to Cedar, otherwise leave my estate! How dare you invade my space. I'm a high estate heir," he growled out. She laughed and put her shirt back on.

"Well maybe I will try Q, hopefully he's not too sprung up on his trash."

"Do not call them that," he yelled. She walked off with a laugh as his phone vibrated. He saw it was Elodie and suddenly his stomach sank. He answered it.

"El," he said his heart was pounding.

"How could you?" She cried out.

"What? What are you talking about? What happened?" His voice was growing frantic

"What? You seriously think this is okay? Some stupid fae rules?"

"What's wrong?" Trevin was pleading. She was so upset and he felt frozen.

"You really take me for a fool, don't you? How long have you been talking to her? At what point did you stop meaning what you said? Did I stop mattering to you." Her voice breaking pained him.

He felt the buzz of a message and checked it. Pure shock washed over him. A screenshot of him with Alena pressing her chest into his face, he was asleep, but Elodie wouldn't know that. How hard had he slept last night? Had she slipped something in his drink? Her pants were on her still, his clothes still on him. He never put clothes back on with Elodie, never would have. All he wanted was Elodie. The screenshot showed it was sent from Cedar's phone. Despair started to pour over him that his own brother had done this and he was going to lose Elodie in the process.

"Please meet me at Sunny Brae. Please Elodie."

"Why? So you can explain more fae rules that I will never understand?"

"Please El. I will meet you at your place right now!"

"Fine. Meet me in 20 at the trailhead," she snapped and hun the phone up

As Trevin ran out of the house, he noticed Cedar's door cracked and heard Alena laugh. A growl of anger slipped out as he changed before he got out of the estate. He would deal with them later, right now he knew Elodie was the priority. His paws pounded hard against the earth to the trailhead. She wasn't there yet. It was a work day, and he hoped she wouldn't be in trouble. Hopefully his dad could pull some strings. He would wait here for hours for her then he would run to her place, her work, he would find her. His heart pounded and his mind raced, he could not believe that Cedar and Alena would do this. Did they not care about rules and repercussions?

The scent he longed for came into his senses and a few moments later her car pulled up. She got out and tears showed her devastation. She wouldn't meet his eyes. *How can she think I want anyone else?*

"El, nothing happened!"

"That didn't look like nothing! She's in your bed naked. I trusted you! Can you actually lie? You only want me and Alena and whoever else?"

"I can't lie, I only want you, I do not want Alena. That was Caleb's phone. How did he even get your number?" he asked with a stinging sensation in his throat.

"How should I know? Ask him. I cannot wake up to messages like that. Regardless of how you ended up in that situation, she is in your bed. Naked."

"She was topless, not naked!" Trevin wanted to scream as soon as the words came out. It didn't matter what her state of dress was, Elodie had seen her in his bed. She glared at him and he could see her eyes water, he could see her sorrow building ready to drown her. "You mean everything to me. Please remember what I asked you to believe time after time. What I needed you to trust me on, that we will have our happily ever after. I went out with the guys and I went home to my room alone. I woke up, and she was in my bed. I didn't sleep with her. I told her to get the fuck out of my room, she invaded my space. El, you mean more to me than you realize."

"Don't call me El," she hissed out, causing him to cringe. "I find it really hard to trust anything any of you say after that. These games you all play. You say I mean more than I realize, yet you can't tell me why or how. I wanted to help you, I wanted to keep you all safe. Everything I did was for you, because I love you, Trev," she cried out then watched his body go rigid, his face washed over with shock then worry. That tether pulled wildly inside her. "You call us liars and fickle, yet you toy with us like we are disposable and I guess we are. Just bones in the dirt eventually, right?

"I knew I loved you that first night we slept together, Trevin. I thought it was real for you too, I knew I'd never feel this way again. That tether, just some stupid trickery. You never wanted me to say it because you don't want it. All of it lies, the only ones you can tell by omission, right. You didn't have to love me. Fine I get it, nothing is forever, but to cheat?"

He could see the thread that bonded them running out of slack and he couldn't grasp it in time. He scrambled to put these puzzle pieces together correctly, but he was out of time. To figure out what was in her, to fight this evil that was engulfing both their homes, time had run out because he had been a coward.

One day he knew he would lose her, she would take her last gasp of air and he would know. He would end up just like his dad. His throat tightened, and he swallowed hard. She was his vowed and he couldn't tell her, he was too scared to tell her. *Why am I such a coward?*

She told him she loved him, and he now had to tell her, this was the bargain he made with himself. It wasn't swaying her because she had made this choice, she had made it so long ago and he never let her say it. Now it was his turn.

"Elodie, I love you. You are the only one I want. This is no lie," he said, looking her right in the eyes. He watched her body tense, and she gasped at him. Her emotions unleashed inside her in fury. *She feels this vowed; she knows we are.* He thought as he watched her. That energy was sure to attract a ton of attention.

"Funny you can say it now. Not after I guided you through an iron maze and saved your life. Or at winter solstice, or opened up that stupid book none of your family can touch. You say it only after you fuck up!" she muttered. No longer fighting the tears. She squeezed her eyes shut and trembled. Trevin watched that energy in her near ready to boil over as her emotions raged inside her. Then she met his eyes with resolve. "I can't let you suck the life out of me like Ricky did."

The wind had been knocked out of him. He couldn't stand to pull her emotions off her when he was feeling too many himself. He trembled and swallowed hard again, watching her pain seep out of her. They both said they loved each other, and he had let her trust in him break because he was a coward afraid of the rules instead of trying to defy them. How could he do this when he had trusted her with his life, when she had proven how much she loved him?

Trevin recalled what his dad had done, played a drunken fool to his vowed to let her go on to live her life while he watched and he was doomed to repeat it. Greenthistle was doomed, had been doomed because it had been built upon lies, and ruled on fear. She could move on, she would move on. She could travel and see the world. Meet up with Charles in Hawaii and tell more stories of their adventures. A mortal would cross her path who would love her for the curiosity and wonder she found. Love her for the magic of the world that she had been blessed with, that his vowed had shown him. He swallowed the cries and screams of pain ripping out of his throat. His face a void mask of emotion he fought to keep up.

"Okay." He fought to keep a calm tone, watching her face change to absolute despair, and he hated it. The instinct in him to nurture her clawed at him, but he fought that too. They stood in silence for a moment, and it was as though the entire earth was holding a breath. As she narrowed her eyes, he saw that cauldron explode and a strong gust pushed him back toward the trail away from her. The trees shook and then almost swayed toward her, as if they wanted to coddle her because he had failed to do so. He failed to protect her, the one they had called back here. Shock formed in her expression that she did that then she quickly got into her car.

Trevin remained frozen. *Bound to them, she belonged to them. She was theirs, not mine.* He snapped his eyes back to her when the car door slammed shut.

"Wait," he said, reaching his hand out and taking a step. "Elodie!" She drove away, and he trembled. His vowed, who had the power of the Old Giants, a mortal? What was she? They were vowed, and she had this great ancient power of the earth in her. She had truly been blessed by the very lands he would inherit one day. Why could he not remember the memory of the blessed one and why had he just let her go? Trevin had been so scared of keeping her from her life but this was her life, the Old Giants had called her blessed one. Elodie was in just as much danger as he was and he didn't know what was coming. He didn't know what she was, nor how to help her because he had been too scared to let her tell him.

"Elodie," he whimpered. "Please, I never lied. You mean everything to me, I love you. I love you! I'm such a coward," he said to himself. Trevin's heart pounded, and the trembling took over his body. "Tell her that, please." He pleaded to the Old Giants and the ferns. The mountain lion was desperately clawing its way out of him. His despair took over, forcing his body to run back into the forest. Giving into feral, he ran fast and hard deep into the forest until the despair and his pounding lungs hurt him. Collapsing in the dirt somewhere in Arcata Community Forest, the mountain lion retreated back into him and he was fae again. The pain now engulfed him as the ferns brushed his back. These ferns that were hers, she was theirs, they wanted her. His eyes traveled up a nearby giant, tracing the lines in the redwood up to the sky. "I let my vowed go. You wanted me with her. I'm sorry. Please. Please tell her I'm scared, I'm lost, I don't know what to do. I love her," he whimpered.

The moisture dripped down from the redwoods and he wanted the earth to swallow him.

He said her name as he cried. Willing the trees to summon her as he was lay in the dirt. There was no way she could safely get him even if they did tell her to run to him.

All those times he saw the trees react to her, she had so much power and she wanted him, she loved him. His own brother had instigated this, had swayed her in a direction, he told her the truth and now he wondered if begging and pleading would further drive her away.

He thought of his dad when he let his own vowed go. He had his mom to coddle him. His dad was lying when she had passed, and had lied to all three of them. Trevin was doomed to do the same thing. Love another that would never compare to Elodie, start a family built upon lies and sabotage. How could his own blood turn on him? Let Alena lie, put himself and her in so much jeopardy? Then he wondered if Cyrus knew? He wondered if Cyrus had helped create the scheme. For what? To play a joke on him? To drive him and her apart? Had Quinn been in on this? His friends, his brothers had done this to him and his vowed? He had let her go? What if his own dad was behind it? Autumn was the only one he felt hadn't had a part in this, the doubt sent a chill through him.

"Elodie," he whimpered again. He couldn't bring himself to get up.

Elodie arrived at school and took a deep breath.

"Get it together, get it together, get it together," she said to herself taking deep breaths. "You were warned. Yet you fell for him anyway. Stupid." She took another deep breath and got out of the car, rushing inside. She had called the school saying she had a car emergency to handle. With a deep inhale, she went in through the office and everyone looked at her shocked.

"Are you okay?" the front desk lady asked.

"I'm fine. Sorry. I finally got a battery jump." She was near erratic and took another deep breath. "I'm here. I'm ready." It was going to be a hard day. The front desk lady nodded apprehensively and Elodie rushed to her classroom. The principal had covered the morning and Elodie forced a smile on her face as she entered.

"Oh I'm glad to see you are here."

Elodie swallowed hard and nodded. "Yes. I am ready to teach," she said, keeping her voice together.

"Great, they just wrapped up their quiz."

"Okay." Elodie nervously laughed. "Time to share our stories." Anything to get her mind distracted from Trevin. This thing inside her was surging, something snapped inside her when he said he loved her. *Did he? He constantly had fae girls throwing themselves at him, could one have sabotaged him?* Then she wondered why he would let that lie linger.

"Ms. Santi." She snapped back to the present moment and looked at Konrad who gasped in shock. She took a slow deep inhale and fought past the pain. She had a job to do, she had to do this, teaching was her only fall back. If she got fired now, it'd be hard to pick up the pieces.

"Yes Konrad?" she said with a smile. *Hold it together, you have to hold it together for them.*

"Do you have a story you can share first?" he asked. She scanned the faces of all her students, seeing their smiling hopeful innocent faces and hoped they would never have their hearts broken too soon. An erratic laugh slipped out.

"I will have one at the end. I want to hear yours. I was so worried I would miss all the stories but I'm so glad I'm here to share them with you." She swallowed back the lump in her throat and sat down. "Okay, I'm going to draw a name to go first," she said, grabbing her stack of name cards.

Her breathing was slow and steady all day, making sure to take deep breaths.

Chapter 53

Trevin dragged himself back to the estate sometime that evening after going straight into his state parks work. He worked late just as an excuse to be in the forest. He didn't want to see Cedar. He didn't want to see Cyrus, Quinn, or Autumn. Straight up the stairs he went with heavy steps and once in his room, he locked the door.

He sat on his bed, his head low, resting his elbows on his knees.

"It's better this way, El. You didn't need to know you were the only one who'd have my heart," he said, wiping his eyes. He looked at the drawing of the mountain lion and the mink with the flower crowns and sighed. He would keep it, and all of her stuff that she had only used a few times. He would keep the solstice gown and her spring equinox gown that was coming up in a few weeks. She had no clue she was invited. That her dress had already been made with Autumn's help of casually asking her preferences. It was safely hidden away in Autumn's closet, where it would never ever be worn. Lord Ashdale had agreed to let her attend and Trevin swore there would be no problems at all. She would stay by his or Autumn's side all night. Autumn was so eager to accept Lord Ashdale's request too. Now he would have to tell her El wouldn't be going and knew how upset his sister would be.

He glanced at the picture of them at the winter solstice. How perfect she looked, how elegant an estate lady she could be. His eyes traced her ears, and he frowned. She was radiant with her hair done like that in her gown. He set it down. He would cherish this too. The winter solstice he got with his vowed. The little mink that won his heart, and he let her walk away because it was for the betterment of Greenthistle. It was better for Elodie.

He laid down and tried to fight his cries.

Elodie slammed her door shut and locked it when she got home. She screamed and threw her keys down.

"Fuck!" she screamed again. She felt her body tremble. Something in her core consumed her and she collapsed on the floor breathing hard. "This isn't real. None of it is!" she cried out. "Trev is no different from any of them. Caleb that bastard!" she cried out. She imagined them snapping at each other, their dad telling them to take it outside and they'd fight then be over it. They would make up because they were family and she was temporary. The pain she felt swelled.

Then sensation engulfed her body.

Evil. Evil lurks. Elodie. El.

Whispers turned to hisses as she pressed her hands to her ears squeezing her eyes shut. Images of a mountain lion, ears back, hissing, clawing out, enraged, flashed in her mind. She tried taking deep breaths as her hands got warm. She rolled over on her back and caught the gleam of something bronzed. The hilt of her dagger.

"Trevin," she whimpered. "Why? Is this how it is for you, easy to disregard us? All these months had to mean something and you just let go?" She frowned, knowing she couldn't talk to anyone about this either. As she lay on the floor, crying, the sorrow eased, the burn in her hands faded. She kicked off her boots and let herself overflow with the sorrow. She got up and crawled into bed. "Trev," she whimpered.

She sniffed and pulled up a picture of them on her phone. How natural it looked even if he had his human glamour on in the picture. *He just stood there, like he gave up. He said okay. Not denying it. Not admitting to it. Omission? Acceptance? Why? Why would he just let go so suddenly, was I really not worth anything to him?*

"Just work through this, you knew it wouldn't work out, and you were so stupid to believe otherwise. You've broken up with people and they've broken up with you, you've moved on. You will move on. You will move on," she said to herself. She glanced at the window. It was still early; she traced the tree line in the distance.

She remembered the first time she had found evidence of Ricky cheating, and how hurt she was, yet she kept going back, not even sure why. She told herself if she had hard evidence as if she were blind to everything else. Then she had walked in on Ricky with another girl, she hadn't had this kind of reaction. Instead, Elodie just turned and left without a word and drove north, always north. She was done with Ricky that second. She sat in her hatch and watched her phone light up. Letting it just ring as she thought real hard about what she was going to do next. The moment she looked straight ahead, north. The ocean to her left and the Old Giants straight ahead of her. She had been restless to get out of Marin, to feel the mist and the ferns, just to reach out and run her hand along them.

Elodie compared that feeling to now and picked apart every single emotion between then and now. Ricky had always made her feel as though that was as good as it would get. Settling for that was something she figured she would have to accept. She stayed through suspicions, but when she saw it right in front of her, the flame had run out of wick, she felt nothing for him.

Trevin though, he was different entirely. Trevin had been a whirlwind of curiosity and passion. The universe seemed to bring them together and he just let her walk away. He spoke of fairy tale romances and it meant nothing.

Never doubt how much you mean to me.

It cannot be undone.

He is yours.

I'm so glad you chose Humboldt.

He will see you.

All his words, and their words played in her head. All the words she wanted to believe, and how broken her heart felt now at the lies they were. She would give anything for that numbness. It pained her to know she would have to talk to his dad about how to handle the bargain. Then to look for a job next year. If she was allowed to leave. If they didn't force her to just stay here.

She looked up at the ceiling and wondered if she had gone crazy. Lord Greenthistle said the other side of the boundary might have affected her but

Trevin was supposed to see her? See what happened to mortals who discovered them? What if it wasn't blacking out for a bit to wake up lost and confused? It was a slow deterioration over time, had Lord Greenthistle done it? Had Trevin told him to?

Elodie didn't know what to do or where she would even go next. Marin felt hollowing, everywhere felt hauntingly lonely because she loved it here and she loved him. She had found a family with Cora, Justine, Charles, with Autumn, and Quinn, and Lord Greenthistle. Even if Caleb and Cyrus didn't like her, they were still a presence she had in this family. The thought of leaving it hurt her heart all over again in a different way than Trevin had. She wanted that life.

She curled up into her blankets and cried, tossing and turning. Sleep was interrupted by dreams of mountain lions being hurt, the Old Giants falling, ravens cawing outside. They were so loud. She got up to change and put ear plugs in, everything seemed louder for some reason and she just wanted to sleep.

When she woke, she wasn't sure how long she had actually slept. The sun finally rose, and she relented. Tiredness clung to her as she got ready and went to the bagel spot then went to work an hour early. Glancing at her lesson plan, she hoped she could pull through the day. Her phone was hardly even an afterthought, and she hadn't even looked at it in the last twenty-four hours. There wasn't much in the way of contact, anyway. Trevin couldn't be bothered, not that she could or would reach out to him. Even if this thing inside her that he and his dad knew about was wreaking havoc on her. The fear he'd not respond, that he'd reject her was too much to bear.

She carried on throughout the day and the next day and the days began to blur together. Flashes of teal light would appear in her vision. Her hands started to glow teal and she was certain she had lost it. Sleep was becoming more and more elusive.

Autumn had reached out once asking if she wanted to meet up.

Elodie didn't respond.

Cora had asked if she was going to the café one night.

Elodie didn't respond.

Cora asked again the next night.

Elodie still didn't respond.

Finally Cora asked if she was okay. All Elodie could manage was a 'yes' before collapsing back on her floor, repeating the same cycle all over again. Her hands burning, his words, their words playing in the mind and sounds getting louder each day. Her hands stayed illuminated longer and terrors played behind her closed eyes in the dark.

Elodie was worried she truly was going crazy. She bounced between this being Lord Greenthistle's doing or that she had been crazy all along. She was too scared to go hiking, to sit on the bed in her hatch listening to the ocean. She was too scared to even walk the path down the street from her place and touch a redwood.

"It cannot be undone," she said, staring up at her ceiling. Then she wondered if she would be experiencing this if they had just locked her into servitude? Would it be better or worse than this feeling? She assumed that her heart wouldn't hurt at least. She didn't want to feel this, didn't want to question her own sanity.

Chapter 54

Some days later, Trevin had not fared much better. Lord Greenthistle became increasingly aware of the absolute defeat in Trevin's eyes. This was not his annoying apathy before Elodie had appeared. This was defeat and pain. Trevin would speak of work things and then go up to his room and not come down for meals. Lord Greenthistle eventually relented, knowing Trevin needed to eat. He assumed it had something to do with Elodie and feared she had hurt him, or that she had left him. He knew Trevin would never hurt her.

Relief finally came to Lord Greenthistle when he saw Trevin and headed to Nightswift's Estate. If she had left him, he hoped the spark in Trevin would not die, but he could tell it was fizzling. He hoped at the very least the old Trevin would emerge. Lord Greenthistle had hoped that Elodie was different. He couldn't imagine her hurting him intentionally, with how much he saw in her when she opened the tome. The absolute pleading he saw in her eyes that she loved Trevin. He checked her whereabouts and ensured she hadn't quit her job after Trevin had left.

"Been a bit down there, Trev." Cyrus grinned with a smugness.

"Not important," Trevin said, looking down. He had hoped being around friends would help even if he was annoyed at them. Cedar walked in a little later and Trevin started taking deeper breaths, feeling his anger brewing.

"It is as though life has been sucked out of you. Did the mortal turn out to be a vampire or something?" Cyrus laughed.

Trev remained quiet. He eyed his glass of liquor. How much had gone wrong in a matter of seconds? How many pieces needed to be picked up with little hope of being mended?

"She left his ass," Cedar said with a grin. "Because she found out about a certain little tryst."

Trevin glared at him.

"Trevin, you bedded the mortal girl and then bedded someone else? I didn't think you had it in you. Wow," Cyrus crooned.

"I didn't bed anyone else. Why was Alena in my room? And how the fuck did you get Elodie's number?" he growled at Cedar, who had a sly smile on his face.

"Looked her number up at work. Pretty easy. Alena spent the night with me and then went to freshen up, and pursue you, apparently. Figured El should know. Communication is important after all." Cedar smirked. Trevin glared and then noticed Cyrus's sly grin. The stabbing sting of betrayal pierced Trevin's heart. *They both were in on this? This was the only way they could tell a lie and let each other think parts were true.*

"I told her no months ago! She just decided it was okay to invade my space, to touch me like that? Against my will! She knew I was with Elodie. Everyone fucking did!" he growled.

"Alena did know, so did I," Cyrus said.

Trevin watched Cyrus's fist tremble. Watched a second of fear pour over Cyrus's face quickly erased by a chill and then that grin that he always gave Elodie took over. All the confusion Trevin felt had diminished with his seething rage.

"Color me surprised when I saw Alena had gotten in your bed. It was only right for Elodie to know, since of course everyone knew about her," Cedar said. Cyrus laughed.

"You both were in on this? You hurt Elodie. Why?" Trevin could hardly fathom how they could do this.

"Trevin! She's a mortal and you act as though she's the end all be all in the universe. Like she's anything important. Be glad she left you. You claim to be all admirable and love her, but I saw your face in Alena's chest. She told me how you pressed into her kiss," Cedar said.

"She said she would have loved to go further, her offer still stands," Cyrus said. "Besides, I remember you said the mortal girl didn't need a bunch of fae messing with her head. I assumed that meant you, too. Let her go, let her be," Cyrus said.

"I am letting her believe a lie! That you both told!" he growled.

"What lie, that you are a fuckboy?" Cedar laughed. Trevin changed and tackled his brother down. Cedar huffed then changed and overtook Trevin with ease. Cyrus watched on in glee at the fight.

"And now you are letting the mortal girl come between family. Tsk, tsk, kitty cat," Cyrus said.

Trevin changed and got out of his brother's grasp.

"Why did you give her your name? She doesn't even know Quinn's or Cedar's. You tried to fill her head with bullshit, too! At solstice, at the bonfire. You better stay away from her."

"I see how trustworthy she is, I see how much that might be beneficial later. Give her a little to get a whole lot from her," Cyrus said and licked his top lip.

Trevin grabbed Cyrus's shirt and pulled his fist back. Cyrus held his coy smile, almost daring Trevin to punch him. Then something like a plea flashed in Cyrus's eyes for one small second. Trevin watched the guilt, shame, sadness, and insanity in it, only for it to be gone as fast as it came. Replaced with joy and amusement.

"Leave her alone! You and Cedar both drove this wedge in. Not her. I don't trust anyone because family doesn't even mean anything!" he yelled, shoving Cyrus away.

Trevin changed and ran out of Nightswift Estate. He ran into the forest. Finding himself in the very spot he had found Elodie in with the bear attack. He wasn't sure where he was running to, but now his paws were locked to this place. She had bled here, had become part of the earth, how blessed she was. That damn thought again. Blessed by the earth, some fairy tale his mom told Autumn when she was little?

He changed and fell to his knees.

Trevin let her go because he was scared. He was scared she might not want life with him one day and she had so many options. The lands had been calling to her, and had vowed her to him. She had wanted him and he just watched her go because he couldn't even trust himself. "Elodie," he whimpered.

Sobbing, he tried to force himself to run to her. He let her walk away. Cyrus and Cedar split them. Trevin and Cyrus used to be so close, closer than he and Quinn were growing up. They may have stopped being as close as they once were but that didn't make Cyrus any less one of his best friends. they always had each others backs, all three heirs did. His friend and his own brother had planted these seeds of mistrust in Elodie. But Trevin, he had let them fester. Had let rust build on those mental gates he would sometimes push open. To stroll through those dreams of her, now overrun with the floss flower and iron. He didn't know what to do. What could he do?

He lay on his back, letting the rain fall on him, and heard the water flow through the creek. His eyes looked up to the Old Giants.

"You brought her here, you gave her magic, and you wanted her to wake up, you guided her home. Guide me, please," he whimpered. Nothing came though, no voices, no words of wisdom or cryptic messages. Just the sound of the creek and small animals nearby. "Elodie," he cried and closed his eyes.

Chapter 55

The next day Elodie had not faired any better. She woke up crying, hearing the hisses telling her to wake up. Images of Trevin screaming and bleeding, Autumn crying, Q and Caleb chained up, and Cyrus screaming in despair. The Old Giants falling and her heart filled with such pain. She fought to hold it together at work. At night, she would become overwhelmed with the hisses and cry out on the floor. Her power was showing in other ways. Every sound was amplified. Someone's TV was up too loud, she could feel the electricity in the air. Ravens cawing as though they were taunting her. She had tried to go for a hike after work one night but the ravens watching her from a tree scared her. She would see more ravens around town. They watched when she went to work, when she got home.

Her phone buzzed, and she didn't care. After an hour, she relented and picked it up.

"Are you okay? I haven't seen you or Trev at the café in over a week."

"I'm okay." she responded and put the phone down. She heard another raven caw and then the flap of its wings.

Soon. El.
Evil is lurking.
Going to strike.

The hissing said.

She pushed herself up and went to the bathroom. Her eyes looked at the bottle of anti-anxiety meds she had been prescribed but hadn't used up here. She needed sleep. Sleep without seeing the world she loved burn. Taking one, she went to bed and nothing came to her that night. Sleep encased her in a dark void and when she woke up, a tired grogginess lingered.

Sitting in the parking lot Elodie wiped her eyes, then noticed a raven looking at her. She glared at it.

"Go on, tell him how much I'm struggling. Let them all laugh," she muttered. Her phone buzzed when she got out of the car.

It was Cora asking her to come over. She ignored it.

Elodie went through her day and found some relief from the kids. When the day ended, she was gathering up her bag and heard a knock on the door jamb.

"Ms. Santiago, do you have a minute?" she heard someone say, and she looked up to meet the principal's eyes.

"Yes," she asked, a little tense.

Soon. Soon he will need you. Soon, El.

The voices hissed, then she heard a raven caw again. A chill slithered down her spine.

The principal frowned, and Elodie could see the concern on her face.

"It seems you are going through some things. We understand you're probably still grieving. It didn't seem as though you gave yourself much time, then with the accident shortly after. We think it might be best for the kids if you take leave for the next week."

"No, I'm okay, really. I'm sorry. I will get some rest and be ready for tomorrow," Elodie pleaded. She had never been in this situation.

"Elodie, take some time, heal what is in your heart. We are not firing you. You're very well liked here. We certainly don't want to lose you." Elodie swallowed hard. "Please, work on any lesson plans you have at home and send them over to us."

"Understood. Thank you." Elodie nodded in acceptance.

"Please take it easy. We all look forward to your return."

Elodie nodded again and packed her things. She walked to her car, ignoring the ravens all together. Once home, she dropped her bag and slid down against her door, wiping her eyes. The gleam of the dagger caught her eye again.

"Trevin," she cried out. She wasn't even sure how many days had gone by. A week? Longer? She didn't know, didn't understand why it felt like she was falling deeper and deeper into despair. There had been painful break ups before but she usually could find peace in the trees or the ocean. That damn tether she had felt, the damn lies they all told. One of them had bound the other and she hated it. Hated that the despair kept growing.

Elodie changed and messaged Cora, still not sure how to talk about what happened.

All that same day Trevin just buried himself in work deep in Humboldt Redwoods State Park. He had ignored his dad's calls when he got back to service. As his sorrow loomed over head just as the Old Giants did, he too now saw Avenue as a sad place. This place made his little mink sad when she was going south. It must have brought her so much joy to be going north. The first thing she would see would be these trees that loved and supported her. They pulsed with a new life because of her. It was how he knew she was still here at least. Though he would not dare go to the café, or her apartment. He was her overseer and he was failing but he just had to let her go. He had crossed a line as much as it hurt him to do, this was them being better. Being apart. He knew he had hurt her and that instinct told him to fix it but she could move on and go see the world. If she did feel this vowed bond, it was better she didn't know now what it meant. She could heal from this hurt.

In all Trevin's hurt he could not see the error he had made.

At the end of his shift, Trevin walked back to the truck and saw a mortal family. A male and female holding a little girl's hand and his heart hurt. He watched the little girl look up at the Old Giants with such amazement, so bright eyed.

"Careful, watch your step," the male said.

Trevin pretended to write something down on his clipboard as they approached. The male gave Trevin a nod. He returned it, schooling his features as best he could.

"Lovely place to work. It is magical here," the male said.

"It is," Trevin said. He smiled at the female and the little girl.

"Thank you, Sir, for keeping these trees safe for us," the little girl said.

Trevin didn't think it was possible to shatter anymore, he fought to maintain composure. He felt as though he had failed. He had failed to keep Elodie from hurting.

"This is my home, these Old Giants are so important to me. To a lot of people." He stopped being unable to get anymore words out without his voice breaking.

"Have a good day, Sir. We are heading south to Fort Bragg," the male said.

"Have a safe drive," Trevin replied with a nod.

As he opened the door to the truck he heard the female talk.

"These redwoods have such an energy to them. It's as though they blessed us."

Trevin stood there for a second then closed the door. He swallowed hard and walked up to one of the Old Giants. His eyes followed up the massive trunk just as he had seen Elodie do. He reached his hand out to touch it and fought the whimper that he had been fighting the entire time.

"Please," he whispered. "Tell her I'm sorry." Then he pressed his palm to the trunk.

Nothing.

Nothing changed in the air, no pulse or current of energy. His shoulders slumped and he closed his eyes.

An image of his mom reading a book to his younger sister in the window seat of the study again. He was sitting next to his dad at the desk, looking over maps of their territory.

"Look at that symbol, the Old Giant atop the crescent moon and three ferns, one for Ashdale, Nightswift, and Greenthistle," Autumn said, leaning over the book.

"That's right. The eight pointed sun is said to have a point for each of the high estate children," his mom said with happiness in her voice.

"Who is the crescent moon?"

"Well, we have to read the fairy tale." His mom laughed.

Trevin ripped open his eyes. He had never seen the symbol in the book his mom held but he remembered that memory. Autumn had described the same symbol Elodie found and they had all forgotten about it. That was so long ago, Cedar was so little. Cyrus's youngest sister, Poppy hadn't been born yet.

He ran to the truck and drove off as quickly as he could. Once the truck and his gear were dropped at work, Trevin took off running home as fast as he could in mountain lion form. His mind raced as fast as his paws carried him. *That sigil, the crescent moon, what did it represent?*

"Three ferns, the three high estates. Eight pointed sun, Greenthistle had three, Nightswift had three, Ashdale two. Eight kids. The crescent moon held it all up, bearing the weight of everything. Blessed by the earth. Elodie. Some kind of fairy tale?" He let her go? Let her cry? Let her think for one second he didn't love everything about her? He roared in frustration and pounded off the earth.

Chapter 56

Trevin barreled into the estate not even changing back into fae until he was at the study doors. He started scanning for that book. Anything to do with lore and fairy tales frantically flipping through pages. Desperately searching for that sigil, that sigil that gave her the code to open the tome. The one that called to her.

A cry of frustration came out when he couldn't find it. Dropping the books on the ground as he grabbed the next one. "Where is it? What happened to it? Why do I keep forgetting this memory? Mom! I don't know what to do!" he cried out, shaking.

"Trevin! What has gotten into you?" Lord Greenthistle gasped at the sight.

Trevin met his dads eyes. "That sigil is in one of these books, I need to find it! I need to know what Elodie is! Where is it?" he shouted.

"Sit down! What sigil?" His dad shut the study door and walked to the desk. "This book with the sigil Elodie used to open the tome?"

"It's in a book Mom used to read to Autumn. Where is it?" Trevin grabbed the book on Falk off the desk and flipped to that sigil, feeling the imprint on the page. "This is a perfect representation of Humboldt right now, the redwood, the three estates, the children of the estates. What does the crescent moon mean? What does it represent? It's holding everything up! The Old Giants, us. Who is it? Elodie and that ancient power in her," he pleaded frantically.

Lord Greenthistle sighed and slowly took a seat.

"Son, calm down please. Deep breaths."

Trevin just stood there, breathing erratic.

"Sit down," his dad said sternly. Trevin did. "Trevin, I'm sorry. I know this hurts you, but you have to accept things are not fair."

Trevin's eyes shot wide at his dad and he shook his head. "No! I know she is connected to this. To this place." He started cracking all over again.

"You've been an absolute zombie this entire week, I know she left you son. I am sorry."

"Left me? No!" Trevin could hardly get the words out.

"Cedar told me she walked out on you. I don't even know for what. I wanted her to be better. I thought she was." Lord Greenthistle sighed.

Tears formed as Trevin shook his head and buried his face in his hands.

"Cyrus fabricated a false story about Alena and I, and Cedar told Elodie, believing it was true. Elodie didn't know any differently. I remembered what you did with your vowed and knew this was my out. To let her live her life while I lived a lie, to do exactly as Greenthistle does. I saw her cry, ask me why and how, and I didn't tell her any truths or lies, just omitted everything, even down to my expression. Hide the fact that something in me was breaking that I can't give her forever and I want to. She said she couldn't be with someone who would suck the life out of her, like Ricky did to her and—" He paused, fighting for a breath.

His dad's expression grew concerned. Trevin could hear his dad's heart rate increase for what might have been the first time ever.

"And all I said was okay, because I was a coward. I couldn't lie or tell her it wasn't good for her. I couldn't tell her she was my vowed, that walking away from this was a huge mistake because I got scared. So I said okay. It was easier to let her hate me than to chain her down here. She didn't reject me, she wanted me, accepted it and this. Elodie decided she would have done anything for me, for Greenthistle, so I let her go. I let her hate me. Free to live her life. Cedar and Cyrus decided for us." He sobbed. "And it's not fair! I love her."

"You never told her she was your vowed?"

"No! I couldn't tell her. I was too scared too. I never let her say she loved me, either. Not until right before she left and I said it back. I was so scared that if I didn't sway her, I would just damn her to be chained down here," he whimpered. "For nothing, because she couldn't be an estate lady, she'd just be a consort. Until she wasn't."

An expression of absolute dread crossed his dad's face. "Trevin, did you remove each other's diadems?" he asked.

"Yes, but I never told her we were each other's vowed. I tried to be careful," he cried out. "I wanted to so badly, but I knew I had to let her live her life. That didn't involve me."

Lord Greenthistle's eyes were wide with sheer panic. "Trevin, words mean little when the intent is so strong. I thought you knew when it was your vowed, it was the real vow tradition. The vow ceremony is no different." He paused. "You vowed yourself to her, but you never sealed the blood bond? It's been pulling you so wildly. You let go of the taut rope and now you are falling hopelessly with nothing to grasp hold of," he said. "I've never heard of a vow ceremony not being completed before. Oh shit. Trevin, the removal of the diadem is stripping yourself bare. Fully embracing your vowed, letting their intent take hold of you. It is sealed with blood. Removing each other's clothes isn't what does it, as long as you are both bare in your natural state. The diadem is a symbol of honor and esteem. That's what starts it, and blood finishes it. The intent washes over you and blood binds it, encases it. And if this power in her is somehow tied to the Old Giants, then you were right, she probably feels it too."

"You never did the vowed tradition with Shirley?" Trevin asked, panicked.

"I knew I couldn't. Why would she ever see a diadem?" he said with a sigh, watching Trevin's eyes shift.

"Mom?"

His dad sighed in shame.

"We did, but the tether never snapped, just our words stuck. I came clean later. She knew about Shirley, but not that she was my vowed, and we were already expecting you. I begged your mother to stay. That I'd raise you with everything you needed to take my place. Your mother and I agreed it'd be best for you, and we did grow to love each other. She was happy, and you were the pride of her life. You were her little boy, and she loved you so much," he said.

"This entire estate is built on lies! No wonder my own brother turned on me. Loyalty clearly resides with Ashdale. Greenthistle makes a mockery of valor. El didn't do any of this. El fought for us, she fought for these lies. She wanted me and I wanted her!"

"Wanted? What do you mean wanted? You don't now?" his dad asked, shocked.

"I can't sway her. That's why I never said I loved her until she said it. I needed her to say it first and she did when I broke her trust in me. She made a choice—she did decide and I never let her tell me. So how do I convince her that the decision she made was the one I want more than anything? It will sway her. Cedar and Cyrus swayed her one way and if I go beg her to listen I'm swaying her another way, and I don't know how to fix it!" he cried.

"You have to set this right. You have to figure out how. Cyrus and Cedar figured out how to victimize you two, you have to decide how to undo it. They tampered with your vowed bond and they will need to be reprimanded for this. Alena too. That girl gained your trust before you had any clue what she was to you. You broke hers, figure out how to get it back."

"I don't even know who I can trust now. My friends and family turned their backs on me. I question if you and Autumn were in on this."

"Trevin, you know I did not lie when I said she was welcome here. Something is in her, something I do not want to lose. I know I indirectly played a part in this too. I was wrong and I am sorry. Autumn had no part in this either. Your sister loves that girl like family, you know this too. But you have to make this right. If you cannot overcome these fears now, ask yourself how are you going to handle the fear in the future?"

"I'm scared she will be taken from me. Or I will be punished if I break these rules. I tried to be so careful and everything fell apart so fast. In literal seconds."

"I will help where I can. Did you notice any power shift? Cedar and Cyrus broke the rules, yet I didn't feel anything."

"No! That's why I don't understand this. She has this power, something in her, they can spin lies and there were no power shifts between estates or family members?"

"Her power got louder after she opened that tome, as if it did something to her. When I checked on her after she collapsed, I felt it loud and strong. She spilled blood here when she was eight, and she spilled blood a few weeks ago. Somehow some kind of tether formed with our entities. Find that fire in you for her. I will do what I can, but this is your vowed. Your mother said you'd make Greenthistle better than it ever had been. Be the Greenthistle that lets their strength and valor shine, just as she showed you how."

"This hurts so badly and so much trust has been lost, with her, with Cyrus. He is supposed to be there next to me. How are we supposed to become high estate lords and lead as brothers, when my own turned on me? Why?"

"This is why you have to fix it, Trevin. You lost her and you lost blood and bonds, your gifts make you wise, but they come at a cost. Fix it. You refused to renounce your role as overseer, do your job."

Trevin knew he couldn't look at Cyrus or Cedar right now. Monday drills were going to be hard enough. Elodie wasn't going to tug back on his and he didn't know how to climb back up to grab hers.

"I don't know how."

"Trevin, if you don't do this, you will hate yourself for an eternity. If you are this confused about what you want, what's going to happen when she is taken from you, for good? Maybe you ought to let her go then. You know what you have to do, at least tell her she is your vowed, tell her the truth and let her decide. It is what you have been trying to do for months now. Let her decide."

Trevin slumped forward. "It hurts. I saw a family on Avenue of the Giants, it could have been her family when she was eight. Avenue south always made her sad because she was leaving these Old Giants. They never stopped calling her back."

"Go get her. I am such a fool. I knew how much she loved you and I doubted her too. I saw her eyes pulse teal before she opened that tome and I have been trying to figure it out ever since."

"I saw them too, that morning after she woke up, I thought I was seeing things." Trevin was tense.

"Go get her. I will talk to Lord Ashdale and Lord Nightswift."

Trevin sighed and then stood up. He dragged himself to his room and looked at the drawing she had made for. Flopping on his bed he tried to run through what he was going to do. He gripped the sheets on her side of the bed.

"Elodie." He sighed, then he heard the faintest flap of wings. Shooting straight up, he spotted a raven fly off. His heart rate picked up again.

"Bastard!" he growled and ran again as fast as he could.

Silent as night, something shot into his neck. Another pinch and he started to veer off course to avoid it. He couldn't tell which direction it came from. The darts hit him everywhere. Then the dizziness set in. He roared and tried to fight back. Disorientated, he fell.

"Elodie!" he cried out. Then his vision went black.

Chapter 57

That night, Elodie stood outside of Cora's house, having agreed to come over for a small get together. It would be her first time seeing them all; they had texted her regularly but she hadn't responded. *This is pathetic,* she thought to herself, that she was acting as though Trevin was her vowed, her soulmate. They were nothing to each other. Nothing more than a foolish mortal getting whisked away by the crafty fae. She had cried every day since that morning at Sunny Brae. Not that she knew how many days ago that had been.

She hesitated with her hand on the front doorknob. "It's a small gathering, just friends. It's not a party. Trev, Caleb, nor Autumn knew about it. I'll be okay." She couldn't handle seeing any of them. Autumn knew something was wrong. Elodie had seen the message asking if something happened. Elodie never responded.

Swallowing the lump in her throat she walked into Cora's house. When her eyes locked on the fireplace it was a struggle to fight back every emotion and force it down. She needed to learn to live without him. Without the magic she had been searching for all her life. One deep inhale and exhale, trying to let the pain go, then she walked into the kitchen.

"Come here. I'm sorry," Cora said, pulling her into a hug.

"I'm so stupid."

"No you aren't. I'm so livid with him."

"I guess everyone knows?"

"Q told Justine who told us. Anna suspected something happened when she realized it had been a week since he had seen you but Charles didn't know."

"Figures. Just the idiot who got in too deep. I knew better too."

"No you are not. I never expected Trev to do this. I didn't think he could." Cora sighed and let her go. "Let's do a shot."

Elodie nodded and followed her into the kitchen. As her and Cora clinked glasses, Elodie tipped the shot glass back feeling the slight burn of the alcohol through her nose. She sighed and grabbed a drink.

"You are here now, you will be okay. Charles is on the patio. Justine is on her way."

Elodie nodded and followed Cora.

She gave Charles a small smile then took a seat.

"I'm glad you came." Charles gave Elodie a warm smile. "It's nice to just have a small group, ya know. I live for these kinds of nights."

"It will be nice to have a quiet evening," Cora said, sitting across from her.

"I'm sorry, Elodie. Anna is worried though. I assume she knows, but I just heard when I got here. You will be ok."

Elodie nodded. "Thank you." A raven's caw made her flinch. She glanced up and saw one in the tree watching her.

Elodie. Wake up.
The danger is here.
Return to us.
The boy is trapped.

Elodie flinched again as the hisses flowed into her ears. She noticed her friends looking at her and panicked trying to think of anything to talk about. "How's work been for everyone?" Elodie forced out as she tried to slow her breathing. She could tell Cora was giving her a look of concern. Elodie tried to ignore it.

"It's been good. The kids are great. The adults are too. I have a client down in Ferndale who has a small dog that howls along with the guitar," Charles said with a laugh. Elodie was grateful for Charles. He never wanted anyone to be sad. She forced a laugh.

The hissing picked up as the raven cawed and flew off.

Soon. Soon.
El, they need you.
The estates. Bound.
His blood will flow.

Elodie flinched again. The hisses in her ears, the raven was so loud. She didn't bother looking at the worry on her friends' faces this time. Her bigger concern was her hands getting warm. Lately when they had gotten warm, they illuminated teal. She set her cup down and shoved her hands in her pockets.

Her ears heard the front door open, two people walk in, and Elodie tensed watching the door. As soon as she heard Justine talk, she cut her eyes down clumsily grabbing her cup. The sound of the sliding glass door was extra loud. She wondered how she could hear further now. Her senses were shifting and had been for weeks, ever since that fall in the creek. She had felt as though she had been in a haze the past week despite her senses being sharper than ever.

"Oh. I'm sorry," Justine said softly. Elodie heard Cora sigh.

"Don't even worry about it. I will see you later," Q said softly.

"Don't. Please." Elodie fought to keep her voice from breaking. She finally met Q's concerned eyes. "You have been nothing but nice to me. I don't want you to alter your life because of me. Stay." She caught Justine's hopeful smile.

"And you have always been loyal and kind to me, El. He's a damned coward. I've told him multiple times," Q said.

"I'm ok. It's really for the best." Elodie cut her eyes down. She again set the drink down feeling her hands get warm.

"Please have a seat, you two," Cora said.

As Elodie tried to steady her breathing she could feel Q's eyes on her. She told herself to ignore it.

"We should do another beach camping trip. What if we did a road trip to Oregon?" Charles asked the group. "I've been debating on going there next anyway, if San Diego doesn't work out. We don't have to go all the way to Portland. We could go to Eugene?"

Elodie knew she was making it awkward. It wasn't going to get easier if she kept acting like this. Taking a slow breath in, she looked up and tried to participate in the conversation.

"That'd be fun. We should! Elodie, we can do it over spring break? That'd be great for the spring equinox!" Justine said, giving Q a questioning expression. Elodie felt a chill and looked away from them for a moment.

"I can check, but you know Pops needs me here for stuff. I will see, though," Q said confidently.

Elodie looked at Charles and frowned. "You aren't planning on leaving soon, are you?"

"I have a few more months, but you know my schedule is similar to yours. School year and all. I suppose I could stay for another summer."

"But what about Anna, and us?" she asked. She knew her voice sounded hurt, and Charles gave her a sad smile.

"Elodie," he laughed softly. "Anna is the girl of my dreams and I don't know how I got her. But you know as well as I do, if not more so, they are rich, they are powerful. Responsibility comes with that. I can't do much for her in the long run. People like us don't work out with people like them."

"You both do a lot for them in the long run. More than you know. They both care deeply for you two, you know. All of you are important to us, so don't let the estate kid title make you feel like you aren't enough for us. You are all more than enough. Regardless of what our futures bring, we will treasure these nights, this life with you all in it," Q said, looking at them. "Stay longer if you can, Charles. She's crazy about you." Charles smirked and nodded. "El, you know you have to stay. Don't leave, ever."

Elodie took a deep inhale and flexed her hand in and out seeing it pulse teal again. She shoved her hand in her pocket. When she looked up she noticed only Q looking at her with shock.

"I'm going to get a refill. Be right back," she said, jumping up and hurrying inside.

Chapter 58

Once she was in the kitchen she flexed her hands again. No glow, no heat, her hands were normal now. When the sliding glass door opened a few minutes later her heart sank.

"What are you doing, El?" Q asked. She had her back to him.

"I'm trying to tell myself it never happened. That none of it was real, because it wasn't to him," she said, her voice breaking.

"It did happen, though. Look at me," Q said. Elodie didn't turn around. "Elodie."

She spun around and met his gaze.

"I'm real, I'm an Ashdale, high fae and a bear," he said, dropping the glamour for a moment and then putting it back on. She took in his features as she wiped her eyes. "And it is real to him too. He's a shell of the person you know. He hardly talks to me, when I heard what happened I told him to go get you. Told him he was a coward if he let this go."

"And he didn't. Because it didn't matter to him. In the end we all know he needs to be with a high fae. Not me."

"He's been searching for a way to give you the choice, to make you immortal, Elodie. You are literally his everything and he's broken. Alena isn't even high fae. He hates her."

"Right. He only told me he loved me after he had his face pressed into her tits! High fae, half fae, nymph, what's it matter. As long as they are not mortal, right?"

"We cannot sway mortals to stay with us. It's not fair to them or us. We cannot keep them from their lives. They have to want it. I told him to tell you this, and he is too scared. He was scared that if he told you he loved you first, it would sway you. If you said it first, he said he would tell you everything."

Elodie's eyes watered. "He never let me say it! He told me he could see it, but I never understood why. What am I supposed to believe? He knows I love him and he doesn't want to hear it. I was going to tell him at solstice, I had never felt more right about anything and he stopped me, interrupted me."

Q sighed and rolled his eyes.

"Okay, I am not going to watch his stupid cowardice continue, rules be damned." He didn't continue until she looked at him again. "Elodie, you are his vowed. That's why he was scared to say it. He was scared he would lock you to him, to that world and keep you from your life. That you would give him everything and he would watch you age. When he lost his mom, he changed. He was permanently scarred from that way worse than Autumn or Caleb. Death terrifies him, and every time you talked about it, accepted it, it scared him. That's why he desperately wanted to find a way to give you that choice. He'd accept it if you didn't want it. But if you did want it, he would do it, and he wants it. You are his vowed."

"What does 'vowed' even mean? Traditions and titles mean little when you all just play with us in your fantasy world." She wiped her eyes hard.

"It means that's our partner, that's the one person we have been searching for all our lives. Our bonded pair. Our vowed is the greatest love we will ever have. Sometimes things don't work out. We get separated, we lose them, and we love others, but never to that point again. They are the person we want to see reach all their potential with and be alongside them for it. We want to be our best selves for them. And you made him want to be everything Greenthistle should be, because you told him that. You showed him he could do it, and he wanted to do it, with you by his side."

"I'm his vowed? His bonded pair?" she said, her eyes welling up, tears falling this time. Q nodded. "How does he know I'm his vowed? I can't be."

"We are drawn to them naturally—they tend to take over our thoughts at first till we can calm that down and you did. He talked about you constantly. The scent is the first indicator. It's a scent only we can smell on our vowed. So I can't smell it on you, Autumn can't, Caleb, Russ, none of us smell it, but he always knows you are near," he said. She gasped.

"Ocean breeze and lavender." She pressed her hands to her mouth, letting tears fall. "He knew it the day I got the iron cuff off him and he didn't tell me? Something in me pulled me towards him, tethering us together, time and time again when we've been close. I felt it at the solstice, but he told me not to say I love him."

"I honestly don't think the love word is the deciding factor in the bond acceptance. I think it's the intent. I can almost see it on you and on him. He was scared it would snap into place at solstice, and everyone would see it, that's why he stopped you. So when he insisted we had to convince my dad to let you attend Spring Equinox, I made a bargain with him. If you got to go, he had to tell you regardless if you had said it or not."

"Did your dad agree to let me go?"

"Yes."

"Trev agreed to your bargain?" Her hands came to her mouth as tears fell.

"Yes."

"So he let go first. It's not breaking a bargain if I'm not there," she cried.

"I'll take you as my lady then. If he's going to be a coward." Q hissed. "At least it will light the fire under his ass to be territorial over you again. He's a fool."

Elodie leaned back against the counter. He was her vowed, and he was going to say it on solstice but he didn't. All this anguish because her vowed gave up.

"You know what else is super shitty about this? He was unaware the photo was taken or Alena was even in the house. Caleb sent it, Russ set it up, and Alena would sleep with everyone if she could. I've had to turn her down many times. She'd probably play with Charles, too. She invaded his space. We went out the night before, and Alena went home with Caleb, Trev went home alone, earlier than us."

Elodie trembled and wiped her eyes again.

"But he still let me go. Even if it was a lie or a game or whatever with everyone, he let me go and he let me believe otherwise. Just said okay. He doesn't want this, or me," she whimpered. "He did lie to me."

"Elodie, he does want you—he doesn't want to trap you. He didn't want to keep you from a mortal life you should have."

"What scent does he have for you?" she asked.

"I don't know, it changes. Sweat, dirt and wet fur if it's a drill day. The same products and stuff I've used before. What is it for you? I've not heard of a mortal scenting a fae, vowed or not."

"Oakmoss and amber. I miss it so much. It's faded from my apartment. I should be grateful, really." She wiped her eyes.

"Elodie."

"Justine isn't your vowed?" she asked.

"No, she's not. I do love her, but I can enjoy this for now, knowing she will move on. Just as Autumn knows Charles will, like Trev thinks you are going to do, but the difference with you is that power in you. It's so loud. Your hand pulsed teal. What happened? How? I got hints of it before, but something happened, Elodie. I don't know what it is, but the Old Giants need it, want it, want you. You belong here, with him, and you know all about everything. You figured all of this out and you saved him all on your own. Your vowed," Q said. "You can't tell me you think he lied about the last five months. Everything you two shared, the looks at the solstice, over one photo with no context from Caleb. Trev loves you, El."

Elodie sniffed and looked at her hand, then she threw her arms around him and he tensed slightly.

"I'm sorry, I just need to know that this is real, that you exist and the boundary and the estates. That Trevin is real and not something my imagination created. I feel like I'm going insane, like my brain was scrambled and I don't know when it happened," she cried out. He wrapped his arms around her.

"We are real. Ashdale, Nightswift, and Greenthistle. Trevin is real and his love for you is real. He is hurting. Before you, he was apathetic and annoyed most of the time. He hardly has the will to do anything now. You are not going insane. Your memory is fully intact, and that's why it hurts so much. Go to him."

"I don't know what to do. How to trust him when I don't know what's real anymore, I don't know what's coursing through my blood. The Old Giants used to whisper in my ears. Now they hiss and scream. It feels like I'm burning up and something is ready to rip me apart and I can't talk to anyone. I feel so hopeless because he always kept me safe. Trev watched out for me. My overseer didn't think I was crazy for this thing in me. Then he let go. He's not here!" she sobbed.

"Fight for it, Elodie. Fight for your vowed. He needs to know you want it. Want that life with him, whatever it might look like."

"I don't know how to look at him. I can hardly look at you."

"But you are right now, confessing everything you should be telling him, everything he needs to know. Tell him."

"He let me go, Q."

"I know. This is a very real thing we have to face. To meet our vowed at forty-five is not something any of us hope for. We can't change it. You are here and he loves you. Fight for that happily ever after. He wants it too."

She sobbed into him and gripped his shirt.

"I'm scared I'm going to find him and he's going to laugh in my face with Alena, with Caleb and Cyrus. They will all laugh at me," she cried out. Q narrowed his eyes and put his hands on her shoulders to look at her.

"How did you know Cyrus's name?"

"He gave it to me at solstice," Elodie said, recalling Cyrus's actions that night. "Would Trevin still keep me safe from him?"

"Trevin will fight Cyrus if it comes to it. Elodie, you have to go to him. Cyrus must have been plotting this. I can't believe he would do this. Give me your keys. I will take you across the boundary right now," he said, starting to walk. She pulled away from him.

"Q, No! He's friends with Cyrus, he's an heir, you are. I already drove a wedge between Caleb and Trev. I can't do that to you all. I don't know who or what to trust. I can't pull you from Justine," she cried out, "And I'm a wreck. I can't."

With a sigh, he knelt in front of her. She backed up a step.

"My name is Quinn Ashdale. I will protect you, Elodie. As the vowed of my brother, Ashdale swears to protect you. I give you my word," he said, looking at her. She gasped. "Let's go right now, to Greenthistle Estate."

"Quinn." She said meeting his rich warm amber colored eyes. He nodded. "Why did you give me your name?"

"In hopes you will trust me, if no one else. Trevin doesn't hate you—he loves you. Fight for him," he pleaded. She shook her head. She was getting overwhelmed.

"Quinn, I order you to go enjoy your night with Justine," she said before running out to her car.

"El!" he called out after her.

CHAPTER 59

At Greenthistle Estate a raven had flown to Cedar and Autumn's windows with urgency. They had heard Trevin rush out of the house but had not thought much of it until the ravens appeared. They saw the study door closed and knew Lord Nightswift and Lord Ashdale were in a meeting with their dad. If the door was closed it was a good indicator to not dare bother them. Estate heirs were the one exception, no one else.

They looked at each other and panicked.

"Surely Lord Nightswift knows?" Autumn asked.

"Probably has his sentries out," Cedar replied.

The raven cawed in haste again and flew a few yards ahead waiting for them.

"Lets go and see what is wrong," Cedar huffed out and changed. Autumn changed as well and followed.

As they ran an unease settled in the air. The Old Giants and ferns felt as though they were trembling.

"We should have told Dad," Autumn said. "This isn't right. Something is wrong."

The raven cawed and flew faster. The two mountain lions pressed on.

"I know but he was in a meeting with the other estate lords. Dad's been nervous the last few days. Trevin might be in trouble," Cedar said with panic lacing every word.

"I have a bad feeling about this. Why did Trevin run out so fast? I heard him scream in the study but when I went to check the door was shut and a sound barrier was up."

"Stupid mortal girl ruined him," Cedar growled.

"No Cedar! She didn't. You hurt them both!"

"He needs to get over it. She is dangerous for him."

"You let this happen to him. He's always looked out for you! And you split them up. You hurt her too."

"What the fuck? Don't blame me for his stupidity!" Cedar growled.

"You haven't even looked at him since you and Cyrus set him up to fail, you haven't been there for him!" she cried out.

"I set him up to get over her. She needs to be in the hold. If dad wants to keep an eye on her, that's the best place for her."

"Cedar! She loves him. He loves her. You couldn't just let them have this?!"

Cedar stopped in his tracks. "Cyrus said she was just trouble, he sensed it in her. You know he was going to hurt eventually, he can't handle two losses like this. Mom then her. I don't know if I even could."

"He's in a lot of trouble and she won't even talk to me. You better make this up to him," she screamed.

"Damn it," Cedar growled. "Elodie."

"You are going to apologize to both of them. Let's find Trevin first. What could have happened to him?" Autumn asked. They followed the raven to the old ruins, swiftly running through the corridor.

Then they both screeched to a halt, gasping.

Trevin was sitting against the old stone wall, his arms strained and cuffed to the wall above his head. His head slumped forward.

"Trevin!" Autumn screamed. She went to run for him but Cedar blocked her.

"This might be a trap."

Trevin hadn't moved.

"Wake up! Who did this to him?" Autumn wept.

"Shhh, no need to weep, little kitten," Cyrus said with a sly tone.

"Cyrus! This is too much?" Cedar growled out.

"Oh Cedar, the little cub, how does it feel to be the third born of the oldest estate? You are destined to serve in your brother's guard." Cyrus walked out of the shadows holding a large crossbow. Autumn gasped.

"This isn't funny, let him go!" Cedar yelled.

"I think it is rather grand. The firstborn, so easy to capture. The oldest estate, so easy to crush."

Trevin groaned and tried to move his arms. He whimpered with the realization that his wrists were cuffed to the wall above his head.

"No," he cried out.

"Trevin!" Autumn screamed. Trevin snapped fully awake at her scream and fixed his eyes on Cyrus.

"Where is she?" Trevin glared. "Where is Elodie?"

"Ravens say she's at home, in her little dwelling above the garage, curled into a ball crying. She claws at her ears, Trevin. You thought I did something to her. Greenthistle did plenty to her already. You broke her, shattered her."

"Fuck you. Let me go."

"Autumn, come please." Cyrus motioned to her. He leveled his gaze at Trevin with a crooked smile.

Autumn was frozen.

"Cyrus!" Trevin growled.

"Come and I will make a bargain with you," Cyrus said again.

"No! Autumn, don't do it!" Trevin shouted. He tried to tug his arms free.

Cyrus pulled a bow out of the quiver and held it in the light. They gasped at the pink shimmer. Trevin's throat went dry. Cyrus loaded it and aimed it at Trevin.

"Autumn, let us see if we can spare him," Cyrus said. Autumn trembled. She swallowed hard and walked up to him.

"Don't agree to anything, Autumn! Don't you dare!" Trevin screamed. "Run, go back home, both of you," he begged. No one moved save for Autumn.

Cyrus lowered the crossbow and held his hand out for Autumn.

"Don't!" Trevin begged.

She swallowed hard and took Cyrus's hand.

"Daughter of Greenthistle, you are lovely. Shame we had a falling out," he said, gazing into her eyes.

"You left me. You got bored," she said, her eyes welling up.

"Is the mortal a good substitute? How temporary he is," he said, turning his gaze to Trevin.

"Let her go and leave Elodie out of this!" he growled.

Cyrus lifted the crossbow.

"If you help him, you have to marry me. We can unite Greenthistle and Nightswift. Let him bleed and you will be free to play with all the mortals you want, Lady Greenthistle," he said, wrapping an arm around her waist. Autumn whimpered.

"Cyrus, stop!" Cedar begged. "Please."

"You know these arrows are lined with floss flower oil, don't you?" Cyrus grinned, running one along Autumn's collarbone. She squeezed her eyes tight and fought the tears as the slight sting of the oil.

Trevin glared at his once friend.

"Leave her and them out of this. Whatever grudge you have is against me, let them go. They have no part in it, Cyrus!" He growled.

"Those gasps of air as the mountain lion ripped the blackbird in two. How I savored them."

Cedar gasped at the change in Cyrus's voice, as though it was not his own.

"Is that what this about, you're blaming me because it was the Greenthistle Estate animal? I was the one there, not Cedar and Autum! Let Quinn decide who he wants to align with," Trevin growled.

Cyrus looked at Autumn. He pressed her waist into him more. "You are stunning," he said with a malicious smile. Autumn cringed when he began to kiss her neck.

"Cyrus!" Trevin screamed.

"This is just going to shift power away from Nightswift!" Cedar said, running toward them. Cyrus put his finger on the trigger and aimed it at Trevin.

Cyrus flashed him a smile. "Now, will the daughter of Greenthistle vow herself to me? Or will she let my only opposition suffer."

Trevin watched Autumn's face contort from fear to bewilderment.

"Autumn, don't. Greenthistle will be yours. Don't lose it," he begged his sister.

His breath left him for a moment as the arrow lined with that toxic oil shot into his side. The blood seeped into his shirt. He flung his head back, knocking his skull against the stone, forming a pounding headache.

"Trevin," Autumn whimpered. He felt his eyes gloss over and tugged on his arms again.

Cyrus laughed as he walked up to Trevin, their eyes meeting.

"Now we watch you live up to your true potential, the Greenthistle disappointment. Then it's left to Ashdale and Nightswift to split. You will lose your estate and your lands, all because you won't fight back. Coward," Cyrus spat. He stepped back and kicked Trevin in the head.

"No!" Autumn cried out. "Please, stop this," she cried.

Trevin groaned and spit out blood. "Cyrus, why? I never wanted to fight against you, we were friends," Trevin strained. "Brothers."

"Have you lost your mind?" Cedar cried out.

"No, I haven't. We know the omens. When one estate is chained and bound, the forest will be born anew. Three courts are said to keep the balance. All we need to do is bind Greenthistle to sever the tether to the last loose end. That newness walking these lands, needs to be eradicated," Cyrus said.

"No. This isn't supposed to be how it goes. You told me he'd get stronger if we got them apart. He'd fight back harder. All you did was split everything apart," Cedar begged. Begged for the first time in his life. "I'm sorry. She just wanted to help. She did help. Don't hurt him please."

Cyrus howled with amusement. "Go on, keep blaming me. It doesn't matter how it's supposed to go, it is how it will go." His eyes fixed on Trevin again.

Trevin trembled seeing the malice in Cyrus's gaze, his eyes, his grin. He had gone mad and Trevin couldn't read anything behind that madness.

"One more tether to snip clean," Cyrus said. "Why not let you watch?"

"Please. Cyrus, please leave her alone," Trevin pleaded.

"Cedar. Step forward."

"No! No!" Trevin struggled. "Cedar!"

Cedar remained still, wide eyed.

Cyrus glared at him and loaded another arrow. Trevin watched him. His breathing picked up.

Elodie is safe, Elodie will forget all about me. She will find home somewhere, she can move far away. Anywhere where Cyrus can't hurt her. Autumn will be free of her bargain and Cedar will find his way. Quinn will be strong; he will carry Ashdale on. Trevin told himself. He flinched when he felt a hand on his shoulder.

"It's going to be okay, let me help you," Autumn said, crying.

"No! Don't, whatever you do. Don't be stuck with him," he said in a labored breath. "Promise me!"

"Trevin," she whimpered, trying to figure out how to remove the arrow. The blood wasn't stopping.

"Promise me! Stop," Trevin gasped out.

"Move away from him, dearly betrothed," Cyrus growled. Autumn froze.

"Stand back. Please," Trevin whimpered. He met her hurt eyes. "Make sure she's safe, Autumn. I order you to."

Autumn sniffed and stepped back from him. "Trevin," she cried out softly.

Cyrus pointed the crossbow at Trevin. Trevin's eyes traced the tip of the arrow, seeing the pink shimmer of the oil. He shook his head.

"Cedar," Cyrus said. "Step forward."

Cedar was still frozen.

"Don't. Please don't," Trevin cried out. The wound around the arrow burned.

"I will fill his body with arrows. He can bleed out, or you can retrieve the little mink for me."

"No!" Trevin cried out. "Leave her out of this."

"What do you want with her?" Cedar asked.

"Little birds say she is struggling, the little mink weeps and cowers down."

"Leave her alone!" Trevin growled.

"She collapses on the floor crying. The little mink wakes throughout the night screaming. She screams your name, Trevin. Trevin. Please, Trevin. Oh how she looks at that dagger, holds it close and begs for you," Cyrus crooned.

"Stop it!" Trevin cried out.

"How much she means to you. How much you mean to her. You let her go. We both know she has a power in her. She has a power we need to snuff out, an oddity," he said. "Cedar, go get her or watch him slowly bleed to death."

"Cedar," Trevin pleaded. Cedar watched in fear, so did Autumn.

"Tell me how little she means to you, Trevin, prove me wrong."

Trevin tried to stop the tears from coming down. He tried to glare. He tried to respond, but he knew, and Cyrus knew, and so did Autumn, and Cedar. They all saw him break at the thought of her gone. She was his, and he was hers and he had tried so hard to hide it. All to keep her safe. He let her go. And she thought he didn't care about her. It shattered something in him. He lost his vowed, his partner, a mortal. He would lose her one day but he didn't want to lose her like this. Not to Cyrus.

"Say she means nothing to you and I will let them go, Autumn and Cedar will be free to go where they please."

Trevin looked at him. He swallowed hard.

Stupid fae blood, lies cannot be told, omission was the truth in this case. She could lie to herself all day and night. She could tell herself she was fine. That she didn't like him, or that she did and nothing bad would come of it. No one would lose a life or spill a drop of blood.

"The mortal"—even calling her that stung, he swallowed hard again—"means." He couldn't get the words out. "She means." He dropped his head. "Elodie," he whimpered out.

Cyrus laughed, a demented laugh.

"Trevin," Autumn said softly. Her words are a small comfort. How he longed to see Elodie's face, her smile, her curious eyes. To hold her close to him and sleep next to her. Those fleeting nights that he knew he'd never have enough of in his immortal life.

"El, please be safe," he said softly to himself. *The patron saint of Humboldt was going to become a martyr because of me. I doomed her. I wanted to give her a choice, but all I did was rob her of any chance she had.*

"Go fetch her," Cyrus said, looking at Cedar.

"She hates me, she won't come with me. I don't even know where she could be," he pleaded. Cyrus turned back to Trevin, and the two glared at each other.

"Cedar, I ord—" Trevin started to say until another arrow shot into his shoulder ripping a roar of pain out of him. Autumn screamed.

"You've tracked prey further with less scent. Drag her back by the scruff if you have to."

Trevin locked eyes with his younger brother as he heaved. "Cedar." he started. "No. No! Please."

Cyrus laughed again riddled with malice.

"No! What could you possibly want from her?" Autumn wept. A smug smile creeped over Cyrus's face.

"Oh, I just want to see why the little mink weeps so much these nights. The poor girl out there all alone. I wonder if she weeps because she knows her life is pointless, a waste. No family to care about her, no partner to fight for her," he said, now glaring at Trevin. "I just want to toy with her," Cyrus said.

Trevin thrashed and screamed out, "I'll murder you."

"Cyrus, you can't. She's his. We don't go after each other's affections," Cedar started, taking a step back.

"His what? His vowed?" They were shocked he knew. "I saw it in you that night when the broken bird took flight again. I saw it in her at the bonfire. I would have made her bleed all over that beach too, letting her power wash away. But oh how she searched for you, Trevin. How she hoped you'd keep her safe. This was far too easy even if Greenthistle did awaken her. You damned her, now she will bleed all over these stones," Cyrus growled.

Trevin gazed into Cyrus's eyes and he didn't think he could break anymore. The pure evil and malice in them. He had never seen Cyrus like this. He lost his vowed and now his brother had turned everyone against him. This couldn't be Cyrus. Trevin thought back to the rage and malice in that mountain lion's eyes over him, how similar a glare in Cyrus he saw.

"I can and I will take her life, because Greenthistle made me, long before he made the Earth Blessed," Cyrus hissed.

Trevin's eyes shot wide. "No! Elodie is Earth Blessed? How?"

"You didn't know? You fool. Every myth and legend has a basis somewhere. Nightswift will take down Greenthistle, we will take down Ashdale. The rule of three is ending and the Earth Blessed's blood will run alongside her vowed, bonded in death," Cyrus said. He gripped Trevin's head and slammed it back against the wall. Trevin was near unconsciousness from pain. He could only hear Autumn weep. He could vaguely see Cyrus lower the crossbow.

"Cedar, go get her," Cyrus growled.

Trevin heard Cedar run out of the ruins and he wept. He shifted his eyes up to the stars. He hoped Elodie was balled up in her blankets, with the doors locked. Or that she was in her car with a backpack heading anywhere away from this place. Away from what she loved. From the land she was tied to.

How badly he had messed up. How stupid he had been to let her go, to not see it. She belonged to the Old Giants, of course she was Earth Blessed. They had chosen her, called to her. She was that crescent moon and had helped them all. How had he been so blind? All he had to do was switch the words around. The Old Giants called her that, everyone did. He could never make her immortal, she already was. She had wanted him more than anything and he let her go, he rejected her. She made her choice and he never let her say it. Every force of nature out there swayed her to be here with him, all he had to do was let her speak. His eyes welled up and his heart hurt with its pounding. Every beat pulsing a radiating pain through his wounds.

His eyes traced up the Old Giants, he felt small and insignificant under them. She was theirs and he didn't protect her, he didn't protect his lands. His home and her home. Her. Trevin slowly dropped his head and tried to slow his heart rate down. "Elodie," he wept.

Chapter 60

Unaware Greenthistle had been bound in those ruins, the high estate lords of Humboldt listened to Lord Greenthistle's plea for alliance.

"So, you are telling me the mortal girl managed to open up this tome?" Lord Nightswift said, eyeing the book.

"Yes, the map was in an isolated patch surrounded by the boundary line," Lord Greenthistle recapped the King Range trip, and the accident with the bear to them. "He panicked, brought her here and begged me to heal her."

The other two gasped.

"Why would he do that? This mortal girl knows too much, throw her in with the hold. It's empty. Indenture her to some kind of work here. She cannot return. I agreed to let her at the solstice," Ashdale said. "Quinn pleaded and begged for her to be allowed at the equinox and I relented, is she going to be a problem?"

"Why does he want her so badly?" Lord Nightswift said. "He was so adamant that he was her overseer. Surely he knows he can not just keep her locked up in his quarters."

Lord Greenthistle sighed again. "No, I was certain we'd have to lock her up, or I'd have to scramble her memory. We haven't had a problem with mortals in our reign at all. I can't find any records of this situation anywhere in the northern territories. I can't ask southern territories or Oregon without raising alarms either," he said.

"What alarms? We have been lucky she held true to the bargain but you've let her go free for too long," Ashdale asked, almost angry. "Why?"

"After she got the iron cuff off him, Trevin must have realized it. I must admit I was grateful for her and her actions. She saved him. I cannot deny, I have grown a fondness for her after what she has done for us all and what she continues to do. The person she makes Trevin want to be and the things they accomplish together, I want to help them. I know she is special—she has a power in her. A strong one."

"You say she's from Marin, alert them and send her on her way. They would have dealt with her already. Why didn't you alert them?" Lord Ashdale demanded.

Lord Greenthistle hung his head low. He pleaded to the Old Giants that his faith in her was not misplaced.

"She saved Trevin's life. She helped him get the map, and open this tome." Lord Greenthistle let out a huge sigh and looked between the two men sitting across from him. "And she is Trevin's vowed."

"No! What are you going to do?" Lord Nightswift asked. "Cyrus must not know, he doesn't like the girl. He spoke of the danger she was to Cedar often. She seemed polite enough, but she is a mortal. Everything is too unstable, her presence included."

"Trevin has been fighting it, he has been fighting himself, trying to not let it be, but I knew it the moment I saw him puff his chest toward me. She doesn't know. Cedar and Cyrus caused them to fight and he let her go. He's heartbroken and shriveling up inside and I can't watch him grow to resent all of this. Trevin hated everyone when we lost Selene, and you know what? Omens and curses be damned. I cannot condemn him to my curse. I cannot have him fill this hole with someone else, who might not be there for him. So I'm begging you to support this choice to trust her. To help me figure out what she is."

Lord Ashdale sighed. "What power do you feel in her? Any trace of fae heritage?"

"None. I've gone back over twenty generations. Nothing. She speaks of the Old Giants as though she knows them and says they've called to her all her life. Trevin says they tend to follow her, the ferns grow brighter. The winds shift for her. She says the Old Giants speak to her. They have since she's been up here."

"What do they say to her? Sounds like she smoked some pot, did some mushrooms, all common things up here. Mortals and fae alike get high on things. Maybe she got some fae hallucinogens, wouldn't be the first time," Lord Nightswift said, annoyed.

"I thought that too, but the drug test from the school district shows she's clean. She drinks, nothing more. Every single one of these shifts in the air is her. It's them communicating with her. The Old Giants tell her she is home. When she opened the tome, they told her to wake up, she's bound to them, she's home. They spoke of the evil in the lands too, he will be the first to fall and one by one they will all follow. It will target Trevin first and then we will follow."

"She could be the evil. She's directly linked to Trevin now," Lord Nightswift said.

"I feared that too, Cedar is convinced she is. I see something else in her, something ancient, something the Old Giants need, want." Lord Greenthistle opened the book on Falk and explained the sigil. The other two narrowed their eyes in confusion.

"So power aside, do you want him to have her? I mean, are you planning on handing him the estate in the next, what fifty years or however long she has? By the time you deem him ready, she might not exist. A mortal estate lady might not be something you even have to worry about," Lord Nightswift said.

"I fear what it might do to him, but I fear what this is doing to him. If she does have a connection to the Old Giants, they might smite me for keeping them apart. Cyrus and Cedar drove them apart, but I certainly played a hand too. I told him to fix it and I hope he is with her. The air is too uneasy tonight."

"Okay, well that's the matter of the girl. You said there were a few matters to discuss. What is the next mountain we have to move?" Lord Ashdale sighed.

"This tome is older than the town of Falk. The map to it is etched into iron," he said, pointing to the book. "In an iron maze, mortals and fae at least around the mid-1800s must have worked together, known of each other. To keep something hidden. I have no records of it. Why? Did fae really indenture enough mortals to do this? Or did they work together, if so, why did they cease to never speak of it? What did they wish to hide?" Lord Greenthistle said.

Lord Ashdale was able to read it slowly and translate it. As he flipped the pages his eyes snagged on a term he hadn't really thought much about, a term he had heard a few times in childhood.

Lord Greenthistle and Nightswift worked to translate some passages but it was such a slow effort..

"This passage strikes me as odd. This section is on possession. It says that 'healing can bind a spirit or demon to the soul. Similarly a dormant Earth Blessed can be awoken in this manner.' With a footnote." Then flipped to the footnote. "The Earth Blessed grow more and more rare with each passing moon, but they are not gone. They are chosen by the Great Mother herself at any time, linked to the entities of a territory, becoming one and the same."

"Earth Blessed? Just faerie tales. I haven't heard that term since I was maybe fifteen?" Lord Nightswift said.

"Fairy tales." Lord Greenthistle jumped up. He had stacked the books up to be put away later but Trevin hadn't gotten through them all. There were still a few more on the shelf. He picked the last one in the section and looked at the contents, finding one titled *'The tale of the Earth Blessed.'*

He flipped to it and a gasp escaped him upon seeing the same sigil with the redwood from the book Elodie had found.

The Great Mother as above, as below, there are those who are to grow slowly.
The ageless, the timeless.
They are the protectors and the watchers; they blend in with the mortals and they run with the Fae Folk.
To the lands, to the flora and fauna, they spoke.
Listen. Listen. Listen for they hold the wisdom old and new.
For they are the Earth Blessed, the chosen and few.
Listen. Listen. Listen to the words they share,
For their magic is rare.

Lord Greenthistle went to the book on Falk that Elodie had given them and saw the same sigil. That moment it clicked for him, this power in her, was of an ancient Earth Blessed. These redwoods called to her, they needed her. She wasn't the evil—she was the good that would fight it. *These Old Giants choose her at eight years old, that calling. Trevin was always supposed to see her. He fought for her.*

"The girl, is she?" Lord Nightswift asked, dumbfounded. "Is she an Earth Blessed? You said you healed her."

"Humboldt has an Earth Blessed?" Lord Ashdale asked, stunned. "Vowed to Trevin?" He then noticed the rubbing of the back of the book. His eyes shooting wide. "What is this? Where did it come from?"

"It's the iron plate on the pack of the tome. Elodie got the ominous voice when she touched it. We got a rubbing of it and I was meaning to transcribe but it got swept aside."

Lord Ashdale took a deep inhale and read the lines aloud.

SECRETS BOUND LOCKED AWAY SOUND.
TRY AS YOU MAY TO PRY,
ON THE EARTH BLESSED YOU MUST RELY.

Lord Greenthistle stumbled back in his chair and put his hand over his face.

"She isn't evil—she is the cure, and it knows she is here. It's going to target Trevin. To get to her! The Old Giants have told her to wake up. They've been warning her this entire time, and she thought she was going insane!" He was near trembling. "I let her believe she was. Oh no! Elodie!"

"She needs to be brought here immediately," Lord Nightswift said.

"We need to look up Earth Blessed more. None of us even thought they were real," Lord Ashdale said.

Lord Greenthistle's heart was pounding. "Trevin. No!" He jumped up, panic-stricken. Every piece of the puzzle locked into place. He tried to call Trevin's phone but it just rang and rang. "Trevin! He's not answering."

"Cyrus isn't either. His phone is off?" Lord Nightswift said. He looked to the window, letting his eyes flash to the raven's eyes, then he gasped. "The ravens are not responding to me. Something is closing them off. What? How?"

"I can't see through any bear, power hasn't shifted." Lord Ashdale panicked now. He dialed Quinn.

"Dad! What's wrong? The Old Giants are restless," Quinn said.

"Where are you? Where are Trevin and Cyrus? Where is the girl, Elodie?" His dad panicked.

"I don't know where Trev and Cyrus are. El was at our friend's house, and something happened to her! Her hand glowed teal. She's distraught over losing Trevin." He went on to explain.

"Get her to unbind you now. We can't find them and they are all in danger," Lord Ashdale demanded.

"She left. She got overwhelmed and left."

Lord Greenthistle thought for a moment about the other thing healing could do. He thought about the mountain lion, none of them could communicate with. The older deeper evil that took so much of his magic to heal. Cyrus and Cedar had split them up, pulled them apart.

Suddenly the blood drained from his face. *The ravens watching her, Cyrus's mood swings, he tried to lure her away at solstice, was he possessed, by my hands? He'd have died had I not healed him.*

"Where are they? Where are Autumn and Cedar?" he asked. "Oh no! The omen! When one estate is chained and bound, the forest will be born anew. The Earth Blessed. Elodie, new, foreign. She's walking into a trap and Trevin is the bait," Lord Greenthistle said, running out of the study and calling for Autumn and Cedar. The house was silent and void of them.

"Autumn! Cedar!" he cried out. "Trevin!"

"Lord Greenthistle, sir, a raven aligned with House Nightswift summoned them with urgency. They ran out not wanting to interrupt due to the haste of the raven," a staff member said.

"We need to get to Elodie. I have to keep her safe for Trevin," Lord Greenthistle said, panic-stricken, then the mountain lion took off running.

Chapter 61

The high estate lords of Humboldt had snapped all the pieces together. Greenthistle had been bound. All the while Elodie stumbled through the insanity that fogged her brain.

She drove home panicked and ran into her studio. Not even turning on the light, she closed the blinds and crawled into bed.

Her thoughts started to take over. Cyrus could enter Cora's and he knew exactly where she was. She just hoped the ward in her place was still held.

"They said I had to let people in. I had to invite them in. He can't come in. That couldn't have been a lie. Please don't let it be a lie."

Her phone lit up with a message from Cora, and a number she didn't recognize. She opened Cora's message and saw that Quinn had covered for her, poorly saying she felt ill suddenly. Knowing she put him in that position, Elodie sighed.

Then she opened the other one. It was Quinn.

El. Please do not run from this. I am not mad you ordered me to but you have to go to him. Why are you not listening to us?

Elodie didn't respond to him. She just let her thoughts run wild as she rubbed her thumb over the pommel of the dagger.

Her hands burned and burned the things she touched, like an electric spark she somehow emitted from her fingers. It didn't hurt her as static electricity would, but it did damage things she was holding at times. Sometimes she would send a jolt through a fork or a spoon the few times she did eat.

The words of the Old Giants remained the same warnings and terrors hissing in her ears. She'd go to sleep, listening to the TV in the owner's house. She had never noticed they had the volume up so high before, she had no common walls, being above the garage. The ticking of the analog clock were becoming torture, and she had to remove the batteries. At night she would stumble out of bed, writhing in terror and those nights she called to him. She tried not to, she tried not to think of him. Remembering how much he calmed her down after King Range and coddled her after she got the tome open. It hurt to think about. His dad said he wouldn't tell them to stay apart. And yet, Trevin didn't want her. She remained alone and scared, huddled up in bed. She had been hurt by him, yet she could not shake the want in her heart, her body. Elodie said his name again. Her vowed.

"Trevin, I'm scared," she cried out, knowing he would not come, that she would remain alone. She was too scared to go outside, knowing what lurked in the woods, knowing Trevin wouldn't watch over her anymore.

"He's my overseer, and he abandoned me. He's my vowed and he didn't want me. Is that even possible? We are better apart?"

Elodie shivered and curled up more, clutching the dagger against her chest.

"Trevin," she whimpered again.

The nights with him came back. The little things he had done like bringing her breakfast before Marin. The big things he had done for her, like carrying her through the end of life in Marin. The tears fell.

Never doubt what you mean to me.

Knows a good thing right in front of him.

I only want you.

You mean more than you think.

"You lied!" she screamed as her hands burned and the sensation crawled up her forearms. "Why did you let go?" she cried out. Images of Alena flashed in her head from the solstice ball. She had long since deleted that image of Alena in his bed. Debated countless times on deleting the entire message thread. She thought about how different she and Alena looked. All the times Trevin had said how beautiful he found Elodie. Quinn said Alena would sleep with everyone if she could. Then she remembered how put off Trevin was by Alena at the solstice while Cyrus was trying to pull her away. *He said he didn't lie, he didn't sleep with her, Quinn had turned her down too.*

Something from that night crossed her mind. "He said he would never chain me down to that side of the boundary. To him. But if I wanted it, he'd give me forever. I did want it, I do want it! He never let me answer for fear that he might have swayed me, that he'd keep me from my life. I don't want to leave. I want this, Trevin. I want you!" she cried out and that tug hit her, some small ray of hope. She thought about the letter attached to her dagger. "He was searching for the words or maybe the courage. The courage to hold what was right in front of him. What had always been in front of him since that first night at Cora's."

She raced through all the pieces. *Never doubt how much you mean to me. Vowed.* "He was scared he was locking me up? Was he searching for an out from me? For me? If Cyrus set this up, Trevin took the chance to not chain me down to him. Yet he did want her in every way possible though, chained and bound to me. *You will be my lady longer than you realize.* Vowed! But how would he know if it was right for me to be chained and bound to him? He wanted to find a way for me to be immortal with him. Vowed."

"Trevin, I want you, I want this, I love you. Come back to me, please," she begged. "I am your vowed, you are mine." She felt that tug in her again. "The bond cannot be undone. We are vowed. Trevin!" she cried out looking at the dagger as if it were a beacon communicating with him. As if she screamed his name loud enough, he would come running.

She turned to the window recalling how often they told her he was home. It could not be undone. He was hers, she was his, Quinn said it was the intent not the words. They were already vowed. She wanted it. Cyrus wanted to lure her away, something evil was in him, trying to pull her away from him.

Her heart raced. A power swelled in her. Her whole body heated now, something boiling ready to spill over. She was going to blast this entire studio apart if she didn't get out into the forest.

"Cyrus knows what this power in me is. He wants to get me alone, away from my vowed who would protect me. Because Cyrus wanted to take my power, and now Trevin and I are separated."

He will fade. Back into the earth, his blood flows.
His family will crumble.
Evil lurks. It will devour him first then the rest will fall one by one.
The blackbird is trapped. He screams.
Little mink! Save the blackbird, save them all.
Lose the mountain lion, lose them all. El!

The voices hissed, and she curled up gripping her ears.

"No, no please! Leave him alone!"

Chained and bound, his blood flows.
Seeping out of him.
Go! Go! find him. Little mink!

Elodie squeezed her eyes shut and then ripped them open sitting up gasping at what she saw.

Visions of Trevin laying lifeless at the base of an Old Giant. Blood pooled around him, the soil taking him back, his eyes opened, void of life. "Trevin!"

She grabbed her phone and texted him.

I need you! Trevin, please, I will meet you at the trailhead!

She clicked send. Not waiting for a reply, she put her boots on and grabbed the dagger then jumped in her car and headed north. The rain started to sprinkle, and the mists crept in.

Every step to the trailhead and the boundary lines ingrained in her memory. She knew how to find it, knew exactly where the trail forked but appeared overgrown. She sped down the street off Old Arcata Highway. No doubt if she left her car too long it would get flagged at this hour. *Not a worry right now.*

When she checked and saw no response from him. Her heart tensed.

What if I have this all wrong, he was fine, he was in bed with Alena or Cassia, or anyone else, not looking at his phone. "No. We are vowed, he wants me. He loves me. How could I not see past his blank expression? He was fighting to keep it up. Trevin, You are mine. My vowed," Elodie declared to herself, staring at the trailhead.

Her phone rang but it was Quinn.

"El! Something's wrong. Unbind me from the order. My dad told me there's trouble! They can't find Trevin or Cyrus, Autumn and Caleb are missing too." His voice panicked.

"There is. The Old Giants keep hissing in my head, they show things, terrors. Greenthistle bound," her voice trembled.

"Unbind me, where are you?"

"The trailhead in Sunny Brae."

"Okay I will leave as soon as you unbind me. I am trying to fight this order but I'm losing the battle."

"I'm sorry. How do I do it?"

"Just say I fulfilled the order."

"Quinn, I deem your order fulfilled."

"Thank you. I will cover all of this with them here and meet you at the trailhead," Quinn said, much quieter and less strained.

"Okay. I'm sorry."

"Don't be. Just be careful. Stay in your car. I don't know what is out there."

Elodie hung up and looked in her sideview mirror at the stairs. She tapped the wheel anxiously.

Knowing she could end up seriously hurt and now, he might not be able to come for her. With no fae, she wouldn't be able to pass through the boundary. Still, she had to find a way.

I need to talk to Trevin! Meet me on the trail please! I'm sorry I was so stupid. Something's happening to me.

She sent the text to Autumn then she stared at the trailhead.

He never said he didn't want me because he can't. It would be a lie and he couldn't lie. She realized his silence was his omission, all he could do. She had mistaken that for the truth.

If she could find a way to get through, she would run to him. If she was all wrong, she'd beg to have her brain scrambled and dropped anywhere.

While her thoughts raced and her heart pounded, she sat there for a second longer then called Trevin. Her stomach lurched when it was answered.

"Trevin!" she cried out not waiting for an answer.

"Hello, little mink." Cyrus's tone had shifted to something truly evil that made her blood run cold. *The blackbird is trapped.*

"No! Please don't do this," Trevin cried out. "Please."

"Are you coming to rescue the little cub?" Cyrus crooned in mockery.

"El, please just go, leave Humboldt, please, you have to!" he cried out in the background; his voice was strained.

"What did you do to him? Why? He's your friend, your brother," Elodie said, her voice breaking.

"Come find out, your escort is on his way, Earth Blessed," he hissed out and the call ended. She gasped and jumped out of the car and started to run.

It was now or never, she had to save him. She had saved him before, she'd do it again. She always would.

Something is wrong with Cyrus. He has Trevin! Find me on the trail. I have to go!

She sent the message to Quinn and jumped out of her car.

Never doubt how important you are to me. His words echoed in her head. She was his vowed, he loved her. He had been alone during all this too and they both had been thrown life lines they couldn't grasp. Trevin was in trouble. The redwoods knew this, and had warned her about this. She had this thing in her, a power she had to use.

"The biggest risk I've taken yet."

Pitch darkness awaited her at the top of the stairs. Mist had rolled in and it was eerily silent, no one would be out right now. When she squeezed her eyes shut his cocky grin appeared. His face made her weak in the knees, because he was fae. He knew how to play by his rules and she had so much to learn about them. She would learn them all, she wanted to because this forest had been calling to her for so long, was it all for this moment? Her heart pounded and her eyes welled up.

She took a deep inhale and looked ahead at the dark void. It was time for her to save him once again. She ran up the stairs and up the incline of the trail.

"What is the Earth Blessed? Cyrus knows but Trevin didn't? His dad didn't? Had he known all along? How?" She ran her fingers on the hilt of the dagger.

Suddenly her boot caught a tree root and she fell forward.

"Damn it!" she said, gritting her teeth then placed her palms down, in damp soft soil and pressed down as she came to her knees. Power shot up from the earth into her hands and throughout her entire body. Elodie's eyes shot wide as another gasp escaped her. Her senses heightened even more. Mountain lions growled, chuffed, roared, ravens cawed, bears groaned and roared, all in unison. She jumped up and found her balance more reactive. She heard more animals, identifying the owls, and the clicks of the beetles. Even the small squeak of a mouse nearby. No doubt the owl heard it too.

Welcome home, Earth Blessed.
You've awoken.

"Earth Blessed? What's happening?" Elodie looked at her hand, remembering the cuts she had gotten on her palm. Both times had been here, in Humboldt. The blood, the deep gashes caked in soil, her blood spilling into the soil. The pulsing current of the earth now flowing through her veins. The same weird teal light she had seen in the soil as a kid that she didn't understand nor told anyone about. "Humboldt's boundary has been calling me back here! If I have boundary line in my blood now, can I pass through on my own?" Swallowing hard she nervously felt her ears, still round, not pointed.

"I'm not fae, am I?" she asked, "There's no way. I have to get to him. I have to find a way to help him!"

Elodie would always find a way to save them, because she needed this place. This was home, she was home. She just needed her mountain lion back.

Swiftly she ran, her steps lighter. The pounding of animals running echoed her steps. Not toward her, but with her. *Earth Blessed.*

She stopped, heart pounding her hands were getting hot, stinging. She balled them up into a fist then felt and saw a pulse of power shoot out of her hands. Her eyes widened again, and she swallowed hard again, bringing her hands up.

With her palm facing down, she rotated her wrist facing her palm up loosely curling her fingers in. Then extended her index finger and watched a vine lash whip out. She closed her fist, and it retreated, then she quickly opened her wrist flat and nothing. She curled her fingers in again thinking about the vine and extended her finger. The vine came back.

"What?" she said with a gasp and a laugh. She repeated it three times and then was overcome with excitement. Forgetting for a moment that everything around her was crumbling down, until his cries flashed in her head, she had to get to him.

Faster and harder she ran, seeing if she could summon the vine as she moved. She smiled seeing it appear. Then she froze dead in her tracks again. Grabbing her dagger in a swift motion she glared. Caleb stood before her utterly and completely shocked.

"Elodie!" She heard from behind her. She spun round to find Quinn, looking just as stunned. She stepped back holding both fae in her view suddenly unsure what was going to happen.

Chapter 62

"Elodie. You really are Earth blessed!" Cedar exclaimed.

"Where is he?" she screamed, her energy swelled.

"Get the fuck away from her, you asshole," Quinn demanded.

"Elodie, please. We have to go. Trevin's hurt," Cedar said, panic engulfing him as his eyes scanned her.

"You and your stupid tricks," she muttered. "I take it you're my escort. How fitting."

"It's not a trick. He's in trouble! We all are! So are you!"

"You!" she screamed out, pushing her magic into the blade. It glowed teal as she gripped it tight. Cedar's jaw dropped and Quinn gasped. "You sent that picture to me."

"I fucked up, I'm sorry. I'm sorry. We can't lie, he can't lie, and he never did. My name is Cedar Greenthistle, Caleb is my mortal name, you have it now. Do what you want with it, but you have to save him! You have to help us! Help Greenthistle," Cedar pleaded.

"You hate me. You wanted me far, far away from him. Now you are my escort dragging me to Cyrus?" she growled out, glaring at him.

"Cedar what have you done? Where is he?" Quinn demanded.

"Trevin needs you, but it's dangerous. Cyrus is dangerous. Trevin never lied to you about that night. Alena pushed herself on him. He wanted nothing to do with her, ever! Cyrus told her to do it and she told me to follow her. They didn't sleep together. I know they didn't."

"Where's Autumn? Why didn't Cyrus send her to lure me into his little trap?" Elodie hissed out, squeezing the dagger tighter.

"Autumn is bound not to. She is unharmed but bound. If she helps Trevin she has to marry Cyrus, or watch Trevin bleed out and she is free. I'm sorry Elodie. I was scared of the wrong things. Cyrus wants to hurt you. He wants to take down Greenthistle and let he and Ashdale split the land."

"No! That doesn't make any sense. Stop spewing bullshit. How are you doing this?" Quinn growled.

"It's all true. Please. Trevin is hurt. I don't know what to do."

"How convenient you have to fetch the one you hate, or did you come to kill me?" she screamed as the blade glowed brightly. Cedar dropped to his knees, and she took a step back.

"Elodie, fuck, will you listen? I was wrong about everything! I'm sorry! He needs you, we all do. Greenthistle needs you. And now, you're, you have that power?"

"What is this power? It's been taking over ever since I got that stupid book open. Cyrus called me Earth Blessed."

"Earth Blessed! You've awoken! Cyrus knew it. He saw it in you?" Quinn said in awe.

Elodie narrowed her eyes. "What does that even mean?"

"We will explain it to you later. Greenthistle needs you, Trevin needs you. He's badly hurt." Cedar jumped up to his feet.

"When one estate is bound, a newness will walk the forest. Elodie," Quinn realized.

"He's using him as bait for you. Your vowed. I'm so sorry. I didn't know I was so stupid," Cedar bellowed. "Cyrus knew all of it. Has known this the entire time. He used me and my unease and turned me against Trevin."

"How could Cyrus do this? He and Trev were so close. He can't possibly want to override Greenthistle. That shifts the power. Nightswift would lose the ravens' sight. Ashdale would lose the bears' strength. No." Quinn panicked. "Cyrus could essentially be the one to scramble minds."

"Cyrus has lost it. He's got Trevin bound in chains. He shot him with arrows lined with floss flower oil. Autumn and I came as soon as we were alerted by ravens, our dads were in a meeting in the study. Cyrus bound us both," Cedar said. Elodie's heart was pounding. "It will bleed him dry!"

"No!" she cried. Instinctively, she felt her ears again. Still round. "So I'm not fae?"

"No, you're Earth Blessed. It means you are connected with the earth—the essence of the earth is in you. She watches out for you, you watch out for her. You harness her power through the Old Giants. They are ancient and old and rare. I thought they were folktales. Trevin was right," Quinn explained

"What? I'm just an odd mortal?" Elodie scoffed, though it was apparent she was overwhelmed.

"Not anymore and you're Trevin's vowed. Humboldt has an earth blessed," Cedar quipped out.

"Vowed. He does want it?"

"Yes!" Cedar panicked. "He does want you. He has wanted you since Halloween, Elodie. I'm sorry. He loves you. I didn't see it. I should have realized it. I never should have listened to Cyrus. I was scared things were happening too fast, and you were there for all of it and I didn't understand why." He turned to run.

"He hurt me, you all hurt me," she cried out, still not moving. Quinn remained by her side as Cedar turned to her.

"I am sorry for everything, Elodie. You were nothing but brave, kind, and strong. You fought for my family. Greenthistle protects you. We will fight for you because you always fought for us. I promise you."

"You will take me to him, across the boundary. Right now?" She whimpered.

"Yes! Please help us. Help him."

"You better fight for her, Cedar. I swore Ashdale to her, I would have every right," Quinn growled.

"I promise you, After he's freed. After he's safe, do whatever you want to me. Just save him please," Cedar cried.

Elodie nodded, and they took off running.

"Can you control the power?"

"I think, but it's driving me crazy. I can't focus, I can't sit still, I'm burning up and my skin stings," she said. "Am I still human?"

"Yes and no. You can still be injured, but you heal faster. They are ageless, immortal. Our parents can explain it better, I think. It's the stuff of folktales and lore," Quinn said.

Elodie noticed she was able to keep up with him now. The ground almost gave her a push.

"You are telling me I'm a folktale? That I'm the oddity. Odd."

"Earth Blessed. Greenthistle's best and only shot at surviving. The omen is you. Not Greenthistle's collapse," Cedar said as they kept running. "When one estate is chained and bound, the forest will be born anew, three courts are said to keep the balance. He never thought he was the best choice for heir. He doubted himself a lot after we lost Mom. It is the first born though, the lands will cling to him unless he falls. He always tried, and he never gave up. You showed him that he didn't need to doubt anything,"

"That's what vowed do, they bring out the best in each other. I don't know how brave you were before but I'd say you are proving to be quite fearless now," Quinn said.

"Cyrus has him chained. Autumn and I are bound. He thinks the lands will be governed by Ashdale and Nightswift. The forest is born anew, yet Greenthistle is still here, still claims it. It's new because there is an Earth Blessed who is tied to the Great Mother. She ran with the fae. She saw and heard the Old Giants here that we don't, mortals don't. You are new and old at the same time. You walk these lands and it's been calling you all this time," Cedar said, coming to a stop at the barrier. "You are this newness who is going to save Greenthistle."

"I always felt a piece of me was left behind. Was lost here, that day I cut my hand when I was eight, and the boundary seeped into me, like it did a few weeks ago when I got the tome opened. I am bound to Humboldt?"

"Yes," Cedar said with a smile and bowed his head. "Step through, Lady Elodie. You don't need us to cross over anymore."

Elodie reared her head back, taking a step back.

"What? Why did you call me that?"

"These are your lands and we need to save your vowed," Cedar said.

"Step through, Lady Elodie," Quinn echoed.

Elodie took a deep breath and stepped over the boundary. The scents of the earth became more intense, the sounds clearer. Then she heard mountain lions cry out.

"Has Cyrus always been this way? Violent? He's to be an estate lord?" she asked quietly. "Trevin said they were friends, close, but why would he be friends with someone so violent? Nightswift will lose power."

"No, he wasn't always this way. He was always clever, cocky, and arrogant, but the mountain lion attack in October changed him. He could have died had Lord Greenthistle not healed him. It was devastating to witness. I will never get his screams out of my head." Quinn shivered. "We were all messed up," He went on to tell of the accident.

Elodie eyed her palm again. "They never found out what it was? In the mountain lion?" she asked, confused.

"No. It was something evil, some old magic. Cyrus healed rather quickly for how bad it was and got more aggressive after that. He's had these mood swings, malicious to nervous, to disoriented and tired."

"I've noticed a lot more blackbirds around. Nightswift, to watch and observe, right?" she asked. They nodded.

What could it be? she thought to herself. *Evil, evil in the lands, the estates need you, Earth Blessed. The blackbird is trapped. Trembling, struggling. Fighting, himself?* The words echoed in her head.

"He's been watching you, he knew. The plan was to drag you in front of Trevin all along. Bastard!" Cedar scoffed. Elodie felt a chill.

They kept going, and the cavern began to open above. Huge redwoods shot to the skies, they hummed and whispered.

Earth Blessed. She's returned. Salvation.
The boy's blood can stop.
Two heirs need you. The mountain lion and the raven, injured.
Hear their cries.
Bind the evil back to stone.
Timeless, ageless, like you. Carry it, bind it.
Bind it back, El.

Bind it back. Falk? The pillar? Is it in Cyrus now? She ran through her thoughts, recalling the book on Falk that mentioned good and bad spirits. *Those skulls around the broken pillar, the dried blood.*

"Your dad healed Cyrus and healed me?" she asked.

Cedar and Quinn nodded then Elodie looked at her hand. Her heart was pounding. They stopped and watched her look ahead with unease. A flash of teal in her vision as Cedar and Quinn gasped in amazement.

"Try to slow your heart rate. What Cyrus has done to him isn't pretty. Do not let these arrows hit you. Cyrus wants you. Get the arrows out of Trevin. Free Trevin, he will be able to fight back, remind him who he is. We will cover you," Cedar said.

"I don't know how to do this."

"You have the power of the Great Mother, you can heal, you can defend. Let him see you, let him see he was right. Remove the arrows, heal him. Let him see everything you feel for him, see what you've become. Vowed want the very best for each other," Quinn said.

She shook her head, confused. Everything was happening too fast—this was too much.

"What if I can't?" she whimpered.

"You can, El. I will walk in front of you. I need to pull your sleeve or something. Make it appear I dragged you here and I will get you as close as I can. When I stop, run for him. Don't stop until you get to him."

"I will run in after you," Quinn said. "Get to Trevin."

"I don't have much other choice, I guess," Elodie muttered. She flexed her fingers and remembered the vine. Cedar watched amazed, and then put his hands on her shoulders.

"El, I was wrong about you, so wrong. You can chain me to a tree in iron and let your magic fly after all this. Just save him, please, let him see you. See him. Tell him you love him. He needs to hear it."

She nodded and held her arm up, bunching the sleeve for him to take. Cedar grabbed it and took an inhale.

"Look scared, I have to act rough," he said. She didn't have to act for long. As he tugged her sleeve, she saw Trevin. Arrows sticking out of his limp body, blood pooling, and his head slumped forward.

"Trevin." No movement stirred from him at the sound of her gasp. Her eyes shifted to Cyrus, and she watched frantically as he screamed hoarsely for help in chains in her mind, screaming for help, his body beaten. *No! He has no control over his own body! Trapped!*

"He's trapped. Cyrus is possessed, and he's trapped!" she said with a gasp.

Cedar looked at her, confused.

"I see the spirit in him. Cyrus is in chains! Save the blackbird, save them all."

"Get to Trev first," he hissed. "You have to! I can't see him bleed out like this," Cedar said, his voice breaking and fear creeping into his eyes. Then it struck her that this was how they had lost their mom. Floss flower. Trevin was going to meet the same fate and she could not fail him. She would not fail him.

"Wait," Elodie cried out. "Don't let it infest you. Be careful. Stay on my side please. I'm begging you both. Stay with me. Uphold your promises."

Cedar and Quinn nodded to her and covered her.

Chapter 63

Trevin managed to slow his heart rate, but he couldn't hold his head up. Numbness and soreness engulfed his arms all at the same time from being chained above his head. His neck was tight and his shoulder burned. He could see the blood dripping, the puddle forming. He felt his tears fall down his cheeks.

She will be safe. Mortals are fickle. She can move on. Power will shift to Autumn, she will fight for her land, he thought.

"It shouldn't have taken Cedar this long. I wonder how far she went. I wonder if Cedar fled. I will hunt him down too."

"Please stop this!" Autumn cried out. "Please."

"You mean this?" Cyrus said, holding the loaded crossbow at Trevin. He didn't even flinch. As tears fell, Trevin watched them splash.

"Stop!" Cedar shouted.

Trevin tried to lift his head, but he couldn't. His senses became engulfed with ocean breeze and lavender. Cedar was back, and he had brought Elodie. *No!*

"I did my part of your bargain. Do yours. Drop the crossbow," Cedar muttered out.

Trevin ripped his eyes open. He heard Elodie whimper. Trevin began to plead. "No! No. Please," Trevin cried out. He tried to tug despite the pain ripping through him. All he could do was cry out when her heard her gasp. "Run! Get out of here!"

"How nice the bear cub joined too."

"No! Leave her alone," Trevin cried, still trying to lift his head.

"Elodie, you're—" he heard Autumn say.

"Please, run!" Trevin cried out, trying with everything in him to pull his head up. He heard Cedar fight, he heard Quinn change with a roar.

"Go near her and you violate the rules!" Quinn growled out.

"El, please run," he whimpered, trying to lift his head. Then his struggling was paused, soft warm hands cupped his jaw and lifted his head.

"Trevin." Her voice soothed his aches. He met her eyes with blurry vision. She rubbed her thumb over his cheek, wiping away the tears. That sensation over his markings soothing him. "Trevin." He focused his eyes, the aura coming off her relaxed him. He wasn't sore or cold. He felt safe and coddled. He saw everything in her eyes, earth and soil of the land, of Autumn's land. How quickly he had died. Maybe it was just to see how blessed she really was. So full of curiosity and wonder. How this mortal girl had stolen his heart. Had shown him things he took for granted. His hands were free now, and he moved to embrace his afterlife. Safe with her. Safe with his little mink.

Pain suddenly radiated out from his shoulder and a whimper escaped him.

"Trevin," she said, panicking. "Look at me."

"I am. I died, but things still hurt. Why?" His words slurred.

"Trevin! Snap out of this. Look at me!" Elodie pleaded. "Trevin, I need you to show me what I am. I love you," she cried out, holding his jaw with one hand now. That thing that strained in him snapped again and this time radiated through his whole body. She loved him. He heard Cedar roar out and Autumn joined in. The loud screech of blackbirds all in unison was deafening. "Trevin, fight for Greenthistle." Her voice cut through the ravens' caws, caressing his ears. "I'll be there. I love you," she said, kissing him softly on the lips. He tried to press into her. He tried to call for her.

Trevin realized he was not dead. His body was still poisoned. His eyes widened, taking her in. She wasn't some ethereal spirit to hold him in the afterlife, she was here holding him, soothing him. She was Earth Blessed. She was his, and he was hers. This mortal girl that showed him earth, showed him his lands in new ways was Earth Blessed. He loved her. Was vowed to her. Would be forever because she wanted him forever, and she had found it herself.

"Elodie, you're my vowed. I love you," he gasped in shock. "Earth Blessed!"

"My vowed." She kissed him again, softly. "This might hurt. I can't really control much, but I have to get these out."

He didn't know what she was talking about until he felt her palm flat around his shoulder, around the arrow. A soothing numbing sensation misted over him and he cried out in pain when she swiftly pulled. Her palm pressed over it for a second. The pain diminished, only some soreness remained. She quickly moved her hand to the one in his flank and pressed her palm against his skin. He took an inhale, and she pulled. Another cry escaped him.

With his hands free now, Trevin cupped her jaw, staring into her glossy eyes. He could see the teal pulsing in them and, through it all, saw all the love and affection she held for him.

"Elodie. My vow—"

Suddenly, Elodie was ripped away from him. She screamed as ravens swarmed her.

"No!" Trevin screamed. He jumped up, still dizzy. Still poisoned but on the mend, thanks to her. Trevin realized how much of his blood was on the ground. How much he had lost. The swarm of blackbirds engulfed her, and she screamed again. Trevin watched on in horror for a moment, panicking and he was about to change. Quinn grabbed him to hold him back.

"Trevin! Don't!" Quinn strained to hold him.

"Cyrus! Fight this!" she screamed. The piercing cry of the ravens filled their ears.

"No! No! I never wanted this!" Cyrus sobbed out. "I never wanted to be this." Then a high-pitched caw of pain. Elodie's entire body pulsed teal, her hands remaining illuminated.

"What is she doing? What are they doing?" Autumn asked, confused. Elodie pushed herself through the swarm of ravens and lunged for one. She grabbed it and rolled on her back, holding the large raven tightly against her. It flapped violently as she held it by the beak, claws reaching out for her. The teal vine wrapped around the raven, calming it down. The swarm of the bird claws cut her body and her face.

"She said he was possessed. She could see him chained up," Cedar said.

"From that mountain lion attack," Quinn followed up, still holding Trevin back. "The bite from the mountain lion. It must have passed through to Cyrus."

"No! Elodie. No!" Trevin cried out.

"Trev! If it goes to you, how bad do you think it's going to go?" Quinn strained to hold him back.

"Little Earth Blessed. You think you can save the blackbird. You want to see how he bleeds. See what I did to your vowed? How his father wept that night that night his face was slashed open. Let me show you all the horrors they kept from you, the horrors that await you, now when your Old Giants burn, so will you," a voice that was no longer Cyrus hissed out. The raven started to fight back against the vine.

"Cyrus, fight for Nightswift. Fight for your lands!" Elodie cried out. With her arms wrapped as tight as she could around the large raven, she rolled up to her knees. She closed her eyes as it cut her stomach through her shirt and leaned over the blackbird. "Fight it, Cyrus, I will fight for all of you," she said, and a glow illuminated the dark. They could see Elodie breathing slow and calm, eyes closed, as the blinding white light came out of Cyrus.

"I'm sorry. I'm sorry," Cyrus cried. "I never wanted this," he screamed and then the screams became encased in a blur. Elodie's bloodied arms released the raven and it flew to her head. She fell on her back and writhed.

"No. No! Stop! You will not harm them anymore!" she screamed and writhed. Cyrus had changed and watched her tremble.

"It's trying to take hold of her! She pulled it out of me! Into her and she's fighting it like I tried to!" Cyrus cried out. He was on his knees, crying. "Please. No. I'm sorry," he pleaded. His body was covered in bruises and welts.

Trevin broke out of Quinn's hold and ran to her. He held her face and saw her eyes lifeless, void of the color.

"Elodie! No!" he screamed.

"Get her to the ferns, to that redwood. She needs the Old Giants!" Cyrus cried out. Trevin grabbed Elodie and ran to the nearest redwood. She just heaved in his embrace. He noticed the cuts all over her as he laid her down in the ferns at the base of a redwood. The ferns trembled and the Old Giant creaked. Trevin's eyes traveled up the trunk, worried.

"Help her please," he pleaded quietly to himself. His heart was pounding. "Elodie."

She struggled to drag her palms flat on the earth.

"Anchor. Contain it. Not me," she groaned. "Stone. Timeless, ageless, like me, not me," she screamed and curled into the fetal position.

Quinn and Cedar pushed a large stone near Elodie, who instantly wrapped her body around it. They watched her push the light into the rock and drag her palm over it, leaving a streak of blood.

"Bound to Humboldt. Old and new have awoken." She gritted her teeth. Then the light was gone and her body went limp.

"Elodie," Trevin said nervously, catching her head before it hit the ground. He pressed a hand to her cheek and was shocked how cold she was. "No! Please. Elodie!" She wasn't responding, and all was silent save for Trevin's cries. Quinn, Cedar, Autumn, and Cyrus watched with such horror and worry. "Elodie, you were never the martyr. Wake up," he sobbed. "I'm sorry. Please, little mink."

With a gasp, she shot up and gripped her heart. Her eyes locked on the rock. Instantly she tried backing away from it, pushing into Trevin.

"Put this somewhere! Get it away!" she panted.

Trevin wrapped his arms around her, the warmth of life returned to her. "Elodie," he said with a whimper, kissing her head.

"I will watch it till our dads get here," Quinn said, walking over to it. Cedar did too.

"Elodie, you are the first Earth Blessed in six hundred years. That thing knew it was you. It saw the power in you," Cyrus said, breathing hard, his eyes watered.

The three heirs looked at each other and Cyrus trembled. Quinn realized he felt stronger. Trevin did too.

The shift of power. Cyrus, possessed or not, had broken the rules on his own free will. He harmed not only the Earth Blessed but another estate member's vowed. He'd hurt an estate heir too. Dropping his head into his hands, Cyrus knew what was to come. He bowed in front of Elodie.

"You saved me?" He looked at her. "I hurt your vowed. I pawed at you and I hurt you," he said. "Thank you. Thank you, I'm sorry."

Elodie remained quiet, still watching the stone, watching Quinn and Cedar. She gripped Trevin's hand hard.

"Cedar did what you bid of him! Release the bind on Autumn now, Cyrus!" Trevin said, growling out.

"I release you, Autumn, of our bargain and our engagement," Cyrus deflated and shrank back into himself. Autumn ran to Elodie and helped support her. Trevin changed into feral and stood next to Elodie. He was even bigger.

"Should you or your estate go near Elodie or my siblings with malcontent again, Greenthistle will act," Trevin roared. Cyrus trembled as his eyes met the furious mountain lion.

Elodie was still in shock at what she had seen, and what she had done. Worry gripped her tightly that the spirit would take over Quinn or Cedar. She pressed a hand against Trevin's body, despite the sting on her palm, she just needed to feel him, to know he was here. He nuzzled her head. Then he stood in front of her and arched his back and flattened his ears letting out a low growl. Her hand slid along his side and she gripped his tail.

Chapter 64

The sound of sentries poured in, weapons drawn. Ravens descended, mountain lions and bears stood ready. The three high estate lords ran in, all panic-stricken, looking around at everyone—Trevin in mountain lion form, Autumn shielding Elodie, Cedar and Quinn in fae form standing next to a rock, and Cyrus shrunken and trembling.

Trevin was prepared to fight all of them if he had to. But Lord Nightswift looked at Cyrus, who was still on his knees and then at Trevin, Autumn, and Elodie.

"I'm sorry," Cyrus cried softly.

"Trevin, stand down. Are you okay, son?" Lord Greenthistle asked nervously, cautiously taking small steps closer towards him.

"You will not take her from me! She is my vowed!" Trevin growled in everyone's headspace. "I will not let her go!"

"We know, just change please. I need to know you are okay," his dad pleaded. "Please. This was my fault, I need to know you are okay, son."

Trevin took an inhale and changed. His dad saw the blood soaking into his shirt and pants, the wounds on his face. He eyed the arrows, crossbow, and the large pool of blood.

The three estate lords looked at him then at Cyrus who still trembled.

"Trevin! The arrows, the blood, floss flower?" Lord Greenthistle asked worriedly.

"I'm sorry. I'm sorry. It's Trevin's, I shot him with floss flower. I tried to fight it. I did such bad things to him. To her. That spirit in me stole my body," Cyrus whimpered. Lord Nightswift knelt down and put his hand on Cyrus's back. "She pulled it out of me. She sealed it back up. Lord Greenthistle bound it to me. I tried to fight it," he cried out.

"Elodie healed me, Elodie fought for us all. She fought for her lands. She belongs here!" Trevin said. He pointed toward the rock. Quinn and Cedar stood by it and nodded. Trevin moved behind Elodie, pulling her against his body.

"Autumn, step aside," Lord Greenthistle said. She froze and Trevin was tense but met his dad's eyes with a glare. "You know she has to understand what this means for her. What being Earth Blessed means. Step aside."

"You will be okay, Elodie, I promise," Autumn said. "Thank you." She took a deep inhale hugging Elodie tightly then moved aside. Elodie backed up into Trevin.

"She really is an Earth Blessed," Lord Ashdale said with a gasp. She started to tremble and Trevin held her steady, as everyone watched her energy surge inside of her and see her wounds illuminating teal.

Trevin locked eyes with his dad, almost challenging him to deny them now.

"She's my vowed. I love her!" Trevin proclaimed it.

"The Earth Blessed has to come with us," Lord Nightswift said.

Trevin remained tense.

The other two lords looked at Lord Greenthistle who still locked eyes with his son. His face was unreadable to most. Trevin could see the emotions in his dad though. He saw pride and relief, but also disappointment and anger in the recklessness of the heirs. Shame and remorse too rest in Lord Greenthistle. Trevin noted his own anger was breaking out faster than he could control.

"You know she will not be harmed. I have told you time and time again, you have to let her be important. You have to let her decide for herself how she will do that. She's been given that choice now. Let her know her options," Lord Greenthistle said, stepping forward. "Trust her just as you always have, Trevin, Let her say what she wants," he said. Trevin sighed and gave her a hug.

"Trevin." Elodie held onto him. He pressed his head into hers.

"The Earth Blessed haven't existed in so long. Answer truthfully and honestly, El. Tell them what you want. You will be okay," Trevin said. She didn't move. "I can't go with you. Orders are orders. You are safe. You saved us all. You decide how to be important going forward," he said with some remorse. She nodded and took a deep breath. "You will be okay, little mink, you are safe. You are home, however you decide it will look. You are home."

"Trevin," she called with a whimper and the smallest smile formed on his lips. The smallest ounce of hope that she would want this life.

"You all are to go home, and lick your wounds. She will not heal you. The Earth Blessed was harmed on account of all our reckless and careless actions. We do not harm mortals, we protect them so that they may protect us and our lands. We cannot abandon the Earth Blessed," Lord Greenthistle said. Cedar and Trevin both looked down. "We do not threaten each other, nor their vowed, we must stand together," he said, eyeing Cyrus and Quinn.

They could all hear Elodie's heart begin to pound as Lord Greenthistle walked up to her and knelt down. He gave her a gentle smile and placed a hand to the back of her head supporting her as she fell unconscious. Trevin pressed his hands to his face, unable to watch. Unable to watch her be taken from him like this.

"All you go back to your estates and stay there until we return," Lord Greenthistle said. They turned to leave, and Trevin took a step as the despair finally hit him. He looked back to watch them take her. Autumn and Cedar pulled him. Nightswift sentries took Cyrus who began to whimper and tremble with the cuffs put on him as they took him to the hold.

Autumn, Cedar, and Trevin entered the estate and got cleaned up. Trevin dragged himself to his room. He wasn't sure how he had any energy to cry. He changed his clothes but didn't bother showering. He sat there and stared at the drawing she had made for him. The little mink and the mountain lion, her mountain lion, his little mink. "Elodie. I hope you come back to me," he cried, sliding down to his knees. Hunger was gnawing at him but he didn't care to eat, he just wanted to drink at this point. Eventually he dragged himself downstairs to find a glass of hard liquor. Small dishes were brought out with haste by the staff who was clearly shaken. As he slumped down on the couch, he leaned forward and buried his hands in his face. Autumn sat next to him and rubbed his back.

"She will be okay. You know she will be safe," she said softly. "She will come back to you."

Trevin didn't respond save for a nod, he was sorting through so many emotions. Anger, shame, sadness, hope, longing.

"I'm sorry, Trevin. I didn't know what else to do. I couldn't watch another arrow go in you. I didn't want Cyrus to hurt her either but I couldn't watch you gasp for another breath. Cyrus or whatever that was in him told me his plan with Alena and I just didn't see what was happening, I'm sorry. I didn't see or didn't want to see her power. I didn't understand why you were being so strong and brave for her and I should have. Cyrus hatched the plan, and I thought you'd get over it like the last mortal," Cedar said, sitting across from him. Trevin remained silent but didn't bother looking at his brother. He didn't want to look at anyone.

"She was running toward the boundary line, for you. She froze when she saw me and held her dagger out toward me. Quinn ran up shortly after. She pulsed her power through it and I knew she only one that would save us, save our home and hers. I dropped to my hands and begged her on your account. I would have given my life for her. I want so much more power shifted off me towards you. I'm sorry for sending that picture to her. I hate myself for letting her believe for one second you didn't care," Cedar said.

Trevin looked at him and scoffed. "Do you know how bad it hurt to watch it all fall apart in seconds like that? Then to listen to you and Cyrus brag about it. To become your literal punching bag? As if I wasn't already worried for her. I don't know who has my back anymore." The rage he felt was apparent.

"I'm sorry. I know I fucked up. Quinn, Autumn, and dad will always have your back. I do to. I promise to protect her. Not just because she's Earth Blessed, or your vowed, but because she's kind and she fought for us. Because she sees the good in people, even the people who choose to not see the good in her," Cedar's eyes welled up.

"I wanted her so badly and I'm so stupid. I should have helped my vowed. I thought I was doing her a favor by letting her go, all I did was hurt her. She belonged to the Old Giants, she is theirs, not mine. Humboldt called to her, and it created her. They chose me for her and I let go," he cried out and buried his face in his hands again.

"She loves you, Trev and knows you are hers, she is yours. She will choose you," Cedar said.

"What are they going to ask of her? What are her options? I don't know if she wants that. Earth Blessed, a folktale, to come to life. A true rarity."

"She's not going to leave your side. You know this. She found us on her own, she pieced it together, and saved you. Saved Cyrus too. She was looking for home, for you," Cedar said.

"Regardless of what she decides tonight, she is part of the family. Lady Santiago is part of this estate," Autumn said. "I am happy to call her sister and I swear to protect her, for the person Elodie is. Never revoke that order on me."

"I'm sorry you had to witness me like that. I promise as the heir, I will fight for Greenthistle, I will fight for your home too. I will always fight for Greenthistle no matter what she chooses," Trevin told his siblings.

CHAPTER 65

Elodie opened her eyes and saw ferns, not exactly sure where she was. With a deep inhale, she rolled on her back and looked at the stars and the Old Giants. She was on a bed of ferns. A raven cawed, and she sat up. A large bear and mountain lion walked out of the brush. The raven descended onto the ground in front of her. All three of the animals were so large compared to normal ones, they all appeared majestic. She felt no fear knowing who these animals were. They all changed into fae forms.

"Lady Elodie Santiago, formerly of Marin," Lord Greenthistle said softly. "Fully awakened Earth Blessed."

The three estate lords bowed their heads.

Elodie looked at them and swallowed hard, bowing her head.

"Yes sir, Lord Greenthistle, Lord Nightswift, Lord Ashdale," she said, trying to be as polite as possible. Her eyes watered and she was worried about what may be asked of her. She was still sitting on the ground.

"Since our children were incapable of being civil, tell us what happened. Speak honestly, for you were given a great gift by the earth," Lord Greenthistle said. Elodie nodded.

"Yes, sir," she locked eyes with him. She would not lie, she had no reason too. Trevin told her not to, to tell them what she wanted. This place was what she wanted. She wanted it to be her home with him. Yet Elodie was fearful, not only for herself but also for these three estates. There was a power shift which caused the three estates to lose balance with each other, with the lands. She hoped to mend it.

Her mind raced and then she looked at each of the three. Then her eyes went to the Old Giants around them. She was Earth Blessed and she was vowed to Trevin and so she would remain. Regardless of how bonds worked, she loved him, and had for some time. She had found a way into his world and she had found a home and a family in this world. This family she knew she would always fight for because the earth in her veins wanted her too. She would fight to keep the three estates sound, and she'd fight for these lands that were part of her now. A gentle wind embraced her, and she remembered it could not be undone, none of this would ever be undone. A small encouragement from the earth, maybe a small chuff from the mountain lion who'd fight for her too.

Elodie spoke of the events of the previous two weeks. How seeing the picture of Trevin and Alena crushed her, how the power started to surge and the Old Giants began to hiss the warnings to her.

"When I pulled the spirit out of Cyrus, I saw the chains release him. The spirit tossed his bruised body aside and went for mine. I could see the skies going stark white, the stars gone, the lands gone, nothing but a bright white void. I could see what was happening, what had happened. That spirit knew about me and had found a great power in me it wanted, so when I pulled the chains off Cyrus, it clung to me. I fought to keep hold on those Old Giants, on this land."

Lord Nightswift and Lord Ashdale asked for her account of the iron cuff and the map to Falk. Elodie spoke of what occurred and they smiled and nodded.

They explained how healing had bound the spirit to Cyrus, and had awoken her dormant earth magic. They spoke of how they pieced together what was happening. Spoke of all they knew of the Earth Blessed, how it was lore and legend all but forgotten until now.

Elodie learned of her responsibility to heal the lands, work with estates and help them as needed. She would be expected to traverse the lands and help them retrieve artifacts as needed. In some cases, she would need to go alone due to iron or floss flower.

In the summer she would spend one week a month at each estate, working and training with each of them. Any environmental changes in the mortal world would be brought to her attention. She would act as the liaison between mortal and fae alongside them, observing both and offering more insight on mortal behavior. Her body would remain in this state, the moment her power had truly awoken, as long as those Old Giants stood. Since Elodie was bound to the Old Giants, the magic that fueled power, it was unknown what would happen if she left the lands that made her. Listening intently, she smiled realizing that she and Trevin had forever.

"You have much to consider, Lady Santiago. You are as the omens say, something new and old all at once. Much of the lore on Earth Blessed has been lost. We are learning too. When we realized what was happening to you and to them, we were terrified. Trevin clearly was too. As you know he does not trust easily, but I am confident you will help him grow into a fine estate lord. Earth Blessed heal even old scars," Lord Greenthistle said. Elodie frowned and looked down.

"Your case is very rare. We have not heard of an Earth Blessed vowed with an estate master or lord/lady. You are the first. You and he accepted the bond, to break it is to reject each other. Yet you are both very young for immortals, you were not born fae or immortal, we are not sure what the bond will do for you. Should you choose to complete the vowed bond, you will be aligned with Greenthistle. The animals of this territory see you as Earth Blessed and will help you. Mountain lions however are at your call, they will come to your aid should you need it. We will show you the call and teach you how to communicate with ravens and bears," Lord Nightswift followed up.

"You may also choose to resume your mortal life. Your memory will be wiped by the Great Mother herself. Your power will be given back to the lands regardless of if you stay here or not," Lord Greenthistle said. His face showed some worry. "If you remain immortal, this life you created for yourself, will at some point in the near future cease to exist. You will watch people you are close with age, move away, pass on, and you will not be in their lives for but a few years. The territory may change, it may get smaller or bigger, the towns you know may not be as they are now. This is what we all know, we have seen many in our lives come and go."

"You will be weakened should the earth suffer. Your life is tied to these Old Giants and these lands. You will thrive as the lands do, and luckily the mortals here wish to let the lands thrive, that may not always be the case," Lord Ashdale explained.

"So, Lady Elodie, we ask you to decide. Remain Humboldt's Earth Blessed, immortal, ageless, timeless. Vowed with master Trevin of Greenthistle Estate eventually to be lady of the estate. Fighting for and with the three estates, the mortal lands, and beyond the boundary. Or resume life as a mortal, live the life you were creating for yourself. Still vowed to Trevin to handle however you two decide. Your other option is to return to mortal life. Your memory erased, free to create a new life, your power removed, free to do as you please," Lord Nightswift said. "The high estates will always watch over as long as you remain here."

Elodie smiled, she knew what she would choose. She knew the risks for her and Trevin, the rarity of her, the inability to blend into nothing. It would be easy to do with the mortals, much harder to do with the fae of other territories. She knew that the three estates would be there for her though and she would be there for all of them. A quick glance at the trees standing tall and proud and then she looked at the three high estate lords.

"I fully accept my responsibilities to these lands, to Humboldt, there is no place I am more at peace. I will do everything in my power to be the lady that Master Trevin and Greenthistle deserve. I will always fight for Greenthistle, Nightswift, and Ashdale," she said confidently, no longer fearful. "This is my home, and I want nothing more than to fight for it alongside all of you, as your Earth Blessed."

The three lords smiled and bowed their heads once again.

"Lady Santiago, on behalf of Ashdale Estate, we welcome you to Humboldt. We thank you for your fight and your dedication to our lands. Ashdale will teach you the honor and loyalty of these lands," Lord Ashdale said with a bow.

"Lady Santiago, Nightswift Estate welcomes you, thanks you for risking your life, and spilling your blood for Master Cyrus. Nightswift will teach you to observe and analyze," Lord Nightswift said. She smiled, and they bowed.

She shifted her eyes to Lord Greenthistle, knowing one day he would entrust his estate to her.

"Lady Santiago of Humboldt Territory, on behalf of Greenthistle Estate, we welcome you and appreciate the blood, sweat, and tears you have poured into our lands and to my estate. I would say Greenthistle will teach you strength and valor, but you already know those traits. We will teach you all that we can," he said with a genuine smile.

Lord Ashdale and Nightswift changed and ran off leaving her alone with Lord Greenthistle.

"Welcome home, Lady Santiago of Humboldt," Lord Greenthistle said, sitting next to her on the ground, knees bent before him. "Welcome to Greenthistle. You will have a room at the estate if you would like, though I imagine you will be in Trev's more. It is encouraged you would keep your current lodging and life as is, for a time at least. Your vehicle will be kept safe but cannot be on estate grounds as there's no road to get it there. We will arrange for safe storage."

"What if I bought a house in Sunny Brae, right by the trail head?"

"That sounds like a good idea, I can see if we can acquire a property," he said. "Having you so near will be good. I assume Trevin will live at both estates part time."

"No, I have enough to buy something with what my dad left me. I think, in some way, he knew I was where I needed to be. He never wanted me to move back. Maybe he knew the Old Giants brought me here too. In hopes that Trevin would see me, they told me he would see it, you all would. I just wished I had seen it in Cyrus instead of being scared of him. I could have helped him before this happened," she said sadly.

Lord Greenthistle put a hand on her back causing her to tense briefly before letting out a steady exhale.

"I am grateful for you, Lady Elodie. I worry for Trevin, knowing he holds these scars from his mother's passing. I thank you for helping him, healing him, and igniting this fire in him. I am grateful he has you by his side. I am sorry for ever trying to stop this bond between you two, for ever making you feel as though you did not belong. Thank you for not shutting him out, thank you for your curiosity. Thank you for choosing Greenthistle, for choosing him. You made a big choice tonight," he said. She smiled wider hearing his acceptance of her. He sighed and his warm smile dropped to a grin. "Since you are aligned to my estate, that makes you my responsibility I suppose, daughter-in-law to be," he said, watching her cheeks heat. "Where would you like to spend this evening? At your home in Eureka or at your home at Greenthistle?"

She looked at him with a hint of unease. "Lord Greenthistle, sir, how does the bond work? Being vowed? I've read about so many variations?"

"The vowed ceremony consists of removing each other's diadems, and then sealing the intent with blood in private. Diadems are a symbol of authority or royal rule. To allow someone else to remove it when you are in your natural state, is a symbol of great trust. The removal of clothing has little to do with it, the diadems and the blood vow are the important things. This bond has been pulling you both violently because it was not completed. I should have ensured Trevin knew how strong intent was when it was your actual vowed. He feels so deeply and seeing him break and curl in on himself after the incident with Alena hurt me immensely. It was like witnessing him after we lost his mother all over again. I desperately tried to find what you were, to find a way to keep you here. You grew on my heart too, seeing how far you went for us and for him, for really no one's benefit but ours."

She nodded, processing everything. "How much blood? Will the iron in my blood poison him?" she asked, worried. He smiled.

"A small incision on the palm. It doesn't take much. It will heal fast for both of you. It will be such a small amount his body will work through it quickly. A thin scar may remain. Some power may pass between you two as well."

"Understood, sir. I want to stay at Greenthistle, with Trevin. I missed him. The last week was hard. I want to see him."

"Welcome home, Lady Elodie. You will have many titles to carry. You will do so with grace as you always have," he said.

Elodie beamed and looked at him.

"We will drop you at your car. Use your talents to find Greenthistle, I will take your keys to Cedar who will take your car home. He will retrieve it for you in a few days. Autumn will be more than happy to help you with the vowed preparations. A revelry can be held once everything has settled," Lord Greenthistle said. Elodie nodded. "I'm afraid I may not be able to pull many more favors for you with the school though. Let's finish out strong, free from doubts and worries. You are home, Lady Santiago." He stood up, as did Elodie.

"Thank you, sir." She looked at him. His hand came to her shoulder and she met his eyes. Pulling her into a hug, Lord Greenthistle slid his hand to the back of her skull bracing her as her vision went black.

When Elodie awoke. she was sitting in her car. It was dark. She panicked for a moment and wondered if she dreamed the entire thing. If he was still in trouble. She jumped out, realizing how much more stable her feet were on the ground, how much easier she could see in the dark. She watched the trees and felt the hilt of her dagger listening. There was no panic in the air. All she had to do was run home, to Greenthistle, to Trevin. She smiled and ran home. When she got to the boundary line she stood for a moment. With a deep inhale, Elodie stepped through and smiled wide. The fae walking by all gasped in awe. She laughed to herself and ran right for Greenthistle Estate.

Chapter 66

Trevin jumped up as soon as he heard the front door open. He froze when he saw the three estate lords and Quinn. Then his heart sank upon not seeing Elodie. He wasn't sure he knew what to say.

"We all need to meet. Let's report," Lord Greenthistle said, concerned as he looked at the other two estate lords. Quinn's head was low.

"Cyrus has been heavily sedated and is back home. He was put in the hold but I think the weight of it all began to drag him down. She spoke of the horrors while she carried that thing. I imagine months' worth of being possessed is taking its toll on Cyrus. Any more sedation and we risked his heart stopping. He trembled and screamed and I just couldn't leave him like that, so I ask you both, let me keep him at home, monitored," Lord Nightswift said with a frown. Lord Greenthistle sighed. Trevin looked at Lord Nightswift with a bout of sadness and loss. He wasn't sure that he could handle Cyrus, nor that he wanted to for some time. Yet knowing his once friend was in that state hurt Trevin immensely. He also feared what Elodie had seen, and what state she had woken up to.

"Master Ashdale's injuries have been cleaned and are healing, but I believe he has things he needs to say." Lord Ashdale gave Quinn a shove toward Trevin. The two locked eyes and the loss and despair Trevin had were replaced with an anger he didn't realize he had in him.

"I'm sorry for telling her she's your vowed. I couldn't watch her break. You should have done it, you coward. She never should have been left alone this week," Quinn said.

"Yeah, I know. You made your point. I fucked up too," Trevin said, trying to hold it together.

"Go get her, you dumbass, that girl loves you and she has for months now. You know that, Trev," Quinn scoffed.

"Apology accepted," Trevin muttered, cutting his eyes down.

"I'm not trying to fight you but don't you dare break her heart now. I told her I'd take her to the spring equinox if you were going to be a coward," Quinn said and turned to his dad before he could meet Trevins glare. "Can we go now? I apologized for what I did wrong."

"That was an attempt, but yes we may," Lord Ashdale said, and Quinn walked out with a minor limp. "I bid you well, Master Greenthistle. I have no doubt that you will take on your new responsibilities brave as ever," he said with a smile. Trevin, Autumn, and Cedar all stared at him confused as he followed Quinn.

"Autumn, Cedar, come please," Lord Greenthistle said, walking toward the kitchen. The three looked at their father with some bewilderment then at each other. "Now," he said sternly.

"You'll be alright. It will be okay," Autumn said quietly to Trevin and walked off following Cedar.

Trevin slumped forward and once again he was alone. He watched the door.

Then as if the Old Giants were waiting, the scent of ocean breeze and lavender engulfed his senses. He froze and his eyes met Elodie's. He stared at her shocked, she was humming with even more Earth Blessed energy.

She was out of breath as if she had run all the way from Sequoia Park, her cuts mostly all healed save for some welts lingering. He was too stunned to move.

"Elodie," he said finally with a laugh that could have been a cry. She lunged for him, hugging him. He wrapped his arms around her tightly.

"I want you. I always wanted you. Greenthistle is home, Trevin, you are home. I love you." She hugged him tight.

"You, aligned with Greenthistle?" he asked, shocked. He gripped her tightly. "My vowed, Earth Blessed. We are going to keep each other safe. We have our happily ever after. I love you!"

"Yes! I'm sorry I ever doubted you. I accept the vow."

He laughed and pressed his forehead to hers.

"Even though I acted like an idiot countless times?" he asked.

She laughed. "We do this together. Always."

He cupped her jaw and kissed her hard. "I wasn't about to let Cedar or Quinn kiss you that night. I felt so much admiration and gratitude toward you after the iron cuff. I will be yours forever, little mink. Our forever," he said. "I love you so much," he said, kissing her again. He led her to his room and closed the door then led her into the bathroom. "All mine. My vowed," he said. She kissed him hard.

He turned on the shower and pulled her clothes off. She undressed him—the very act that vowed them months ago—and her eyes lingered on the scars on his shoulders and waist.

"I didn't heal them right. Trev?" Worry washed over her. He held her hands.

"You saved my life. I will wear them as a reminder that you saved us all, that you are here. I'm going to keep our home safe for us."

He pulled her under the water and held her close, letting the steam rise around them. She held him just as tightly.

As they washed away the remains of the ruins from each other, they could not help but explore each other all over again. It certainly was not their first time but tonight it felt as though they could walk a new path together.

Once they were finished he wrapped her in a towel and gently brushed her hair. She looked at him with such endearment. He smiled warmly back at her.

"You are being so gentle, your touch is so soft. I hope you are not worried about any injuries I had. They are healed," Elodie said.

He leaned in and kissed her then kissed along her jaw and up to her ear, "I certainly am glad they have healed, because as soon I get you on our bed, it is going to be a long night of showing you just how much you mean to me."

His teeth grazed her ear and a lustful breath slipped out of her.

With that Trevin wrapped his arms around her and carried her to the bed, where he wasted little time showing her just how much he missed her.

Tomorrow night they would be vowed.

They would start their new lives together.

Her and the three high estates of Humboldt.

The little mink had found her mountain lion again and she was home.

One summer evening, they were meeting the estate lords at Sequoia Community Park in the very place she told them all this was home—this was where she belonged. The stone that held the spirit was safely monitored in the zoo where it would be maintained and protected. Trevin walked out of the bedroom and grabbed his hoodie and her windbreaker. He saw her flipping through her sketchbook and smirked at the mountain lion, bear, and raven all wearing flower crowns.

"Ready?" he asked.

With a nod, she set down her sketchbook and stood up to kiss him. "Any idea what this meeting is about?" Unease lined her voice.

"No, sometimes we do have to meet here. We did before the mountain lion attack. You know they do when checking in with the halflings and such who work in town."

"Yeah, I suppose a neutral meeting place is good, I'm just glad they didn't pick the King Range," she said, causing him to laugh.

"I'm sure I've had enough iron exposure for a lifetime, an immortal lifetime."

Once at the park they walked to the spot, and Elodie's stomach dropped. She gripped his hand, feeling the tree's pulse. No voices though. Trevin gave her hand a squeeze back.

The high estate lords walked out with tight-lipped expressions. Trevin pulled her closer, ever ready to keep them together.

"At ease, Master Greenthistle," Lord Ashdale said. "We have concerns about an upcoming situation."

Elodie let out an uneasy sigh.

"The regional conference is coming up. Trinity County has informed me there is talk of a peculiar individual in Humboldt's territory. One that a young master may be vowed to. Marin expressed interest also," Lord Greenthistle said. Elodie looked at them nervously and Trevin held her.

"They will never take her from us. From the Old Giants," Trevin declared.

"We knew this was coming, let us make a plan."

Elodie and Trevin nodded. Whatever they needed to do they would do it, together.

Elodie and the high estates will return to
traverse the next trail.

Acknowledgements

You made it! To the end of the trail. This one at least. I am so grateful that you dear reader were here for my very first publication. So thank you for picking this book up, and spending some time in Humboldt with Elodie and the crew. I hope you find magic out there on the trails, or at least keep an eye or an ear out.

This story was not going to be told, at least not in this way with these characters. I was in a creative rut with another project when talk of NaNoWriMo 2022 started in a Discord full of wonderful bookish people and I said I would be there for support. Then I went to a Halloween party and one line of dialogue spurred my idea for the opening scene. So I wrote that the moment Elodie and Trevin crossed paths and then the book began to tell itself. It certainly has undergone a lot of changes from my original idea.

I want to thank a community of Discord people who wrote their stories along with me and cheered me on. To the writing corner, thank you and to the mods of that insanely busy sometimes chaotic Discord, thank you. To everyone who has swapped countless snippets with me, thank you too.

To my Editors: Kristen Hamilton, thank you for all your hard work on this beast and cleaning this up. Could not have done it without you. Emma who dealt with an even longer mess, thank you. Maddi, thank you for the additional help.

A big thank you to my fellow author friends both near and far for the insight, talking me through my moments of self doubt, and listening to me talk about a million what if scenarios that never actually made it to the book. I loved getting to meet your characters and visit their worlds. Brittany Czarnecki, Elyzabeth Trickey, Shea Robinson, Ciar Pfeffer, JJ Wright, Max Musings, M.D. Casmer, & Nelle Nikole. Special thanks to Adalyn Grace, Skyla Ardnt, & Rachel Moore for your fantastic discords and writing advice. Allison Shaft, Rachel Griffin, and Adrienne Young for also writing stories about magical places on the West Coast.

Obi Kaufman who is also an inspiration and whose beautiful field atlases were referenced many times while writing.

To Sadia and all the other beta readers, know that I am grateful for you and for bearing with me through these drafts.

Special thanks to Tegan Weissman who released *Eden Weeping* around the same time and probably knows the entire story of Secrets without even needing to read it. Debut book buddies! Thank you too for bringing the estate heirs to life with your fantastic artwork!

Brie Ann for being the best and most supportive Alpha reader I could have asked for and being excited for all those bonus what if scenes I wrote too. This seriously would not be where it is with you and your love for Quinn. He will get his novella! I can not wait for your book. The story amazing and I love it already.

This book would not be here if not for National and California State Parks. A massive shout out to Eureka Books, Los Bagels, Just My Type Letterpress and all the comforts of Humboldt. Also to Sabrina at East Village Bookshop for your constant support on all my endeavors.

To my family who made sure I had the opportunity to travel as a kid, to my sister for instilling a further degree of wanderlust and opening this door to Nor Cal for me. To my brother for furthering my love for the ocean.

All my friends who have sat quietly and listened to me when I would not shut up about this book and Humboldt. Darren, Kim, Missy, Emily, and Christine specifically. Danica for always hosting your amazing Halloween Parties. Mei & Deanna for the Humboldt Trip in 2022.

To Cindy and DK, thanks for being some of the best hiking buddies out there who listened to me talk about this even more.

To Danielle, for being the best bestie and also listening to me tell you the entire book and the sequel over coffee, brunch, thrift stores and road trips to the trees.

Joe, my love, thank you for always accepting my hyperfixations. Your unending support to let me create and explore this area we call home and willingness to join in sometimes means the world to me. I am so lucky to have a partner like you.

Also once again to you dear reader, Thank you.

Kelly Virens is a fantasy author with a love of all things trees, oceans, hiking, fantasy, and fae. Born and raised in San Diego, California, with a two year teaching stint in Japan, she relocated to Northern California to find home in all the amazing areas nearby. When she is not writing, she is usually off hiking or exploring somewhere in the Northern California region where she finds inspiration. Following a hike, she always stops by a nearby bookstore and a coffee shop. Her imagination is usually dreaming and scheming new things to write, draw, or make. Follow along with her explorations on Instagram with her personal account @fireflirt and her bookstagram @KellyVirensBooks

Check out more Secrets of Old Giants content and find the playlist below

linktr.ee/portfireflirt